The Assassin's Honor

The Honor Series
By Robert N. Macomber

At the Edge of Honor
Point of Honor
Honorable Mention
A Dishonorable Few
An Affair of Honor
A Different Kind of Honor
The Honored Dead
The Darkest Shade of Honor
Honor Bound
Honorable Lies
Honors Rendered
The Assassin's Honor

The Assassin's Honor

A Novel of
Cmdr. Peter Wake, Office of Naval Intelligence, USN

12th in the Honor Series

Robert N. Macomber

Pineapple Press, Inc.
Sarasota, Florida

Inquiries should be addressed to:

Pineapple Press, Inc.
P.O. Box 3889
Sarasota, Florida 34230

www.pineapplepress.com

Library of Congress Cataloging-in-Publication Data

Macomber, Robert N.
The assassin's honor / Robert N. Macomber. -- First edition.
    pages ; cm. — (Honor series ; 12)
    ISBN 978-1-56164-798-9 (hardback : alk. paper) — ISBN 978-1-56164-795-8
(pbk. : alk. paper)
    1. Wake, Peter (Fictitious character)—Fiction. I. Title.
    PS3613.A28A9 2015
    813'.6—dc23

2015021726

Design by Jennifer Borresen
Printed in the United States

This novel is respectfully dedicated to the dean
of Florida's contemporary novelists
Randy Wayne White
My friend and mentor, who long ago listened to my dream
and didn't laugh.
Over the ensuing years he has provided me with remarkable
rum, intriguing conversations, helpful introductions
around the world,
and great advice about this bizarre business.

Thank you, Randy. You turned out to be right on all of it.

Robert N. Macomber

A Preliminary Word with the Reader

I think a little background about Peter Wake and this novel, the twelfth in the Honor Series, is in order for both new readers and for longtime Wakians (self-named fans of these novels). *The Assassin's Honor* is set in late 1892 and early 1893. President Benjamin Harrison (Republican) has just lost re-election (his beloved wife Caroline died two weeks before the vote) and President-elect Grover Cleveland (Democrat) will be inaugurated on 4 March 1893. Cleveland was already president from 1885 to 1889, but lost his re-election bid to Harrison. Now, Cleveland is coming back to be commander in chief. The country faces serious economic, social, political, and foreign policy challenges.

Commander Peter Wake is fifty-three years old, and has been in the U.S. Navy for twenty-nine years, beginning with his combat duty in the East Gulf Blockading Squadron in the Civil War. His twenty-eight-year-old daughter Useppa has been a Methodist missionary in Key West for the last nine years. His twenty-four-year-old son Sean is an ensign in the navy and at sea in the U.S.S. *Yantic*; he graduated from the Naval Academy in 1890, a feat his father never accomplished.

Wake's dear friend and trusted colleague, Boatswain (usually pronounced and spelled "Bosun") Sean Rork, for whom Wake's son was named, is now sixty-one years old. Born and raised in County Wexford, Ireland, Rork shipped out to sea at age thirteen and has been there ever since. He joined the U.S. Navy in 1861 at Boston after jumping his previous ship. Rork is the kind of fellow you want beside you when drinking in a pub—or fighting for your life in the alley behind it.

Wake and Rork have served mostly together since 1864. From then until 1881 they served in ships, mostly frigates and gunboats, in the West Indies, South America, and the Mediterranean. From 1882 until 1892 they served in the newly established Office of Naval Intelligence, the first foreign espionage agency of the United States. This work took them to

Southeast Asia, South America, the Caribbean, the South Pacific, and Europe. It was sordid, shadowy, perilous work, shunned by most naval officers as beneath the dignity of an officer and a gentleman. Wake didn't like it at all, especially some of the things he had to do, but he is the kind of man who will get the mission accomplished.

Now he is out of that work, and back in the clean air of the ocean, as a proper naval officer should be. His career, so long stymied by his lack of formal academy education, wealth, and political supporters, has finally gotten on track. In his personal life, melancholy for so long, he has found contentment.

But Wake is about to learn that the past is always right behind you, even when you prefer to forget it.

1

The Unpleasant Truth

Patricio Island, Florida
Friday evening
5 May 1893

I have learned the truth is the rarest of possessions. So rare that it is often hoarded, frequently denied. Seldom is it shared, even when it is kind or even crucial to do so. That thought echoed in my mind when Maria asked the question. With a petite finger, she had been lightly tracing the remnants of the wounds I've accumulated over the last thirty years. The brush of her lips over the scar on my right temple was followed by a whisper, the words trembling with tears, "Peter, when will this madness end, so we can live in peace?"

Holding her closely against the chilly night, I decided to tell her the unpleasant truth. There would be no deceit with her, even of the gentle kind.

"It ends when they think we aren't a threat anymore. And that may be a long time."

She nodded slowly, for it was simply confirmation of what

she already knew and feared. Our future would be as dangerous as the recent past. "At least we are finally together, Peter, to face whatever comes."

The mood clearly needed to change, so I conjured up some mock naiveté just to hear that delicious laugh of hers. "Really, madam, aren't we supposed to be doing something other than *talking* tonight?"

Molding her body to mine with tender caresses that conveyed far more than words ever could, her laugh emerged as a subtle blend of naughty and nice. But even as I smiled in appreciation, her desperate question brought memories from the chaos of the previous six months. Disturbing memories.

They began at an anchorage in Jamaica.

2

The Summons

U.S.S. Bennington
Kingston, Jamaica
Thursday morning
8 December 1892

Even in December, at the start of the dry season, the indolent climate of the tropics can sap one's energy by midmorning. Around me, the men working on deck in the sun moved slowly, wasting no motion, the sweat on their bare backs streaked with grease and coal dust. Officers had no special immunity from the climate and were starting to wilt as they paced the bridge wing and pulled at their white chokers, which by custom they were expected to wear. The senior petty officers, the oldest and smartest of any in the ship, had already sought the shadier places, from which they silently watched over everyone else.

I am well versed in tropical weather and have suffered my share from it. But the muggy air held no deleterious effect on me this time, for within my constitution was an energy no temperature or humidity could diminish. For months, while steaming through the sun-broiled Caribbean, I'd looked forward to what each day would bring. This was, of course, a pleasant symptom of my present status—after twenty-nine very long years, I had finally reached the pinnacle of a naval officer's ambitions: independent command at sea of a newly built ship.

Not only that, but my personal life knew happiness for the first time in eleven years as a widower. Genuine love had reentered my life, giving me hope I wasn't doomed to a bachelor's loneliness for the rest of my mortal life. Hard as it was for a cynical soul like me to admit, the future was actually positive, and my chronic melancholia of the past had become merely a memory.

Leaving the shade of the bridge wing above me, I strolled forward along the main deck to survey my steel domain. The recently commissioned 3rd class cruiser *Bennington* rolled gently at anchor off the Royal Navy Dockyard in the harbor of Kingston, on the south coast of the British crown colony of Jamaica.

Gleaming in the sun, she was quite a sight to behold. A beautiful manifestation of the ship designer's blending of art and science, her lines bespoke speed and her guns showed determination. *Bennington* could outrun anything bigger and outfight anything her size. It filled me with gratification when British officers came out several times a day to ogle my vessel, conjecturing about her abilities and potential missions. For the past twenty-five years, it had been American officers envying the Royal Navy's ships.

Half my officers and men were ashore on liberty, enjoying the notorious delights of the city's waterfront taverns on Harbour Street. Hopefully, the officers were patronizing less vulgar establishments than the crew, but I knew some of the more rambunctious young gentlemen were, no doubt, exploring places which were less than genteel. It was all to be expected, and time would tell whether my preliminary admonitions to them about safety and propriety had taken effect.

With her population thus reduced, it was relatively quiet

aboard the ship. No throbbing of engines came up from below, for *Bennington*'s boilers were at minimum pressure and the ship herself was relatively dormant. Those sailors remaining in the ship were kept busy by the disagreeable duty of swabbing the weather decks and interior spaces, for we had refueled the day before and coal dust had infiltrated everywhere.

My tour of the main deck completed, I repaired to my cabin to sift through a pile of paperwork waiting for me. Twenty minutes later, I was going over division reports when the signal officer, Ensign Yeats, brought me a coded telegram sent out to the ship from the cable station ashore, via the U.S. consulate.

"Captain, it's marked urgent, and it's from Flag, North Atlantic. Not copied to any other ship or station—it's just to you, sir."

Flag, North Atlantic. That meant my superior, the legendary Rear Admiral John Grimes Walker, commander of the North Atlantic Squadron. I was expecting a routine ship-movement order, but not an urgent message. Yeats had deciphered it into plain language, a short task, for it was in Walker's typical no-nonsense style.

XX—GET TO KW IMMED—XX

The squadron, scattered across the Caribbean and the northern coast of South America, wasn't scheduled to rendezvous in Key West until ten days hence, on December 18. Then we would begin our annual three days of gunnery practice and evaluations at the nearby Dry Tortugas Islands. After the gun drills were completed, the squadron would steam in various battle formations to the naval station at Pensacola. Arriving there by the twenty-fourth, a lucky few of the officers and men would board trains to head home for Christmas with their families.

But this wasn't a squadron-wide order. Obviously, something serious had developed. What? If it was that serious, why wasn't the entire squadron summoned? The Kingston newspaper had displayed no momentous headlines lately. In fact, the region was relatively calm, without any new developments other than the usual litany of petty local assassinations, revolutions, coups, war threats, and political blustering. Certainly nothing involving the United States or the Europeans was on the horizon.

Whatever the reason, one never dawdled when Walker sent one an order to move immediately. Accordingly, I issued orders changing the sultry day from routine to rigorous. The Blue Peter crew recall signal was hoisted, the whistle sounded, and a blank signal gun fired to bring *Bennington*'s people from shore; the on-watch engineers started raising steam; the bosun's men hove the anchor's cable short and began to bring the ships boats and booms aboard; and all departments secured their areas of the ship for sea

The initial recipient of these commands was *Bennington*'s executive officer, Commander Norton Gardiner. He was clearly upset by this intrusion into his personal plans, for he possessed special invitations from the local swells. The first was to a polo luncheon at Torrington House by the Kingston Race Track. Later in the evening, he was to be a guest at a high society soiree at Wadston Plantation in the cool hills above the city. For the previous two days, Gardiner had repeatedly bored me with the details of his sartorial preparations, telling me how much the local society reminded him of his family's circle of sophisticated friends in Boston.

That did not impress me. I also was originally from Massachusetts, but arose in far different circumstances. Born and raised in a seafaring family on the coast—culturally quite distant from the comfortable salons of Boston—I thought of high-class social functions as pure fakery and senseless drivel. They were something to be occasionally endured by a professional naval officer, but certainly not anything to be enjoyed. So, with that prejudice firmly established in my being, I will fully admit a certain perverse pleasure was derived in the disruption of Gardiner's anticipated hobnobbing with the British colonial upper crust, whom I found even more obnoxious than the American version

Nonetheless, with scowling face and sarcastic tone, Gardiner did his duty and got *Bennington* ready for departure. Four hours and much grumbled commotion later, all our men were aboard, some of them suffering from a bit too much liberty while ashore. Officers and men assumed their stations, smoke poured out the stack, the anchor was in its stops, and our signal gun boomed out a salute to Queen Victoria's empire as we steamed past Fort Charles at Port Royal Point, bound for the Windward Passage between Cuba and Haiti.

Using all the mechanical power we could muster, and all the sail we could carry, *Bennington* traveled the 732 miles from Kingston to Key West Naval Station in a little over fifty hours, a record time for the squadron. Upon our arrival in Key West's outer channel, the station's signal mast informed us that I was to report to the admiral directly upon mooring.

Accordingly, eighteen minutes after the main hook was let go in Man of War Anchorage off Fort Taylor, I landed at the naval wharf near the foot of Duval Street, ascended the brow of the 2nd class cruiser *Chicago*, the admiral's flagship, and entered his day cabin. It was precisely 10:00 a.m. on the tenth of December, in the year 1892.

I remember the date and time vividly, for that was the moment when a chain of events was set in motion that changed my life forever.

3

The Reason

Key West Naval Station
Saturday morning
10 December 1892

Somewhat breathless at my hasty arrival in the admiral's
palatial quarters, I was announced by a pale-skinned junior
lieutenant on the squadron staff. He glanced at me with an odd
mixture of pity and envy as he knocked three times, then opened
the door and reported to the admiral, "*Bennington* has arrived,
sir."

Sitting at his large desk, Walker wasted no time in polite
preamble, his long gray forked beard flapping like semaphore
pennants as he gruffly greeted me.

"Thank you for getting here so quickly, Wake." Pulling out a
pocket watch, his gray eyes glanced at it and added, "Impressive
transit. I suppose you have very little fuel left?"

"Correct, sir. Only forty tons of coal out of three hundred
and seventy. At three tons per shaft per hour, I have only six
hours full-ahead steaming left."

"Machinery and boiler condition?"

"Satisfactory for right now, sir. But she'll need a maintenance overhaul soon after this last run. The usual—boiler tank, flues, tubes, and lines."

"Ammunition and guns?"

"Full load out in all calibers, and all bags and casings look good. Every gun is operative, sir."

"Provisions?"

"Short, sir. We didn't have time to take enough onboard at Kingston."

His brow furrowed as he continued, "Yes, well, time is of the essence on this matter, so the boiler overhaul will have to wait, but we can get you coal and provisions right away. Now, sit down and listen closely."

Choosing a straightback cane chair instead of the more comfortable upholstered wingbacks, I felt the old pounding in my chest. A mission at sea. It had been years since I'd felt that sensation.

A slight smile showed for a second on the admiral's face, then disappeared as he spoke. "You've been out of the Office of Naval Intelligence for years now, but this situation will bring back memories and, I hope, some of those arcane skills you were so good at."

The last comment made my stomach feel queasy. "Arcane skills" probably meant some of the more disagreeable things I'd had to do on ONI missions—things I'd tried to forget.

The admiral leaned back with a long sigh. "Yes, well, you were in Venezuela about five weeks ago, mid-October, I believe, so you know the general situation there regarding the Germans, their railroad and other commercial enterprises, and the turmoil with the new local president, if I can be so generous as to use that term. Correct?"

My reader understandably may not be versed in Venezuela's convoluted history, so I will digress briefly about what happened in 1892. The country was sadly typical of Latin America. Foreign investors, mostly German and British, built and controlled most of the transportation and communication systems there, exerting tremendous pecuniary influence over the country's politics. The previous national leader, a liberal reformer named Pulido, had been removed from office on October 7 by the grand-sounding "Legalist Revolution." That particular crew was led by a distinctly nonliberal fellow named General Joaquín Crespo, who had been the country's head man some years earlier.

At first, the Germans tentatively backed both sides in the conflict, waiting to see which would prevail before donating larger amounts to the frontrunner. Once Crespo started winning, the foreigners, particularly the Germans, started backing him seriously.

"Yes, sir, I'm familiar with the place," I said. "President Crespo is consolidating his hold over the country following his coup. There are still remnants of opposition on the Caribbean coast and in the interior, but they are dwindling fast and the civil war is effectively over. The country is relatively calm now, and the Germans are officially supporting Crespo and are loaning him a lot of money. Our government just recognized him as well."

"All true. And what do you know of the Red D Line steamer *Philadelphia*'s recent role in all this?"

"Nothing, sir. Except she's American flagged and works that route out of New York, and occasionally New Orleans."

"Yes, she does. A month ago, shortly after you'd taken *Bennington* over to Costa Rica to calm the ever-faint hearts of American merchants there, *Philadelphia* was at her usual port call in La Guaira, Venezuela. She took aboard as a passenger one General Mijares, ex-governor of Caracas and sworn enemy of Crespo. Mijares was fleeing to the United States, but the ship was delayed in sailing. General Crespo got word Mijares was on the steamer and sent troops onboard with orders to snatch his antagonist away to a dungeon.

"*Philadelphia*'s Captain Chambers protested there was no court-issued warrant and thus it was an illegal search of an American ship—thereby bluffing the soldiers off his ship without getting their man. Chambers then weighed anchor and rapidly exited the coast. He deposited General Mijares in New York, but not before a supposedly accidental gunshot in the first-class bar salon almost killed the general, which would have been very convenient for Crespo and his new German allies. Nothing could be proven, of course. So far?"

"Understood, sir."

"Very good. Now, to get to the point. While on another voyage, that same steamer put into Key West five days ago—Monday, the fifth—needing to recoal on her way from La Guaira, Venezuela, to New Orleans. It wasn't unusual, of course, since this island is right on the course. A quick, routine port call of only one night. However, while she was at the commercial coal dock adjacent to us, something very unusual was discovered aboard the *Philadelphia*. It was that discovery, and the accompanying evidence, which is the salient issue for us today."

Admiral Walker looked at me and paused, his bewhiskered face showing perplexed consternation, not a typical expression for him. He clearly wanted me to ask the obvious question, so I obliged him.

"And what was that, sir?"

"The dead body of a passenger, Wake. Not your average passenger, mind you. Quite an unusual man, actually, who ended up quite unnaturally dead. I've spent forty-two years, man and boy, in Uncle Sam's navy, and I have seen and done it all. You know I am not given to exaggeration, but this situation has me baffled and concerned. And that's the reason why you have been ordered here so abruptly."

Some passenger died? This was why my men and I pushed ourselves and our ship to the point of total fatigue to get to Key West so quickly?

I swallowed my sarcasm and merely said, "Sir, I still don't understand why *Bennington* was needed here."

The admiral shook his head slowly, looking down at his desk. Then he looked up at me. "It wasn't your ship I needed, Wake. It was *you*."

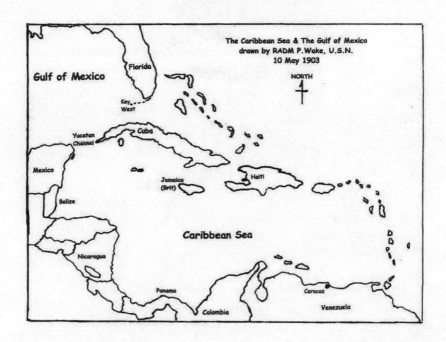

The Caribbean Sea & The Gulf of Mexico
drawn by RADM P. Wake, U.S.N.
10 May 1903

NORTH

Gulf of Mexico

Florida

Key West

Yucatan Channel

Cuba

Mexico

Belize

Jamaica (Brit)

Haiti

Caribbean Sea

Nicaragua

Panama

Caracas

Colombia

Venezuela

4

The Enigma

Key West Naval Station
Saturday morning
10 December 1892

The intensity of the admiral's stare matched his tone.

This was getting a little overdramatic, I thought, but I humored him. "Yes, sir. So they found an *unnaturally* dead body . . . but why do you need me?"

Now that he was in the meat of the matter, the pace of Walker's narrative picked up speed. "I'll explain. The morning of *Philadelphia*'s arrival, one of the first-class passengers, a Mr. Simon Drake, age fifty-three and traveling alone, was found dead in his cabin by a steward. There was no obvious sign of foul play on the body, according to a shore doctor functioning as the coroner, who ruled it an apparent heart attack. He allowed the body to be immediately embalmed and buried, this being the tropics.

"On the face of it, Drake's death was routine and didn't warrant official attention. Passengers die naturally every day on ships. Nothing unusual about that, or so everyone thought at the time. Ever heard the name—Simon Drake?"

"No, sir." But I had noted that Drake and I were the same age. Heart troubles. Hmm. Was the pounding in my chest something more than nerves?

Walker harrumphed and nodded. "Yes, well, I didn't know Drake's name either. But maybe we should have, from our time in intelligence work, as this is where things get interesting. The steamer's purser checked his records and informed Captain Chambers that Drake was an American who worked as a senior telegraphist in Caracas for the German railroad firm there. Now, not many clerical fellows can afford a first-class cabin, so the captain thought it a bit out of the ordinary.

"Then, when the purser was packaging up the personal belongings in Drake's cabin, he found a couple of intriguing items and notified his captain. One of them was hidden inside a pillow case—a four-inch-square section cut out of a German nautical chart. It contains a coastline the purser and captain didn't recognize, with a place name, *Xel-ha*, underlined. It also has the words *Dzul* and *Verabredung* handwritten next to it."

"How do you know it's actually a German chart, sir?"

A flicker of annoyance darkened his face. Admirals aren't used to being interrupted. "It has German words printed on it—*Karibisches Meer*—which even I know means Caribbean Sea. It shows a north-south coast, so it could be in Venezuela near Puerto Cabello, where there has been some conflict between the government army and some of the left-over anti-Crespo rebels."

"I see, sir," I said, though I really didn't.

He resumed. "And now the second item. Inside the cabin's safe, which was found to be locked, there was a piece of common note paper containing several lines of numbers separated into groups. It appeared to the captain to be some sort of coded message."

Coded message? Now I was beginning to understand the urgent summons.

"Captain Chambers and I are old acquaintances, and when we were having dinner the same evening, he mentioned the situation. Said it was a bit of a mystery to him. When I expressed an interest in seeing those items, he gave them to me. After perusing them closely, my interest was piqued even more, so I sent my squadron intelligence officer and the staff surgeon over to the steamer to have a look in Drake's cabin, to see if anything was amiss. That was something the shore doctor evidently didn't do before rendering his verdict on the cause of death. The intelligence officer contributed nothing; he's new at it and nearly useless. But the surgeon returned with a significant observation—the odor of garlic, a lot of it, on Simon Drake's bed pillow."

"Garlic, sir? I don't understand the meaning."

"And neither did I, Commander. The surgeon says it's a telltale sign of arsenic poisoning. It turns out arsenic mimics the general characteristics of a heart attack. A check with the purser revealed no actual garlic was found in the cabin. The surgeon spoke with the steamer's cooks and learned there was no meal with large amounts of garlic served on the ship during her most recent voyage from Venezuela. Therefore, the garlic on the pillow must have gotten there by Drake breathing on it as he died."

"That *is* a curious development. A postmortem examination of Drake's body might shed light on it, sir."

Walker's beard shook in the negative. "Surgeon says it's too late—the embalming ruined the body for that type of examination."

"Bad luck."

"Yes, bad luck, indeed, but I am still faced with an enigma. An American citizen who works for the Germans in Venezuela has in his possession a small part of a German chart depicting an unknown coast, as well as a coded message—and then he is murdered on an American ship, probably by a professional who knows the dark art of assassination by poisoning. So what does it all mean?"

"I have no idea, sir," I admitted.

Walker's eyes narrowed. "Commander Wake, I have a feeling something nefarious is afoot, and the Germans are hip-deep in it. Our country, or at least this region, will surely end up being involved in whatever it is, to an uncertain end. And that means that *we* in this squadron will be involved. Furthermore, I think time is short before this thing, whatever it is, comes to fruition—otherwise, why murder the man? So I intend to discover exactly what is going on here and either stop it or spread the alarm, before it gets further out of hand."

He exhaled loudly as his tone grew exasperated. "This, however, has not proven an easy task, for it turns out not a single soul on my staff can read the confounded German language with any proficiency, so I don't know the English translation of those mystery words on the chart. None of my staff recognizes that coast, either. And I have discovered none of them, not even the newly arrived signal and intelligence officer, have ever worked on foreign code deciphering, either out in the fleet or up at the naval intelligence office in Washington."

I wasn't surprised. I'd heard the new intelligence man, a lieutenant commander with over twenty years in the navy, had only recently started in the field of naval intelligence. I didn't envy him his assignment, for the admiral never suffered ignorance among his subordinates gladly. Few in the navy were wary of the Germans yet, even after our confrontation with them at Samoa in '89. Most eyes were focused on Spain and Cuba.

"Any German passengers or crew on *Philadelphia*, sir?"

"Captain Chambers and I thought of that, too. No, none on the manifests. And no one disembarked at Key West either—it was just a temporary coaling stop. She's gone now. Left the next day."

"And ONI's opinion of the coded message, sir?"

"On top of everything else, the telegraph station here is temporarily out of service due to a break in the line between here and Punta Rassa. I've sent the original coded message to ONI by armed courier, via steamboat to Tampa's telegraph station. But it will take more than a week, probably ten days, to get the information up there and the translation of the message back to me. That's too long—I want this enigma solved now. I kept an exact copy of the numbered message on the notepaper, but unfortunately, I don't have the expertise around here to give me answers."

He slapped his right hand down on the desk as a sly grin emerged.

"Ah . . . but all was not lost for me, for I did have *you* down there in Jamaica, didn't I? Actually, you're the perfect man for the case, especially if the code does turn out to be German. You're the only man in Uncle Sam's Navy who has seen them in combat close up, and you've got the wound to prove it. You're the one who stole the German navy's code from them at Samoa in eighty-nine, you're well versed in their activities in the Caribbean, and you know this region's coasts better than almost any officer in the squadron. So now, Commander Wake, you know why you were summoned posthaste. You're the man who's going to figure out this enigma and tell me what it means."

The admiral stood and handed me a dark blue U.S. Navy Department dispatch envelope. "The items are inside. Take them back to your ship. Report back here in three hours and tell me what these people are up to in our area of operations."

5

The Message

U.S.S. Bennington
Key West Naval Station
Saturday morning
10 December 1892

Ignoring the inquisitive looks from my officers and men, I descended to my cabin directly upon returning aboard *Bennington*. Once in my sanctum, the numbers would be tackled first, for they might explain the chart.

There were three lines of numbers, separated into groups. The first line had five groups, the second had four, and the third had five. It was obviously a coded telegraph message, but not in the standard European commercial, military, or diplomatic code. Most of those were in five-digit groupings of numbers. These groupings had only four numbers each. The admiral's premonition was right.

It was the secret code of the Imperial German Navy.

From my safe, I extracted my copy of the 1888 German naval code, painstakingly copied from the original lead-lined code book. During one of my last clandestine missions at the Office of Naval Intelligence, in March of 1889, that code book had been surreptitiously removed from a reef near the wreck of the S.M.S. *Adler*, flagship of the German squadron in Samoa.

The Germans still didn't know we had it. From what we heard later, they assumed it was lost in the wreck. I had the only copy outside of the Special Assignments Section of ONI, of which I had once been the senior officer. ONI is located within a small office in the bowels of the State, War, and Navy Building, across the park from the president's mansion. ONI functions as his trusted resource for understanding—and influencing—events around the world.

The first number group was the mathematical formula to start deciphering the rest of the message. There were eight German formulas, some of which were quite complicated. But I was in luck; according to what I saw, this was one of the simpler ones. The formula would consist of only addition, subtraction, and division, in that order, utilizing each number in the initial group as the operating feature.

Following the formula, the number groups changed into a complete new set of integers. I had now completed the first phase of deciphering the message.

Comparing the new number groups with those on the secret code list before me, I found the letter of the German alphabet represented by each numeral or pair of numerals. There was an additional complication. Unlike English's twenty-six letters, the German alphabet has another four letter-diacritic combinations, for a total of thirty letters.

At the end of the second phase of deciphering, the translation from numbers into letters, I came up with this message in the German alphabet:

TÖTU NGAB SCHU SSDE
ZEMB ERSE CHZE HNXX
ESWI RDKR IEGB EEND ENXX

The double *X*s were endings of sentences, a standard practice in all navies. The final phase would be to get the correct sequence of letters formed into separate words. Consulting my German-English dictionary, as my knowledge of that language is woefully lacking, it took a while to find the words formed by the letters. It gave me the following:

TÖTUNG ABSCHUSS DEZEMBER SECHZEHN XX
ES WIRD KRIEG BEENDEN XX

Converting the message into English, a chill went through me. I repeated the entire procedure three times to make sure I had it right.

Unfortunately, I did.

THE KILLING HAPPENS DECEMBER SIXTEEN XX
IT WILL END WAR XX

Next I turned to the small section of chart. The coastline on it was oriented vertically, with the sea to the right, or east. Depths were in meters. Perusing my large area chart of the Venezuelan coast, I narrowed the north-south coastal possibilities to the western shore of Lake Maracaibo; the Caribbean coast northwest of Puerto Cabello; or the west coast of the Gulf of Paria, across from Trinidad. However, there were no Venezuelan places on my chart titled *Dzul* or *Xel-ha*, and nothing geographically matched the fragment.

Again consulting the German dictionary, I found the word *Verabredung* meant "rendezvous" or "appointment." Next I looked up *Dzul* and *Xel-ha*, but neither were in the book. They didn't sound French or Spanish to me, but for some reason they seemed vaguely familiar. I wondered if they might be Dutch, for that country had island colonies off the coast of Venezuela.

Then I remembered, and cursed my stupidity. Because of the admiral's report about Simon Drake, I'd been thinking about

Venezuela, but was completely wrong. Those words weren't European, and they weren't even from that part of the Caribbean.

In fact, they were from an area almost a thousand miles away from Venezuela. Dredging up memories from a cruise along the Caribbean coast of Central America the previous September, I remembered Xel-ha was a village on the Mayan coast of Mexico, the Yucatán Peninsula. It was only a couple days steaming from Key West.

Now that I had the correct location, I recalled the other word's meaning. Dzul wasn't the name of a place, it was the name of a man—the current leader of the Mayan independence army, which had been fighting the Mexican national army for the last fifty years in something called the Caste War. It was a simmering conflict few outside of Mexico knew about. Occasionally, it would boil over into a pitched battle, but even then the U.S. press didn't deem it worthy of American readers.

Now, however, there were outside players in Mexico. Porfirio Díaz, president of Mexico, had enjoyed good relations with Germany's chancellor, Otto von Bismarck, for some time. Díaz and Bismarck had signed an immigration agreement several years prior, after five decades of immigration had already brought thousands of Germans to Mexico, mostly around the Gulf coast. More Germans were heading there. Two communities of them were in Yucatán, near Mérida.

Bismarck, ironically, was in retirement and out of the equation, sacked by the young Kaiser Wilhelm for being not aggressive enough internationally. Now that Wilhelm had no one to restrain him with wise counsel, German naval and commercial efforts were quickly expanding around the world, causing conflicts with other countries.

I recalled that the Mayan warriors had bought weapons and supplies through traders in neighboring British Honduras. Did this message and chart mean the German navy was going to rendezvous with Dzul, form some sort of alliance, and take over supplying him? For what purpose? Was it to secure an area for the Caribbean naval base they had wanted for years? Or was Dzul the target of the killing, at the bidding of the Mexican government?

The chronometer on the bulkhead showed I had less than an hour before I was to give Admiral Walker an idea of what was happening. In the meantime, another pair of eyes was needed to look over this problem. Turning to the row of speaking tubes beside my desk, I opened the lid on the tube connected to the wheelhouse. "This is the captain. Pass the word for Bosun Rork to report to my cabin."

I knew someone would be assassinated in six days, but three crucial questions were still unanswered. Who? Where? Why?

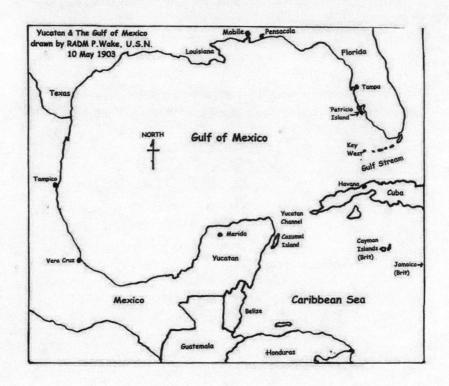

Yucatan & The Gulf of Mexico
drawn by RADM P.Wake, U.S.N.
10 May 1903

Mobile
Pensacola
Louisiana
Florida
Texas
Tampa
NORTH
Gulf of Mexico
'Patricio Island
Key West
Gulf Stream
Tampico
Havana
Cuba
Yucatan Channel
Cozumel Island
Merida
Cayman Islands (Brit)
Vera Cruz
Yucatan
Jamaica (Brit)
Mexico
Caribbean Sea
Belize
Guatemala
Honduras

6

The Enemy

U.S.S. Bennington
Key West Naval Station
Saturday afternoon
10 December 1892

A knock sounded twice at my door. The nervous voice said he was the messenger from the officer of the deck. With my permission, a young sailor entered. Taking in everything at a glance, his face was a study in competing emotions: envy at the relative luxury of my quarters, and terror at being inside them. He knuckled his brow and began his recital.

"Ah . . . Seaman Bundle, Captain, sir, with a message from the officer of the deck. Mr. Manning presents his respects and reports the naval station just signaled *Chicago* and *Bennington*—a German warship entered the channel ten minutes ago. She's the . . . Genays . . . ayn . . . now. . . or something like that. Sorry, sir, but I just can't pronounce them foreign names."

The morning was turning out to be rather interesting. It had been quite a while since a German warship visited Key West.

"I believe she will be the *Gneisenau,* Bundle. She's a well-armed corvette-cruiser and Germany's West Indies station ship. Pass along my compliments to Mr. Manning and tell him I want my gig ready in ten minutes."

As Bundle departed, Rork arrived. Bosun Sean Rork is a curious study, worthy of a closer glance.

Born and raised County Wexford, Ireland, in 1831 he left that blighted isle at age twelve and grew up fast at sea on a coaster working ports on both sides of the Irish Sea. His sad childhood back in Wexford was something he never really explained to me, other than to deflect my inquiries into humorous anecdotes about girls, the church, and the despised English. By the late 1850s, Rork was a grizzled bosun working the Atlantic trade between Liverpool and Boston.

In January of 1863, after his desperation could be held in check no more, he had a life-altering decision to make. Either kill the maniacal new mate in the ship, or jump ashore and see what life in America would bring. Wisely, he chose the latter option, but after five months' search there was no work for a foreign seaman; all the maritime jobs went to locals, for to be without a seaman's exemption meant you were subject to be conscripted into the army. And that meant going south to live in the mud in disease-ridden camps, all the while being subjected to mindless army discipline, when not getting shot at by the Confederates.

But there was another opportunity at hand—go to sea for Uncle Sam. Rork joined the quickly expanding U.S. Navy, made bosun's mate immediately, and never looked back. We met in the East Gulf Blockading Squadron in the summer of 1863 and served against the Confederates in Florida and the West Indies for the rest of the war. That experience formed a friendship that has strengthened over decades of shared danger and despair on assignments around the world. Rork is a good man to have beside you in bad situations.

Such a friendship was not only rare between officer and

petty officer—ours was the sole example I've seen—it was severely frowned upon by the notoriously hidebound naval establishment. That didn't bother me a bit, for I was a persona non grata with those fools myself, not having attended the naval academy and thereby become a proper "gentleman." One attribute Rork and I did have, however, was that we always accomplished the mission, albeit occasionally with innovation which deviated from regulations.

Rork's only major faults are a fondness for women and rum, necessitating a keen watch over him lest either lead him, and sometimes me too, into ruination. Unlike me, he was never married, has no legitimate children and, as he says, is a truly free man.

Admiral Walker was one of the few in the upper naval strata who appreciated what Rork and I had done for the country, and the admiral never harassed me about my old friend. Actually, I always thought him a bit envious of Rork's comparative freedom and love of life.

I bade Rork to close the door and then sit down, something enlisted men never were invited to do in a captain's quarters. When he had done so, I handed over the piece of chart and the deciphered message. Then I told him what I'd learned from Walker and deduced from the chart and message.

"So now I want you to examine those, Rork, and give me your opinion."

He read the message through twice, tracing the numbers with his finger, then studied the chart closely. Looking up at me, the ghost of a smile showed on his weathered face. "Ooh, lookin' like a wee bit o' the old times, back in the shadows again. Been a while since we worked an ONI mission, sir."

"That it has, Rork, and good riddance to it. So, what do you make of it all? The admiral wants answers in less than an hour."

"Ah . . . so that's why we ran here so bloody hard. Well, sir, methinks you're right as rain about the Mayan boyo Dzul. An' bugger all if this don't have an evil sound to it. But it does plague me mind with more questions than answers. Just who sent this message, an' to who is it sent? Is Dzul the Heinies' target, or one o' their mates? Aye, an' mark me words, sir—this is big. Me eyes see crazy Kaiser Willy's hand all o'er it."

"I agree, Rork, something evil's stirring. And yes, for this afternoon, at least, I guess we're back in our old business again." The clock showed one thirty, so I said, "I brief the admiral on this in half an hour."

I pointed out the stern gallery toward *Gneisenau*, which was letting go her anchor a quarter-mile away. Her yards, ratlines, and weather decks were manned by sailors in white, standing at parade rest. Spars and rigging were taut and squared in perfect seamanlike fashion. The German navy was small, but impressive. And growing larger.

"Rork, I need more information, so you're going ashore immediately and you're going to befriend the German ship's petty officers over pints when they get their liberty. Then you're going to find out what they know about their destination and mission. Report back to me no later than the end of the second dog watch. That'll give you about five hours by the time their liberty section gets ashore."

I handed him a ten dollar greenback, which quickly disappeared into a pocket. Once he'd secured the cash, Rork rubbed his false left hand and began unscrewing it from its base plate, revealing a wicked-looking five-inch marlinspike underneath. The phantom aches still bothered him, nine years after he lost that hand to a sniper in Indochina, and he massaged the stump of his forearm beneath the prosthetic base plate.

His right eyebrow cocked upward and a devilish grin creased his face.

"Aye, sir, methinks a wee bit o' skullduggery is jus' the thing to liven up the day. An' five hours is more than enough time to make the likes o' them Heinies me very best mates."

Boom . . . boom . . . boom . . . *Gneisenau*'s thirteen-gun salute to Admiral Walker echoed across the anchorage. The last time I'd heard a German warship fire her guns, they weren't firing saluting blanks. They were shooting a Maxim gun for real—at *me*.

This had been only three years earlier, on a beach in Samoa. War between our countries was inevitable at that point. We only avoided it by Divine intervention, in the form of a hurricane that destroyed both countries' squadrons and killed 221 sailors. The jagged scar on my right hip throbbed, a sharp reminder of that damnably accurate German Maxim gun, and a needed addendum to Rork's orders.

"Rork, remember, drinks and yarns only with these German fellows. No threats, no fights, and for God's sake, don't refer to what you and I did in the South Pacific."

His face transformed into an innocent mien, which I knew to be entirely insincere from almost thirty years' experience with the man. Rork hadn't had an innocent thought since he was ten years old.

Rescrewing the India rubber hand back in place, he said, "Aye, aye, sir. Nary's the worry, 'tis ordered an' will be done. This'll be easier than slippin' off Mary O'Shanassey's garter on a Friday night. After two pints o' ale an' a glass o' gin, them sea-weary lads'll be putty in me hands. Why, they'll think o' me as their newest bosom buddy, a true brother o' the ocean, an' a man to be trusted with their innermost secrets an' prides."

"It's Sunday, so where will you go that's open?"

"Only waterin' hole open is Annie's on Front Street—used to be Curry's Saloon. "Aye, an' methinks Annie's is jus' the right place to steer 'em. That way, what the lads don't gab to me, they'll whisper to me dear ol' friend Annie upstairs, an' that's sure 'nough. Ooh, but she do have a way with Jack-Tar, no matter his flag."

"Annie Wenz, the madam?"

"Aye, one an' the same. The temperance people failed to close her down."

It didn't surprise me. Wenz was formidable when angry, and

the most successful madam in Key West. One of the temperance people was my daughter, Useppa.

"Yes, well, no fights with the Germans, Rork," I repeated.

He stood up and showed me his sincerest look of complete agreement, knuckling his brow with his right hand. "Sir! Nary a blonde hair on their big square Kraut heads'll be put out o' place. An' that's me solemn promise," he glanced up, "as Saint Peter's me witness."

"Good." I handed him a small envelope. "First thing when you're ashore, get a boy to take this note to Useppa over at the church. I was hoping we both could have dinner with her but, of course, it's out of the question now with all this going on. She'll be not be pleased with our sudden departure, but I suppose I'll have to just put it on the list of her grievances with me."

My daughter Useppa had been a Methodist missionary in Key West, teaching the island's black children, for the last eight years. Hers had been a difficult life; learning to live with a crippled leg, losing her mother to female cancer when she was fifteen, helping to raise her younger brother Sean, having a frequently absent naval officer for a father, and losing her fiancé Raul, a Cuban Methodist pastor, to a Spanish bullet when she was twenty-one. After that tragedy six years earlier, she'd plunged into her faith with an even more zealous passion that had no tolerance for backsliders.

Our relationship was polite and pleasant, having regrettably grown somewhat distant over the years. She tried, but couldn't quite hide her disappointment in me.

The main contention was that I wasn't as vigorous in my Christian faith as Useppa thought I should be. She disapproved of my behavior regarding drink, my humor, and was particularly offended by a love affair I'd had four years earlier. All this disapproval—I thought of it as "an obsession"—usually manifested itself in her preaching to me about the various moral sins I was currently committing, something no father wants to ever hear from his daughter. It is especially embarrassing when I realize she might very well be right. My rebuttals to these harangues rang a bit hollow, I'm afraid, and any attempt to defuse them with light-hearted wit simply engendered yet another frown of dissatisfaction with my incorrigible attitude.

As ridiculous as it might sound, I had the distinctly uncomfortable feeling that at age twenty-seven, my dear little girl Useppa had somehow taken on the role of my mother, and I was the irredeemable lad heading to hell in a hurry.

Her godfather Rork, who actually *is* incorrigible, naturally thought this all rather entertaining and recommended for some time not to take it seriously, that she would grow out of it. She hadn't.

Rork took the envelope and smiled. "Aye, said an' done, sir. An' don't ye worry a wee little bit, she's a Navy man's daughter an' will understand. Next time here, we'll be havin' a fine relaxin' dinner with our dear lass."

7

The Motive

U.S.S. Chicago
Key West Naval Station
Saturday afternoon
10 December 1892

I ended up late for my briefing to the admiral. When one is the captain of a ship, there are many demands on one's time, most of them of a spontaneous nature. Some can be delayed, but not for long. The necessity for me to deal with the admiral's enigma trumped the routine duties and decisions of a commanding officer, even the more important bureaucratic responsibilities accompanying a warship's return to a naval station. But it hadn't stopped my executive officer from expecting me to fulfill them, for he had fulfilled his.

Commander Gardiner was fuming with frustration, a condition in which he seemed to spend most of his existence. That his irritation had reached a boiling point was clear from his cloudy expression upon entry into my cabin. This was, no doubt, aggravated by the fact he, as the number two officer of the ship, was kept waiting while I met with a mere noncommissioned petty officer.

Gardiner walked in just as Rork was departing, casting a glare at the bosun as they passed each other. Rork didn't help himself any by bestowing a polite smile on the executive officer and, in his thickest Irish brogue, pleasantly offering, "Af'ernoon, sir!"

That amiable greeting elicited a low grumble in response. Foul mood enhanced, Gardiner started in on his business even before he sat down, with an attitude bordering on disrespectful.

"Captain, I have been trying for hours to get in here to see you and go over these division head reports and requests. Can we please go over them now? I have the master-at-arms' prisoner and punishment report; captain's mast disciplinary requests from the division heads; surgeon's sick bay list; paymaster's commissary and supply accounts and requests; gunnery officer's ammunition and guns readiness report; signals traffic from the station ashore; chief engineer's machinery readiness report, bunker report, fuel request, and his repair and maintenance requests. Also there are the watch, quarter, and station bill changes, liberty ashore allocations; and several officers' ship visit requests. As per my duties, I've made decisions on all these things, but need to apprise you of them."

Need to cover your stern, is more like it, I uncharitably thought as he started in again. Holding up a hand to stop a continuation of the monologue, I pointed to the bulkhead. The clock showed thirteen minutes until 2 p.m.

"You are right, of course, Norton, but I'm afraid the admiral outranks you, me, and *Bennington*'s administrative issues right now. He's expecting me at four bells, so I've got only a few minutes to get there. I don't hear any emergencies in your list, so we'll go over all of that when I return from the flagship. I should be back in an hour or two."

"Aye, sir," he said mechanically, departing without saying anything further and, most notably, without asking for my permission to leave.

This was followed within seconds by Seaman Bundle again,

the quarterdeck messenger timidly reporting that my gig had capsized when the forward boat falls were let go prematurely. It was presently being righted and bailed by the coxswain, the messenger said while stifling a grin, adding that the coxswain and the officer of the deck sent their apologies for the delay.

"Any other boats alongside and ready for use?"

"No, sir. The duty launch is over at the station landing. Should we call her back for you, sir?"

Damned bad luck—I would be late for the admiral. I was sure Rork, for whom the coxswain worked, would make certain the boat crews would never make that mistake again.

"No, Bundle. The gig'll be ready sooner. You're dismissed."

And so it was several minutes past two o'clock, or four bells in sailors' jargon, when I arrived in Admiral Walker's cabin. His irritation was apparent.

"Well, Wake, I see you are finally here. So tell me, what have you determined about the mysterious coast on the chart segment, and that coded message?"

I concisely explained the facts I had discovered and added that I had sent Rork ashore to obtain information from the *Gneisenau*'s petty officers on liberty.

He nodded, then asked, "This place is in Mexico, you say, not Venezuela?"

"Yes, sir. All the evidence points to the Caribbean coast of the Yucatán Peninsula of Mexico."

"Killing . . . an assassination. Serious indeed. And they've already proven with Simon Drake they can murder quite effectively and anonymously."

"Yes, sir, they did. These are definitely professional assassins, part of a sophisticated scheme, not some ragtag gang of *bandidos*."

"This Dzul fellow, what do you know of him?"

"Not much, sir. He's the leader of the Mayan rebels, apparently a native religious zealot who calls himself a Christian and, from what I can recollect, a bit ruthless."

"How so?"

"Some Mayans wanted to reach an agreement with the central government a short time ago, but he said no, then went after the moderates who proposed it. Rumor had it he killed them, but that is unconfirmed."

I held up a hand to make my next point. "And there is the conundrum, sir. It is very difficult for me to believe the Germans actually would support a man like him, at least openly, and I have no idea why they would want to rendezvous with him."

"We must understand their *motive,* Wake, and it will take us to the heart of the matter. Money's involved, we can be sure of that."

"Yes, sir, no doubt. The Germans have a lot of commercial money involved in the Caribbean and Latin America. The American hemisphere is a major foreign trading partner for the Hamburg firms, probably *the* major trading partner, and their trade is increasing everywhere. But the Mayans don't have anything valuable in their area, except sisal for making cordage."

I shook my head in irritation at my own inability to deduce any reason for the Germans' rendezvous with Dzul. Airing the thought process aloud, I reiterated my knowledge of German influence inside Mexico, seeking a clue.

"Admiral, the German government has been currying favor with the Mexican federal government for several years in order to get commercial advantages in the country. President Díaz and Chancellor Bismarck were friends long before Kaiser Wilhelm II took the throne and subsequently dismissed the chancellor from office. There is a sizable German immigrant population—mostly farmers and tradesmen—all over coastal Mexico."

A recent article in the *New York Times* came to mind. "Just a little while ago, Baron Bleichman, one of the big Hamburg bankers, was in Mexico to study the potential for railroads with a view to investing in them. At the end of his trip, he publicly said he would recommend the idea. So why would the Germans jeopardize it by having a rendezvous with Dzul, much less kill him? Why get involved at all with the Caste War?"

Then it struck me. For the second time that day, I'd been overlooking the obvious.

"Admiral, I just had a thought. The Germans have been trying for five years to get a naval station somewhere in the Caribbean so they could protect their country's considerable commercial trade in the region."

"Yes. Go on."

"Well, sir, they've tried the eastern Caribbean repeatedly at Curaçao, Venezuela, and St. Thomas, failing to secure an agreement each time, and that island they stole and tried to make a naval base, Klein Curaçao, turned out to be a failure. So maybe they're changing target areas. Maybe they're opting for the western Caribbean?"

Walker didn't seem warm to the idea. "Perhaps . . ."

"Sir, here's my logic. If the Germans had a naval station on the Caribbean coast of Mexico, they would control the Yucatán Channel, chokepoint of the major shipping route to the Caribbean and South America from all the Gulf coast ports of Mexico and the United States. Not to mention dominate the local countries from Mexico to Costa Rica. But the real object of their efforts is something far more important."

"Good Lord, the canal . . ."

"Yes, sir. The Germans want to be in a position to control access to the canal at Panama."

8

The Hypothesis

U.S.S. Chicago
Key West Naval Station
Saturday afternoon
10 December 1892

Walker's face creased in thought as he got up and walked to the Caribbean chart on his bulkhead. "Wake, you just might have something there. Are there any decent harbors on the Mayan coast?"

I joined him in perusing the chart and pointed toward the Yucatán area.

"Some small ones are along the mainland, but they're not nearly deep enough for a proper naval station. But wait, sir—the island of Cozumel lies about eight or ten miles off the coast. It's large, about five by twenty miles, and not crowded—or important to the central Mexican government. And though there's no harbor at all, the western side is a lee from the prevailing Caribbean winds and an open anchorage can be found at San Miguel, the main town. The Germans could establish machine shops, coal depots, and some large docks along the shoreline, which is deep enough for major warships to get in close."

The admiral looked at the place on the chart and nodded. "Is this Dzul in control of that island?"

"Not sure, sir. He controls the Mayan mainland in the area, only eight miles across the water, so he probably does have influence at Cozumel, if not outright control."

Walker's finger followed the coastline down the chart. "So if the Germans wanted to establish a base there, they would need two things politically: stability in the area and permission of the Mexican central government."

I immediately saw his line of thought and extended it. "And assassinating Dzul would eliminate the perennial instability of a rebellious local leader, thereby helping the Mexican government end the Caste War. And in exchange for that, President Díaz gives permission to the Germans to lease the land, probably for decades, and build their Caribbean base."

"Precisely, Wake. The Germans simply go there under the pretext of helping Dzul, probably by offering to supply him guns. They lull him into a meeting, then kill him, probably by poisoning him in a way that doesn't point back to them, as was done to Drake, thus negating the risk of inciting the natives. Then they install a local man in charge who is amenable to their wishes. After that, they quietly slip in some military advisers in mufti and enough modern weaponry to keep the local populace under control."

"Just like they did in Samoa, sir, when they deposed King Malietoa Laupepa and installed Tamasese as king."

"Yes. Simple, low profile, and effective."

I thought the scheme brilliant. "And Díaz won't complain, will he, sir? It's a quiet quid pro quo for ridding him of a war that's drained the country for generations. Thus, the Germans get their base of operations, and the Monroe Doctrine isn't triggered because it wasn't done by brute force and, after all, they are only leasing the land. A neatly done fait accompli, which our leadership in Washington must accept."

Walker's eyes narrowed. "The Germans don't even recognize the Monroe Doctrine and have continually ridiculed it, calling us the United States of *North* America. The Latin countries love hearing *that* sort of talk. And just to make sure the Mexican government remembers the quid pro quo, the German navy shows up in the form of *Gneisenau*, which just happened to put into Key West today. It really is shrewd, isn't it, Wake? They've already got colonies across Africa and the Pacific, and now they'll finally get the beginning of one in the Americas."

The admiral was hot on the trail by then, and pounded the Caribbean coast of Nicaragua on the chart. "And, of course, that base would just happen to be right around the corner from the potential trans-isthmus canal across Nicaragua, wouldn't it?"

I knew Walker was a big proponent of the United States building its own canal across Nicaragua. Many thought it could be a sea level canal and easier to build than the French effort through the mountains in Panama. That endeavor had failed wretchedly, cost twenty thousand lives, and resulted the project's promoter, Ferdinand de Lesseps, being under investigation for bribery and fraud.

"Nicaragua is a good point, Admiral. It's probably their prime underlying motivation. Berlin is thinking well ahead. It'll take years to survey and build that canal. By then, the Germans will be well ensconced, both commercially and militarily."

Walker's reply reflected grudging admiration. "Machiavelli had nothing on these gentlemen in Berlin, and this is just one part of their grand worldwide scheme. Oh, I bet Kaiser Willy's probably on pins and needles right about now, waiting to see how this turns out. It'll be a very nice Christmas present to him, and that current toady of his, Chancellor Caprivi, will probably get some big medal for pulling it off. I wish Bismarck was still in charge over there. He had sense."

The admiral sat back down in his chair and waved for me to do likewise. With pursed lips and drumming fingers, he thought for a while. "Now, what about this Simon Drake fellow? What's your opinion on his real role in this, and why he was poisoned?"

"All we have so far is supposition, sir. But here is my hypothesis," I said. "It is logical to assume Drake probably socialized with the German diplomats and businessmen in Caracas, so he could've heard some snippet of conversation about a potential base in Mexico during evening cocktails. And somehow he came into possession of that chart fragment. I think it's logical to assume it is stolen, torn out of the chart."

The admiral nodded agreement as I continued. "Drake worked in the German telegraph company, so when he saw an odd naval code message, he put two and two together and came up with four, figuring it was about to happen. They guard that naval code pretty closely, so I doubt he knew the true message and the details of who and when, but he might well have already deduced what and why. Then he would have understood the plan was about to unfold."

"So with all that was at stake, they killed him to keep the secret. Operational security, as it were."

"It does look that way, sir. Maybe he was on annual leave and headed back to the United States when the Germans in Caracas discovered what he had. If he ever was able to tell the press when he got to the U.S., the game would be up and Germany would suffer a major loss of face in Latin America. It would've ruined their political and commercial efforts all across the hemisphere. Time was of the essence, so according to their logic, Drake had to be killed—by someone on that ship during the voyage. That person had to have been slipped aboard before they got under way from Venezuela, since the steamer touched at no port between there and Key West."

"Hmm. An American citizen murdered on an American ship in American waters by order of a foreign power—that would light up the New York papers, and Washington as well. It's all supposition, as you say, but it does sound plausible. Still, we've not enough evidence to report this theory as confirmed fact to

Washington just yet."

The admiral was right, for the Harrison administration was in its last few months and the president was still in mourning for his recently deceased wife. Harrison would have no appetite for confrontation with a European power in his final weeks. The new president-elect, former president Grover Cleveland, would take over in March. And I knew from personal experience with Cleveland he wanted no part of a confrontation with any foreign country.

I asked, "If we are right, sir, this happens in only six days. So what do we do now?"

The look in Walker's eye gave me a pretty good idea of the answer. And I knew I wasn't going to like it.

9

The Mission

U.S.S. Chicago
Key West Naval Station
Saturday afternoon
10 December 1892

Before replying to my question, Admiral Walker had more inquiries about the Yucatán Peninsula. "Are there many American citizens on that coast?"

"None to speak of, sir."

"That's good—and one less thing to worry about. Do the Mexicans have a cable station in the area?"

"There's one at Mérida, the main town of the peninsula, sir. It's located up in the interior of the northwest part, about twenty miles inland from the Gulf of Mexico coast, and connects the area with Mexico proper."

"How long to get there from this Mayan coast?"

"From Xel-ha and Cozumel to Mérida's port at Progreso, it would be twenty-four to thirty hours transit under steam, given good weather, around the top of the peninsula. Otherwise, it's at least a week, probably more, to go overland through the dense jungle."

"Too far and too long. Is that the closest cable station?"

"No, sir. The closest cable station would be down the coast at the town of Belize, in British Honduras, about a hundred miles south from Cozumel—it's against the prevailing current and maybe twenty hours steaming time. The British cable goes across to the Cayman Islands and onto Jamaica. From there it goes to Cuba, and then up here to Key West and the United States."

"I see . . ." The admiral paused for another moment of deliberation while examining the calendar on his desk.

Next came his command voice. "Very well, Commander Wake, here are your orders. The Key West station commander will give your ship top priority on everything. As soon as *Bennington* is coaled and provisioned, you will head at best speed for Xel-ha and Cozumel. Time is short. How long will it take you to get under way?"

I thought of Gardiner's lists and tried not to groan. Liberty for the crew would be cancelled yet again. We would need all hands to load the coal, and all the depot workers to load the provisions.

"We'll shift *Bennington* to the wharf when I get back onboard. By working all night, we can be under way at dawn, sir."

Walker knew what it would take, but he showed no gratitude. Instead, he plunged into the details of my task.

"Once there in Mexico, you will meet this Dzul fellow and ascertain the situation with him and the Germans. Then you'll head quickly to Belize and cable me with what you discover. I'll expect the report as soon as you have something solid— and in any event, *no later* than nine a.m. on the fourteenth of December, four days from now. You will receive further orders by return cable once I have your report. Questions?"

"Yes, sir. I have several."

"State them."

"Aye, sir. What is the official reason for our presence there? Should I warn Dzul of the plot? What are my rules of engagement, vis-à-vis the Mexicans and the Mayans? What are the rules regarding my relations with any German citizens or German warships I might find there?"

"Good questions, Commander. I'll take them in order. One, you'll be there on a coastal navigation survey to study the currents and reefs in the Yucatán area. Two, yes, warn Dzul of the plot. Three, as far as this Mexican government versus Mayan squabble, stay neutral, but obviously you will defend your ship and men, or American citizens ashore, if they are attacked by *anyone*. And fourth, as to the Germans . . . hmm . . ."

Walker drummed his fingers on the table while considering the issue. His mien was as grim as death, for he full well understood the weight of his words and the slender limb on which they were placed. "You will exercise the utmost diplomacy and social interaction with them, in order to gain the most intelligence of their intentions."

The admiral eased his expression with a chuckle. "Use your gentlemanly charm, Peter, just as Rork is using his Gaelic wits with his own German counterparts in the grogshops ashore as we speak. Make friends with them."

"What if they are using force against the natives, sir?"

The chuckle ended abruptly. "That's different. If you see any overt German naval or military actions against Mexican civilians, warn the Germans to stop, for they are violating the Monroe Doctrine. If they do not end their action, it is contrary to the accepted behavior of civilized nations and you will intervene to stop it, Commander Wake. I'll not have them doing here in the Americas what they did in the South Pacific. Understood?"

"By civilians, that includes even Mayan Indians, sir?"

"Yes, they are still Mexican citizens and thus our nation's friends."

That was a stretch. Nonetheless, I was about to say "aye, aye," when a thought intruded. "And just in case of the off chance the

Germans engage in action against the Mexican naval or army forces? Do I intervene on the side of the Mexican government?"

"Yes."

"Understood, sir." Another thought came to me. "Sir, what if the Germans use an American-flagged ship to provide weapons or supplies? Or mercenaries, for that matter?"

"You will inspect all American-flagged vessels in the area. It is your right and duty to compel them to stop and be boarded. If you find any evidence of filibustering or smuggling, seize the ship and bring it to Key West."

Our eyes met for a moment. Perhaps sensing my *unspoken* concerns, the admiral added, "And don't worry, I'll put all these instructions in your written orders. Look, Wake, I can't sit here and conjure up ahead of time every possible scenario or combination of circumstances which might happen over there. You'll have to use your judgment if something we haven't discussed comes up."

"Aye, aye, sir."

"Now, as for your operational needs once you get to Mexico. There's a collier putting in here in tomorrow and offloading to the depot. I'll extend her charter, keep some of her coal onboard, and send her to Cozumel Island. Top off your fuel bunkers when she arrives, so you're ready for anything. She'll wait there for ten days, in case any of our ships have need of her coal in the near future. Anything else you need?"

"Yes, sir. Could you please send *Bennington*'s mail in the collier? The station boat told us on the way in the next squadron mail wasn't due for another couple days."

"That will be taken care of," Walker said, then added, "By the way, I've been informed your personal life has taken on a new . . . rather unique . . . dimension lately. I think we should talk about that, and what it might mean for you."

"Not sure what you mean, Admiral," I said, knowing precisely what he meant and not liking it.

10

The Lady

U.S.S. Chicago
Key West Naval Station
Saturday afternoon
10 December 1892

"Well, Wake, I hear you have a new lady in your life. I suppose you're eager to hear from her. Getting the mail to you will help, won't it?"

It was said nonchalantly, but I knew better. John Grimes Walker never spoke without meaning. Not many in Washington were aware of my increasingly close relationship with the cousin of the Spanish ambassador to the United States. In the mounting tension between the two countries over Cuba, it wasn't something I, or she, advertised.

The admiral was a keen observer, and even keener interrogator, and I registered that he was watching my reaction closely. His spies were everywhere, both out in the fleet and back in the Washington bureaucracy. There was no use in denying the facts.

"Ah, well . . . yes, sir, I am eager to hear from her. It's been awhile. Maria writes often, but her mail seems to always be one port behind us."

"Maria is her Christian name? And her family name?"

"Maria Ana Maura y Abad. Her husband died several years ago."

"A Spanish lady, then. She lives in Washington?"

"Yes, on both points, sir. She's lived there for eight years. Her husband was in commerce and they lived in New York before Washington."

"Hmm, well, that's certainly intriguing, isn't it? I imagine she has close connections to the embassy in Washington, and the government in Madrid as well. Society and kinship, and all that."

I didn't like where this was going. Grimes never *imagined* anything—he knew she was part of the Spanish elite and immersed in Washington diplomatic circles.

"Yes, sir. She's a distant cousin of the new Spanish ambassador, Enrique Dupuy de Lomé; lives next door to the embassy; and gets invited to diplomatic events."

"And I'd bet she hears some interesting things in those conversations," he added with a deceptively whimsical chuckle. Anyone who didn't know him would think it an innocent comment. I knew better. Walker had crossed the line. Now I was angry.

"You actually want me to *use* Maria as an informant?" I asked with incredulous rage. Gripping the chair's armrest, I willed myself to remain calm.

He waved a hand, as if I had made a ridiculous allegation. "Oh, no, of course not, Wake. That would be more than a bit crass. But, of course, she might voluntarily pass some little tidbit along. As you well know, even seemingly inconsequential things can sometimes solve riddles."

"She doesn't pass anything confidential or inconsequential along to me," I explained, pointedly omitting the required "sir" for the second time. "I am *not* using her for information."

I will admit I *had* used women for information on occasion, sometimes with regrettable consequences—but none with whom I had a relationship. Admiral Grimes was one of the few who knew who, where, and when those professional occasions had occurred, but he caught my tone loud and clear now, and quickly went full astern.

"Yes, well, whatever. I'm sure you know I meant no offense. Just it's a shame you're such a long way from Washington and not scheduled to return anytime soon. In fact, you're headed to the Med in a month, so you probably won't see her for quite a while, will you?"

Walker's artificial concern angered me even further, so it was with a modicum of satisfaction I countered with, "No, sir. It turns out I probably will see her. Her last letter said she was heading from Washington down to Cuba to visit relatives. From there, in early January Maria's catching the steamer back to Spain. She should be there when *Bennington* arrives at the European Squadron in late January."

"Really? Now that's an interesting development. Good for you. From what I've heard she is quite charming, intelligent, and beautiful—a formidable combination of qualities. Tell me something, is it serious between you two?"

I replied warily, "Possibly . . ."

Indeed, I had been thinking of a future with her, for my life before Maria had been desperately lonely, and my more recent relationships with women had been temporary respites, and ultimately devoid of true affection. Eleven years of being a widower had taken its toll on me, and the thought of merely existing all alone through my final years was depressing.

There were serious drawbacks to the idea of a marriage with this particular lady, however. We were both widowed, but that was our sole commonality. Maria, as accomplished and beautiful a woman as I had ever known, came from an ancient Spanish family. Jewish until the reconquest of Spain by Christian monarchs Ferdinand and Isabella in 1492, they converted to Christianity in order to avoid expulsion—or a worse fate. Four hundred years later, Maria was a devout Roman Catholic who still revered her Jewish roots. Independently wealthy, impressively educated, and quite comfortable among high society, she was connected by bloodlines to the elite of a country many Americans thought of as a decadent enemy, either potential or actual.

On the other hand, I was an Episcopalian turned liberal Methodist, necessarily frugal with money, had never attended any college, was painfully uncomfortable in the presence of the upper social strata, an official persona non grata in Spanish-occupied Cuba, and was integrally involved in preparing our navy and nation for possible future naval action against her country.

Though both she and I fully understood and had discussed these daunting factors, we subordinated them to the improbable affection, genuine respect, and aching love that had grown between us. Still, it required the naiveté of youth to think love could overcome brutal reality and create a truly contented marriage, and I was long removed from my youth.

The admiral's face tightened. "Possibly? Yes, well, here's a word to the wise. Obviously, a union between you two would be culturally and politically . . . challenging, to put it mildly. My suggestion is you should marry into a proper American naval family, like I and so many officers have. It would stand your career in good stead, Wake. And let's face it, now that Admiral Porter has died and the senior leadership of the navy is changing, your career will need some help once I retire in a couple of years."

The admiral regarded me for a moment, then said, "You haven't exactly been one of the good old boys, have you? You never went to the academy. You never won any laurels in glorious open battle. You have no rich family behind you. You never latched onto a rising politician. And after I'm gone, you won't have a mentor looking out for your welfare and career."

He saw I was about to argue and wagged his stern face sagely.

"No, Wake, listen to me. Marriage to a foreigner, and a Spanish one at that, would play right into the common impression about you among the naval aristocracy—and yes, that is exactly what it is, even though we deny it to Congress—in Washington that you aren't really one of them."

I said nothing, trying to keep my temper in check. I hated to admit it, but he was absolutely correct. I was one of only three nonacademy mid-level officers left in the service, and therefore many of my colleagues considered me as something less than an officer and a gentleman. That, combined with my dislike of inane small talk, hypocritical politicians, stupid bureaucrats, and faked courtesies prevalent at society affairs, meant I hadn't been "seen" in Washington much, even though I'd been officially stationed there from '81 to '89.

In addition, the clandestine nature of my intelligence work during those years precluded any recognition of what I had accomplished in that difficult field. In fact, quite a few senior officers thought that sort of work to be completely unbecoming of a gentleman, and something no decent officer would lower himself to do. Thus, most officers looked down upon me, some with pity, and some with contempt. Marrying Maria would confirm their opinion.

Even Rork had shown concern about her, warning me, "Peter, me boyo, the loneliness is gettin' the best o' you. Think clearly on this—with your head an' not your heart."

Admiral Walker cleared his throat. "One more thing, and then I'll end this whole matter. As part of your espionage work, you have employed falsehoods to get unwitting people to give you sensitive information in the past. So consider this—how do you know you're not a target of the Spanish now? There's a real possibility she's trying, quietly and gently, to turn you into an unwitting informant, or even a double agent. You have a large store of knowledge about our operations and plans. Just think about it as a possibility, Wake. That's all I ask."

"I've already considered the possibility, and she's not."

His eyebrows flickered up as he sighed. "Very well, Commander Wake, I hope you're right. No more on that subject.

"Now, back to the matter at hand. Before you get under way, I want to hear what Rork learned from his new German cronies today, so send that old Irish rogue over to me in person. I haven't seen the big rascal for some time, and for some reason I can't really fathom, he cheers me up."

"Aye, aye, sir," I said with trepidation, imagining Rork briefing the admiral on his drinking assignment ashore— directly afterward, when my Irish friend would be still under the influence. *No good can come of that interview*, I thought as I exited the cabin.

Little did I know.

11

The Report

U.S.S. Bennington
Key West Naval Station
Late Saturday evening
10 December 1892

Rork's return to the ship, hours after the coaling had begun, was not greeted pleasantly by his begrimed peers, especially when the word spread he smelled like a brewery when saluting the quarterdeck and reporting to the officer of the watch. I happened to observe the scene from afar and could tell by their expressions that the petty officers were seething with anger. That Rork's subsequent arrival at my cabin would be the topic of much additional negative speculation, I was certain, for he was already thought of by some as the captain's toady.

"Well, Rork, what did you discover?" I asked when my cabin door was shut.

Rork remained standing. He was glassy-eyed, but not drunk. Well, not completely drunk. Like most senior petty officers, he had a substantial capacity for maintaining a façade of semi-sobriety after ingesting a large quantity of alcohol.

There was a slight slur when he spoke, though. "Well, sir, they're a lively bunch, them Germans. Needed a romp ashore, that they did, an' their kraut-eatin' lips got nice an' loose by the second round. Told me they started at La Guaira in Venezuela, an' stopped for a port visit at Colón in Panama, an' another one at Bluefields in Nicaragua. From here they're bound for Tampico, up on the Mexican central Gulf coast."

"What's their mission, officially?"

"They say they're doin' the annual conscript registration o' German émigré lads for their national army back home. Round up all these fellows an' take 'em onboard to get it done. On top o' the paperwork, their sawbones looks the boyos over an' says yea or nay on their fitness."

That was believable. The German Navy did that, or tried to do that, all over the world once a year, except inside the United States and Europe. By German law, any male German citizen of military age anywhere on the globe could be called upon to return and fight for their country in time of war, or imminent war. This manly duty, however, wasn't always appreciated by Germans who had emigrated overseas to find a better life than they had back in the old country. Many had intermarried with the locals and been assimilated with the locals for years, with far more ties to their new home than to the old one.

"Are they running into any resentment by the German families?" I asked, for such resentment might lead to some interesting potential for recruiting ONI informants.

"Aye, that they are, sir. They say not so much in Venezuela, where the Heinies are relatively recent arrivals an' stay to their own kind, but over in Central America there's been some bitchin' from the families that've been there awhile. They don't fancy their sons goin' off an' dyin' for Kaiser Willy. Can't say I blame 'em there."

"No mention of Dzul, Drake, the *Philadelphia*, the Mayans, or Yucatán?"

"Nary a word, sir. I steered the talk that way, but not a one o' 'em took the bait."

"When are they getting under way for Tampico?"

"Well, methinks that's a funny thing, sir. They originally told me they'd be in port a couple o' days. Seems the Heinie officers wanted to have some time to have a look-see ashore here— probably to spy on Uncle Sam's Navy—an' all hands thought it a capital idea. They were plannin' on havin' some memorable jollies. But it looks like the notion just got dashed all to hell."

"How's that?"

"Well, I tell ye, sir, just as we were getting' down to some serious drinkin' a messenger boy from their ship comes in, all in a fluff. He whispers in the senior petty officer's ear—an' then that worthy gets all worked up an' says something in Kraut lingo that made the rest o' 'em haul their sheets an' leave, quick as you please. Senior lad said to me, 'thank you,' but he said it like he was lookin' at a whore in church clothes. An' then he joined the other buggers an' went off at a clip. Never even bought *me* a round, the cheap bastards."

"They left suddenly?" I found it an interesting development. "I presume you followed them."

"Aye, sir. An' right to the boat landin' they went—in formation, o' course—swingin' them arms an' stompin' along at the quick march. I could see they was eyein' our *Benny* pretty close as they went by her on the wharf, especially our guns. They were missin' one o' their mates, but didn't stick around for him. Took their ship's launch from the boat landin' straight to the ship in the anchorage. Ah, but there's more to the tale, sir."

Rork loved to tell about his jaunts ashore and, depending on how much swill he'd drunk, had the tendency to drag the tale on and on. I've learned over the years to be patient. "Continue."

"Well, wouldn't ye know it, sir, but a wee bit later, here comes the wayward lad him ownself. Aye, an' he was drunk as a lord an' towin' none other than dear Annie herself. An' she's none too happy with him, an' latched onto his arm like a limpet. He looked to me to be a senior quartermaster's mate, by the sleeve insignia. By all her fuss, I fathomed he hadn't paid the girl. Bad move on his part."

Bad move, indeed. He was lucky Annie didn't gut him like a fish.

"And so?" I prompted him.

"Ooh, Annie was in an ugly mood, sir. She never lets go o' a man 'til she's got his coin in *her* hand. You get laid, you pay the maid—that's her motto. Well now, she had this poor bugger all aback tryin' to escape from her, an' failin' miserably cause she had 'im right by the ballast stones. Finally he finds a wee bit o' gold coin in his pocket an' slaps it in her hand."

Rork shook his head. "Then she changes her tune, an' gets all cute-like. You know how Annie can be. She rubs on him an' says, 'And just when will ya be back here, my darling Gerhardt?'"

Rork shook his head sadly. "O' course, now the simple fool's smitten again, don't ye know, and he says back to her in that Kraut accent, 'Ve go. Must meet a ship at Mexico. Back in two weeks. I see you then, Annie?' She says back, 'Yes, but with all yer money up front next time, dearie.' An' then he jumped in a bum boat an' headed out to his ship."

"Thank you, Rork. Is that it—learn anything else from Annie after the man headed out to his ship?" I asked. "I presume you both returned to the bar."

"Aye, sir, figured it was part o' me duty to take Annie back an' find out what she knew about those Germans. Well, to make a long story short, it turned out the ol' girl didn't know much at all. She told me ol' Gerhardt wasn't a talker, either in his beer or in her bed. So that's the whole lot o' it, from stem to stern."

"So where's my change from the bar bill?"

"Sir, really . . . there was a boatload o' those Heinies to buy for, an' full three rounds o' drinks. An' then there was ol' Annie, an' you know she's no lightweight when it comes to drinkin' an' such."

"Neither are you."

Rork cast a downward gaze. "Well, not to brag, but bosuns do have a certain reputation to keep up, sir. Wouldn't do to let me profession down, now would it?"

"So, no money left?"

"Nary a penny, sir. But every bit was spent in the service o' me beloved Uncle Sam an' his loyal navy."

I wasn't surprised. "Yes, well Rork, just so you know, that was *my* money, not Uncle Sam's. Anyway, to summarize, they all suddenly departed for their ship, and from a navigation petty officer, you learned there's another ship involved when they get to Mexico, and they'll return here in two weeks?"

"Aye, sir. Methinks that ship's a merchie probably. Ain't another German warship in the Caribbean right now. An' methinks further it's maybe a private filibuster endeavor. Maybe one o' our flags, out o' Texas or New Orleans."

"Why?"

"Just a feelin' in me bones."

"Mercenaries. Well, it's a possibly. Or maybe out of Central America. By the way, did you send that letter to Useppa's church?"

"Ordered an' done, sir, even before me time with the Germans."

"Thank you. Oh, Admiral Walker wants you to personally brief him on what you found out."

Rork's face clouded. "Oooh, the admiral him ownself wants *me*, sir? Don't quite fancy the sound o' that. 'Tis the admiral gunnin' for me about the little lady o' the night thing in D.C. two years ago. On me mother's grave, sir, she told me she'd be gone by daybreak, an' I had no idea she'd be lollygaggin' in me bed during the admiral's inspection."

I shook my head. "No, Rork, you're not in any hot water on that—he got over it a while ago. For some inexplicable reason, he likes you. Just be brief with him and then get back here to work on the coaling. Your absence has surely caused all kinds of rumors to circulate among the officers and the men. Neither of us needs that."

His face split into that ridiculous grin of his. "Aye, methinks our lads're a wee bit jealous, for somehow they've the idea me whole time ashore was for gettin' drunk an' bedded. 'Tis a mystery to me how they came up with these ideas, but not to worry, sir. Sean Rork can still pull his own load, an' then some. This ol' Irish carcass'll out-haul the whole lot o' 'em."

12

The Departure

U.S.S. Bennington
Key West Naval Station
Sunrise, Sunday
11 December 1892

The sun's arrival was a sight to behold, greeting *Bennington*'s worn-out men with a beautiful parade of burnished copper clouds scudding along on the southeast trade wind. This tropical panorama went unnoticed by most, however, for the work of getting the ship underway trumped nature's wonders, and the men were too damned tired anyway.

Lieutenant Gideon Lambert, the ship's gunnery officer and current officer of the deck, showed no such physical debility. On the contrary, though the Iowan had been awake all night like everyone else, myself included, he was still a steady source of questions and commands to the petty officers around him that morning. I found it noteworthy that his comments weren't bothersome, but practical points needing to be made. It was at this moment that I made a decision regarding our departure.

Lambert had fifteen years in the navy and was experienced at handling the ship, but still, taking a warship off a wharf in a crosscurrent, right in front of one's captain and the squadron's admiral, is enough to make the most composed naval officer nervous. It didn't help any that Commander Gardiner, who had taken a disliking to Lambert, was silently watching him like a hawk from the port bridge wing.

An important part of being the captain of a warship is being a teacher, training subordinate officers to take over if the senior officers are incapacitated. The situation that morning somewhat duplicated the stress that went with combat and would be an excellent teaching opportunity. This was a bit unorthodox, but I knew Lambert could do it. However, I wasn't sure *he* if knew he could do it, and so I ordered him, as officer of the deck, to take *Bennington* out to sea. I would be there beside him, and I would take the responsibility if things went wrong. He would get the accolades if they went right.

I walked over to Gardiner and briefed him on my plan. He disagreed, saying either he or I should take the ship out from the wharf, for he thought Lambert too timid, especially for the difficult athwart current that usually runs strongly at that wharf. His objection struck a nerve with me, for when I had briefed him an hour earlier on our confidential orders from the admiral, he'd expressed open doubt as to their wisdom or necessity. Now he was unsupportive of my wish to have Lambert get some practice at ship handling under difficult conditions. I thanked him for his candor, for a captain must never quash it from his number two, and said my orders still stood. Gardiner said "Aye, aye, sir," in a perfunctory manner and I walked away, noting it for the future.

Behind Lieutenant Lambert stood Ensign Theodore Pocket, the junior officer of the deck. Pocket was an '89 graduate of the academy and a bright fellow. Lambert was keeping him very busy, but I saw the ensign didn't get flustered.

The navigator, Lieutenant Commander Warfield, whom I often wished had been the executive officer, reported his recommendations to me from inside the chart room.

"Captain, the transit is approximately three hundred and five miles. The course will be just north of southwest, to a position five miles off the Colorados Reefs at Tobacco Point in western Cuba, thence southwest along the reefs to Cape Antonio at the very western end of Cuba, thence west-southwest to the southern point of Cozumel Island."

"Very good. Time?"

"Maintaining ten knots steaming speed, our estimated time of transit to the south end of Cozumel Island will be thirty-five hours and thirty minutes, which assumes an average three-knot current against us in the Florida Straits, a one-knot countercurrent assisting us along the Cuban coast, and a two-and-a-half-knot current against us in the Yucatán Strait. This makes our estimated time of arrival to be just after first dog watch, about six thirty tomorrow evening, which will be in the dark, one and a half hours after sunset at that longitude."

Warfield paused for questions. I had none, so he continued with his report.

"Current conditions have the wind at Force Four, moderate breeze, nor'east to easterly, sir. Tide is at full ebb of two and three quarter knots, with an hour and a half until slack water. Once we reach the outer mark, I recommend a course of two-five-two, west-southwest, full fore and main sails set, and revolutions for a speed of ten knots."

"Thank you, Commander. I concur," I replied. To Lambert, I said, "Make it so in the log."

Lambert acknowledged and then rattled off his report. "Captain, the ship is fully manned and loaded, steam is up and the shaft is ready, all lines are singled and ship's lines ready to be taken in, the quarter forward spring line belongs to the station and is ready for casting off, and the ship is ready in all respects to get under way."

I was about to acknowledge the lieutenant when a shout came down from high aloft, "Lookout to the bridge! The

German warship off the starboard beam is weighing anchor!"

"Very well, lookout," answered Pocket as we all swung our gaze to starboard, looking past *Chicago*. Out in the anchorage, *Gneisenau's* anchor was already weighed and she was gathering speed toward the main channel, a dirty gray plume of smoke belching from her funnel against the pale blue sky.

"Thank you, Mr. Lambert," I replied, my eyes still on the German ship. "You may commence getting off the wharf and under way on the recommended course."

Then, to everyone around us, I announced, "Mr. Lambert has the conn."

"Aye, aye, sir," chorused the officers and men.

The quartermaster brought over my glass so I could study the foreigner more closely. She had weighed smartly and turned south into the main channel without fuss. Her officers were clustered on the port bridge, watching us just as intently, reflections from the rising sun glinting off their telescope lenses.

Across the wharf, on *Chicago's* port bridge, the admiral was observing us. He waved to me, then pointed toward *Gneisenau*. I nodded back, imagining the questions in his mind were the same as those swirling through mine: *Why her sudden departure? For what destination? Is the assassin onboard her now?*

Lambert began his orders. "Stand by your lines! Take in the forward bow spring line, after bow spring line, stern line, and the quarter-after spring line. Hold that starboard quarter-forward spring line." Pocket echoed the command down to the main deck. I heard Rork pass the order to his men.

Bennington's starboard side was being held on the wharf by the ebbing current and easterly wind, both of which were pressing against the port side of the ship and presenting Lambert with an interesting challenge. He seemed to be handling it calmly. "Take in the bow line," he directed the men on the foredeck.

Once that was accomplished, he ordered the helmsman, "Rudder amidships." Then to the man at the engine telegraph, he said, "Port engine stop. Astern slow on starboard engine."

The man acknowledged the order in the neutral tone common to petty officers on the bridge. Slowly, the ship edged against the wind and tide, the quarter-forward spring line stretched taut, vibrating with the tension of holding the ship parallel fifteen feet from the wharf.

Lambert's next command would be the crucial one. If bungled, the ship's starboard forward half would be swept back down on the wharf—right in front of the admiral.

"Stand by on the starboard quarter-forward spring line. All engines half astern." The rumble faded, then quickly built again, the deck shuddering as both engines increased the shaft revolutions. Their propellers bit into the water, rushing water forward past the bow. A cloud of black smoke erupted from the funnel, to be scattered into wisps by the wind.

Down on the main deck aft, sailors watched as the sole remaining line stretched even more, becoming a thin strand, shaking with the strain. *Bennington*'s starboard side moved farther away from the wharf.

Rork cleared the others from the deck around the starboard quarter bitts, for if the line parted, it could whipsaw a man in half. The starboard quarter-forward spring line was figure-eighted three and a half times around the bitt, and Rork himself stood gripping the tail of the line, using his good right hand. I could see the line beginning to smoke as it tightened against the iron horns of the bitt, while Rork focused on the bridge, waiting for the signal to let go.

Gardiner was grumbling beneath his breath, alternating his glare between Lambert and me.

Lambert waited another fifteen long seconds—about five more than I would have—and as I was about to step in and give the order, he coolly said to Pocket, "Let go the starboard quarter-forward spring line, *smartly.*"

Pocket roared the command to the main deck. Rork let go the end of the spring line and stepped away. The ship, no longer restrained, surged backward into the harbor. The line ran off the bitts and out through the chocks, flying over to the wharf where the naval station's line handlers had already ducked behind cover. The eight of us on the bridge held our breath, waiting to see what would happen forward.

All attention was on the starboard bow, for that was the location of danger and this was the moment of truth. While moving astern, *Bennington* also slid sideways, downcurrent, toward the end of the wharf. Two seconds later the bow cleared the timbers on the wharf's corner with ten feet to spare.

"Good thing we don't have a bowsprit or we would've lost the rig," Gardiner muttered to Lieutenant Lambert, to my displeasure. It was petty, unworthy of an officer in his position.

"All engines stop. Left full rudder," said Lambert, ignoring Gardiner's comment.

The helmsman and lee helmsman repeated the order as they executed it. By the time the engine room telegraph lever had been rung to "All Stop" on its dial, *Bennington* was away from the line of wharves and her bow had swung to leeward, pointed down the channel.

When the ship lost her sternway, Lambert continued his orders. "Rudder amidships. All engines ahead slow. Steady on course two-zero-zero. Steer nothing to the left of course two-zero-zero."

Gneisenau was well ahead of us in the outer channel, nearing the line of reefs that separated the islands from the Straits of Florida. Then she was gone, Fort Taylor's bulk hiding her from us. In another ten minutes, *Gneisenau* would be in the open ocean and free to settle onto her course. From that I would know her probable destination.

But what was her mission?

13

The Mystery Man

U.S.S. Bennington
Key West Naval Station
Sunday morning
11 December 1892

Over on *Chicago*'s bridge, a grinning Admiral Walker waved to us. I recognized *Chicago*'s captain pointing out something on the wharf to another officer. Beside them, a signalman was pulling out code flags from the locker, preparing to hoist a message.

Suddenly, Rork's voice boomed out from the port side of the main deck below the bridge, "Sorry we missed ye, me dear! Next time for sure!"

Leaning over the rail, I followed his line of sight. Standing at the head of the naval wharf was my daughter Useppa, her hand fluttering a blue scarf in farewell, auburn hair waving around her face in the breeze. I felt my heart stop, for she looked just like her mother did at that age.

A man, dark haired and thin, stood close to her. Very close

to her. Probably a pastor, I decided. But no, he was standing too close for that. And then they were gone from my sight as we moved away and *Chicago*'s superstructure blocked the view.

Hopes and worries flooded my mind. My heart always considered Useppa a little girl, but my brain reminded me she was twenty-seven now and alone in the world—a spinster. My son Sean was a naval officer, two years out from the naval academy and recently passed the examination for ensign. He was well started on his career, but what would happen to my daughter?

The lee helmsman reported to Lieutenant Lambert the shaft revolutions from the engine room. I forced myself back into the present moment.

"Well done, Mr. Lambert," I said.

The trace of a smile crossed his face for a second. "Thank you, sir."

"My only suggestion is to let go the quarter-forward spring a couple seconds earlier. It almost parted."

His stoic mien returned. "Aye, aye, sir."

"Message from the admiral, sir," interrupted the duty signalman. "It reads: 'Well done. Good luck.'"

I'll need it, I thought, as I noted Gardiner's expression turning sour.

As we passed Fort Taylor and altered course to due south, down the outer channel, I saw the German warship's course. It wasn't the correct one for Tampico, which would have been due west. The German was heading southwest.

Yucatán.

Pocket reported from the port bridge wing, "Mr. Lambert, the pilot boat's approaching to pass us, close on port bow. She's returning from picking up the harbor pilot on *Gneisenau*."

I noticed the ensign pronounced the name correctly and wondered if he could speak the language. Then I thought of something—U.S. Navy vessels didn't use a pilot at Key West, but foreign warships were required to use one, and many times their bridge officers imparted subtle bits of information to the pilot.

"Mr. Lambert, have the pilot boat hailed to come alongside," I said. "I want to speak with the pilot in my cabin. And please send word to my steward to bring some breakfast for two to the cabin."

We were well past the reefs when the pilot, an old grizzled salt if ever there was one, entered my quarters and introduced himself. "Captain Rolle, sir, senior harbor pilot. You wanted to see me, Captain?"

The Rolle family was originally from the Abaco Islands of the northern Bahamas. They had been in Key West for generations as schooner captains and wreckers. Captain Rolle still had a faint trace of a British accent.

"Welcome aboard, Captain Rolle, I'm Commander Wake, captain of *Bennington*. Please sit down and share my breakfast. I wanted to ask you about the shoaling by Whitehead Spit. Is it getting worse?"

He was wary. This sort of invitation, especially in the outer channel, was unusual from a U.S. navy captain. The sunburned skin around his eyes crinkled in appreciation, as if I'd made a joke.

"Well, thank you, Captain Wake. Don't mind if I do take a bite, this looks good. Aye, sir, the shoal has been getting worse ever since the storm in June, but you knew that." His gaze narrowed. "You've been in and out of here many times since then."

"Yes, well, I just wanted to make sure. Say, I think I saw you on the German ship up ahead. What's she like?"

Rolle never stopped chewing the fried eggs in his mouth as he replied, "Well-handled and in excellent condition. Curious thing, though, they asked the very same thing about this ship."

"Did they really? Anything else curious about them?"

A gulp of coffee was followed by, "Nothing, except for the fellow our pilot boat brought out to them. Older European man, maybe German, maybe Russian, I don't know. Said he missed the last launch out to the anchorage before the ship weighed, so he asked if the pilot boat could take him when they went out to get me."

I chuckled and shook my head. "Guess he was in trouble for missing ship's movement, wasn't he? Probably was passed out in a trollop's bed when the sun came up. Did they put him under disciplinary arrest?"

"No, I think not. Officers weren't upset with him a bit. He's not in the navy, I can tell you that."

"How do you know?" I asked.

Rolle shook his head. "This fellow was dressed like a store clerk, and sober as a Baptist. Very quiet. No color in his skin. No sway to his walk. Uncomfortable on the boat out, my crew tells me, and when I saw him board the ship he looked out of place. Oh yes, he's a landsman if ever I saw one, through and through. Acted untouchable, like a passenger. Carried a valise and case."

"Did you hear a name?"

"Never got introduced to him. Neither did the pilot boat crew. You surely seem interested in him, Captain. Who was he?"

Captain Rolle was no fool, and knew something was afoot, so I was semi-candid with him. "I have no idea. We don't get German warships at Key West often. I was just wondering why they are here. And why they left so suddenly."

"So was I, Captain. So was I," agreed the pilot as he gulped down the last of the coffee. "Never learned why they got under way all of a sudden this morn. They were supposed to stay for three days."

I ended on a relaxed note. "Yeah, well, there's probably nothing to it. They needed a liberty port for the men and Key West is convenient and safe. The fellow who came out to the ship is probably just some German merchant who missed his packet steamer, saw the opportunity, and hitched a ride. Warships get those requests on distant stations all the time. I know we do."

"Maybe," said Rolle.

I could tell he didn't believe it any more than I did.

14

The Yucatan

Yucatán Channel
Monday afternoon
12 December 1892

We lost sight of *Gneisenau* while off Cuba that first evening, shortly after sunset. I expected as much. Though we were faster under steam alone, she was larger and faster downwind under sail and engine.

In order to escape the eastbound main current of the Gulf Stream and its progenitor, the northbound Yucatán Current, *Bennington* steamed close along the northwest coast of Cuba to use the westbound countercurrent—but not too close. We were careful to maintain at least four miles of distance offshore, a mile beyond the Spanish territorial limit. Each hourly position fix was double-checked by both officers on watch. Our vigilance in this regard was reinforced by a steam cutter from *La Guardia Costera* that paralleled us inshore as long as we were within sight of the island.

No one on board *Bennington* except Rork knew why I was

69

so adamant about our exacting course. The others were not privy, and hopefully would never be privy, to the fact Rork and I were considered personae non gratae by the Spanish authorities, following a rather violent end to our last ONI mission there four years earlier. In fact, there might even be warrants for murder waiting for us there.

Once we left the Cuban coast at Cabo de San Antonio and headed southwest across the Yucatán Channel, the seas built to gigantic proportions, every bit of twenty feet high. This was the product of a thirty-knot northwesterly wind, which arrived later that day. Blowing across the Gulf of Mexico, it collided with the strong current coming up from the Caribbean to the south. Fortunately, we had no thick cloud cover shutting down visibility completely, only scattered squalls bringing even greater winds and rain.

Unfortunately, however, there was no pattern or slope to the seas as we headed south-southwest—with the wind but against the current. The waves rose suddenly straight up like wet gray sea monsters. Occasionally a rogue wave would outdo the rest, a predator rearing up to tower over us before falling down on our foredeck and washing its way aft, submerging everything. The sea forced itself through any aperture, no matter how tiny, to send a jet of water into the gun deck, crew berthing, galley, and mess spaces. Within an hour, everything in those areas was soaked and water sloshed fore and aft along all the decks below.

Ten minutes of steam-driven bilge pumps per hour became fifteen, then twenty, and I worried about the engine and, most especially, about the condition of our four boilers. The strain on *Bennington*'s mechanical apparatus was mounting, and the hourly reports by the chief engineer were getting more pessimistic. His men in the gyrating engine and boiler rooms were doing their best to keep everything functioning, but each hour added to the toll on the components.

It was impossible to sleep, eat, or work without holding on for dear life with at least one hand at all times—a condition that

soon tires the strongest of men. This was aggravated by the speed
necessitated by our orders. Under reefed fore and main sails,
and with the shaft turning for ten knots, the motion of the ship
was increased to the discomfort of all in her as she smashed into
another watery ridge every sixty seconds. And when our stern
was lifted out of the water by the roll of the waves, the entire hull
shuddered with the cavitation of the propeller in the air.

None of this was appreciated by the men, half of whom had
not a minute of liberty in Key West. Those who did get a taste of
that first ale had their freedom ashore cut short when *Bennington*
suddenly shifted to the coal dock. They were even more upset
about what they viewed as a theft of their personal free time.

For the initial day of the voyage, the men were busy cleaning
the ship, just as they had after our departure from Kingston. I
studied them intently to ascertain signs of disaffection beyond
the usual complaining over lost liberty. On the next morning,
Norton Gardiner was going over division reports with me when
he alluded to seeing and hearing some serious disgruntlement
among the men. When I pulled him aside and pressed for
specifics, he backed away from his insinuation, saying it was just
an impression.

On the second day, I had just finished my luncheon—alone
in my cabin, as is usual for a captain—when Gardiner arrived
in a troubled state, saying the ship needed to slow down, for the
crew's endurance was near the end.

I thought it odd, for the sea conditions, while rough and
miserable, were nothing beyond that which veteran sailors know
on many occasions in their time at sea. The ship was still sound,
without any major damage or malfunctions, and ready for
anything which might be required. None of the crew had been
injured beyond some contusions and minor lacerations.

I decided to start out even tempered, for I remembered from
my own experiences that executive officers have a lot of pressure
upon them. "Don't worry, Norton, the men can handle it. We all
can. This is a warship, after all, not a yacht. Besides, in another

couple of hours we'll be out of the main current and these seas from the opposing wind and current will diminish."

That logic failed to impress him. His next comment crossed a crucial line.

"Look, Captain, this whole thing is ridiculous. We're punishing our men and our ship for what? Who cares if the Germans want to parley with some tribal peasants and kill off one of their *bandido* leaders? In fact, who cares if they make niceties with the Mexican government and get a naval station? If they want to get involved with those uncivilized scum, that's their problem. The wardroom is sick of this kind of thing, going from one banana republic upheaval to the next. These Latin Americans are worthless and always will be."

"Really?" I said, curious about what would come out of his mouth next.

"Yes, sir. What we should be doing is cementing our friendship with the European powers in the Caribbean, not trying to thwart them. Modern civilized countries are our natural allies—not a bunch of uneducated, un-Christian, mongrel thugs who dress up in generals' uniforms and call themselves, 'President of the Republic,' or some other such nonsense." He blew out a breath in exasperation. "This is just one more of the admiral's half-cocked notions."

The foundation for Norton Gardiner's resentment toward me and the admiral was understandable enough. He had been executive officer under the previous captain, and had thought— no, he had been absolutely convinced—he would be given the command when it became available. In fact, he had assured the wardroom officers it was a certainty. His seniority in grade was also two numbers ahead of mine, though he was five years younger and had three years less time in the service than me. This was due to his early promotion to commander, courtesy of his political connections.

Norton Gardiner was everything I was not—academy graduate, independently wealthy, sophisticated bon vivant and raconteur, and the scion of a politically influential family in Boston who was allied with the senior senator from the state. Most of his limited sea duty had been in Europe, where the navy cruised along the coasts to show the flag and attend cocktail parties. Very little of my naval career had been in that elegant part of the world. The majority of his time in the navy had been on staff assignments at headquarters, or at naval yards, or teaching at the academy. He had been in *Bennington* from her commissioning, however, and thus was a "plank owner," with the attendant pride of ownership. He considered her *his* ship.

But Norton Gardiner didn't realize his grand prophecy. An uncultured newcomer arrived to take command, while the true gentleman who actually deserved the honor had suffered a gross humiliation in front of his subordinates. It was as mystifying as it was humiliating to Gardiner.

There were two attributes I had that he did not. The first was that I had actually commanded a ship against the enemy in war. The second was a solid record of accomplishing dangerous missions, most of them clandestine and completely unknown to both the public and the majority of the naval officer corps.

Gardiner's disappointment had worsened over the months since I'd taken command, occasionally emerging in unguarded comments and facial expressions. I allowed those to go without rebuke, for I hoped his attitude would improve. He was no longer bothering to disguise his feelings, though, and now he had gone too far. It was time to stop it cold.

I waited all of twenty seconds before replying, the entire time looking into Gardiner's smug face, trying to gauge whether he was just stupid or actually Machiavellian. Was this a plan to goad me into overreacting with theatrics, or to entice me into agreeing with his assessment of the admiral's orders in a moment of camaraderie? It was impossible for me to determine by studying that cold countenance, a situation I found even more disconcerting.

Taking out my pocket watch, I informed him, "Commander

Gardiner, you have just committed insubordination. I will give you ten seconds to recant your statement and make amends."

The cold expression vanished. His eyes flared with rage. "What! Are you serious?"

"You now have five seconds."

His demeanor abruptly dissolved. "Wait! Sir, please wait. Captain, I meant no disrespect to you or the admiral. I just thought we were airing personal opinions, sir. I've been in the navy for over twenty years, sir, and have never uttered a single word that was insubordinate."

"After serving four months with you, I find that hard to believe, Commander Gardiner. And I further find your reply was not a sincere apology or amendment of your original statement. Leave this cabin at once and attend to your duties, *without* the negative attitude toward your superior officers and their decisions. I will decide your fate later."

He leaned across my desk and began to plead. "Captain, really, I—"

"Get out of this cabin and do your job, Commander Gardiner, while you still have one."

I sat there for some time afterward, assessing the state of affairs and my options. I could have Gardiner restricted to his quarters and transferred immediately upon return, but it would cause turmoil in the ship. No, it hadn't gotten that bad. Besides, we were going into harm's way and I needed every officer and man to be focused. Memories of a similar predicament came to mind.

Back in 1869, I was the executive officer of a ship commanded by a man who was eccentric in the extreme. His behavior changed into outright lunacy and forced me one night to make a decision, the one which no naval officer wants to even contemplate. I relieved the captain from command and continued with our mission. Subsequently, I was court-martialed for it, surviving the proceedings with honor and career intact, but enduring rumors and innuendos of mutiny have followed me ever since.

Now the scenario was the opposite—I was the captain. And the problem man was the one officer aboard on whom I had to completely rely and trust. The admiral expected me to go ashore and meet Dzul, but dare I leave the ship in Gardiner's hands?

As I considered the issue, *Bennington* abruptly hit a particularly large sea, stopping her as if she'd hit a granite reef. All loose items lying about in my cabin were flung up into the air and against the forward bulkhead. I and my chair were capsized to the deck, where I managed to land squarely on my bad right shoulder. To top off the day quite nicely, above me the preventer chains of the lantern parted, allowing it to smash into the deck overhead and shatter the glass, which then showered down around me. Little shards embedded into my hair and clothing.

I quickly rose to my feet, not wishing for the steward to see me in such a sorry state, for I knew what would be around the ship in minutes: *I found the captain sprawled on the deck—he was either seasick or drunk, I don't know which.*

The Yucatán Channel was living up to its reputation.

15

The Ruins

Isla Cozumel, Mexico
Monday evening
12 December 1892

Lieutenant Commander Warfield's original estimate wasn't that far off, for we arrived at Cape Celarain, the southernmost point of Cozumel Island, in the dark at 8:35 p.m. The wind was still strong and had gone a bit westerly. The sky had grown completely overcast, with no stars in sight and occasional showers of rain. The land was a faintly darker line on the horizon several miles to the north. Having no landmark or star to fix our position, our location was only an approximation—most definitely not a comfortable situation for a ship captain on a strange coast.

Lieutenant Manning had the deck. I ordered him to get the ship hove to, with enough revolutions on the shaft to keep her bow into the waves and wind from the northwest, which had moderated somewhat by the proximity of the mainland in that direction. I was sure in the morning light we could get a better

·

bearing on the island to our north and thus fix our position precisely.

At precisely 11:12 p.m.—such things are recorded in men-o-war's logs—the duty messenger arrived at my cabin in inform me a ship was in sight off the port bow, about a mile west of us.

Thirty seconds later, I was on the rain- and wind-lashed bridge deck outside the wheel house, peering through the night glasses into the gloom. The other ship was barely discernable, fading in and out of sight, her running lights tiny pinpricks of red and green

"It's the Germans, Captain. So much for their Tampico story." Gardiner came up beside me in the dark. His face was a mask, imparting no clue to his thoughts.

Seconds later, I heard confirmation from the poor soul assigned to the swaying main top. "Lookout to bridge! I think she's the German ship from Key West, sir!"

Manning was still on watch. "Any new orders, Captain?"

Like everyone aboard, he had surmised the reason we were in Mexico had something to do with the *Gneisenau*, just not what it was or why. Actually, I wasn't certain myself of what I would do next.

"Her captain's getting up more steam," said Gardiner while looking through the glass.

"Yes, I agree, sir," offered Manning to the executive officer. "She's bearing off to the west, toward the Mexican mainland. She's bigger than us, and can muscle through easier."

I shook my head. "But she's square-rigged. We can steam-sail ahead easier with our fore and aft schooner rig, gentlemen, and thus fore-reach on her, especially on this point of wind."

When she'd first arrived at Key West, I studied my reference material on *Gneisenau*'s characteristics. They included an important point, which now became salient. In ONI's *Principal Characteristics of Foreign Ships of War*, it showed that while *Gneisenau* was a bigger ship with slightly larger caliber guns, *Bennington* had a much larger engine and two shafts to the Germans' one.

"Our steam plant is more powerful than hers, gentlemen. Mr. Manning, kindly set double-reefed fore and main sails, and have all engines ahead full. *Gneisenau*'s top steaming speed is twelve knots and with all the windage aloft she'll be even slower, so I want shaft revolutions for fourteen knots to get close to her."

Manning nodded excitedly. "Aye, aye, sir. Course?"

"Follow her course. Close to with half a mile astern of her, then conform to her speed. I do *not* want to lose her in the dark this time."

"Aye, aye, sir."

"They'll know we're following them if we're that close, sir," Gardiner said, somewhat unnecessarily.

"I want them to know," I replied.

"Bridge there!" shouted the lookout aloft. "Another ship is barely in sight, broad on the port bow, well beyond the German!"

I called for the officer of the deck. "Mr. Manning, who is aloft on lookout?"

"Able Seaman Benion, sir."

Benion had been in the navy for seventeen years. Every time he'd worked his way up to a promotion, he lost it soon afterward to drunkenness, both afloat and ashore. I needed a better set of eyes up there. I noticed the junior officer of the watch examining the Germans from the port side of the bridge.

"Young sharp eyes are called for right now, Mr. Manning. Please send Ensign Yeats aloft with a night glass. I want a good description of the other ship."

Ten minutes later it was delivered with a thump as Yeats jumped down to the deck from his climb. "Other ship is a steam collier, sir! Looks American to me and low in the water. She's bound westerly, a mile or so ahead of the German."

I evaluated the new information. It was too soon for our collier to have arrived. How many colliers would there be on this remote coast? She was probably the ship the tardy German petty officer had mentioned to Annie Wenz at Key West. Both the *Gneisenau* and the collier were bound to the west. Xel-ha and Dzul were in that direction. The ships would be there the following morning, the thirteenth of December—time was running out.

While Manning was busy getting the sails set, Gardiner leaned close to me and said, "With all due respect, Captain, we are now in Mexico's territorial waters, and openly chasing a warship of a major European power. May I ask if we have gone to a war status? The officers will want to know."

He made his inquiry with a tone of curiosity, as if he were merely an observer to the whole affair, not a participant. I could just imagine the wheels turning inside his clever head, however. *He's already building his defense for the court-martial—and his testimony against me.*

"War? No, we are not at war," I replied quietly. "But we must always be prepared for any eventuality, at any time, in the execution of our national policy. This is a warship, not a diplomat's yacht that looks pretty and cruises from cocktail party to cocktail party."

"Thank you for the clarification, sir. This should turn out to be very interesting."

It was. Through the night, *Gneisenau* slowed and followed directly astern of the merchant ship, matching the collier's slower speed of only five knots against the wind and waves. *Bennington* followed suit, so when the eastern sky finally lightened behind us, the ships were still in a column, a mile apart from each other, a few miles off the low mainland coast.

Dead ahead of the ships, a crumbling moldy-gray stone structure was silhouetted above the jungle, near a shallow inlet of sparkling jade-colored water, which curved around behind the beach. Illuminated by the first rays of the sun peeking through the clouds, it was an incongruous and slightly ominous sight. The chart confirmed we had reached our unusual destination: the ancient Mayan ruins of Xel-ha.

There was no harbor. One after another, the three vessels

let go their hooks just off the sandy beach in front of the ruins, in calm water formed by the lee of the Yucatán Peninsula. The primary ruins seemed to be some sort of a palace, built up from layers of squared-off terraces to a height of perhaps four stories. Around it was structure of several lower terrace elevations, and in the periphery were scattered several groupings of thatched huts. On the sandy beach a few canoes were pulled up, with locals milling around, staring at the modern warships suddenly intruding into their home.

The collier, whose name we could see was the *Marie,* of Portland, Maine, was closest inshore. The German cruiser anchored three hundred yards outboard of her, and we Americans were anchored outboard of the German by an equal distance.

I knew what was expected next. There are strict rules regarding the protocol between foreign warships. Breaching those rules is a dishonor not only to the other ship, but to the country. I had no wish to get diverted into a diplomatic dither over social graces on which Europeans, and Americans like Gardiner, place absurd value.

Fools have actually gone to war for such things.

16

The Naval Necessities

Xel-ha Anchorage, Mexico
Tuesday morning
13 December 1892

In the situation we were facing, the latest ship to arrive—
Bennington—sends a boat containing an officer to the
existing naval occupants of the anchorage—*Gneisenau*—to
render greetings and inquire as to the rank and the seniority
within grade of her commanding officer, and also to provide
the same information about their own captain. Upon receipt of
the information, the officers of both navies would know who
was senior, and thus the courtesies would begin. We were only
minutes behind the Germans, but that mattered not—we were
the new arrivals, and so our boat shoved off.

Many naval officers reveled in the pomp, having been
inculcated in the stuff at the naval academy. Gardiner, naturally,
was among them. I learned long ago to keep my opinions on the
matter to myself, lest I ignite the zealous wrath of my brethren
and even more accusations of not being enough of "a true naval

gentleman" by the blue water aristocracy. Yes, it is ridiculous, I know, but that is the way it is.

After the boat visit, Lieutenant Lambert reported back that FregattenKapitan Heinst Blau had been promoted to the German equivalent of commander on the twelfth of February, 1883. He thus had six months of seniority in rank on me and was the senior naval officer present in the anchorage. Lambert assumed a carefully bland expression as he presented this information, but a peripheral glance at Gardiner revealed a brief smile crossing his usually enigmatic face.

I gave the expected orders. "You may have the watch begin the usual professional courtesies, Mr. Lambert. And kindly inform our German colleagues I will visit *Gneisenau* and render my respects in one hour."

"Aye, aye, sir."

"See anything of note aboard her?"

"Yes, sir. One thing stuck out. When I went onboard, I noticed they had ready ammunition lockers opened and the gun covers cast off at the secondary batteries. I think they wanted me to see all that. The officer on the quarterdeck was polite, but not friendly."

"To be expected," commented Gardiner. "They are suspicious of our intentions."

I ignored him and asked Lambert, "See any civilians onboard?"

"No, sir."

"And what did you learn about the collier?"

"*Marie* is owned by the New York company of Strauss and Wilcox, sir. Needs maintenance, but not as bad as some I've seen. Captain Anson Wilson, commanding. Old and tired, with a drinker's nose and eyes, but appears to be professional. He says they arrived at the north end of Cozumel Island from Havana yesterday afternoon, looking for the German cruiser. *Marie* had been waiting for orders at Havana for three weeks, under charter to the German government through the consulate at La Guaira,

Venezuela. She's carrying a full load of eleven hundred tons of anthracite coal. They were supposed to fill *Gneisenau*'s bunkers somewhere at Cozumel Island, then head off to Roatán up in Honduras to coal a couple German merchantmen waiting there."

One may recall that three weeks earlier would have been around the time the packet steamer *Philadelphia* left La Guaira with Drake aboard. Several more ideas occurred to me just then, and Lambert was just the man to carry them out.

"Mr. Lambert, I have five additional tasks for you. First, please inform the duty watch to place the following order in the log. While we are at this place, I want all boats departing or arriving at *Gneisenau* observed closely but covertly, night and day, to see if there are any civilians among the boats' passengers. *Observe only*, Mr. Lambert. Notify me immediately when it is found to be the case. We will employ a guard boat at night, both for the purpose and, of course, to protect *Bennington*'s men from the temptations of the shore."

"Aye, aye, sir."

"Second, inform my steward we will be inviting the German captain and two of his officers to luncheon in my cabin at one o'clock. Something typically American, like grits, for the meal. Commander Gardiner and Lieutenant Commander Warfield will attend the luncheon and need an invitation. It will last until at least three p.m. and the uniform will be tropical white dress."

"Aye, aye, sir."

"Third, please make sure *Bennington* is squared away and looking like a proper man-o-war."

"Aye, aye, sir," said Lambert. Then, with a sly grin, he added, "Should I do anything particular with our guns, sir?"

As the ship's gunnery officer, Lambert was especially fond of his "persuaders," as he referred to our main battery of six-inch guns. The secondary battery of light six-pounder quick-firing guns were his "little babies."

"Some quick-loading drills would look impressive."

That made the lieutenant's grin spread from ear to ear.

"Impressive, indeed, sir. Aye, aye. What's the fourth thing, sir?"

"I want you to quietly go ashore while the German officers are having lunch with us. Your official reason will be to inquire about the history of the ruins, for a report to go to the Smithsonian Institution in Washington—which you will, in fact, compose. Your real reason, however, is to find the local head man and make arrangements to get a sealed confidential message from me to a man named Dzul—he is the regional leader—and make sure they know the message is extremely urgent. I will give it to you in a few minutes. Understood, so far?"

"Aye, aye, sir."

"Good. Questions?"

"No, sir."

"Very well. Just for your information, this man Dzul is also the chief Mayan rebel leader in these parts. The message is a request for an immediate meeting with me tomorrow morning at ten a.m. in the lagoon away from sight of the warships—but do not tell anyone in the village of that."

"Yes, sir. And number five?"

"On your way to shore, have a private talk with Captain Wilson of the *Marie*. A very serious private talk. Inform him his country's navy needs the coal in his ship right away in Key West. He will get under way today, right after you leave his ship, and upon arrival at Key West he will report to Rear Admiral Walker in *Chicago*. There will be no financial loss, and in fact the U.S. Navy will pay him one and a half times what the Germans had contracted for, once he presents the German invoice as proof. I will give you a cover letter signed by me for Wilson to present to Admiral Walker."

I said my next words slowly. "Lieutenant Lambert, you will make sure Wilson agrees to this and complies immediately. No hesitation. No explanation to the German warship. I will personally explain it to the Germans for Wilson when they come to lunch. Understood completely?"

"Yes, sir."

"Very good. After you get all this done and return to the ship, report back to me on your results."

With the same grim look as when he had taken *Bennington* off the wharf in Key West, Lambert carefully repeated each of my instructions and I acknowledged them.

As I turned to go below, I added, "Remember, Mr. Lambert—it is imperative all this gets done *quietly*."

"Aye, aye, sir."

As he turned to go, I thought Gideon Lambert just might be the kind of man ONI could use in the future. This would be an excellent test of his abilities.

17

The Required Visit

Xel-ha Anchorage, Mexico
Tuesday afternoon
13 December 1892

It turned out my impression was correct, for Ensign Pocket did understand a bit of German, so I had him come along with me to the *Gneisenau*. He was to scrutinize the German warship, not let on he had some of their lingo, and listen to their conversations, alert for any signs of preparation for impending battle. He was also to see if a civilian was onboard and look for indications of a meeting with the locals ashore.

Our arrival was received in the precise Teutonic fashion I had seen in the Pacific. As I climbed the boarding ladder, a crescendo of action erupted when my head rose above the main deck. Petty officers twittered their pipes, a line of side boys came to stiff-backed attention, the officers of the watch clicked their heels and rendered the salute, and all aboard stopped what they were doing, stood up straight, and faced the quarterdeck. The Royal Navy of Queen Victoria herself would be hard pressed to surpass the performance.

While my junior was immediately diverted to the German wardroom—there to be plied with gin and other intoxicants in the reciprocal of what Rork had done at Key West—I was shown to the commanding officer's cabin.

A warship captain's quarters function as more than his home. It is also his office and his diplomatic salon. The space is designed to impress foreign visitors, not just with the hospitality of their host, but by the grandeur and power of his navy. The intent is intimidation in its most subtle form.

The Kreigsmarine of imperial Germany had certainly succeeded in that effort with the captain's cabin of *Gneisenau,* which proved to be an even more luxurious version of my own embarrassingly lavish quarters. Palatial is not too strong a word for it—plush red carpets, soft black leather sofa and chairs, dark blue satin curtains, polished coffee tables, intricate nautical artwork on the paneled bulkheads, magnificent crystal and china displayed around the cherrywood dining table, and a desk fit for an admiral. Rear Admiral Walker would be jealous of the place. I reminded myself to give him a detailed description, just to see his reaction.

As protocol required, I introduced myself upon entering the cabin. "*Guten morgen, Kapitän.* I am Commander Peter Wake, captain of the United States Ship *Bennington.* Regrettably, sir, I cannot speak German beyond a simple greeting, and I fear I may have not even said that especially well. I look forward to making your acquaintance, and offer any and all assistance while we are in your ship's company."

The captain, a barrel-chested man of medium height with thin lips and eyes, and his number two, a thin man with nervous mannerisms, both greeted me with profound handshakes, as if we were long-lost friends.

"Not to worry, Commander Wake," replied the captain. "I can converse in the language of Shakespeare, for I trained at the academy at Dartmouth with our cousins, the English. I am

FregattenKapitan Heinst Blau, the captain of *Gneisenau*. And this is KapitanLeutnant Otto Eichermann, my executive officer who, like you, can also only speak simple greetings in your language. Welcome onboard our humble ship. May I offer you some refreshment? I am happy to report even after traveling four thousand kilometers, our gin is not that bad."

I dislike gin intensely, can't even stand the smell, but Brits and Germans love the stuff and it is de rigueur to accept a taste when offered.

"Thank you very much, sir, but only one small glass, please. I have a lot of reports to go over and then some disciplinary decisions to make when I return." I shrugged—one navy's captain commiserating with another. "I find a clear head is better for these things, particularly the disciplinary decisions."

Blau nodded sympathetically. "Ah, yes, naval discipline. It is the unforgiving, but necessary, foundation of any true warship. Where would we be without it? You know, we saw your ship at Key West, Commander. How ironic we are both here now. May I ask what brings *Bennington* to this backward area of Mexico?"

I gave another shrug, as I lied through my teeth. "Oh, our assignment here is just the mundane and never-ending work of coastal survey, sir. Charting the currents, and also sending some ethnological reports about the Mayan ruins to the scientists at the Smithsonian Institution."

I let out a commiserating sigh and added a baited hook to the conversation. "And, no doubt, right when I am busy with all these others things, some missionary or trader will probably demand passage back to the United States, which I will have to provide. That happens all the time to us. I suppose you have German citizens demanding passage on your warships, too?"

Blau didn't bite the hook. "No. That would be strictly prohibited, except in an emergency."

Hmm, I thought. *What would constitute an emergency, then?* Then I got to the main point. "Ah, yes, you are fortunate in that regard then, sir. So what brings your magnificent ship here?"

"Coaling from the collier we met here on this savage coast last night. Then we go onward with our mission to register our countrymen who live along the Mexican coastline. It is an annual duty." Blau shook his head in self-pity. "Yet another example of the unappreciated work performed by the navy for the fatherland."

"I didn't know German émigrés lived here."

"They are scattered along the coast, but mostly to the north of this place."

"Really, I thought in this coast of Yucatan there is only the rebel leader Dzul, and his Mayans. Interesting fellow—do you know of him?"

Blau immediately said, "I do not know the local bandits of Mexico. I am here for my assignment, disagreeable as it is."

The whole thing sounded like a lie to me, but I nodded in solemn agreement. "I think no one back in our homelands really understands or cares about what we have to endure out here in the savage areas of the world."

"So true," Blau said. "They are comfortably ignorant."

I bowed slightly and said, "I will be disposing of my administrative duties by the end of the morning and would be greatly honored if you would be my guest for a luncheon in my cabin at one o'clock, sir. Please bring two of your officers along. It will be an excellent opportunity for the officers of our two navies to get acquainted."

It was Blau's turn to bow. "It will be our great pleasure, Commander Wake. Thank you for the kind invitation. We very much look forward to seeing a ship and crew of the American Navy. Your ships are so unique, but then so is your country, of course."

He said it with a smile, but it came out as condescending.

"It's always a pleasure for us to entertain, though I must say in advance we aren't as splendidly furnished as you. Our accommodations are rather Spartan in comparison. Our Congress and president prefer their warships them that way . . .

for the obvious reasons, of course."

Captain Blau bowed curtly in response, all the while maintaining his damned smile.

18

The Luncheon

Xel-ha Anchorage, Mexico
Tuesday afternoon
13 December 1892

Norton Gardiner had his faults, but he did have the ability to put on a good show for visiting brass. This he had done for the British in Jamaica and Barbados, the Dutch in Curaçao, and the French in Martinique. I ordered him to do so for the Germans.

When the official welcoming pomp was done, Gardiner guided the obligatory tour of our ship—with a close look at her guns. They received approving nods from our guests, who were then shown to the table in my cabin. The Germans did not disguise their surprised low impression of my quarters. The cabin was simplistic when compared to European counterparts, for in the U.S. Navy the captain, not the government, furnishes his living space.

I opened the luncheon with a toast. "To His Imperial Majesty, Kaiser Wilhelm the second, ruler of the worldwide empire of Germany. May he enjoy a long and successful life."

Blau responded in a booming voice. "And to His Excellency Benjamin Harrison, President of the United States of North America! May he also enjoy a long and prosperous and peaceful life."

I caught the dig, loud and clear, though no outward indication of intentional insult was apparent on part of the German. He had done it quite nonchalantly, in fact. Blau's round face was beaming, the limiting descriptor "North" was not accentuated, and the other German officers didn't appear to react. Not so with the Americans, however. Gardiner looked confused, Warfield glowered, and I felt my jaw tighten.

I looked in Blau's eyes and said with a smile, "Thank you, sir. I will be sure to pass along your precise words to the president. Please know the navy of the United States of America stands ready to assist you in any way we can while you are in *our hemisphere* of the world, of which we are very proud. Our presence is everywhere, so please be assured we will be there to help wherever you visit."

With only a partial understanding of English, the two junior Germans didn't get my meaning at all. But FregattenKapitan Blau did. For just a fraction of a second, his expression clouded.

"It is my turn to thank you, Commander Wake, for your kind offer of assistance. But I do not see where it will be needed. Our mission is quite simple."

He surveyed me and I gazed back at him, but no one spoke. The awkwardness was broken when the meal's opening course, some sort of vegetable soup, was brought out by the stewards. I gestured for everyone to begin.

Following the soup was a plate of buttered and salted grits with melted cheddar cheese. Blau wrinkled his nose, then said in his British-learned accent, "How very exotic. The grain I do not know, and I have not tasted such cheese since I was in Devon."

His smile came out as a leer. "By the by, Commander Wake, I must say your name seemed so familiar to me when we first met. I knew I had heard it before, but could not recall where or when. Then it struck me a moment ago. Were you in the Pacific a few years ago, in eighty-nine?"

Did he know what I'd done at Samoa? How close our countries had come to war?

"Why yes, I was. But, of course, it's really not unusual at all in our navy. Our officers serve in various squadrons all over the world. In any event, I was out there only for a short while the last time. Were you there then, Captain Blau?"

"Yes. I had the honor to serve in *Adler*, under Commodore Fritze. But I also was out there only for a short time. I departed for home just before she and her sisters were sunk at Samoa."

That sounded like he did know what I'd done, or at least suspected. An interesting piece of intelligence to file away. I was formulating a quick and innocuous comment when the duty messenger suddenly arrived.

"Sir, an American collier has arrived on the northeast horizon. She's steaming directly for us."

Blau watched me intently as I said as casually as I could, "Thank you, messenger. Present my compliments to the officer of the watch. Commander Gardiner, would you please go up and look into that for me, then you can come back and enjoy your lunch."

Gardiner popped up in a very un-casual manner and excitedly said, "Aye, aye, sir." I could see that Blau duly noted the reaction.

This, however, was interrupted when a second messenger arrived from the quarterdeck and reported, "The collier which was at anchor, *Marie,* is preparing to get under way, sir."

So Lambert had done it. A pleasing development.

To a frowning Blau, I pleasantly commented, "It appears your fuel supply is leaving, Captain. There must be some sort of misunderstanding. In my experience it is a common failing of merchant captains. Say, do you have enough steam up to get under way and catch her?" I asked, though I knew the answer.

"No."

"Oh, what a shame, indeed. Regrettably, the collier that is approaching us now has only enough coal for our ship, and due to my operational requirements I simply cannot reduce my intake to spare any for you."

He sat there, staring at me. Finally, after he stewed for several seconds, I made a generous offer, "I tell you what, sir—in the interests of our countries' friendship, as soon as I return to Key West, I can notify your consulate in New Orleans by cable to have some coal sent down here for your ship, if you'd like. You should have it in three or four weeks, I would think."

He didn't seem pleased, so I came up with an alternative. "Or, of course, *Gneisenau* could leave this coast and seek coal over in Cuba, either at Havana or at Santiago. If there's none there in Cuba, you might find some in Jamaica. We were just there, as a matter of fact, and I think they still had some available for friendly foreign navies. And say, the British queen is pretty close to your Kaiser Wilhelm, isn't she?"

"Yes. Queen Victoria is the Kaiser's grandmother."

"Well, this is a truly distressing turn of events, isn't it? It's a good thing you were only engaged on a routine German emigrant registration assignment, and nothing important was interrupted. Right, Captain?"

"Yes," came the even-toned answer.

"What ever will you do, Captain Blau?" I asked as innocuously as I could.

The German's reply was rather guttural, through gritted teeth. "It appears I have no real choice, does it, Commander Wake? I will have to leave the coast and find coal in Havana."

Commander Warfield was smiling sympathetically for his European colleagues as I cheerfully concluded with, "Well, I wish you all good luck, Captain Blau. For now, though, let us enjoy the rest of this wonderful luncheon. It's so valuable to break bread with one's brothers of the sea, don't you think? It allows us to understand each other much better."

Several minutes later Gardiner returned from the quarterdeck and reported, "Mr. Lambert reports all is well, sir. *Marie* is hull down on the horizon, bound northward, apparently toward New Orleans. Oh, and the arriving collier will be alongside in an hour and a half. The sea's laid down nicely and we won't have trouble coaling."

"I see. Thank you, Commander."

The timing worked out nicely, for it would be about an hour after Blau and his minions returned to *Gneisenau*.

"More tea, Captain Blau?" I inquired. "I fear it's not as good as the British version, but it's all we have."

"No."

And thus the remainder of our international tête-à-tête continued in awkward silence, for it seemed our German guests had lost their appetite for food or for conversation.

19

The Turning Point

Xel-ha Anchorage, Mexico
Tuesday afternoon
13 December 1892

The stack of envelopes on my desk was at least ten inches high, half of which bore the scent of a lady, the other half the moldy smell of bureaucracy—all of it delivered via our guard boat when the newly arrived collier grew closer. As she came alongside to top off our bunkers, I begrudgingly began the examination of my correspondence with duty over pleasure.

A brief personal note from Rear Admiral Walker shared the latest intelligence he had learned, which wasn't much, but did match what we had surmised. The admiral had received a report about a man who had gone out to the *Gneisenau* in the Key West pilot boat the same morning we'd left. He was one Carl Nicolay, and not much was known about him.

Registering at a cheap hotel on Petronia Street near the Bahamian Quarter on the afternoon of December fifth, Nicolay listed his occupation as businessman and his home as Hamburg,

Germany. The hotel clerk said Nicolay rarely spoke, and then in a low tone with a thick accent. The register showed he'd arrived aboard the steamer *Philadelphia* and was waiting until a ship came into port bound for Charleston. Nicolay ate his meals in his room and never frequented the bars. He passed the time quietly until suddenly leaving the morning *Gneisenau* got underway, paying his bill in cash without a word.

It appeared to Walker this Nicolay man was Drake's assassin, and I concurred. I further assumed his name was an alias and the Charleston story a false trail. Was he now targeting Dzul for the Germans? It certainly seemed so.

In addition to Walker's message there were the usual supply, paymaster, and ordnance missives from their respective departments and bureaus in Washington, all of which would need attention and replies. I was about to wade into them when the report came from the officer of the watch that *Gneisenau* was getting steam up.

Next, Lieutenant Lambert came in and reported on his efforts in reverse order. Captain Wilson fortunately was an astute man and understood the unspoken threat to his future livelihood, instantly agreeing to head the *Marie* for Key West without getting permission from Blau. He was as good as his word, for while Lambert was stepping down into his boat, the collier was already getting steam up.

The message to Dzul was sent through a local mulatto trader whom Lambert met ashore and decided he could trust. The man told Lambert he knew the Mayan leader and Dzul would probably meet with Lambert's captain the next day, out of curiosity if nothing else.

The boat surveillance of *Gneisenau* had yielded no sighting of a man being taken ashore, so presumably Nicolay was still on the German warship, and now his mission was interrupted. Lambert suggested he could have swum unseen in the dark from the German cruiser to a local bumboat, which I granted was a possibility, but a distant one.

And finally, Lambert had even managed to obtain some rudimentary information about the Mayan ruins, the better to maintain our façade. He would write the report directly after his briefing to me. All in all, I decided the young officer had done quite well.

I had Gardiner see me afterward and told him what I'd learned. His opinion toward the mission had not changed, but I was pleased to see his outward attitude had modified. He respectfully suggested we not do anything rash until we could prove what he called "mal intent" on the part of the Germans toward the Mayans.

After the executive officer exited my cabin to supervise the coaling—which we were not in absolute dire need of, but which had to be started while Blau's cruiser was still in sight—I turned to those scented letters still piled on my desk. It was my custom from the war, years earlier, to read the oldest of my wife's letters first, then the most recent. This way, I could quickly know any bad news on the home front. I followed that practice now, with Maria's letters. There were two from her in the pile, one from five weeks earlier and the other from a week prior.

Her lovely endearments, combined with her perfume emanating from the pages, filled the opening page of the earliest letter and made me ache with desire. I could hear her speaking those words, sense her close to me, feel her touch.

Washington City, October 28th, 1892
Darling Peter,
I am so lonely without your presence. Your love for me is real, of that I am sure, but I long for the solid weight of your physical nearness, the reassuring sound of your voice, the gentle touch of your rough fingers, the delectable taste of your lips on mine. How intensely unfair it is for a grown woman to yearn so much and be so denied.

Nonetheless, I know our love will endure, and be all the stronger for these trials. And when we once again embrace, every wound will

*be healed, and every tear forgotten, in the ecstasy of that moment. I
dream and I plan for it, and that vision gets me through this dreary
existence in the cold atmosphere of Washington and its diplomatic
circus.*

*This place is not only without true human warmth for me, it is
politically perilous for anyone daring to love across social boundaries.
This very morning, I caught my maidservant gossiping with the
carriage driver about me—actually about us. Your naval superiors'
well-known distrust of my compatriots is more than equaled by the
loathing for* norteamericanos *by many in my embassy. I have no
doubt the driver passed along, with his own lewd embellishments,
the fact that the ambassador's cousin is having a liaison d'amour
with a naval officer of the despised* yanqui *barbarians. I fear not for
me, my love. I am, after all, the widowed lady of a Spanish hero,
and am untouchable in the legal and social sense. No, I fear for your
reputation and ability to progress professionally, for this growing
rumor will inevitably make it to your leadership's ears.*

*I am so disillusioned by the mounting hatreds and hypocrisy
between our countries, fed by the rabid press in both capitals. The
acrimony against the independence movement in Cuba is heating up
again because of all this, and the most fantastic schemes are discussed
over after-dinner cognac and cigars in the most nonchalant manner.
Like trained parrots, the junior men echo their enthusiastic approval,
no matter how stupid or cruel the idea.*

Maria had long been in favor of Cuba being granted full
independence and afterward maintaining a normal international,
and close commercial and cultural, relationship with the
mother country. She thought, and I agreed, the bond would
strengthen if both Cuba and Spain were respected equals, free of
recriminations. Her opinion was the minority among the Spanish
elite, however, and I was well aware of her growing despair at
how the Cuban situation was unfolding, so I wasn't surprised by
the tenor of her note, but I was surprised by the acceleration of
Spanish fears and plans. Then I read the next paragraphs.

As an example of this insanity, just yesterday I passed by the smoking room and heard two of our military attachés saying the authorities in Madrid and Havana have confirmed the Cubans in the United States are finally uniting under one leader. They did not say his name, but said the man in question has great influence not only with exiled Cubans, but with all of Spanish-speaking America. They then said, with an amazement that betrayed their complete misunderstanding of the American ideal of liberty, that this man was even gaining adherents among the Anglo people of the United States.

At that point, one of the attachés added a fact which frightened the rest of them—a Pinkerton surveillance report had confirmed the Cubans had taken in great amounts of donations and were planning to amass arms and supplies in Florida. The senior man, a colonel, predicted the long-simmering guerrilla conflict would soon erupt again into large-scale war on the island. The junior officer, along with several of the diplomatic staff, suggested drastic action be taken now to peremptorily eliminate the threat this persuasive leader posed, or the newly united Cubans might impress the U.S. Congress enough with their sophistication and sincerity to obtain yanqui *military support.*

My curiosity could not be held at that point, and I peeked around the corner to see the colonel wave his hand dismissively, saying there was no need to worry, that an operation had already been decided upon and initiated, and the threat would be eliminated soon. He then proudly said the empire would remain whole and the Cubans would remain in their proper place.

I didn't hear what the drastic action was, for they stopped talking when one of them noticed me watching from the hallway and the door was instantly closed. But by the sound of it, I think it involves violence of some sort toward the Cuban leader <u>inside</u> *the United States. May God forbid these short-sighted men ever carry out their schemes—especially here in this neutral country. I fear the outcome for all of us if they do. This is but one example of the delusional lunatics around me here.*

Oh Peter, I wish you were here to take me away, if only for an evening, from this madness. I am desperate to be held by you, and to be able express my affection in more than mere words.

And just so you know, I am taking this letter to the post office myself, to preclude prying eyes, for I think they are reading my letters going out with the embassy's mail.

With love and longing,
Maria

The letter was a bombshell, stunning me to insensibility for a moment. My stomach clamped into a knot as I perused the letter again, visualizing her writing it, trying to discern any hidden meanings. That she realized her mail might be scrutinized by the staff said a lot about her situation and her nerve in circumventing it.

Maria hadn't mentioned names, but I knew that particular colonel and his aide from the Washington cocktail circuit. They had both served against the rebels in Cuba, as had most of the Spanish army's officer corps during the twenty-four-year-long insurrection for independence, both during the years of open combat and those of smoldering espionage and sabotage. Over delicate flutes champagne, I'd heard the Spanish officers dispassionately discuss the rebels in dismissive tones, calling them "creole mongrels, who were devoid of civilized behavior, and deserving of no respect or mercy."

And I knew the Cuban rebel leader to whom she referred: José Julian Martí, the most accomplished poet, author, journalist, and orator of all Latin America. Exiled from his native island by the colonial authorities, he had subsequently lived in Spain, France, Mexico, Guatemala, and Venezuela, before settling in New York City for the last twelve years. From that metropolis in the nation of free speech, Martí spoke and wrote to urge Cuban exiles in the United States and elsewhere to unite in their support for a free and independent Republic of Cuba.

In addition to his international status, Martí was a dear friend of mine. In fact, I owed my life to him for the assistance he had rendered to me while I was on intelligence missions inside

Cuba in '86 and '88. Martí was the best hope for an independent Cuba to be democratic, honest, and energetic, free from the tyrannical oppression seen elsewhere in the Hemisphere.

I had been completely wrong about everything for the last four days. I'd made a terrible mistake, a fatal error of judgment about the target and the perpetrator.

The perpetrator was Colonel Isidro Marrón, of the dreaded Spanish secret police. The target was my friend José Martí—and he was going to die in three days.

20

The Ruse Revealed

Xel-ha Anchorage, Mexico
Tuesday afternoon
13 December 1892

The bridge messenger reported *Gneisenau* had weighed anchor and was steaming northeast at twelve knots—so Blau had chosen to refuel at Spanish Havana instead of British Jamaica. There he would meet with the German consul and complain up a storm, which would then be sent on to Berlin and eventually Washington. There would be complaints and recriminations to deal with later, but what was done was done, so I continued checking the correspondence for something else of value which would help me understand Marrón's plan.

Quickly tearing open Maria's latest envelope, I found it contained only a brief note saying she had accelerated her travel plans. She was leaving for Cuba immediately, via train for Tampa, thence the Plant Line steamer *Olivette* for Key West and Havana. Once in Cuba, she would spend the Christmas season with another of her cousins, and then take a passenger ship for

Spain, where she would see me in January, when *Bennington* arrived in the Mediterranean.

There was no mention of the plot to kill Martí, but there was a postscript alluding to it.

I apologize for the haste of my journey, but I need to flee from the political madness around me here, for it has gotten worse. I want to be with gentle people who long solely for peace in Cuba and in Spain. The violent talk by pompous little men sickens me.

I considered the timing of her note. It took three days to travel by train from Washington, D.C. to Tampa, a trip I've made many times over the years. From there, *Olivette*'s transit was overnight to Key West for a port call, departing the next afternoon with another overnight passage to Havana at dawn. Five days of travel, if the weather was good and there were no complications for the train. The letter was dated December sixth—seven days earlier, and two days before I received the admiral's summons while at Kingston. If Maria had departed Washington the day after the letter was written, she might very well be in Cuba by now.

In her mind, Cuba was a safe haven with friends and relatives, and a tropical refuge from the onset of the cold North American winter. For me, Cuba was the home of the enemy, the realm of Marrón's clandestine Special Section of the Orden Público, and a place of shadowy peril.

I returned to studying the murder of Drake. Somehow, an elaborate ruse had been planned and carried out, with both German assassin and Mayan victim conjured up as a decoy from the true operation. The evidence uncovered in Drake's cabin and the ensuing events, all logically pointed toward Venezuela, the Germans, and Mexico. Each piece fit perfectly.

There was no link to Cuba or Spain. Not one.

Then I looked at each component with a freshly critical eye. The section of the German chart had been found stuffed in a pillowcase on the bed. I'd assumed the chart was Drake's, but anyone, including the killer, could have put it there.

The message in German naval code was locked in the cabin safe, thus unavailable to the killer. But the message didn't specify the target or the perpetrator. I'd assumed it was a German operation, because the message was in German.

And I had assumed the Germans killed Drake to prevent him from alerting the world to what I thought might be their plans to build a naval base on the Caribbean coast of Mexico. *Gneisenau's* appearance at Key West, her sudden departure, picking up Nicolay, and her subsequent arrival in Yucatán, all supported my theory.

But what if the message was merely a report to Berlin of what the Germans had learned about what the Spanish, with whom they had close ties, were about to do in the U.S.? That intelligence would meet with quiet approval in Berlin, for the Germans were pro-Spanish in Cuba. A victory by a fellow European monarchy over her Cuban colony would ensure stability for the growing German commercial investments on the island and serve as a warning for German colonies around the world.

And if the Spanish discovered the Germans knew about their operation against Martí, there would be little fear of them having that knowledge. The Spanish knew the Germans would stay mute publicly, for it was in their own interest.

My previous theory about Drake still seemed valid when looked at with Cuba in mind—working in the German telegraph office, he came across an unusual cable message which, combined with snatches of overheard conversations, made him deduce what was about to happen.

For the Spanish, Drake was more than a loose end, he was a loose cannon. Unlike the Germans, Drake would not stay mute. His going to the press would be a disaster, preventing the Spanish plan from coming to fruition, and igniting the wrath not only of Washington, but all of Latin America.

My new analysis logically led to the question of how the Spanish stopped Drake. Once he got to the U.S. mainland it would be too late. They had little time and few options to stop the threat to their operation.

I saw the method instantly, for I've done similar things—against the Spanish, inside Cuba. It was a classic false flag ploy, designed to lead any suspicion about the perpetrators in the wrong direction. The reader may well ask, why not make it look like Cuban rebels had done the murder? The answer was two-fold: there was no ready motive, for Key West is extremely pro-Martí and Cuban independence; and Americans were beginning to be suspicious of German expansion in the world, particularly in the Western Hemisphere. The Germans were convenient suspects.

The Spanish assassin must have boarded in Venezuela. Was that planned ahead of time, as his transport to the United States to kill Martí? Or was it a last-minute decision?

Once Drake was dead in his cabin, the assassin needed only to plant the German chart section in the pillowcase, complete with notations in German about meeting the Mayan rebel leader Dzul. Add to that the open knowledge the Imperial German Navy was touring the Mexican coast on their annual emigrant registration mission, and the lie gained the weight and momentum needed. That was all it took to shift the blame.

It was damned impressive, really, when one realized how quickly they had to react to the threat, prepare the men involved, and execute the operation. There was only one entity in the Spanish intelligence apparatus which had the ability to pull it off.

I knew that group well, Marrón's sinister little group with the mission of eliminating the island's independence movement. They were attached to the uniformed men of the Cuerpo Militar de Orden Público, a police regiment centered in Havana. Marrón's agents were extremely effective at penetrating the Cuban patriots' organizations with *agents provocateurs*, at employing complicated plots and ruses, and in using methods calculated to instill terror, such as assassination.

But the Orden Público didn't only function on the island.

They had expanded into other places where Cuban exiles fomented their homeland's independence from Spain. Most ominously, the Orden Público's Special Section operated surveillance and assassination agents against the Cuban rebel leadership inside the United States. Yes, this entire scheme was typical of them, and most especially, their leader, who was known in Havana as "The Henchman."

Marrón had been my nemesis since 1886, when Rork and I narrowly escaped with our lives from his Havana interrogation dungeon. Six months later, his thugs came to my home on Patricio Island in Florida to kill me and my family.

I thought I'd killed Marrón during a mission in Havana in 1888; I was quite certain of it at the time. But later intelligence reports, including one passed along from Martí, showed the colonel had survived, albeit with a disfigured face to remind him of the experience.

I sat there at my desk, feeling sick in my gut and trying to remain calm while trying to formulate some sort of a plan of action. Martí was the target—but where? He had written me in early September from Santo Domingo, where he was trying to rally support for the Cuban cause. His note indicated he would be in Florida later in the year and perhaps we could meet for dinner if I was in the area. I went through my files and found the letter, but it revealed no dates or locales, only that he was to be in Florida from late November through mid-December.

But where in Florida? Cuban exiles were everywhere, particularly in Key West, Tampa, Ocala, Saint Augustine, and Jacksonville. Martí had visited them all in the past and presumably was doing so again. Key West would be where I'd start. First, I needed to brief the admiral and check ashore for word of Martí's itinerary. Then we'd find my friend and warn him.

We had to get under way immediately.

21

The Source

Xel-ha Anchorage, Mexico
Tuesday afternoon
13 December 1892

"Pass the word for the executive officer to come to my cabin," I said into the speaking tube connecting to the bridge.

When Gardiner arrived, I forwent any preamble and gave him his orders.

"I have just received new intelligence that completely alters the situation, Commander, so the plan has changed. First, send Mr. Lambert ashore and have him find his contact man to cancel the Dzul meeting. Next, ready the ship to get under way immediately for Key West. Understood so far?"

"And will this be another high-speed run, sir? The boilers . . ."

I interrupted him. "Yes, it will be."

"So what am I supposed to tell the officers when they ask the reason? Are we chasing the Germans again?"

I decided right then not to take him into confidence about the details. Norton Gardiner, of Boston's Beacon Hill, was completely incapable of understanding the reasoning behind my sudden decision, the fact it was based on subtle information contained in my foreign lover's letter, or the enormous consequences of Martí's assassination.

"The reason is secret and will remain so until I decide it can be divulged. No, we are not chasing the Germans. And I don't have time for a discussion right now—just make it so, Commander. And have Bosun Rork come here. That is all."

The moment he departed my cabin, I heard Gardiner transform his hatred of me into growling to the officer of the watch for Lambert and Warfield to "Get to the bridge this instant for new orders!"

Soon the shouts of petty officers mustering their work details rang about the ship. Arriving in front of my desk five minutes later, Rork assumed his usual pose of patient subordination, though I noted his right eyebrow was slightly raised in anticipation. I had no doubt the whole ship was abuzz with the captain's latest abrupt decision.

I pointed to the pertinent paragraphs on the second page of Maria's earlier letter and said to him, "Read this, Rork, and tell me what you think."

As usual, he read it twice. "Well, damned if it don't look like we were played the fool, sir—lock, stock, an' barrel. 'Tain't the square-heads at all, is it? Nay, the Spaniardos an' Cubans, yet again. Our old game."

"That's what I thought also. Just wanted your thoughts. Damn it all, Rork—I made a terrible mistake thinking it was the Germans in Mexico."

"Yer not alone on that score, sir. The admiral an' me thought it was the right answer, too. Bloody well done false-flag op, it was."

"Worked on me. And now we've got to rectify this and do it quick."

He rubbed his false left hand. "But ooh, it makes me spike itch. Marrón an' his crew o' poxy bastards've got our ol' friend Martí as their target, an' we've got wee little time to stop 'em, don't we? The quartermaster says he's laying a course for Key West."

"Yes, we're heading there immediately. I'll explain to the admiral and we'll find Martí's whereabouts."

"Aye, an' nary o' them'll be easy," said Rork with monumental understatement.

Once he'd departed for the foredeck, I turned to the next phase in my alteration of strategy—one needing a certain amount of finesse. How I would explain to the admiral I had been wrong in my hypothesis about the message, that I had angered the Germans by thwarting them, and it was now imperative we save Martí's life?

José Martí was of absolutely crucial importance to our relations within the hemisphere and our country's future; far more than some peasant rebel in a remote stretch of Mexico. His assassination inside the United States would have unforeseeable and catastrophic consequences.

The admiral would not be pleased by the pending diplomatic row with the imperial German government over my rerouting their chartered collier, but he would understand the significance of Martí, of that I had no doubt. The major dilemma I faced in briefing him was going to be his first question: "And how did you determine any of this is the actual situation, Commander Wake? You were certain before about the Germans in Mexico . . . "

I was definitely not, under any circumstances, going to mention Maria. That would merely confirm his prior suspicions about her and reignite his hopes to use her as an informant. No, Walker would have to trust me when I told him a confidential source conveyed information illuminating the true nature of Drake's message. I dared not even tell him where the source was located.

It would not be easy to stand up under his scrutiny or wrath, for John Grimes Walker had formidable powers in both areas. He had been privy to several of my intelligence sources in the past and would expect that privilege now. But I had to preserve my darling's anonymity, for with a monster like Marrón involved, her very life depended on it. Would Walker guess her identity anyway? I would have to convince him not to idly speculate on my source's identity with anyone, a delicate task to accomplish with an admiral.

The swirl of worries kindled memories of the first time I saw Maria in the summer of 1892 and the regrettable way we parted that evening.

22

The First Evening
of the Rest of My Life

French Embassy
H Street
Washington, D.C.
Thursday evening
14 July 1892

I t was the evening of Bastille Day and I was at one of
Washington's most famous diplomatic cocktail parties
of the year—the French embassy's annual celebration of the
French Revolution's storming King Louis XVI's home in 1789.
Though many of Washington's elite had already fled the capital's
humid summer, quite a few also endured another ten days of
it just so they could attend the French party. Everyone who
was anyone sought an invitation, and hundreds of the city's
favored personages received the gold-embossed summons in the
distinctive blue envelope.

Still a part of the North Atlantic Squadron staff, I had been

temporarily sent up to headquarters in Washington for the
month of July to facilitate the diplomatic and training functions
of an upcoming squadron tour of South and Central America.
The French party was a disagreeable part of this task—as stated
before, I heartily despise formal affairs and wearing the full dress
uniform—but I was expected to cement goodwill ahead of the
visit of our squadron's ships to Martinique, Guadeloupe, St.
Barthélemy, St. Martin, and French Guiana. The assignment
required me to hobnob with the cultured class at the champagne
bar, pretend I enjoyed their company, and use my embarrassingly
fractured French to repeatedly compliment my hosts and their
country. My cause was greatly helped by the fact that I had worn
one of their awards—the Legion of Honor—since 1874.

Halfway through the ordeal, I was standing with champagne
flute in hand, desperately trying to stay awake as some old fellow
from Martinique, in faded striped trousers, tails, and sashes,
mumbled inane somethings in French about the glories of the
Napoleonic wars when he had been an ensign. Then I saw her.

Crimson satin gown trimmed in black lace over a perfect
figure, long dark hair covered by a simple black mantilla veil,
expressive dark blue eyes, confident bearing—the whole effect
was just stunning. She came closer and I could see her smooth
skin was perfectly accentuated by unusual jewelry: a carnelian
onyx and emerald necklace, earrings, and bracelet, in an ornate
Moorish motif. It was not only unusual, it was very expensive
and probably at least four hundred years old, from the Muslim-
Jewish era of the Iberian Peninsula, before their expulsion in
1492 at the hands of the Christians.

She caught me watching her from eight feet away while
she tried unsuccessfully to get the bar steward's attention. A
cautious smile briefly crossed her face, then she turned away, as
if embarrassed. Her age was difficult to determine with accuracy,
for the smoothness of her skin, the flash of her eyes, and the
lightness of her step indicated a playful demeanor, so unlike the
stodgy matrons who formed the majority of the female attendees.

But the smile lines of her mouth and eyes showed life experience, as did a quiet strength. I guessed at forty to forty-five; not too young to be offended by an approach from my fifty-three-year-old person.

Immediately observing no escort was in sight for this damsel in distress, which I found astonishing, I executed a perfect parade ground column-oblique-left away from my chattering old companion and shaped a course toward the obviously more convivial company at the champagne bar. He never even noticed my absence.

Now, at this point let me say I fully realize the cynics will probably assume the lady was well accustomed to getting men to do her bidding, and probably was in the employ of some entity to accomplish just that, with the goal of obtaining useful intelligence as a byproduct. They will think me, an officer with an extensive history in the secret service of his country, a valuable target for such an effort, usually known as a "honey trap." But I would remind them that I, far more than the average man, have had to deal with many such predatory females in my life, particularly during my clandestine service around the world. Having employed women as honey traps against adversaries, and had them attempted against me, I am quite experienced at discerning them, even when beautifully disguised in satin gowns at soirees. This was not a honey trap.

She obviously was Spanish, but French is the language of diplomatic cocktail parties, so I ventured forth in that lingo and asked if I could help her. "*Bonsoir, madame. Puis-je vous aider?*" At least, that is what I tried to say.

Barely able to politely stifle a laugh at my terrible accent, she fluttered an ornate little fan quickly past her face and answered in remarkably fluent English. "Thank you, Commander. Yes, I would appreciate your aid, since I need something cool to drink in this heat and the steward seems to be dominated by the Dutch ambassador and his entourage at the moment."

"It will be the work of only a moment, *madame*."

Three steps away, I interrupted the Dutchman and his fellows by canting my head toward the lady and saying, "Gentleman, a disaster has occurred. My beautiful companion is thirsty and I must divert the steward away from you to obtain her refreshment."

All eyes gazed admiringly at the lady, followed by a chorus of "Certainly! But of course!" The barman hopped to his duties with a will and produced two chilled glasses filled to the top for me.

Bowing to her in my best imitation of a European swell, I handed a glass to the lady. "Madame, your relief from the heat of a Washington summer has arrived—I hope you enjoy it. May I introduce myself? I am Commander Peter Wake, of the United States Navy, at your service."

She favored me with a smile that spread effortlessly across her face and was pleasantly genuine, unlike most of the others in the room. Now I could see the dark eyes were actually indigo blue. They sparkled wonderfully, transforming her whole persona from dangerously mysterious to gentle friend. It was as if we'd known each for years and shared a joke. Then and there, my heart melted and I had to learn more about her.

"Thank you so much, Commander Wake. I think you just saved my life!" She extended a hand. "I am Maria."

Full Spanish names are complicated, giving recognition to names, and sometimes the pedigrees, of both maternal and paternal families. I was intrigued that she was so informal, almost American. Kissing her hand, I asked, "Just Maria?"

She bowed her head slightly in contrition. "Most of your countrymen are confused by our traditional introductions, but I see by the awards on your chest I was mistaken about you. Obviously, you are a man of the world. My formal name is Doña Maria Ana Maura y Abad."

"Maura, as in the Spanish political leader?"

Antonio Maura was well known to be a liberal on the matter of Cuba, favoring not independence, but full autonomy within the Spanish empire. I had asked the question as neutrally as I could, but she reacted with wariness. Not many Americans knew of Maura.

Her eyes lost their mirth, boring into me as she answered, "Yes, he was my late husband's cousin. They grew up together on the island of Majorca."

I retreated immediately, wanting to return to our amiable start, but I thought I should let her know I could sympathize with her condition. "I am sorry for the loss of your late husband, Señora. It is so very difficult to cope with. I know, for I lost my wife eleven years ago to female cancer."

The edge to her tone and gaze faded. "And I am sorry for your loss. Guillermo passed on to heaven four years ago. He was my beloved husband for twenty-four years."

Memories of my family flooded me and I suddenly felt old. "Linda and I had seventeen years together. We have a daughter and a son. Both are grown and on their own. And you?"

"Two sons, who are grown also. The oldest is a Franciscan priest on his first assignment at Havana, and the other has started work in the national government in Madrid."

Hmm, I had contacts among some priests in Havana. "They must be a great comfort for you. Señora, my curiosity is piqued and I must ask how you learned English so fluently."

"I studied with a tutor from the British school in Majorca for six years. My father expected me to know French and English in addition to my mother tongue. Five years ago, Guillermo was posted to the embassy here in Washington, so I have had a good opportunity to practice the American version of the English language."

I was wondering why she stayed in Washington as a widow when she fanned her neck and face and added, "Ah, the summers of Washington . . . does it seem excessively hot in here to you? It seems to be getting even hotter than this afternoon."

It was indeed beastly hot in the jammed ballroom, and my starched collar was driving me mad. "I agree completely. Perhaps another chilled champagne will help? Once we are thus fortified,

I suggest we then walk out to the balcony, where there might be an evening breeze."

My technique was admittedly a bit clumsy, and she regarded me dubiously. After several seconds she said, "I agree."

23

The Blunder

French Embassy
H Street
Washington, D.C.
Thursday evening
14 July 1892

There was no breeze on the balcony, but there were dozens of guests also seeking respite from the ovenlike atmosphere inside. We walked to the corner of the balustrade and looked out over the city lights.

She started the conversation with a standard device of ladies at a soiree—ask a man to talk about himself. "Your French Legion of Honor I recognize, Commander, but the others are unknown to me. I think they are not from Europe, and am certain they come with fascinating explanations. And please, call me Maria."

"Only if you please me by calling me Peter."

"I shall, Peter. Now, do not be shy and please tell me about your medals, or I shall be forced to start calling you Commander Wake."

A brief explanation is in order. I have to wear my medals when attending such formal events in Washington, because the diplomats of the countries that awarded them know I have them and expect to see them on me. It is considered a gross national insult to forgo them in public. In my case, however, the true stories behind the medals are confidential. Very confidential. The medals inevitably incite questions, which require me to present a sanitized version of the events, for the real version would probably physically sicken the ladies or politically anger the gentlemen of the cocktail crowd. Most interestingly, I've discovered even the diplomats of the awarding countries are not privy to the real reasons for my medals.

"Maria, your wish is my command. Well, let's see here. The Legion of Honor was for some work in North Africa almost twenty years ago. This is the Order of the Sun, from Peru, and is for some aid I rendered them during a war they had with Chile a decade ago. This Royal Order of Cambodia is from King Norodom for some assistance I provided him nine years ago. The Royal Order of Kalakaua is from the King of Hawaii for helping him a few years ago. Unfortunately, that good man died last year. The Hawaiians are a noble people."

"You seem to provide a lot of assistance to people, Peter. But your descriptions were too brief. I think you are the most modest man in this building, maybe in Washington. I find that very unusual, and quite charming."

Clinking her glass with mine, I then preempted any follow up inquiries with a question of my own. "Thank you, Maria. And now I have a question. Why did you stay here in Washington after Guillermo died? Washington can be so duplicitous. It's not my favorite place, and I would think you would be more comfortable back home in Spain."

"Yes, it would have been the proper thing, the expected thing, for a widow to do. But Madrid is as full of insincere politicians, treacherous aristocrats, and mindless bureaucrats, as Washington. Peter, as ludicrous as it sounds, a six-year-old little boy is our king, his Austrian mother is the regent in charge of our royal house, our conscript armies are fighting insurgents in every colony, and a brutal prime minister who clings to a faded façade of an empire is in charge of our country.

"The United States, for all its corruption and duplicitousness, is a breath of fresh air compared to Spain right now. I am a proud daughter of Spain, but for now I prefer to live a bit longer in the fresh air of true freedom."

Her comment emerged slowly at first, but gained intensity as she spoke. This lady was no pretty wallflower decorating the Spanish diplomatic corps; she was a modern, confident woman with very definite opinions.

I decided to explore those opinions. "I hear the Liberals under Sagasta might return to power this fall, so perhaps Spain will see better days. Antonio Maura is one of them, I believe."

"From your lips to God's ear—we can only hope the Liberals regain power in Madrid. And yes, Antonio would be part of the Liberal administration, probably the Minister for Overseas Colonies. He could bring sanity to our long-festering Cuban trouble. They deserve independence."

"But Mr. Maura only favors autonomy within the empire, not full independence. The Cubans will still fight for independence and thousands will die in the war."

Her answer came in the form of an accusation. "And many in this country *want* the Cubans to fight Spain."

"Some, yes."

Her eyes grew darker, as cold as her tone. "And *some* want the United States to annex Cuba."

I had crossed the line into politics, a colossal blunder, and wanted to return to more pleasant topics, but not before I set the record straight.

"Yes, Maria, but many do not want to annex Cuba, or anywhere else. I am one of those. I also think it is time for Cuba to be a free independent nation. I hope they don't have to fight for it, that Spain graciously grants them independence without further bloodshed, and thereafter maintains a close relationship based on goodwill."

"Then you are in the minority, from what I see and hear in this city."

Before I could reply, or even think how to reply, a tall gentleman in the sash and medal of a Spanish civil order marched toward us. His rapid Spanish to Maria was in the Andalusian style—something about the *chargé* and his wife asking for her. After delivering his message, he cast me a disdainful glance.

Her mood altered by my impertinent queries, the lady introduced me to the interloper in a perfunctory manner. A perfunctory reply was grunted in my direction as he took her arm and escorted her toward the ballroom.

As she left, I heard, "We must continue this conversation about my country sometime, Commander Wake. I find it disturbing, but educational."

With that less-than-sterling appraisal of my skills as a raconteur, she disappeared from view. I was left standing there charged with electricity at the thought of seeing this mesmerizing woman again. The next time, I vowed, politics would not be part of the conversation.

24

The Return

Key West Naval Station
Wednesday evening
14 December 1892

U nlike the earlier voyage, *Bennington*'s transit from
Cozumel Island to Key West was downwind,
downcurrent, and fast. With time running out and a life—
and possibly a war—hanging in the balance, it was a welcome
development. Upon entering Man-o-War Anchorage at Key
West, I was pleased to see two of our squadron, *Essex* and
Atlanta, had already arrived for the annual gunnery rendezvous,
with the guard boat officer saying the others would be arriving in
the next several days. Another pleasant sign. Then we rounded
Essex, and what I saw was most certainly not.

Gneisenau wasn't at Havana.

Instead, she was right there in front of us, the officers on
her bridge staring and pointing at our arrival. Anchored close
nearby her was the large Spanish cruiser *Reina Regente.* I was well
acquainted with that formidable ship, having been chased by her

while in a stolen Spanish patrol boat in Cuba four years earlier.
To add even more spice to the trouble brewing, Lieutenant
Lambert reported that *Chicago* had German and Spanish
captains' gigs alongside her.

Obviously old Blau was smarter than he appeared and,
though he could only have been in Key West for a few hours
ahead of us, had wasted no time. Presumably *Reina Regente*
was already visiting the port. The wily German was innovative,
increasing the international repercussions by using the Spanish
captain as his witness while complaining to Rear Admiral Walker
about my stealing his collier in Mexico. A quick glance at my
executive officer showed him standing there watching the scene
like the proverbial cat who ate the canary, for his nemesis—me—
would soon depart the ship in disgrace, once the leadership in
Washington discovered what I'd done. He was probably planning
his promotion party.

With a bit of luck, the admiral could cook up some placating
story that somewhat matched the one I gave Blau. Walker would
have to improvise, of course, and that was something admirals
hate to have to do. By their age and rank, many are no longer
nimble of foot or thought. Walker was a notable exception to the
rule, so I had hope.

In any event, I needed to get over there to *Chicago* as soon
as possible and salvage what I could of the Blau situation, in
addition to briefing Walker on the Martí factor. This meant yet
another unconventional decision for *Bennington*'s inhabitants to
question.

"Commander Gardiner, we're not anchoring. I'll take us
alongside the naval wharf, across from *Chicago*." I waved aside his
look of protest. "Yes, I know the station commandant assigned us
to anchor out, but I need to see the admiral immediately. Signal
the station we're coming in and we need to top off our bunkers
immediately."

This was, of course, a gross breach of naval protocol, but
it was *my* gross breach of naval protocol. Another charge in

the current list against me. Gardiner answered with the most enthusiastic "Aye, aye, sir!" I'd heard from him since I first came aboard.

As we approached the wharf, Gardiner was positively cheery as he declared in a voice loud enough to be heard down on the main deck, "Looks like the wharf crew isn't ready yet, Captain. Ah, but wait, I see the flagship's sent some men over to help. Good thing, too, we'll need all the help we can get with this strong flood current running. And damned if this southwest wind isn't making it even worse."

Unfortunately, though his glee was perturbing, his assessment was entirely correct. The strong wind and current would send us away from the wharf. *Chicago*'s deck watch sent men running to the bollards on the opposite side of the wharf to help handle lines, and flagship's bridge was crowded with officers watching the show. In my ship, the officers and petty officer on the bridge were studiously not watching my reaction to the executive officer's comment.

But I knew I was in the corner of every eye when I replied, "Thank you for your advice, Commander. Duly noted."

I judged the docking of the ship to be an excellent opportunity to teach Gardiner a lesson in humility, and far more importantly, a lesson for my junior officers in close-quarters ship handling.

"This will be simple gentlemen," I announced as we closed to within one hundred yards of the scarred wharf end. "We will approach at dead slow on a forty-five degree angle and put the starboard bow to the wharf, about two-thirds of the way down, then secure with bow and spring lines. Keeping the rudder amidships, we will then go slow ahead on the starboard engine and slow astern on the port engine. That will twist the stern up current and upwind toward the wharf. Put a good line thrower on the stern."

Gardiner said, "Aye, aye, sir. That'll be Bosun Watson, best I've ever seen. I'll send him aft."

Watson, in my opinion, was the second-best line thrower aboard, after Rork, but I refrained from commenting. Things went well until the bow was thirty feet off the wharf.

At this moment three things happened. Gardiner reported the Spanish and German gigs had shoved off from the flagship, an unnecessary interruption I presumed was intended to rattle my nerves. Rear Admiral Walker appeared on the port side of his main deck, evidently after seeing the foreigners off the ship, and was grimly surveying the scene. And lastly, a gust of the damned southwest wind blew against us, stopping our forward momentum instantly. *Bennington*'s bow immediately slid sideways to leeward, away from the wharf.

"We've lost steerage way, Captain," observed Gardiner lightly. "We're drifting down to Tift's dock."

Now, to the non-nautical soul who may be reading this account, an explanation will be in order. Asa Tift's dock is 120 feet (on that day, downwind and downcurrent) east of the naval wharf. It is a tight fit, with little room between, to put a ship at each wharf when there is no wind or current to contend with. Thankfully, there wasn't a steamer at the Tift dock at the time, but 120 feet is not a lot of room to maneuver a 250-foot warship with a 36-foot beam. And at that point, we only had seconds before colliding with Tift's dock.

"We'll have to go full astern to get out and start over," Gardiner announced while shaking his head in mock sympathy.

"No, Commander Gardiner, we won't," I replied and turned to the men at the wheel and engine telegraph. "Slow ahead on port engine, dead slow astern on starboard engine, left standard rudder."

These men, a quartermaster's mate and a seaman, acknowledged the orders as they instantly fulfilled them, for they, unlike Gardiner, understood what was needed. The engine telegraph bells rang up the commands and water began churning around us. Everyone on the bridge was stone-faced—except for my second-in-command.

"What are you doing!" gasped Gardiner. "We'll hit the wharf ahead of us!"

"Watch and learn, Commander," I tried to say as pleasantly as I could, though my stomach and nerves were agitated into knots. Glancing aft, I called out to Watson and his men, "Watson, stand by on the starboard quarter lines!" Then I called out to a big-bearded petty officer on the bow, "Kouskee, send over the bow messenger line!"

He knew his business. A monkey's fist knot, trailing a light line, instantly flew out from our starboard bow and arced to the wharf, where *Chicago*'s men caught it and used it to haul the heavy main bow line up to the wharf deck. There was a good man in charge who didn't wait for orders but began dragging the line to a bollard near the foot of the wharf.

This was the moment of truth. "Dead slow astern on port engine. Dead slow ahead on starboard engine. Left full rudder."

Bennington's bow was now secured, albeit still a ways from the wharf, but our stern was unsecured and out beyond the wharf, in the stronger current and wind. I ignored Gardiner's shaking head and mumbling, and ordered, "Slow ahead on starboard engine."

The engine order bell rang and I felt the ship surge forward, getting the stern inside the end of the wharf and out of the worst of the wind and tide. But now the bow was closing rapidly with the bulkhead along the shoreline at the head of the pier. "Stop starboard engine," I said, waiting for fifteen long seconds before adding, "Stop port engine." The churning water and vibrating deck ended.

To Watson I shouted, "Send over the stern line!"

The stern messenger line flew over to the wharf as the ship slowed her forward speed. That damned bulkhead was still getting closer though. The eyes of the quartermaster's mate alternated between me and the bulkhead.

"Send over and take a strain on the forward spring line!" I ordered. "Take the bow line to the capstan and heave around!

Send over the after spring line!"

Bennington finally stopped twenty feet from the bulkhead, and sat there parallel to the naval wharf, fifteen feet off our starboard side. Soon the capstan was doing its work and the bow edged close alongside the wharf. It was followed by the stern.

I turned to the executive officer, who still stood rooted in the same place, by the chart table, and said, "Commander Gardiner, please have all lines doubled up, set fenders, secure engines, shift the colors, and make ready to coal ship. I'll be with the admiral. When I return, I want to see you in my cabin. That will be all."

Then, without waiting for him to process the import of my final words and come up with a cynical reply, I departed the wheelhouse.

Outside, the sun was nearing the horizon, searing the marching lines of dark clouds with fiery edges of copper and gold, and making a beautiful sight. In my hurried condition, my mind vaguely processed it as an indicator a storm was coming, but my main attention was on my destination across the wharf. I dashed down the ladder to the main deck and, without waiting for the brow to be set up, leaped down to the wharf and made my way across to *Chicago*.

A storm, indeed—for Rear Admiral John Grimes Walker was certainly the human equivalent.

25

The New Plan

Key West Naval Station
Wednesday evening
14 December 1892

The wrinkled brow, tired eyes, and wan expression told me the admiral wasn't angry, he was disappointed and exhausted. That made me feel even worse, for I respected this man more than most. I stood before his desk, looking down at him, waiting for the inevitable.

"Well, Wake, you're in trouble yet again, aren't you? Should I expect the Mexican government to be in line demanding your head along with everyone else?"

"No, sir. The Mexican government is outside of this matter."

"Well, that's something, at least." He let out a long weary breath. "It has not been a good day, Wake. In fact, it's been a deuce of a long, lousy day. At four o'clock this morning the officer of the watch informed me a gunner's mate from *Atlanta* was arrested for drunken assault on an undertaker—an undertaker, of all people—and the sheriff of Key West is in an uproar."

Well, that one wasn't my fault, so I waited.

"This afternoon, one of your brother captains informed me his ship was unready for the gunnery drills and another one informed me they were delayed by some local dispute in Panama and would be late for the rendezvous. Incredible!"

Walker's eyes were blazing, and I was happy I wasn't one of those two captains. But he hadn't mentioned me yet, so I knew the fire was about to get hotter. He leaned forward and pointed a finger in the air.

"All of that would be quite enough to ruin my day, of course, but wait, there was more to come. And, naturally, it involves *you*."

"Sir . . ."

He didn't let me talk. "Yes . . . you. This evening an irate German captain and his Spanish sidekick showed up in this very cabin."

"Sir, I can explain."

"Oh, you'd better! The two of these pompous asses, *after* draining a glass of my personal wine, started complaining about how you stole German-contracted coal in Mexico. This Blau fellow next proceeded to threaten me with accusations that your actions have been an international provocation, an insult to the Imperial German Navy's honor, and none other than the great Kaiser himself will be greatly enraged and personally protesting to the President of the United States immediately. The Kaiser will demand immense satisfaction, starting with your naval career, and possibly mine."

He paused and took a breath.

"Oh, and there was more, Wake. Blau said the cost incurred by the Imperial German Navy will run into the thousands. Guess who will be billed for that? It was a very impressive performance on his part. I doubt whether even you could have done better."

The admiral glared at me, then said, "So, in an effort to calm Captain Teutonic Drama down a bit, I told him he could coal here absolutely gratis, at this very wharf, courtesy of the United

States Navy, starting right away."

Walker paused again, shaking his head in contemplation of the situation. Yet again, I took advantage of the lull and began to try and clarify the situation, but the admiral still wasn't ready for that. He unloaded another salvo.

"Now here is where it gets really ironic, Wake. I had just given orders for the Germans to coal at this wharf when who should appear? The long-lost Commander Wake! And then, just to rub salt into Blau's wound and compound the Kaiser's coming enragement, you blissfully ignore the naval station's orders to anchor out. Oh no, instead, you chose to steal Blau's berth at the wharf, and his coal for the second time. And now, you show up in my cabin right after our foreign guests have disembarked, and you've got that look on your face," the admiral let out a long sad sigh, "the one I know only too well. My day is bound to get worse. Far worse. Isn't it?"

"Well, sir, the situation has changed considerably, and that's why I'm here. I was wrong in my initial assessment of both the target of the assassination and of the perpetrators of the assassination."

"All right, explain what happened."

I didn't waste his time with remorse over barging in and taking the berth, but started my narration with our arrival at Cozumel Island and the ensuing events. The admiral kept a stolid visage throughout, even when I related how I had co-opted the Germans' collier away from them. When I reached the point where *Bennington*'s collier arrived in Mexico and I received my delayed correspondence, I slowed down, for this was the part which worried me.

"As you will recall, sir, I maintain correspondence with acquaintances all over the world as a result of my intelligence missions since eighty-one. Jesuits, Freemasons, Asian and Pacific royalty, politicians in Europe and South America, foreign intelligence agents and naval officers, writers and artists, performers and merchants—I've tried to keep a diverse selection of information coming in."

"Wake, please speed this up. I know about your global circle of bizarre friends."

"Yes, sir. Well, part of the correspondence lately was from an unwitting source who provided an insight into an upcoming Spanish operation. The operation is to stop the Cuban rebel organization, which has finally consolidated and strengthened, from mounting a coordinated massive military campaign for independence of the island. Their goal is to decapitate the organization and thus re-fractionalize it."

He understood straightaway and said, "Your friend José Martí."

"Yes, sir. He is the target. It was a false-flag disinformation ploy. And it worked."

"All this was concluded from an insight gained from an unwitting source?"

"Yes, sir. Ancillary information from an unwitting source."

I could see the inquiries forming in his mind, but he held back, so I went on.

"This kind of operation could only be accomplished by Colonel Marrón's Sección Especial, of the Cuerpo Militar de Orden Público."

The admiral's jaw tightened. "Marrón, again. So how did they deceive us?"

"The basic premise we partially uncovered here in Key West several days ago is still correct, sir—there will be an assassination of a rebel leader. But I erroneously attributed it to the Germans, against the Mayan rebel leader in Mexico. The scrap of chart was a plant by the assassin. The fact it coincided entirely with the coded message in German means the Spanish knew the Germans had somehow gotten wind of their plan and were passing it along to Berlin, so they made the Germans look like the suspects. It was simple, and I bought right into it."

I didn't add the admiral did too. Admirals don't like to hear that sort of thing—especially from mere commanders.

He grumbled something as I continued. "However, with this new insight, we now know the real target is José Martí. The Spanish don't know we know. From our previous information, we know the assassination will be on December sixteenth. Martí wrote me in September that he would be on a speaking circuit in Florida in December, though he didn't say where, so now we also can be certain that the assassination will be inside the United States, and probably here in Florida."

I glanced at the clock on the bulkhead just as the bell struck to begin the second dog watch. Six o'clock. In addition to his other irritations, I was keeping the admiral from his supper. "So, in summary, sir, we now have only two days to find and warn Martí and stop the assassination. If we don't, and Martí is killed on American soil, the press will call for war. That's a war we in the Navy, and also the leaders of the Army, are not prepared for right now."

"Who is this unwitting source?"

"Someone who is in mortal peril should their name ever get out, sir. Drake's murder proves it."

"You didn't answer my question, Commander."

"I cannot answer that question, sir, in order to protect the source. It's a matter of honor."

The instant I said that word, I regretted it. The admiral shot up to his feet, his face a contorted purple mask as he pointed at me. "*You* . . . dare to lecture *me* . . . on the subject of *honor?*"

I was sure the Marine sentry outside the admiral's door heard, and within minutes it would be around the flagship and across the wharf to my ship—*Did you hear? The admiral laid into Wake about honor!* That juicy bit of gossip would nicely reinforce Gardiner's visions of my imminent professional demise.

When an admiral stands, juniors stand, so I calmly rose. Knowing my career truly was over if he took it the wrong way, I replied, "Sir, you must surely realize after all these years I've served under you I meant no disrespect, absolutely none, and I would never lecture you on anything, much less honor. I made the statement as something both of us, as men who really do try to live by a code of honor, would understand. The source is a decent person, who had no idea of the peril I have subjected them to, and I am relying on your trust in me, validated by a decade of crucial secret missions around the world under your command, to help protect that life."

His tone was quieter when he answered. "This correspondence, a letter I presume, is the sole basis for your new theory?"

"No, sir. It instigated my new theory, but it also ties together previous information we had deduced, and our understanding of Martí and Marrón."

"So why did you not suspect a Spanish assassination of Martí when you examined the evidence before?"

"Because Martí has been telling his people not to do anything overt against the Spanish. The struggle for Cuba's independence has been in a clandestine phase for years. Martí and his senior generals know they are not ready yet for large-scale war, but the hotheads in the lower ranks still want action. He has urged them to quietly build their support structure of finances, munitions, supplies, and manpower instead, so all will be ready when the time comes for a coordinated return to general war on the island. The Cubans aren't ready for war again."

"Why don't the Spanish know that?"

"The egos and paranoia in Madrid and Havana. They think the rebels are stronger than they really are. Their fear is turning into panic, and that is driving this decision to kill him, even if they have to do it inside our country. The source's letter gave me important insight into that."

"An unwitting source, you said, with no other descriptors or details. So there is no quid pro quo, no expectation of protection, and no ability of the source to protect themselves?"

I answered cautiously, for he wasn't using a masculine pronoun for the source. I wasn't going to lie to him and use that pronoun, so I'd kept it generic and hoped he would delude himself.

"No, sir. The source doesn't understand the import of the information, or that I am using it to make decisions. This makes the information even more valid, in my opinion."

"I see, Commander," said the admiral. "What if the source is appearing within the Spanish circle of trust, but is actually a triple agent, working for the Germans? They then feed information to the Americans, which decoys them away from the Germans as suspects. Ladies, in particular, are renowned for it, as you well know."

Damn. That was that—he'd deduced the source.

"Double or triple agents are always a possibility, sir. But in my best judgment, this is not one of those situations."

Walker sat down and motioned me to do so as well. "Peter, I sincerely hope the dear lady remains safe, and I'll say nothing about her. You have my word of honor on it."

"Thank you, sir."

"All right, Commander," said Walker decisively. "I concur with your new assessment—within two days the Orden Público will assassinate Martí somewhere in Florida. What exactly do you propose to do?"

"Not many options, sir. We warn the local Cuban groups here in Key West right away, then send warnings by cable to his probable venues in other areas of the state; Tampa and Ybor City, Jacksonville, Saint Augustine, Ocala, Pensacola."

He nodded his concurrence. "That will be a problem. The new cable northward to the Florida peninsula is still out. They say the cable ship is en route to make the repairs. But we just got word yesterday there's a problem ashore, north of Punta Gorda. A sink hole, on top of everything else we've got to contend with, has swallowed the poles and cable."

"Then it looks like I'll have to head to Tampa and use their cable station. But first, I'll get *Bennington* out to the anchorage. That way *Gneisenau* can come in and coal. It might help the political situation with the Germans."

"Maybe . . ."

"Second, I need to find Martin Herrera or José Poyo, two of Martí's revolutionary colleagues over at the San Carlos Institute, on Duval Street. They'll know Martí's schedule. Once I know where he is, we'll get under way for Tampa directly and from there I can warn Martí by cable wherever he is."

"Very well. Anything else, Wake?"

"Yes, sir. One thing—a personnel matter that needs to be decided right away."

Walker cast a look to the overhead and groaned. "Let me guess. Norton Gardiner."

26

The Good of the Service

Key West Naval Station
Wednesday evening
14 December 1892

After *Bennington* coaled and anchored out, I had Gardiner visit my cabin. "Get your gear together, Commander Gardiner. You're going ashore and won't be returning to the ship."

"I don't understand. Why?"

"You're being transferred to the Boston Navy Yard, where you'll be equipment officer under Captain Selfridge, the commandant."

His face transformed into a pinkish red hue. "That's an insult! I'm leaving *Bennington* now? This way? Is this because of our stupid conflict last week and your obvious jealousy of my class and status? People from your station in life can never really understand the burdens of wealth, can they?"

"No, it's for the good of the service, because of your gross incompetence, Commander Gardiner. I need an executive officer

136

I can trust, which eliminates you, for you are not trustworthy in either seamanship or leadership. The fact you are going to Boston is a gift of charity toward you by the admiral."

"Charity? The admiral! You and Walker cooked this up so I'll be disgraced in front of my family in my home city, sent there to be an underling with a menial office. My family is expecting me to be given a proper command and they will not stand for this at all. They are very close friends with Senator Lodge, and you and Walker will regret this. You both will be ruined. Count on that. Ruined!"

His performance disgusted me, but I was not about to get into a shouting match with the likes of him. I kept my demeanor calm, which seemed to madden him even more.

"Yes, actually it was charity, Commander. If you would rather go to Mare Island Naval Yard in California to spare your ego any humiliation, I understand there is a vacancy there for an *assistant* equipment officer."

To preclude further whining, I judged it time for the coup de grâce. "And as far as Senator Lodge goes, perhaps he might be interested in learning what I just learned ashore—you have had marginal evaluations for the last ten years, you were never considered for command of *Bennington* or any other ship, and you have been passed on from one station to another as a political payback for your family's campaign donations. Your assignment to this squadron and in this ship was the last chance to prove that your skills were worth everyone putting up with your character flaws. You failed. It's over."

Gardiner started to say something, but I cut him off. "And if you do or say anything even remotely insubordinate from this moment onward, I will have you arrested instantly and court-martialed. Do you understand?"

He didn't answer, so I said, "This was where you should've said, 'Yes, sir.' And where I would've said, 'Good luck.' But you didn't, so get out of my sight, get your gear sent down into the boat, and remove yourself from this ship."

That did the trick. The petulant arrogance vaporized. He sat there, dumbfounded.

"I said, get out!"

In a daze, he made his way to the passageway and out of my sight. I called for Lieutenant Commander John Warfield to come to my cabin.

He arrived in a hastily donned working uniform, with the middle button undone and a pencil behind his right ear. "Yes, sir?"

"Sit down, please. I have some substantial news for you."

He lowered himself into a chair, regarding me as one might a strange dog, uncertain whether he was going to be bitten or licked. It was a feeling around superiors I knew only too well and I couldn't help but inwardly chuckle. Did I really have that kind of reputation? I hoped not.

"Effective immediately, you are *Bennington*'s executive officer. Commander Gardiner has received a new assignment at Boston Navy Yard and is going ashore as we speak. You will move into his quarters straightaway and work out a new officers' watch bill."

Warfield was understandably stunned for a moment, but his recovery was rapid and he answered in a steady voice, "Ah, yes, sir. Thank you, sir."

"My yeoman is typing the order for distribution to all divisions this evening. Whom do you recommend for your former billet as navigator?"

"Lieutenant Lambert is the best of the lot, sir. He'd do fine."

"And for the new gunnery officer to replace Lambert?"

"Manning, sir. He knows the guns well."

He showed no hesitation in the recommendations, I was pleased to see. Warfield knew his brother officers in the ship.

"Very well, make it so. I will be going ashore soon, myself. Not sure when I'll be back, it might be late. When I do return, I will brief you on the past and present particulars of our mission, which are very confidential. The ship needs to be ready for getting under way as soon as possible. No liberty ashore for the crew, I'm afraid, but as soon as we can, they'll get several days ashore, wherever it is we end up."

"Yes, sir."

"I know this is a lot to absorb so suddenly, John. But you are a good officer and have shown me you can handle it. Go ahead and brief the wardroom about this change at supper. However, I want you to make sure there are no negative comments regarding Commander Gardiner or his departure. I will not stand for any of that sort of nonsense."

"Aye, aye, sir."

"You must have a thousand questions in your mind. Any I can answer right now?"

"None that can't wait for our meeting later, sir."

I stood, which prompted him to do so as well. Holding out my hand, I said, "Not much time to offer my congratulations, I'm afraid. Please know I am glad to have you as my number two."

"Thank you, sir."

A check of the clock showed it was getting late. "And now I must go ashore. We'll talk later, John."

We both got down to business, Warfield heading for the bridge and me racing down the ladder into my gig, where I told the coxswain to hurry. That he did, and when we rounded the bow the boat moved heavily through the chop of the anchorage, for the southwest wind was rising. The straining boat crew kept their eyes averted from mine, but not before they registered I was in civilian attire, unusual for a captain ashore in Key West. The smell of rain was in the air and I peered through the darkness, trying to ascertain the shape of the clouds. They were low and in long lines. Squalls from the southwest and west. A bad sign.

Seeing my uneasiness, the coxswain commented over the splash of oars and waves. "Storm a-coming, sir. And a bad 'un at that. Gonna be a rough night, sure as hell's hot."

Key West

27

The Mysterious Cuban

Wednesday evening
14 December 1892

Those squall lines brought thick showers that soaked me as I ducked from building to building along Duval Street. Few people were out and about; those who were traveled buttoned up in their carriages. Key Westers are intimately experienced with foul weather and I saw several places with storm shutters closed.

Just after crossing Fleming Street, I reached the new Cuban society building known as the San Carlos Institute, a stone structure that replaced the old frame one at Fleming and Carlos Alley. That place of revolutionary fervor was destroyed by the fire of 1886, an event indelibly imprinted in my mind for many reasons. My watch showed 8 p.m., quite late for a Tuesday evening, but there were lights on inside the Institute and I pounded on the door.

A rotund elderly man with eyes that had seen it all answered. After a top-to-bottom evaluation of this fool standing in the rain and disturbing the peace, he deigned to allow me a skeptical,

"*Buenas noches, señor.*"

I asked if Mr. Poyo or Mr. Herrera were there and provided my name. He replied in English, informing me the gentlemen were off the island. I stressed it was most urgent I speak with a leader of the Institute, for I had information they would want to know immediately.

Evidently I passed muster, for he asked me into the foyer, blue tiled in traditional Spanish motif, and bade me wait, saying he would find someone in authority. A moment later, that person turned out to be a slender gentleman of intelligent features, expensive attire, and middle age. His penetrative gaze, magnified through a pair of spectacles, reminded me of Martí's.

He was introduced by the doorman as Dr. Mario Cano, a lawyer from Havana and a member of the Institute. The prefix was an indication of his occupation as a lawyer, a normal appellation in the Spanish culture. I was impressed by Cano and thought I could transact my business quickly. Cano bowed slightly and was about to speak when a commotion behind him showed someone else was about to join us.

My daughter Useppa appeared from around a corner and gave me a big hug, exclaiming, "Daddy! What in the world are you doing here?"

I was completely caught off guard. Suddenly, I recognized Cano as the man I'd seen on the wharf standing beside Useppa the day we'd departed. *Possessively close* beside her then, as he was now.

A lawyer from Havana? Red flags went up in my mind, for Cano's profession uses deceptive words to camouflage mal intent or guilt.

Useppa had never mentioned him in her letters. Did this mean their obvious "friendship" was of recent beginning? Her fiancé, killed six years earlier by Spanish agents in Key West, was also Cuban and a member of the Institute, though he was a Protestant pastor and a decent gentleman. Was there a connection between the two men beyond the apparent? Was my daughter still mixed up in the extremely dangerous world of Cuban revolutionary intrigue?

I felt a surge of anger toward Cano. He should know better than to involve her in that world. And so should she.

"No, what precisely are *you* doing here, young lady?" I asked indignantly, for now I didn't like the look on Cano's face. No longer vaguely pleasant, it appeared deliberately inscrutable. Actually, it was damned smug. My suspicions grew by the second. My daughter was still fragile after her beau's death, and I didn't like Cano's looks, or his profession.

"Especially at this time of night," I appended, speaking in the Cuban's direction.

My demonstration of paternal concern for my little girl's welfare got me no accolades or concessions, however. Instead, I got a lecture.

"Oh, Daddy, for goodness sake. *You*, with *your* sordid history, should not be chastising *me* about propriety. There is absolutely nothing improper going on here. It was a meeting of a committee of the Institute, which asked me to stop by and speak about my work at the Douglass School, since we have some Cuban Negro children there."

A true daughter of her Irish-blooded mother, she was worked up now and cast me an indignant scowl of her own. "And Mario, for your information, is a gentleman of the highest caliber and a decent Christian. As for me, I am a grown woman, a lady, and I am perfectly safe with him, anywhere, anytime, of *my* choosing!"

As the man in question silently watched this scene of familial rebellion play out, I thought I detected a slight bemused look on his face. Yes, there it was, the right corner of his mouth slightly raised, in appreciation of the show.

Fathers cannot win in such situations, especially when the daughter is a grown woman. So, ignoring her broadside, I switched targets and subjects.

"Dr. Cano, I am here to transmit a special message to José

Martí. It's quite urgent and of extreme import, but I just arrived from sea and don't know his location."

My daughter looked at me warily, then relaxed and said, "Mario, you may remember me saying Daddy is a close friend of Martí." With a protective squeeze of Cano's arm she added, somewhat condescendingly, I thought, "You can trust him."

I was about to remind her who was the daughter and who was the father, when Cano spoke for the first time. I noted he had very little accent, as if he was quite comfortable in our language.

"Martí is not here in Key West, Commander Wake. He was here for nearly a month, but left by steamer five days ago for engagements in Tampa, Ocala, and Ybor City. I will be taking the steamer on the seventeenth, if this weather permits, to meet him up in Ybor City next Monday. I can pass along your message at that time verbally, or in writing, whichever you wish. If it is confidential, you may trust it will remain so."

The years in espionage taught me there were frequently several layers of meanings, for reasons good or bad, in many people's statements, and one had to peel them away to discern the actual core of the issue. The man before me was a prime example.

So he had a meeting with Martí himself in Ybor City? Was Cano in the Cuban Revolutionary Party as well as a member in the San Carlos Institute? Probably, for many members were. But he lived in Havana, so if he was a revolutionary, he must be covertly so.

Or perhaps he worked for Colonel Marrón? The colonel was very good at infiltrating revolutionary groups with agents provocateurs. Conceivably, Cano could be the assassin. Using my daughter as a trusted referral would be a logical route for an agent to get close to Martí. And if he was working for Marrón and the secret section of the Orden Público, he would know all about me, and therefore, Useppa.

He'd said his meeting was Monday, the nineteenth. That would be three days too late. A ruse to disarm my suspicion—or was it the truth, indicating he was legitimate? Or was it a clever test of my reaction to the date, to see if I knew it was three days too late?

Oh yes, this Cano fellow was slippery, indeed.

"Exactly where is Martí right now?" I demanded.

"Daddy . . ." warned Useppa in a whisper.

"I do not know, sir," replied Cano. "I believe he probably is in either Ocala or in Ybor City today, for he has an important speaking engagement there tomorrow night. He stays at the home of Paulina and Ruperto Pedroso on Thirteenth Street."

It was common knowledge Martí stayed with the Pedrosos when in Ybor City. The old black couple were like doting grandparents to him, and he was devoted to them. His love for them exemplified his attitude toward race relations and his hope for a unified free Cuba.

Useppa glared at me, her words hissing with anger. "Daddy, Mario is not one of your junior subordinates—stop treating him like one or I will send you away until you behave like a gentleman."

A retort came to mind, but I refrained. She was right. I was using the wrong method to get information. I didn't like or trust Cano one bit, but I had to admit his relationship with Useppa had clouded my judgment on the best way to learn more about him. It was time for some honey-flavored humility, not vinegar.

"Yes, well, you're entirely right, dear. My anxiety on this matter got the best of me. You have my apologies, Dr. Cano, for being so impolite."

"Not anything to worry about, Commander," he said, rather unconvincingly. I saw Useppa nudging him, then he smiled openly for the first time and added, "Say, we were just about to get dinner over at the Duval Hotel. I would be honored if you could join us, and I know Useppa would greatly enjoy it."

Was Mario Cano a friend or foe? There were two categories of foe. Was he, in fact, the assassin of Drake and Martí? Or was he, instead, a parasitic threat to my daughter's happiness, a Latin scoundrel out for something different? Either answer made him my enemy, and demanded more information about this mystery man. But both required something I didn't have—time.

I smiled politely in return. "Thank you, Dr. Cano, but I don't have much time at all, and so must say goodnight and goodbye for now."

Useppa said, "Daddy, please don't go. The Navy can wait for an evening. I have something important to tell you."

She was understandably proud of her work at the school, so I asked, "Really? What is it?"

Useppa beamed with delight. "Mario and I just got engaged!"

A sledgehammer could not have stopped my heart quicker. "What?" I asked, hoping I'd misheard.

Through gritted teeth she informed me, "I love Mario. He loves me. We are getting married this coming spring." She took a breath, and said, "Please come to dinner."

She was absolutely serious, her mother's determination clearly evident in her eyes. With the realization that I had no say in the matter other than to accept it as a fact, I willed myself to remain calm and said, "Useppa, I guess my opinion or consent hasn't been asked for. As for dinner, I need to get under way immediately. There's a storm arriving tonight. And I'll see you both when I return to Key West in a couple days."

"With Uncle Sean? I want Mario to meet him too."

And I wanted Sean Rork to gauge Mario Cano as well. "Yes, dear. Sean will be here with me. We'll all go out to dinner then, but I must insist on being the host."

That altered the ambience entirely. My daughter was delighted.

"Wonderful, Daddy! Thank you. We'll have a splendid time."

Useppa gave me another big hug, afterward cuddling Cano.

They did look good together, I grudgingly admitted. Maybe this Cano fellow wasn't so bad after all.

Their happiness reminded me of my second encounter with Maria, one which ended far better than the first.

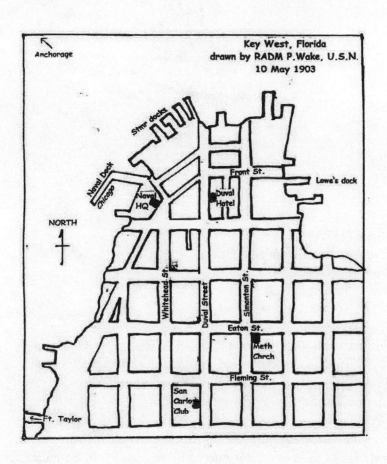

Anchorage

Key West, Florida
drawn by RADM P. Wake, U.S.N.
10 May 1903

Stmr docks

Naval Dock

Chicago

Front St.

Lowe's dock

Naval
HQ

Duval
Hotel

NORTH

Whitehead St.

Duval Street

Simonton St.

Eaton St.

Meth
Chrch

Fleming St.

San
Carlos
Club

Ft. Taylor

147

28

The Kiss

British Embassy
Connecticut Ave & N Street
Washington, D.C.
Friday evening
22 July 1892

It was yet another formal affair in full-dress white choker—
my fifth that summer and pure torture in a sweltering
Washington July—and my presence was due to an elderly
superior's distaste of all things pertaining to the English. He
particularly despised, as he described it, their "perennially
arrogant condescension toward us." I was bluntly "volun-told,"
as we say in the navy, to attend so he wouldn't have to go and
associate with "those people my father and his father had to fight,
twice. Perfidious Albion!"

Evidently, this duty had been passed down the line from
officer to officer because no one wanted to go. It is damned hot
and humid in Washington's July.

For the record, I have no aversion to the British at all,

in informal company. My aversion was to being miserably uncomfortable wearing a damned formal uniform and enduring an hour or more of stupid chatter. However, I was in Washington on temporary assignment, had no junior assigned to me to unload the duty on, and I needed the captain's cooperation on the work I was doing. Thus, I acquiesced to the doddering old twit.

And this was how I found myself standing in the embassy's drive, waiting for a break in the procession at the entrance to make my way inside inconspicuously.

I found out there was no break. The United States hosts thirty-six foreign embassies and legations in Washington, and that of Her Majesty Queen Victoria is the most senior, ornate, and prestigious. When the British give a party, all the others attend, to stand there idly and to see and be seen. Therefore, the line of landaus, coaches, phaetons, and cabriolets reached all the way around the block. There was no way I could walk inside while the ladies and gents of the glittering class were making their grand entrée. Even I knew that would be *tres gauche*. I must wait to enter with the sycophants, hangers-on, posers, and assistants of the middle level.

So there I stood, next to the stone columns of the embassy's portico, the sole representative of the United States Navy present. Trying to stay out of the amber glow of the giant lanterns I felt, and no doubt looked, like some uniformed minion waiting for someone to tell him what to do. Someone finally did, in a charming accent.

"Please rescue me for the second time, Peter. I am shamefully without an escort, for he has not appeared yet and no one seems to know where he is."

It was Maria, alighting from an open landau with another couple stepping down from the other side. The man of the couple was in an elaborate uniform but I couldn't make out his rank.

With apologies for my lack of fashion knowledge to any lady

reading this account, I will endeavor to describe the exquisite vision Maria presented that clammy, windless evening. Amidst the turmoil in the portico, she was an oasis of cool, confident beauty, the beau ideal of a modern lady. Dressed in a green silk gown trimmed in white lace, with golden necklace and earrings, I saw she did not use a bustle or a long trailing hem, a look which I had learned was *passé*. Her hair was done up in what I believe is called a chignon, with a gold comb fastening it. She managed to actually look somewhat comfortable, unlike the other ladies, who wore harried and painful expressions when they thought no one was watching.

My perusal was completed in mere seconds and I was by her side in a flash. With a bow, I took her hand and said, "Doña Maria, it would be a great honor and pleasure to escort you inside. And, I must say, it is I who has been rescued, from a night of abject boredom among pretentious men, by a beautiful lady."

She curtsied and took my arm and, treated as a couple, we strolled past the liveried doormen in style, smiling generously to the servants the whole way. It was immense fun play-acting a grandee, and even more fun when the real Spanish grandee from the landau cast a worried look toward us.

In the outer parlor, we were shown to the refreshments— gin cocktails, even the smell of which I dislike—and then ushered into the main ballroom, where a red-coated majordomo announced our presence to the assembled diplomatic world. And oh, how the assembled world reacted. Ladies whispered knowingly and gentlemen opined to each other with furrowed brows. The content of their discourse was obvious—a mid-level American naval officer escorting a Spanish lady of noble connections? Why had she sunk so low?

By the little giggle she made, which only I could hear, I knew Maria was enjoying the fuss. The constant stares began to wear thin for me, however. I suggested to Maria we retire from the limelight to somewhere less noticeable, to which she said, "Why Commander Wake, that sounds like an attempt to get me alone."

"Good, it's what I wanted it to sound like."

I reconnoitered behind a large hanging tapestry of an eighteenth-century English king and queen—otherwise known as a musty old rug on the wall—and found a servant's door, which opened onto a garden. There was a dim glow by lantern light, just enough to walk by. Beckoning Maria to follow, I led the way through the manicured hedges to a group of chairs by a table. We sat down amid some pink flowers I guessed were azaleas.

Overhead, the stars were emerging as a powdery dusting across the night, barely visible in the loom of the city. Inside the building, a string quartet had begun a French-sounding tune, the music wafting in the air, which was sweetly scented by Maria's perfume and some Confederate jasmine nearby. The romance of the scene, the years of loneliness, and an unfamiliar feeling of uninhibitedness, all combined in my psyche to reduce its usual reticence with ladies of wealth in social situations.

In a state of pure abandon, I put my hand over hers on the table and said, "You are truly stunning tonight, Maria, and I am very glad I came. You made it worthwhile."

"Was this an assignment to be endured, like last week?" she asked as she put her other hand atop mine. "You certainly did not appear to be having a pleasurable time back in the ballroom, Peter."

"Yes, it was," I admitted. "And I couldn't get out of it. But if I only had known you'd be here, I would have immediately volunteered and fought off all others to have the pleasure of this moment."

She smiled shyly. "I did not want to attend, either. But I was asked to come because the chargé d'affaires's wife, Madame Sagrano, is ill and they needed another lady to balance our party. I think that is a silly reason to be here, but now I also am glad I attended."

"You are? When we last parted, I got the impression by your comments you thought me crude."

"Well, you *were*, Peter. But I knew you were not trying to be crude. Actually, I was intrigued by you. My final words last week were for the benefit of the man who interrupted us. I needed to protect my reputation and knew he would repeat them around the embassy, for that fool gossips like an old woman." Maria grimaced as if she'd touched something disgusting. "He is a worthless toady , and nothing more."

"We have our share of those too. I really wasn't trying to be crude."

"Yes, I am sure of that now. You were merely being *real*. It is a quality quite rare at these events. Most are so busy posturing they do not know how to be genuine anymore. I may be wrong, but you appear to be as sincere a person as I have ever met— though I think there is still much you have not told me about those medals."

Her look was one of curiosity and challenge, and extremely alluring. I surrendered to the moment. "There are times not to talk, Maria."

Leaning close, I took her face in both hands and kissed her gently. She responded in kind at first, then more fervently. Soon we were entwined and oblivious to our surroundings.

Thus occupied, I failed to notice an intruder slipping up on us in the dark. Well, I say intruder, but we were in *his* embassy. It was the assistant Royal Navy attaché, a congenial fellow with whom I had spoken occasionally in the past. He discreetly cleared his throat and whispered, "Good evening, Commander. Ah . . . hem, His Excellency and some other people will be coming along through here very soon."

I heard someone conversing behind him. It turned out to be the ambassador himself, Sir Julian Pauncefote, who was showing off the embassy's garden to some of his guests.

Suddenly, servants were padding around hastily lighting lanterns and torches, and our hideaway transformed into an illuminated display of flowery splendor. We quickly disengaged and, led by the naval attaché, headed off into some convenient shadows, far from the ambassador's party. It was a close-run thing, but Maria and I managed to escape the attention of our esteemed host and his bored-looking guests when he began a detailed monologue on the growing cycles of the Chinese flowers in the garden. My Royal Navy friend waved goodbye to us and then dutifully joined his boss.

That left the lady and me standing in the dark, feeling decidedly juvenile. She giggled first, and before I knew it, we were both trying to stifle our mirth as we made our way, hand in hand, down the path in the dark. It had been years—decades, actually—since I had giggled, and it felt wonderful to know I still could.

Another seating arrangement appeared and we took advantage of it, cuddled in a kiss that was all the more delicious for its furtive nature amid the distant voices. Everything about Maria aroused my passion and interest, and as I sat there I didn't want to let her go. By her behavior, she agreed wholeheartedly. So we stayed there together a long time, saying nothing and yet saying it all.

Finally we had to leave, for the soiree was ending, but not before promising to meet for lunch the next day at a little tavern I knew in Georgetown, far away from the disapproving stares of Washington's diplomatic elite at the Willard or National. There was so much to discuss, to learn about each other.

As she turned to leave, Maria's words were like music to my ears. "Now I know you are very real, Peter Wake, and I rejoice you have entered my life. Until tomorrow . . ." She touched her lips and smiled. My heart melted again, completely smitten.

Any doubts about her feelings for me were gone. In some way which I have never fathomed, Maria was in love with me, albeit at second sight.

29

The Maelstrom

Key West
Late Wednesday evening
14 December 1892

My departure from Useppa and her beau was accelerated
by a squall line blasting down Duval Street. Making my
way block by block north toward the harbor, I registered the
wind was clocking to the northwest. That meant it would be
rising in velocity soon, into a full gale. And it meant no boats
would be able to take me back out to *Bennington*.

At the wharf, *Chicago* was ablaze in lights and a hive of
activity as officers and men made preparations for her to get
to sea, for the wind was pushing her hard against the wooden
fenders in a shrieking cacophony of pain for the steel hull. I
could see and feel the wharf recoiling each time the big cruiser
smashed into it. Among the officers on her bridge, I saw Rear
Admiral Walker, standing there like Noah with his beard flapping
in the wind. If Gardiner was there, I didn't see him.

My coxswain didn't hesitate when I reached the boat landing, where the waves tossed the launch up and down four or five feet. Jumping down as the boat rose up, I felt a strong arm pull me with a blue curse from sliding off the gunwale into the water. The instant I collapsed on the thwart we were away from the wharf, with additional language from the coxswain as foul as the weather to which it was addressed.

The wind had piped up fast into a full gale, a wall of solid air and rain, with gusts blasting even stronger. Pulling hard against the seas and wind, the men were exhausted in minutes, but we still had a mile to go. I took an oar from a sailor who suddenly cried out in pain and was clutching at his ribs, and yelled for the coxswain to keep the bow into it. I'd been ashore far too long and now the anchorage was a maelstrom. If we tried to turn back, the launch would broach and swamp, and we'd all be in the water and swept away into the Gulf of Mexico to our north by the current.

That flood tide current was helping to kick up the seas, but also helping to move us against them. After what seemed an eternity, a shaft of light reached out from somewhere ahead. Sweeping across the cauldron of the anchorage, it moved toward us, before settling on the boat. Bathed in an otherworldly light, every movement of our straining arms and contortion of our anxious faces played out as if in the limelight of a stage. I had the ominous feeling God was in charge of that searchlight Himself and this was the judgment day, with the verdict on my life very much undecided.

While trying to synchronize my oar with the others, I took quick glances over my shoulder to search ahead for our ship. Through the spray and rain I saw several steam vessels in the anchorage ahead moving, most heading south, which was downwind toward the Straits of Florida. One was moving north, toward Northwest Channel and the Gulf of Mexico. A couple ships were staying put, with every deck light burning brightly and black clouds roaring out their stacks. They were steaming at slow turns of the propeller to ease the pressure on their anchor cables. At our distance, I couldn't make out which one was ours, but the coxswain spotted her a quarter-mile away.

It was a quarter-mile too far for the men in our boat, for we were all completely emptied of strength. Of the ten men in the boat crew, six, including me, were crumpled along the thwarts, arms and legs no longer functioning. The four left, including the coxswain who had left the tiller and was working an oar, were failing fast.

Someone yelled, "That ship is coming for us!"

One of the vessels heading north had turned, a dicey maneuver in those conditions with reefs all around, and was steaming our way. She slowed and formed a lee close so we could get alongside. I heard orders in German and realized she was *Gneisenau.*

Blau's voice boomed through a speaking trumpet. "You want to come aboard?"

"No," I answered, wondering if he realized I was in the boat, "but we could use a tow to *Bennington!*"

"Ya, vee do that!"

A line snaked out in the air and the bowman secured it just before the tow took strain and the boat surged ahead. The German ship circled toward *Bennington* and we cast off the towline just to windward of our ship, to drift down the remaining fifty feet to our home. Both ships exchanged blasts on their steam whistles, ours in "thank you" and theirs in "good luck."

Warfield's hulking shape was at the entry port when I hobbled through, every part of my body hurting. The dream of stretching out in bed filled my mind like a beckoning narcotic, a vision I was trying to ignore.

"I thought you all were goners, Captain," he blurted out. Then, with a tinge of apology he added, "This damned storm's gotten up far worse than I'd predicted. Good thing the German turned to help. We were trying to weigh the anchors and get to you, sir, but they're stuck in deep as hell."

"Don't worry about it, John," I gasped while clinging to a stanchion. "I didn't think it'd be this bad either. And yes, we were lucky Captain Blau helped. He just finished coaling at the pier."

A shouted report came down from officer of the deck on the bridge. "Lookouts report *Atlanta* and *Essex* are through the main channel and south of the island, sir! The German and Spanish cruisers are southbound in the main channel now, sir. *Chicago* is getting under way at the wharf."

All eyes went toward the wharf. Walker and his men had done it. The flagship was free of the wharf and the land, her bow swinging to the southwest and the main channel. She was following *Gneisenau* and *Reina Regente* to run downwind through the channel and get under the lee of the Florida Keys. I concluded the two foreign warships would probably shadow Walker's ships for the next week or so, and thus be in a position to observe the squadron's upcoming gunnery practice. That would give them valuable intelligence as to the true state of the American Navy's combat readiness.

Well, I decided, that was going to be the admiral's problem. I had enough other things to worry about.

My pocket watch showed it was now almost midnight on the fourteenth. Time had run out for doing anything else but proceeding directly to Tampa. Making the 260-mile run from Man O War Anchorage at Key West to the Tampa docks usually took twenty-four hours—in fair weather. But the weather was the opposite of fair, and getting worse with each minute.

I staggered like a drunk along the deck to my cabin. Once there, while gradually recovering the use of my wrenched arm muscles by flexing them gently, I reviewed my options.

The secondary channel into Key West is the twenty-foot-deep Northwest Channel, which leads into the Gulf of Mexico and is the normal route to go north to Tampa. The nor'wester gale was blowing right down the channel. *Chicago* and the foreign cruisers drew too much water for the channel, but *Bennington*'s fourteen feet could proceed through the meandering center of the passage, though it would be a very risky navigation challenge in the rain-shrouded dark and against the brute force of the storm.

I calculated the timing. If we stayed in comfortably safe, deep water by going south out the main channel, then steaming west sixty miles toward the islands of the Dry Tortugas, there to turn north and head for Tampa, it would add about eighty miles and at least half a day. On the other hand, if we slogged up Northwest Channel into the teeth of the gale, we would save time and distance, but it would be extremely dangerous. Foolhardy would be a more appropriate description.

Even so, that was my decision, for time was paramount.

30

Nothing Is Easy

Key West
Midnight Wednesday evening
14 December 1892

I called for Commander Warfield to come to my cabin. As I changed my clothing, I briefly presented him with the facts of how the entire situation had unfolded, from Jamaica until then. His face grew grimmer as he took in the explanation for all our apparently bizarre endeavors of the prior week.

Warfield's only comment was a cryptic, "Well, now I understand, sir."

Then I gave him my plan of action, afterward asking for his candid evaluation. True to form, he presented an analytical summary of the salient points.

"It'll take some time to get our anchors up, sir. Once that's done, we can make it through Northwest Channel, even in this bad a storm, *if* we go slow and the searchlight functions well. We'll have both the tide and wind against us on this side of the Keys, so we'll make no more than six knots during the ten-mile transit. Once we're free of the channel, we can make maybe twelve knots against the storm, but I'd count on ten over the bottom. That puts us at the docks in Tampa at approximately three o'clock in the morning on Friday, the sixteenth."

I nodded my concurrence. It was the same time of arrival I'd estimated. Warfield held up a hand while shaking his head. "However, there is a major factor involved here we haven't spoken of yet, sir. The engineer officer reports three of our four boilers are in dire need of overhauling—boilers A, B, and C— and the fourth one not far behind. He told me it would take at least four days to flush and clean the almost four hundred tubes inside each boiler. The pressure readings prove his point, sir. I've read the reports myself. We are straining the boilers and engines as if under war conditions, and Lieutenant Angles is very concerned."

I'd been worried about that very thing. Warfield next spoke as if he was reading my mind.

"The ship and boilers are new, or they probably would've blown the safety valves already, sir. If two or more boilers *do* end up tripping their safety valves, we'll be stopped dead in the water right then and there. In the midst of a storm. The only alternative at that point would be to sail downwind back to Key West. I recommend we maintain steam for ten knots and no more on this transit to Tampa, sir. It'll help lessen the strain on the boilers."

He'd presented it well, the facts without hysteria. Lieutenant Edward Angles, the dour engineering officer who kept to himself and his mechanical beasts below, had been telling Gardiner and me the same thing for a week.

But one more run was needed. Then we could lay up and overhaul the boilers, a nasty job for the men who tended them. As for being in war conditions, I considered us in war *preventative* conditions. We had to go.

"Thank you for bringing that up, Commander. It is a valid and important point, but a risk I must take."

"Is all this really worth the risk, sir? For a foreign rebel leader, not even an American? If and when we fail, your career will be over. Thirty years for nothing."

The man was genuinely concerned for me. It brought memories of another time and place, far away and long ago, and another man who was concerned for me because of a decision I'd made.

"John, I learned an excellent lesson almost twenty years ago from a wise Mohammedan scholar in Northwest Africa. His name was Mu'al-lim Sohkoor, and he was the royal scholar to the king of Morocco. This was at a time when I faced an overwhelming Tuareg enemy, had little time to rescue hostages, and had few assets to use. Just before I had to make a decision about what to do, Sohkoor told me, very quietly, something I have never forgotten since: 'You are a warrior, Peter, and for a warrior, there are times to risk everything. It is true that when a warrior does take a risk, he may lose everything in defeat. But always remember that if a warrior never takes a risk, he will always know defeat.'"

Warfield asked, "So what did you do, sir?"

Intense visions flashed in my memory. Once again, I felt the doubt in my mind, the intense pain of a chest wound, and despair of Rork and I knowing we were about to die, somewhere in the middle of nowhere in the Sahara Desert. Remembering made the wound begin to throb as if reopened, and I absentmindedly massaged it. I suppose I was grimacing, for Warfield was looking at me oddly.

I didn't tell him about the memories or sudden pain, but simply said, "I risked everything—the life of myself, my partner, and several others. We were wounded very badly and almost died, but we accomplished the mission, and the innocents were saved. John, I don't want to seem melodramatic, but Martí is the innocent in this situation. He must be saved to do his work. The future of this hemisphere needs him."

Warfield nodded pensively. "Aye, aye, sir."

"Good. So we'll still go, but we won't push the engines any more than absolutely needed. I accept your recommendation of ten knots of speed. That should still get us there in time to prevent this assassination. I want the safety valves inspected right now to make sure they are working well. Also, have Lieutenant Angles provide steam log hourly reports to the officer of the deck, with immediate notification to both you and me if anything looks like it's getting beyond control."

Normally, the hourly steam log, which detailed temperatures, pressures, and oil and water levels, was reviewed at the end of each watch by the watch officer, with the executive officer and captain getting daily reports.

"Aye, aye, sir. Concerning the safety valves—I had them inspected an hour ago and they are functioning well."

"Excellent. All right, I'll meet you on the bridge in ten minutes. In the meantime, set sea watches, secure for heavy weather, and start weighing the anchors, starboard one first."

Warfield stood. "Aye, aye, sir. Ship is already secured and watches set. Anchors are already hove short." At the door, he said, "Oh, one more thing, sir. The station delivered our mail bags when we first arrived at the wharf and you were with the admiral. You've got several official and private envelopes on your desk."

"Thank you. I'll see you in ten minutes."

Then I looked at the mail and groaned. More things to read, more decisions to make, more worries. What I really wanted to do right then was lie down on the bed, so enticingly near. Just five minutes to rest my aching bones and muscles. Five minutes.

A deep thud sounded from forward. A second later, a speaking tube in the rack of three beside my desk whistled. It was the bridge. I opened it and said, "This is the captain. What happened?"

"Warfield here, sir. Number two anchor cable just fouled on the steam windless. They're putting nippers on the cable to take the strain while they clear the fouled cable on the drum. We're also hauling in on number one to help."

That was dangerous work on a pitching bow. The cable nips probably wouldn't hold for long and a cable lashing around a deck kills and maims at blinding speed.

"I'll be right up, Commander Warfield. In addition to what you're already doing, get ready to buoy the cable and let it slip if we have to."

Damn it all to hell and back! What friggin' else will go wrong? Those were the thoughts roaring through my mind after Warfield's report. The bed, and any respite for my bones and muscles, would have to wait.

Both I and the ship rose at the same time, knocking me off balance. Lurching across the deck, I grabbed at the chronometer on the bulkhead for support and almost fell over, further aggravating my outlook on how things were going. Once the wave passed astern I adjusted my mindset about potential future setbacks, for I had enough hard-won experience to know better than to dwell on that sort of thing. It was a pointless waste of time and effort. Whatever would happen, it would probably be the one thing I never anticipated.

Nothing is ever easy on a warship.

31

The Pressure Builds

Southeastern Gulf of Mexico
Early Thursday morning
15 December 1892

Unfortunately, Warfield was right. It did take a long time to get those hooks dislodged and hauled up to their catheads. After almost two hours, and three men hurt with lacerations while freeing the fouled cable, I was about to order the anchor cable slipped and buoyed when both anchors were finally weighed. *Bennington* swung northward into the teeth of the gale and began punching into the seas.

Tremendous clouds of spray flew aft from the bow as she smashed into waves every thirty seconds. Jagged reefs lined the channel close on either side for the first couple miles. The swinging beam of light illuminated their frothing walls of coral rock just waiting for us to make a mistake—or for those boilers to fail.

Standing beside me, Warfield called out the course orders, maintaining a calm demeanor throughout, an image so unlike his predecessor. His composed manner was contagious among the bridge watch, the members of which peered through the watery gloom to find the next channel mark and keep an eye on those reefs, keeping any sound of fear or false cockiness out of their verbal reports.

When we cleared the outer mark of the channel at 2 a.m., I complimented Warfield and all hands and stopped by the sick bay to check on the injured men. They were resting and expected to recover quickly. Now we were in open sea and away from dangerous reefs, I went to my quarters to focus what little energy I had left on the newly arrived correspondence.

Four were from the Navy Department, the Fourth Auditor Section, to be precise. Those were the stuff of bureaucratic functionaries and the bane of ship captains. As such, they could be ignored when matters of real import were at hand. I pushed them aside.

The other three were personal, including one from Maria. They were far more important than a clerk's request for expense documentation.

I opened Maria's first. The envelope was light, containing only a brief note dated December ninth. She wrote from Richmond that she had left Washington and was on the train, bound for Tampa.

The date was the ninth? That meant she would have been in Tampa by the eleventh, a Sunday. The Plant Line steamer usually left Tampa on Wednesday. But the storm would've delayed it, so that implied Maria might still be in Tampa. With any luck at all, I could get to Tampa, warn Martí, and see my love—all within the next twenty-four hours. It seemed the situation was beginning to brighten!

The second was from my young impetuous friend Theodore Roosevelt, currently causing mayhem in the federal Civil Service Commission at Washington, which he was actually trying to turn into an efficient agency for the good of the people. Roosevelt, whom I'd known for six years, was a force to be reckoned with, as many a politico had discovered, usually to their chagrin, particularly in his present position. He continually railed against cronyism, criminal corruption, and professional incompetence.

His note was to the point. Namely, when exactly would I be back in Washington? He had urgent things—there were no other kind in Theodore's energetic world—of a naval nature to discuss. It would take place over dinner at his club.

Dinner discussions with Theodore were generally an endurance contest as to who would override whom in the conversation, with Roosevelt the frequent winner. But, on the other hand, they were never dull and often enjoyable. His note ended with one of his favorite exhortations in French: *Honneur au courage malheureaux!*—Salute to ill-fated courage!

The third missive was from Tom Moore. Commonly known by everyone as "old Black Tom" to distinguish him from other Toms in the area, he was born a slave at Gamble Plantation up on the Manatee River, seventy miles north of where I had my home. Of indeterminate age—possibly sixty—Tom made his living after the war by building fishing vessels among the islands of the lower Gulf Coast of Florida. One of those islands, Patricio, is where my bungalow home, as well as Rork's, is located.

It was a sad letter, for he had found the body of the caretaker of my island, old man Whidden, slumped in a chair in his cottage. Whidden, an ancient former Confederate who had looked after the island since 1883 when Rork and I bought it, had been getting feebler by the day, so the news wasn't totally surprising. Tom said he gave Whidden "a reel Christian burial near his hut, compleet with words from my own Bible, even tho that old coot Whidden aynt deserved em."

Tom reported that he was staying on at Whidden's place and overseeing the island until I or Rork returned or wrote and decided what to do. He then offered to take Whidden's position on the island for, he said, he felt it was time for him to settle down in one place. I liked and trusted Tom, and was inclined to accept, but since the island was jointly owned, a talk with Sean Rork would be in order first.

I returned to Maria's letter. As always, I sat there staring at the curves of her handwriting, taking in the faint scent of her perfume, imagining her little idiosyncrasies, and remembering our last time together, in September. It had been quite a courtship, accelerating exponentially in depth and time.

Politically and socially unacceptable as was our growing relationship, we reveled in every minute of it, though we took great pains to keep it confidential. The furtive nature made those moments we could be together even more special, delicious really, with both of us acting like young lovers whose parents had forbidden us to see each other.

By the time August came along, we knew our mutual life histories and dreams. Both having been married, we had no fantasies or misunderstandings about the opposite sex's behavior or weaknesses, and dismissed mere romantic infatuation as naïve foolishness. Actually, we had grown quite comfortable with each other. No pretenses were needed or shown—sincerity was enough. Meals, walks through parks, symphony concerts, even diplomatic cocktail soirees, all were looked upon as opportunities for us to share laughter, knowing glances, and quiet understandings.

There was one threshold we did not cross, a silent agreement we would not complicate our emotions, or risk discovery, by taking our love *dans le boudoir*. This, I will fully admit, was not easy for me. I am not a saint, but bitter experience and intuition told me we'd better not.

So, after two months of intense passion, quiet resolve, and heartfelt connection, and in spite of my misgivings about the odds of success for such a marriage, I felt almost as if we already were married, in spirit if not in consummation. I felt at ease with my personal life, and had hope for the future.

In mid-September my time in Washington ended. I was recalled to the fleet and given command of *Bennington*. It was agony for me to be away from Maria without a solid plan for reunion to look forward to, and her letters became the only surrogate for our need for intimacy. But even those communications had to be guarded in nature, lest our secret get out through those who might have access, benign or mal intended, to our mail.

I steeled myself to turn away from thoughts of Maria and plunged into my administrative responsibilities—the disagreeable ones centered around documentation and authorization. At four in the morning, I was still immersed in getting caught up with my neglected paperwork duties when Warfield knocked on my cabin door.

He reported all was well with the ship and we were still making nine to ten knots against the thirty-five-knot gale, the wind now veering due north. Our position was fifty miles west-southwest of Cape Sable at the bottom of the Florida peninsula, and sixty-five miles south of Cape Romano, near Marco Island. On the crucial issue of the boilers' pressure, all four were holding steady between 139 and 141 pounds per square inch, far below the designed maximum of 160 pounds and the safety valve level of 150 pounds.

I thanked him and sent him off-watch, for Lieutenant Lambert had relieved him on the bridge for the next four hours. All being well with the ship, I succumbed to exhaustion and fell into my bed, which had been beckoning me for hours.

The gauzy amber light of a storm-filtered dawn filled my cabin two hours later when the tube beside me whistled again. It was Lambert, and the news was not good.

"Pressure in A Boiler has been rising, sir—it's now at 146. B Boiler is at 142. C Boiler is steady at 139 and D is at 140. Commander Warfield, Lieutenant Angles, and the senior boilermaker are down in the boiler rooms checking them now."

"Very well, Mr. Lambert. What is our course, speed, and position right now?"

"Course is due north at zero degrees, speed is nine knots, position is approximately forty-eight miles south-southwest of Cape Romano and forty-two miles due west of Cape Sable, sir."

The air was noticeably cooler, so the warm front of the storm had passed and we were now on the cold backside. *Bennington's* motion seemed the same to me, the bow smashing into seas and the hull shuddering each time, so apparently the damned storm wasn't letting up. "What's the weather, Mr. Lambert?"

"Glass is steady at twenty-eight-point-six, sir. Wind is still out of the north at a steady thirty-two, gusting to forty knots. Seas are eight to ten feet out of the north at thirty-second intervals, with no breakers. No damage to ship, boats, or equipment so far. No casualties since freeing the number two cable when weighing anchor. And the sick bay steward reported ten minutes ago all three of those men are resting easy, sir."

"Very well, Mr. Lambert. Good report. I'm heading down to the boiler rooms."

When I arrived in the ship's belly, the blistering heat and roaring noise of the fire boxes and boilers was, as usual for me, overwhelming and disconcerting, for this part of a modern warship was alien territory for an old canvas man like me. I never could find it fascinating, unlike many officers, but I did understand it was now vital. Canvas aboard men-o-war was going the way of the dinosaurs. New ships being designed had no sailing rig at all. In the new century just ahead, we'd all be at the fickle mercy of machinery.

In a dark corner, farthest away from the boilers, Warfield and Angles were shouting into each other's ears in animated debate, their faces intense in the flickering light. Bare-chested coal heavers, by far the strongest men on the ship, were tossing a shovelful every minute onto the grating inside the boxes. The boiler man, a thirty-year veteran in filthy overalls, was crawling around the far side of the B boiler tank, getting far closer to it in that heat than could his captain. His apprentice, a youngster clearly made nervous by the presence of so many officers in his metal cave, was passing and receiving various fitting tools as the boilermaker tested the integrity of our number two tank by tapping and twisting like a doctor on an obese and recalcitrant patient.

Warfield came over to me and said into my ear, "We're going to have to shut down A and B boilers. The A boiler is now at 150. B is at 145. We've got to find the problem. Angles thinks it's a steam leak, because the water level's low but there's no fluid leakage below the tank. He says once the tanks get cold, it'll take five or six hours to search and spot the leak. Eight or nine hours total."

"That'll slow us to just steerageway at revolutions for five knots—which will mean staying stationary in this wind!" I said, a bit too angrily.

"Got to, sir. Can't risk an explosion at this point."

Grudgingly, I admitted he and Angles were right. There was no alternative.

"Do it," I ordered.

32

The Race

Southeastern Gulf of Mexico
Thursday
15 December 1892

We sat there and wallowed, barely staying even against the wind and seas. After letting the boilers begin to cool down, Angles and his men searched for the leaks, which were discovered by waving a broom in front of tanks and piping, and waiting until it disintegrated from the invisible jet of leaking steam.

The leaks were found along the upper middle seams of both A and B boilers. The seams were then riveted tighter and appeared to hold well. The cause of all this was the boilers' feed pumps, which weren't transferring enough water from the condenser back into the boilers. This allowed a superheat to build and thus fatigue the seams, which had already been weakened by scale deposits that had built up because of the lack of preventative maintenance. In other words, this chain of events started because of my earlier decisions to postpone the boiler maintenance.

Next, Angles's men had to disassemble all three pumps to find out which had failed and why. It was the number one pump, which had developed a tiny leak in a valve seal. The seal was replaced.

By now I am sure one can understand the level of my mechanical ability and comprehension, and therefore would be not surprised that when Lieutenant Angles went into a long, detailed recitation, eyes shining with pride, of his solving the of the hows, whys, and whens that composed this litany of failures, I utilized the last of my dwindling supply of patience and simply said, "Very good, Mr. Angles, and when can you get us moving again?"

"We've already gotten the fireboxes lit, and we should soon have enough steam, sir. Then all four will be on line."

"Good. Then make it so, Mr. Angles."

At long last, all our boilers had enough steam to move the pistons in the three large cylinders to turn the two long shafts that turned our two propellers.

The engineer counseled caution against too much pressure too soon, for these were crude repairs done at sea, so *Bennington* steamed at less than her full capacity. Even though the wind had diminished to a steady twenty knots and the seas to six to eight feet, we were making no more than eight to nine knots over the bottom.

By four o'clock Thursday afternoon, we had only made it northward to a point five miles west of the snow white beaches off Captiva Island. There were still about eighty miles to go. I estimated our arrival at three a.m. the next morning. That would be Friday, the sixteenth, the day the assassin would strike, according to the coded message. We still had time, but not much.

One hour after I made that calculation, another factor intruded. The weather had cleared in the cold crisp air and the lookout spotted a warship, then another warship, on the southern horizon astern of us. Over the next hour it was clear they were gaining on us, and equally clear who they were: our anchorage mates from Key West, *Gneisenau* and *Reina Regente*.

Warfield, the only man aboard other than Rork who knew the entire convoluted state of affairs, looked at me. "Well, I'll be damned. Look at them. I thought they would be staying in the Keys to spy on our gunnery skills, sir."

I looked aft, then east toward the coastal islands. "Yes, I was hoping for that too. The fact that they're on a northerly course this close to the Florida coast means there's only one destination for them."

"Tampa."

I nodded. Both warships had "bones in their teeth"—bow waves bursting high in the air from their ships' speeding into the seas. "Two or three hours 'til they're even with us, do you think?"

"Yes, sir. At the most. They're doing a good twelve knots or more."

That unwelcome news opened up an entire new category of questions for me.

Had the German ship transferred Drake's suspected assassin to the Spanish ship while at Key West Harbor? Did Captain Blau really have German immigrants to document in Florida? Was the fact of the two foreigners steaming in company just a mere coincidence, or part of the plot? Did the Spanish cruiser have the assassin onboard, or was she just making a routine port call? Spanish cruisers periodically made port calls around the Gulf of Mexico, especially at Key West and Tampa, where there are large Cuban-Spanish communities. But I could not assume these ships didn't carry the assassin. I had to assume the worst.

"What do we do now, sir?" asked Warfield.

More quick calculations. The *Gneisenau* and *Reina Regente* were going to get to Tampa ahead of us at this rate and we still had no other way to warn Martí or his people of the killer's coming.

Unless I could somehow stop the German and Spanish warships.

To the officer of the deck, I ordered, "I want to know when those ships close to within half a mile. I'll be in my cabin."

"Aye, aye, sir," was the neutral reply, though I could see excited curiosity in his eyes. Within minutes the word would spread from deck to deck—their unpredictable captain had something up his sleeve and there was no telling what was coming next. Of course, the lower deck's evaluation of this news would be colored by their recent lack of liberty ashore and increase in work load. I was sure they would not view it positively, but simply as more evidence of my lunacy.

To Warfield, I said, "Come to my cabin, Commander. I have an idea I want to go over with you."

When we were seated in the privacy of my cabin, I broached the plan that was hatching in my brain. It was, to say the least, unorthodox. Or perhaps lunacy.

"John, we need to stop or slow those ships, since one of them may well be carrying Martí's murderer. Here's an idea as to how."

He listened intently, then asked, "I don't know, sir. This is damned dangerous for Lambert. He could die doing this."

"Yes, it most certainly is dangerous, which is why he'll have to be a true volunteer. I think he will, once the entire situation is explained to him. And we'll keep him under close watch the whole time he's doing it, to minimize the danger."

Warfield still wasn't convinced. "If the Spanish or Germans catch on, it might be construed as an insult to their flag and start some kind of international mess. The admiral won't like that, sir. Not to mention Washington."

"No one will be hurt or killed, nothing will be damaged, and no country will be humiliated or dishonored—so no, it is not illegal or an insult according to international law. Just a routine training exercise. And while it is playing out, the wind and seas will lay down further and veer to the east, and our boilers will have time to slowly build steam to maximum safe pressure. That will ensure at least sixteen knots for *Bennington* when we start up again, which is more than the German and the equivalent of the Spaniard, since her bottom is foul and engines are undermaintained. And it means we'll beat them there."

When newly commissioned five years earlier, *Reina Regente* was rated at twenty knots, but my intelligence operations in '89 and '90 showed she was considerably slower now due to lack of proper maintenance.

"Yes, sir," he said guardedly, "that's possible. Of course, it'll have to be kept very quiet, sir. Only Lambert, you, and me can know about this. If it ever got out . . ."

"I concur entirely, John. This will work, though, because once we've delayed them and then can start back on our way at six or seven o'clock tonight and are steaming at sixteen knots, we'll be in Tampa in eight hours, around three a.m., if the wind goes easterly enough for us to get our fore and aft sails up for a broad reach along the coast."

Warfield let out a breath and grinned. "Well, sir, I must admit it's something those devils will never suspect, and will just have to go along with."

"Very good. Let's get Mr. Lambert in here and brief him."

33

Force Majeure

Gulf Coast of Florida
Thursday
15 December 1892

Lieutenant Gideon Lambert's broad Iowan face lit up like one of Lewis Carroll's famous cats when he heard me present the plan, and his critical part, should he accept it. Feeling I should dampen his youthful excitement with some sober reflection, I ended with a sincere addendum, meant to give him an honorable way out.

"This is not only out of the norm for an officer, it is extremely rigorous for the man who fills the role. Gideon, I don't want you to say yes without thinking about it for half an hour. You have my word of honor no one outside us will ever know if you feel, for whatever reason, you're not the right man for it. I expect an *honest* answer."

"I don't need half an hour, sir. I think it's a brilliant idea, and I am fully capable of accomplishing my role. I was an athlete at the academy—football and baseball."

"Remember, if I do pick you, it means you can't tell anyone what you did. This is a clandestine assignment. Understand?"

"Aye, sir. Full and well."

A knock at my door heralded the young bridge messenger, who managed to survey the cabin while staring straight ahead at the bulkhead—memorizing who was where, their facial expressions, and any other information which would be pertinent when he told his mates later on what was going on in the captain's cabin.

The report emerged in nervous rapid-fire fashion. "Captain, I have a message from the officer of the deck. Mr. Yeats reports the two foreign warships are now half a mile astern, three points over on the port quarter. He estimates them steaming at fourteen knots along the same course as us. Wind and sea conditions are laying down, veering northeasterly. He also says Mr. Angles told him all the boilers are holding well at one hundred and thirty-five pounds of pressure, sir."

"Very good, Dumphries. Present my compliments to Ensign Yeats and there is no reply needed. You may go."

I turned to Warfield and Lambert once the door closed. "Well? You both ready?"

"Let's do it, sir," acknowledged Warfield.

"Aye, sir," said Lambert. "Ready."

Nearly everyone on the bridge, and down on the main deck, was staring at the cruisers astern when Warfield and I entered the bridge and the quartermaster announced the traditional warning, "Captain and Executive Officer are on the bridge."

They all got back to being busy with their duties as I said to Warfield, "Wind's looking better. This would be a good time for the topmasts to be sent up, wouldn't it?"

"Aye, it would, sir. We can get some canvas up. Mr. Lambert is about to come on as officer of the deck, but I see he's out and about right now, so I'll have him attend to that."

"Very well, we'll set lowers and topsails once it's done."

"Aye, aye, sir," Warfield replied to me, then told Ensign

Yeats, "I see Mr. Lambert is down there on the main deck by the foremast. Have him get with the bosun of the watch and send up the topmasts directly, and then make all ready to set sail. He may relieve you when that is done."

I could see but not hear the word being passed forward, and then watched as Lambert began gesticulating and pointing to the spars and shrouds that needed to be shifted in order to raise the topmasts up—they'd been brought down in the storm to reduce our windage—so our sailing rig was full sized again. The bosun mustered his men and within a minute or two they were hauling away on halyards and shrouds.

Meanwhile, the men of the oncoming watch were arriving at their stations on deck and in the bridge, and those of the off-going watch were briefing them on the situation for their specific areas of responsibility. Yeats announced to the men around him that he was remaining on watch until relieved by Lambert, who was supervising the work on the main deck.

By this point, Lambert was standing atop the bulwark by the port fore shrouds, his left hand gripping the lower ratlines while swaying effortlessly with the exaggerated motion of the ship through the seas. He was looking up as the topmast ascended and the men on the foretop began to secure the topmast butt in its step. His rhythmic swaying took him out over the water and inboard over the deck.

The foretop man yelled down that all was well aloft, and the deck men tensioned the upper forestays and shrouds. Once that was completed and our foremast was in no danger of falling, Warfield and I walked aft to the chart table and conversed nonchalantly about the peculiarities of tidal currents in Tampa Bay.

The ship's bell struck and Yeats oversaw the turnover of the men in his watch. The daily evolution of existence aboard a man-o-war continued in its prescribed routine manner, for the bell dictated time and life aboard.

It also provided the signal to Lambert.

"Man overboard!" came the shout from forward.

"Man overboard to port! Lieutenant Lambert is in the water amidship!" was the cry of Ensign Yeats on the port bridge wing.

"Get that life ring in the water!" roared a petty officer on the main deck.

"Where away is the man?" asked Yeats frantically. "I've lost him!"

This was answered by several men, along with subsequent refutations since what they thought was Lambert was just a whitecap. Someone then confirmed he was thirty yards off the port quarter.

"The Captain has the deck!" I announced in the middle of the commotion, striding to the center of the bridge. I immediately gave out a string of orders. "All engines ahead slow. Left standard rudder—come to course one-seven-zero. Drop buoys and rings. Man the ready boat. Fire the signal gun and hoist code 'X' and code 'Y' for those other ships to assist."

I looked astern, but couldn't see Lambert myself. Warfield was scanning the sea with his binoculars. He quietly said to me, "Can't see him, sir. He must be well astern of us by now."

Loudly, I ordered, "Commander Warfield, get down to the boats and have both ready to launch the second we sight him."

"Aye, aye, sir," he called over his shoulder as he dropped down the ladder.

"That's him!" called down the lookout aloft in the maintop. "Two hundred yards off the port beam."

No one on the bridge could spot Lambert. The lookout repeated the range and bearing as *Bennington* turned to the port. Then he reported losing sight of him.

And now an explanation of the preceding narrative is due. Those who have maritime experience may wonder why, once I was certain the man overboard was clear of the propellers, I did not circle the ship to the windward, or to the right, and thereby form a lee for him. It is easier to see a man in the water when looking downwind than when looking upwind, into the white caps and breaking seas.

The answer is that my plan was for Lambert—who had stuffed his pockets surreptitiously with kapok fiber in order to be more buoyant—to enter the water on the port side so I could turn the ship to port. This maneuver accomplished three things: it turned our propellers away from Lambert; it allowed us to turn into and block the path of the other warships, who were astern of us off the port quarter; and it put us between the sun and Lambert. The reason for the third point will become apparent shortly.

Boom! The signal gun went off just as the signal flags soared up their halyard and streamed to the wind. The hoist of the international code flag "X" meant "man overboard." The "Y" flag had two meanings: "I am putting boats in the water" and a command-request for the Germans and Spanish to do so as well.

The entire operation had taken only three minutes, but it effectively obstructed *Gneisenau* and *Reina Regente*. It also had the added benefit of degrading their machinery a bit, for both foreign ships had to put a huge strain on their gears and clutches by ringing up "full astern" on their bridge engine annunciators in order to stop in time. This was evidenced by the smoke pouring out of their funnels and propellers furiously thrashing the water around their sterns.

If they hadn't done so, they would've collided with *Bennington*, which was now dead ahead of them and slowing down. Still, they might try to continue on their way, so I decided to lend some additional inducement, not to mention confusion, to their situation.

"Fire that gun again and hoist the signal!" I ordered Yeats.

Down on the main deck, Warfield was doing his bit in the charade, for as soon as we had slowed, our launch and whaleboats were in the water, and every available man was lined up along the deck rail, looking for Lieutenant Lambert.

As I expected, Captain Blau's crew were top-notch. It didn't take them long. Flags bloomed out from their masts.

"The Germans acknowledge and have a boat in the water, sir," related Yeats. "And there is the Spanish acknowledgment, sir. They are putting a boat in the water too."

"Is that Lambert?" called out Lieutenant Manning, standing there in his undergarments having rushed up from below. He pointed toward the east. No one could confirm his sighting.

"Mr. Yeats, I want to know from Mr. Angles if full steam can be gotten up and ready in all boilers, but I want the shafts still turning at slow ahead for right now. Also, left standard rudder— come to course zero-seven-zero."

He acknowledged and repeated my order, then saw to it by calling into the speaking tube to Lieutenant Angles in the boiler room. The reply came seconds later.

"Mr. Angles reports the boilers are holding well at half steam and he sees no problems with having full steam in ten minutes, sir. He'll engage the gears when ordered."

I checked my pocket watch. Ten minutes. Yes, that would work out well. It was almost time for Lambert's next action. And more confusion for the enemy.

"Mr. Yeats, please signal the other warships we have at least one man overboard and are declaring *Force Majeure*. Send a signal to *Reina Regente* to please have their boat search to the west, and signal *Gneisenau* to please have their boat search to the south. Inform them our boats will search to the east and north. Then add a thank you for their assistance."

Force Majeure was invocation of an ancient law of the sea— the right of any vessel to request and expect help from another ship due to a disaster. No warship would ever refuse to respond, unless at war with that country. Of course, no warship would ever invoke *Force Majeure* falsely to another country, unless at war.

In my judgment, saving Martí's life was worth my deception.

The scene around us had transformed considerably in the last few minutes. From the sight of three ships steaming bravely ahead into the wind and seas on a sunny afternoon off the

Florida coast, with the Germans and Spanish overtaking the American ship, the momentum had completely reversed. The foreigners were drifting downwind well to the south-southwest while *Bennington* was turning her bows back around to the northward. Our two boats were already in the area where I estimated Lambert would be, but not precisely where the signal said they would be.

All we needed was to know Lambert's exact location in the lead gray waves. The sun was lowering in a rapidly darkening sky, but enough light remained for Lambert's signal. And we had an hour after that until the sun disappeared entirely at five thirty.

Warfield showed up in the bridge and nodded toward the nearly deserted starboard bridge wing. I met him there and whispered, "You sure the coxswains know what to do?"

"Yes, sir. Get him in the boat quietly so the other ships can't see what's going on. No signals, no shouting. Then come back to us and get the boats hoisted up while *Bennington*'s underway and increasing speed. They'll get it done."

"Very well. Remember, the second those boat falls are hooked on, you've got to get them up because we're going to full speed very quickly."

"Aye, aye, sir."

The ship's bell was sounded once—extra strongly, just like Lieutenant Commander Warfield had quietly ordered the bosun of the watch a few minutes prior—to signify the first half hour of the first dog watch was completed. It needed to be louder than usual, so it could be heard far away from the ship.

34

An Unusual Signal

Gulf Coast of Florida
Thursday
15 December 1892

"Deck there!" came an excited yell from the lookout aloft. "A flash of light just showed two points off the starboard bow, a hundred yards out!"

Ensign Yeats piped up while peering through a long glass, "There, I see it! Yes! I think that's Gideon!" He glanced at me, then quickly added, "I mean Lieutenant Lambert, sir. The launch is close by him. I think he's using a helio-reflector. I didn't even know he had one."

He didn't. I'd given him mine. Turning my binoculars on the area, I saw two more flashes—fleeting reflections of the sinking sun—winking to us from the southeast. They were aimed right at *Bennington* and away from *Reina Regente* and *Gneisenau*, which were now almost two miles away to the south.

"Yes, I see him now too, Mr. Yeats. Well, I'll be, that was damn good thinking on Lambert's part. And he managed it just in time to get back aboard for dinner."

"Should we signal the other ships to discontinue the search, sir?"

Yeats loved to work out the complicated codes needed in flag messages. I answered in a calm paternal tone. "No. No signals just yet, Mr. Yeats. Let's make sure of the situation. Once Mr. Lambert's aboard and all is well, I will order a signal of thanks for the other ships."

I then added, "Also, please notify Mr. Manning he will be standing Mr. Lambert's watch and will relieve you as soon as he can be ready. I want you to get down to the main deck and escort Mr. Lambert to the sickbay for examination once he gets aboard, and then make sure he get a fine dinner afterward. He'll need it after that little dip in the water."

On a warship, when the captain says *as soon as one can be ready* it means *do it immediately.* Manning was due to relieve Lambert at the end of the two-hour first dog watch anyway, so coming on duty early wasn't that much of an inconvenience, and I wanted Yeats off the bridge, lest he pester me some more about signaling those other ships.

Lieutenant Manning showed up and properly relieved Ensign Yeats according to naval tradition, who dashed down the ladder to be there when the boat came alongside.

"Mr. Manning," I said, "you now have the deck. Turn to course three-five-zero with all engines ahead slow. What is the steam report for the boilers?"

He checked the report from the previous hour and answered, "One hundred and forty pounds in all four boilers, sir. Mr. Angles reports no problems and all boilers are ready for maximum pressure and revolutions."

"Very well, then the moment the forward boat falls are hooked and begin hoisting I want a steady increase in turns for sixteen knots on the course I just gave you. I will be in my cabin."

If Manning was wondering why the ship wasn't waiting until

the boat was up and chocked before increasing speed, he didn't look or say it. He also didn't ask about signaling the other ships. Instead, he only gave the age-old reply, "Aye, aye, sir."

Soon *Bennington* was charging north-northwestward along the coast at sixteen nautical miles per hour. The deck and topmen were setting up the main and mizzen topmasts, so soon all three masts would be ready to carry full sail to enhance our speed even further.

To the west, the sun was no longer a blazing white spotlight capable of reflecting off a heliograph, but a luminescent ripening mango in a dark blue and violet sky. To the east, a couple of dim lights showed eight miles off the starboard bow at the new phosphate dock on Gasparilla Island.

The Gulf of Mexico around us had turned gun-metal black, ruffled by a decreasing moderate breeze and waves from the northeast. A week earlier the men had been stripped to the waist in sweltering heat at Jamaica, but now we needed coats over our shirts in the cold air. Five miles to the south, red and green specks showed where *Gneisenau* and *Scharnhorst* were finally realizing the search had ended, but had yet to get their boats in and turn northward.

Warfield sat in the guest chair by my desk, looking decidedly pleased.

"Only our stern is toward the Germans and Spanish, and no lights are showing on deck or from ports, sir. Mr. Angles has Hammer Wilcox and his boiler men minimizing any sparks from the funnel. I told Angles it was a battle training exercise, as if we were at war with the foreigners behind us. He thought it an excellent idea."

"And Lambert?"

"Giving heliograph lessons in the wardroom and enduring ribald jokes about his clumsiness. He's fine, sir."

"The rig?"

"Should have all lowers and uppers set and drawing inside of ten minutes, sir. With all sail set on this close reach, I'd estimate another knot or two in speed. We'll hold that reach until we get to Anna Maria Island, then take in sail as we turn northeast into Passage Key Channel. That's a narrow channel for us, sir. I've never taken a ship through there in the dark."

"You're right, it'll be dicey—but I know the way. Learned it back during the war, going after the blockade-runners when they'd make a dash on moonless nights. The Germans and Spanish draw too much water. They'll have to enter the bay by the main North Channel, past Egmont Key. They'll also have to pick up a channel pilot. All that will add six more miles and much more time to their transit. And once they get near Tampa, they're too deep drafted to get up into the river to the docks in downtown. So they'll have to anchor a couple miles south, near Depot Key, out in Hillsborough Bay, and take a launch into shore."

"I don't know the tidal situation there, sir, but if it's high, we can get up into the river."

"Yes, if it's high, but I'm wondering now, what with this northerly wind. That'll lower the water levels.

"Well, if the tide does serve, I'm estimating we'll be at the waterfront in Tampa at three-forty five a.m., sir. Which dock will we use?"

"We'll use the government dock at the mouth of the Hillsborough River, right in in the middle of Tampa. That should either be unused, or we can raft alongside, if a Revenue Cutter Service cutter is already there. It's only a couple miles from Ybor, the town where Martí will be. I'll go ashore and fulfill the mission while you stay aboard."

I let out a sigh and put my feet up on the desk, a gesture signifying the briefing was over and we could both relax. "And with any luck, we can warn Martí tomorrow and the men can have liberty tomorrow night. They have earned some fun ashore. So have you, John."

Warfield took my cue and leaned back in his chair. "It has been a hectic week, sir. Never thought I'd be on this kind of mission, especially in my own country."

"I know what you mean. I thought I was done with espionage. Has there been any accurate conjecture among the officers or men?"

"Lots of silly rumors, but none the wiser on the facts, sir." Warfield laughed. "So far, the main conjecture is about how lucky Lambert was, after being dumb enough to fall off the ship."

I could just picture the good-natured heckling in the wardroom, but had no doubts the lieutenant would keep his mouth shut. "Oh yeah, that little anecdote will follow him for the rest of his career. I've had several to endure myself."

A captain leads a solitary life, maintaining an authoritarian image constantly. It felt good having a number two I trusted enough to be able to let down my guard and relax, if only for a few minutes.

That's when a knocked sounded on my door, followed by the messenger's voice.

"Sir! Bridge messenger Carson with a report from Mr. Manning!"

"Enter," I replied as both Warfield and I straightened up.

The boy presented the message. "Mr. Manning presents his respects, sir. He says a light has been seen flashing in code to the southwest, but it's not from either the Krau . . . I mean the German, or the Spanish, ships. He had Mr. Yeats called up to look at it and Mr. Yeats says it's in navy code, but it doesn't make any sense to Mr. Manning. So Mr. Manning requests your presence on the bridge, sir."

Warfield and I glanced at each other, both perplexed. *Another* light signal? It must be a ship, but as far as we knew there were no other U.S. Navy ships anywhere north of Key West.

"Very well, Carson. My compliments to Mr. Manning. I'll be right there."

When Warfield and I arrived, the bridge was crowded, for most of the wardroom had assembled upon hearing of this mystery and were busy with various theories regarding the strange light message. That we'd been in a race with the Germans and Spanish was obvious to all, and now this new development was giving a more menacing connotation to the race. There may not have been conjecture in the wardroom before, as Warfield had reported, but there was plenty of speculation among the officers now.

When my presence was announced by the bosun of the watch, the area silently vacated as the off-watch officers all found somewhere else to go. With Yeats beside him, Manning briefed Warfield and me out on the port bridge wing. The lieutenant pointed to where I could see a light twinkling in the distance.

"Captain, we first saw the light about fifteen minutes ago. As you can see, the light is not from the *Gneisenau* or the *Reina Regente*, who are directly astern of us."

"Yes, I see that."

"The flashing light looked like a message in navy code to me, so I called Mr. Yeats topside to see if he could make it out."

Yeats then took over. "It *is* a message, sir, and it's being sent by a man experienced with Morse, but not using our standard navy code. I checked it with the ONI code, but it doesn't make sense in that either, so I think it's a personal cypher-substitute message with the letters of the words unified. I have no idea what they are trying to tell us, sir."

Warfield put down the night telescope and said, "Can't see anything of the ship—too dark now. She appears to be closer than the foreigners, though. I'd say about three miles to the southwest. How the hell did she get this close without us spotting her before, when the sun was still up?"

It was a good question, which Manning answered. "Sir, I think they came up directly astern of *Reina Regente*, and just passed them a little while ago."

That indicated they came from either Key West or points to the southwest, such as the Yucatán. I asked Yeats, "Is it the same message being repeated, or are there different messages?"

"Same message constantly repeated, sir. I wrote it down in

the signal log."

We walked inside to the chart table, where the red-glassed night lantern shed its diffused glow. Yeats showed me the log page. It had spaces to record the time, location, and ship sending the signal—but the last part was blank as yet. Then it spelled out the Morse code letters of the message.

USEPPAMANYBOR

Manning, Yeats, and Warfield watched my reaction closely, which I confined to an order, since I really didn't know how to explain the signal in a way that didn't sound crazy.

"Mr. Manning, please accomplish the following: reduce our speed to ahead slow, maintain this course, and prepare for a boat to come alongside from that vessel when she gets close. After we embark the person from the boat, we will resume full ahead on this same course."

"Aye, aye, sir," he said, clearly bewildered, a state shared by the others.

"Commander Warfield, please join me in my cabin."

When he had done so and closed the door, I explained, "It's from a man named Mario Cano."

I had no intention of getting into Cano's relationship to me or my daughter.

Warfield was as mystified as the officers on the bridge. "Don't know that name, sir. Does he work for us?"

"Not really sure," I muttered, mentally conjecturing various explanations of what Cano might be up to. "But I'll be finding out. I want you to get him in my cabin the instant he steps aboard. He is not to converse with anyone."

"Aye, aye, sir." Warfield eyed me warily, as one would a senile favorite uncle. I didn't blame him. He changed the subject. "That's a pretty fast ship he's on."

"The only ship on this coast that can go fast enough is *Olivette*."

Warfield had been in the squadron only for a few months and wasn't familiar with the coast or the shipping. "Don't know her, sir."

"She's a sixteen-hundred-ton Plant Line luxury steamer running between Tampa, Key West, and Havana. Launched about five years ago. I heard ashore in Key West that she was delayed making her run south to Havana by the storm. Now it's abated a bit, I presume she's back on her schedule and trying to make up for lost time. Probably got into Key West last night, sometime after we left."

Then, wondering aloud, I asked myself, "But she should be heading south from Key West to Havana. Why is she steaming so fast to the north? Somehow, Cano got her captain to do that . . ."

35

Complications

Gulf Coast of Florida
Thursday night
15 December 1892

The throb of increasing shaft revolutions rumbled like nearby thunder when Warfield showed up in my cabin doorway twenty minutes later. I knew from his grim face something was amiss. Then I saw who was right behind him— my future son-in-law, the mysterious Dr. Cano.

Warfield reported, "Sir, the situation is not exactly what we thought it was. But to start off with, this is Mario Cano, an attorney from Havana. He says he knows you."

"Thank you, Commander Warfield. I'll handle this from here. Make sure all is well and we are making best speed."

When Warfield had closed the door, Cano spoke up in a nervous voice, "Good evening, Commander Wake. I'm glad you understood my message."

He was still standing, for I had not invited him to sit and relax, and had no intention to do so. "Doctor Cano, why are you here? I really don't need any more complications right now."

"I am truly sorry for this unusual intrusion, sir, but exigent circumstances have developed that made drastic action necessary."

We were interrupted by the bridge messenger, who reported, "Mr. Manning presents his respects, sir and says the *Olivette* has reversed course and is steaming south at about sixteen knots. The German and Spanish ships are now about three miles astern, continuing northbound, and staying even with us."

"Very well, Carson. No reply. You're dismissed."

I studied Cano again. "As I was saying, Dr. Cano, why are you here? And please omit the legalese. Get to the point."

"The Spanish are out to kill Martí, in Ybor City. I was informed of this last night, after we parted. The telegraph cable was still out, so I couldn't use that to warn Martí. The only ship available was the *Olivette*, but she was going south. So I made a large donation to *Olivette*'s captain. It turns out he is a supporter of Cuban independence also."

"Let me understand this clearly. *Olivette*'s captain steamed at full speed for over a hundred miles in the opposite direction from his company route, just because you bribed him? Why didn't he take you all the way to Tampa?"

"It was a *very* large donation, sir. The man has a big family and many expenses. And, of course, I told him the reason, so he wanted to help save Martí's life. But he couldn't go the entire way, for he had to be at Havana at dawn. I thought we could catch up to you."

There was more to it than Cano had said. Far more. But it was minor compared to the main issue. "Why exactly do you think the Spanish will kill Martí tomorrow night?"

"Lieutenant Roldan, who works for a secret unit of the Spanish Orden Público based in Havana, is the man in charge of their espionage operations in Key West. I found out he and some of his thugs are in Ybor City right now. They will kill Martí during his speech Friday night and make it look like a rival

Cuban group did it."

"How do you know this?"

"From a confidential informant, the identity of whom cannot be revealed for obvious safety reasons."

I studied Cano closely. He gazed back at me. He was in the espionage business himself, that much was sure, and because of it I couldn't trust anything he said or did.

"Who do you work for, in addition to the San Carlos Institute?"

"I am only a member there, one of hundreds, sir. I attended the meeting because of Useppa's presentation. I am also a member of the Cuban Revolutionary Party, and I help Martí when I am able. Beyond that, I have no political affiliations."

"Is my daughter involved in any of this?"

"No, sir. Not at all. Though I did tell her what I had learned and how I planned to get to Tampa and warn Martí."

"This all was a very ridiculous scheme, Dr. Cano. Bribing a steamer captain to race well out of his way to rendezvous with a warship for a ride to Tampa?"

"Yes, sir. I knew the odds were against me, but I was desperate. And it worked, for here I am. Martí must be saved, sir. Useppa said you would understand that."

A thought entered my mind. "Dr. Cano, do you know why the German cruiser and the Spanish cruiser are heading north from Key West along this coast?"

"Rumor in Key West is the *Reina Regente* is going to Tampa, but I did not hear the reason, Commander. I presume it is to facilitate Roldan's escape after the murder. I do not know about the German ship."

"Do you how Roldan will have Martí killed?"

"No sir. I would think they will shoot him."

"Maybe. By the way, did you notice a Spanish lady, very attractive, in her forties, on the steamer?"

"Not that I saw, sir. In fact, there were very few ladies aboard. It was mostly businessmen."

"I see. Well, anything else, Dr. Cano?"

"I've told you all the information I possess on the subject of Martí. There is something else, though, of paramount importance, on my mind, sir. It's very personal."

What next? I wondered tiredly. "Go ahead, what is it?"

"You know we are engaged, sir, but I want your official permission and blessing to marry your daughter. We have known each other as acquaintances for three years, and have been courting for a year. We love each other, are both Methodists, want a family, and will live in Key West after we marry in the spring. I can give Useppa a good life, sir. She wants to give you a grandson, and I would be greatly honored to be your son-in-law."

I was completely taken aback. Seconds went by as my anger at his impertinence rose exponentially. Then I exploded. "Good Lord above, are you crazy, Cano? You damn near hijack a steamer, stop a U.S. warship in the middle of the night, waltz aboard with a fanciful story of skullduggery in order to get a ride to Tampa, and now 'officially' ask to marry my daughter? You actually want my *blessing* after all this?"

He gave me a sheepish smile. "Yes, sir. I actually do."

Apparently, Cano was a complete lunatic who had somehow inveigled his way into my poor daughter's affections. Ignoring his cheeky comment, I shouted for the orderly to fetch Warfield.

When he arrived, I said, "Commander, please get somebody to escort Dr. Cano to the wardroom right away. Dr. Cano, you will remain in the wardroom until we arrive at Tampa. You may eat and sleep there—that is all. Our discussion is not for dissemination to anyone."

Warfield, who I was sure thought *me* a lunatic by this time, hustled Cano out and reentered my cabin a few minutes later. He looked like he'd seen a ghost.

"Ah, sir, there's something else we need to discuss. Actually, it's *someone* else. Another man came aboard tonight from *Olivette*. He's waiting outside, in your passageway. Dr. Cano said he didn't have a chance to go over it with you."

What the hell now? I asked myself. *This mission should've been simple.*

"Who would that be, pray tell?" I asked Warfield.

"Commander Gardiner, sir."

36

Rum and Ribald Songs

Gulf Coast of Florida
Thursday night
15 December 1892

That explained Warfield's worried looks. I suddenly felt worn-out.

"Very well. Sit down and tell me what's going on, John."

"According to the man himself, here is what happened. When Commander Gardiner disembarked *Bennington,* he reported to the squadron staff and confirmed his transfer, then demanded to see the admiral. Denied by the staff captain, he went ashore and checked into the Victoria Hotel. After what he described as a disgusting dinner, he went over to the naval station and spoke to the duty officer, asking about transport northward from Key West. This yielded nothing, so insisted on speaking to the station commandant privately, who is Commander John Winn, as you know. Evidently, Commander Winn had to come in to his office from his home."

I'd known Winn for years and could well imagine the scene.

He was a good man, and not the type to put up with Gardiner's antics.

"Well, sir, according to Gardiner, it seems his interview with Commander Winn lasted a grand total of three minutes and was not amiable. Winn then told his duty officer to write out transit orders for Gardiner to leave Key West as soon as possible for Navy Headquarters in Washington by any means available."

"So Gardiner alienated yet another senior officer, who was glad to be rid of him."

"Yes, sir. Here's where it gets really interesting. The station duty officer, that young lieutenant who just started got transferred in, got the message quite loudly and clearly from his boss. Well, as luck would have it, ten minutes earlier, this lieutenant had heard on the docks that *Olivette*—docked next door—was just about to leave, heading north on a special unscheduled transit, before heading south to her usual next port at Havana. It seemed to be the perfect solution to his problem. He told Gardiner about what he'd learned and suggested he present his orders to the *Olivette* and tell them the U.S. Navy would reimburse them for his passage."

"Smart lieutenant."

"Indeed, sir. Once Gardiner got aboard and the steamer had departed, he met Dr. Cano in the first-class salon and they had some drinks together. Dr. Cano told him *Olivette* was only heading north far enough to find *Bennington* so he could get a ride to Tampa, and she would turn and head straight for Havana right afterward. So now Gardiner had no option but to come aboard *Bennington* or end up in Cuba."

"Amazing," I said to myself. "I'm afraid to ask, but is there anything more?"

"That's pretty much it, sir. And Commander Gardiner is not amused by being back aboard. He's angry at Cano, who he says was drunk in the first-class bar, and at *Olivette*'s people for misleading him. Oh, one more thing, sir. When he came up our Jacob's ladder, somebody in the crew made a disparaging remark.

We don't know who. Anyway, Gardiner demands to see you immediately, sir."

I waited thirty seconds, willing myself to calm down, then said, "Show him in."

"Captain Wake, I want to speak to you in private," said Gardiner the moment he entered. The arrogant tone instantly eliminated what little calm I had remaining.

"First of all, I don't care about anything you *want,* Commander Gardiner. Secondly, you will stand at attention and remain that way for the duration of this interview, which will be short. Thirdly, Lieutenant Commander Warfield is the executive officer of this ship and he will stay. Now, present your travel orders."

He did, with a sour expression. They were standard, except for one addendum—the words "expedite" and "by any means available" were included in a request for travel assistance from any naval, military, or federal officers.

"You are back aboard this ship due to exigent circumstances, Commander Gardiner. We will be arriving in Tampa this morning and you will immediately disembark the moment the gangway or gig is lowered. Until then your gear will be sent to Lieutenant Commander Warfield's former cabin from when he was navigator, and you may rest there." I turned to Warfield. "Present my regrets to Mr. Lambert, and tell him he will bunk in with another officer of his choice."

"Aye, sir."

Back to Gardiner. "Remember, you are merely an officer in transit and will have no duties or authority in this ship. There is no need for you to be anywhere other than in that cabin, or in the wardroom for meals. Understood?"

"Am I under arrest . . . *sir?*"

"No, not yet. However, your behavior aboard will influence my decision on the issue."

The sour look morphed into a sneer. "Captain Wake, this is completely unwarranted and contrary to the dignity of an officer of my rank, and I officially protest in the presence of this witness. I want my protest documented in the ship's log right now. I also intend to file formal charges against you when I arrive in Washington. You are warned, sir, not to abuse me any further."

"Request regarding the log entry is denied. Your intention to file charges is duly noted, and welcomed, by me. I can't wait to testify, though I will have to wait my turn in a long line. Anything else?"

"Yes, there is quite a lot else, sir. That . . . that . . . that damned Cuban *pal* of yours . . . *bribed* the steamer's captain to dump us off with you. How does someone like him get passage on a United States warship? And not only that, but during the entire voyage from Key West he got drunk in the bar, drinking rum and singing ribald songs—in front of gentlemen in the first-class bar!"

Cano didn't seem under the influence at all when he came aboard. I had experience in the matter and would've been able to tell. But still, a devout Methodist drinking in a bar? I wondered if my daughter, the temperance princess, knew her beau allowed alcohol to pass his lips. Maybe the fellow wasn't so bad.

More importantly, Cano had kept his mouth shut about knowing Useppa and me. Evidently, Gardiner thought Cano was an intelligence operative. So be it.

"Really, so he was drinking rum? Which rum was he drinking?" I asked with mock horror. I couldn't help it. This was the one bright spot in my day. Besides, you can tell a lot about a man by the rum he drinks.

Gardiner didn't understand the sarcasm, but Warfield struggled to suppress a chuckle. "You know very well how those kind of people are. It was some sort of rotgut rum from Cuba. He had the rest of them drinking it too."

"Matusalem?" It is the finest sipping rum of Cuba, which means the finest in the world. It also happens to be my favorite. Rork's too.

"Yes, that's the name of it," grumbled Gardiner, who then

huffed, "*True* gentlemen know to drink only a small gin, especially in a fine establishment, but Cano had them all swilling rum and howling those wretched songs."

Well, well, points for Cano. The man had depth and understood cuisine.

"Fascinating story, Gardiner. Now, is that all? Or is there more whining? I'm tired."

"No, it's not all! Oh, I can assure you the truth will be told when I get to headquarters, and the highest authorities will hear of your transgressions! Charges will just keep adding up, Captain."

Obviously, Gardiner thought his threat would impress me. It didn't. I'd had internecine battles with far more devious and ruthless officers than he. It was time to deflate his hot air.

"And you, no doubt, will have great glee in telling everyone in Washington all about my many transgressions. Good. I suggest you start with the senior admiral of the navy. He gets whiners like you all the time. You'll find him on the second deck of the State, War, and Navy building. It's the very plush office in the northeast corner. You'll have to make an appointment, but it shouldn't be a problem for an officer and gentlemen of your high caliber and influence. Or perhaps I should write a memorandum requesting you get an audience?"

Angered beyond words, a condition I was rapidly approaching myself, Gardiner stammered out something negative. He was about to resume his tirade when I resumed mine.

"But while you are here, Commander Gardiner, there will be no further whining. You've had your say, and now you will do precisely as I say. That is all. Lieutenant Commander Warfield, you will now escort him to his temporary quarters."

When the door closed, I closed my eyes and took several deep breaths. Tired as I was, my mind's agitation wouldn't let rest come now. Instead, it swerved off course and conjured up the image of Cano joking and singing in *Olivette*'s first-class bar, amongst the white tie set, who were probably all drunk as coots and warbling right along. Except, of course, for Commander Norton Gardiner, officer and gentleman of the United States Navy.

Warfield returned a few minutes later. "Got Gardiner in my old cabin, sir, and he's still fuming. He's going to include me now in the complaint about the conspiracy against him. The Cano fella's stretched out on the settee in the wardroom. He didn't seem drunk to me. Said he had two glasses to be friendly. Also said he did teach some folk songs—his terminology—to the other gentlemen in the bar."

"Gardiner's against anyone who isn't Boston Brahmin. Just ignore him. Listen, I'd hoped to get right into downtown Tampa, but the wind's been too steady and strong out of the north and northeast. It's certainly lowered water levels in the upper part of Hillsborough Bay. That channel up into the Hillsborough River at the city of Tampa is shallow and narrow anyway—now it'll be too low, even for us."

"Anchor out and row the gig in, sir?"

"I thought about that, but no, we'd have to anchor too far out, at least two or three miles out. Instead, we're going to head to the new docks over at Port Tampa on the west side." I spread out a chart of Tampa Bay. "Let's go over it."

"I've never been in there. Is there a government wharf we can use there, sir? I thought it was all commercial docks."

"Yes, it is all commercial docks. And we're going to barge our way in and moor at one of them."

Warfield's face clouded in concern. "That'll be trouble, sir."

I shrugged. "Put it on the list."

"Isn't that pretty far from Tampa by land, sir? On the chart it looks like eight miles or so. Long walk."

"Good point. Yes, it's almost ten miles from the riverfront docks downtown. But there's a railway from Port Tampa northeast to downtown Tampa, and another from downtown Tampa the two miles out to Ybor City, where Martí will be."

"How can you get a train at three in the morning, though?
Won't they'll all be closed down for the night?"

"Rork and I will find a way," I stated flatly.

37

The Night Race

Tampa Bay, Florida
Before dawn, Friday
16 December 1892

Two pairs of double gongs of the bell sounded—meaning 2
a.m.—and the junior officer of the middle watch dutifully
turned the hourglass. The quartermaster noted the sea and sky
conditions in the logbook, the lookouts rotated their positions,
and the bosun of the watch, Rork, prowled the main deck,
looking for anything amiss or anyone not ready for what was
about to be expected of them.

We could barely see ahead and around us in the cloudy
gloom of a quarter-moon as we charged northward, two miles off
the beach of Anna Maria Island. Ahead lay the channel through
the shoals of Passage Key Inlet, shallowest of the three broad
entryways into the vast expanse of Tampa Bay. The only problem
was to find it. I remembered well the same feeling from thirty
years earlier, only then it was wartime and there was an enemy
involved.

A look at the two sets of running lights four miles astern made me wonder—did I once again have an enemy in this same place? A far more sinister and ruthless one?

"Bridge there!" hailed a disembodied voice from aloft. "I see the end of this island up ahead. It's two points off the starboard bow. I think I see a house on the point. Another small island is about a mile off to the north of the point."

That made sense. The north end of Anna Maria Island curved around to the northwest, with Passage Key a mile northeast of the point.

Lambert, the officer of the deck since midnight, approached me on the starboard bridge wing. "Sir, foremast lookout reports . . ."

"Yes, I heard him, Mr. Lambert. Thank you. We're getting close, and will be slowing and turning soon. Get your bridge and deck people ready and alert the engine room there may be quick bell changes for gears and turns."

"Aye, aye, sir."

I glanced inside the wheel house. By the Dante-esque illumination of the small red night lantern, I saw Warfield hunched over the chart, measuring our speed against his watch by moving a set of dividers. He shook his head and chuckled as he caught sight of me watching him. "No less than sixteen and a half knots average! She's hot tonight, sir."

"That she is. Let's keep her from getting high and dry too."

My quip got the hoped-for laugh from Warfield and the men. I beckoned him outside. "Steam pressure still doing well?"

"Yes, sir. Still steady at one hundred thirty-eight to one hundred forty on all four boilers."

I nodded, then took the night glass and studied the small wooded island on the starboard bow, explaining to him as I peered through the night, "There is Passage Key. Damn, the ebb is very low and still flowing out. There's a new quarter-moon so we'll have even more serious low water, in addition to the wind factor on the tide. Could be too low. If Passage Key Inlet looks too dicey when we get close in to the first bar, then we'll back away and shift course to the bell buoy at Southwest Channel, then go through there."

"Aye, sir. Bosun Rork reports we're still darkened. No lights showing and no funnel sparks visible."

"Very well. Let's get this done."

I moved to the area forward of the chart table, near the starboard bridge door, where I could be heard by everyone and also see outside.

"This is the captain. I have the deck. Mr. Lambert, take in all sail, slow all engines to dead slow ahead, eliminate any funnel sparks, and quiet the ship."

Lambert repeated the order verbatim and then set the watch to carrying it out. A methodical flurry of activity instantly ensued all over *Bennington,* from the engine room to the mast heads. Eight and a half minutes later, Lambert reported, "All sail is taken in, engines are ahead slow, course is steady at north-northwest, and ship is quiet, sir. North point of Anna Maria Island bears east-northeast, approximately two miles, and we are in five fathoms of water. Bearing of ships astern remains at due south. Range is approximately three and a half miles and closing fast, sir."

"Very well. Commence right standard rudder and come to course zero-nine-zero degrees. I want constant soundings."

The order was repeated and as the bow swung to starboard, toward Passage Key, I soon heard Rork, swinging his lead line by the foremast chains, and calling out his report of the fathom depths in a low chant. "By the mark, four!" "Nigh on four! Hard sand." "By the mark, three!" "Deep three, hard sand!"

Bennington's hull drew fourteen feet of water, so she needed sixteen feet to float through and not foul the intake pumps—if the transit through the shallows was brief and the bottom wasn't loose silt or sand. Two and two-thirds fathoms was what we needed.

"Deep two!"

That meant it was about seventeen feet deep. The next sounding didn't come from Rork, it came from the ship when her bow touched the shoals with a slow thud.

"All engines back full," I said as calmly as I could. With the ebb still running strong, two minutes aground was enough to set us on the shoal until the next high tide, at least seven hours away. Lambert was on the command immediately and within seconds the deck rumbled as the propellers dug in and pulled her astern, off the shoal.

All eyes watched my reaction, which I was determined to make unruffled.

"Very well done, Mr. Lambert. Please stop the starboard engine and go slow astern on the port engine. I want her backing around to starboard. Stand by for new course. We're going through Southwest Channel, which is also too shallow for our foreign friends. Speaking of which, what is the bearing and range on the German and the Spaniard?"

"Both are due south, approximately three miles and closing fast, sir," piped up the junior officer of the deck.

Bennington was now gradually backing southwest then south, toward our adversaries. As I surveyed the taut faces around me, I silently counted to twenty.

"All engines stop," I ordered, then waited another five seconds before continuing my orders, "All engines ahead slow. Course is three-one-five, due northwest. Steer nothing to the east of the course, if you please. Mr. Lambert, the outer bell buoy for Southwest Channel will be dead ahead by half a mile. Green buoy number one should be a mile out, about a point on the starboard bow. It is the important mark. Let me know when both are spotted."

Lambert repeated the order and added a spirited, "Aye, aye, sir!"

This élan was echoed by his subordinate helmsmen as they, in turn, received the command. Warfield glanced at me in the gloom and smiled. Ol' *Benny* had a different atmosphere about her now.

Certainly, my reader knows there was no war going on at this time, but the thick tautness in the ship was closely akin to the tension encountered in combat. That there was a race against the Germans and Spanish was obvious to all in *Bennington*. That it had to do with something more serious than sport was equally plain.

For the first time since her commissioning, the sailors of *Bennington* were bonded in a common struggle against a visible common foe in their homeland, and they would do everything they could to prevail over them.

"By the mark, four! Hard bottom." Rork called.

Lambert quietly said, "Egmont Key bearing northeast, sir. Range is one mile." Then he added, with a touch of awe, or maybe surprise, "Oh, there's the bell buoy on the bow, and there, there's the channel mark, sir! A point on the starboard bow—just where you said it would be."

"Mr. Lambert, that came out wrong," growled the executive officer.

Lambert recoiled, then quickly added, "No disrespect intended, sir. Sorry."

"Understood, Mr. Lambert," I said. "It helps that I've been on this coast for thirty years."

The time had arrived to begin our turn to the right so we would not cross into the beam of red light from Egmont Key lighthouse. Shining to the southwest, the red beam warned ships in the main shipping channel to the northward about the shoals we were about to cross. *Bennington* would be silhouetted against the beam for the ships astern, giving away our position and plan.

"Mr. Lambert, come right standard rudder to course zero-four-five, due northeast. All engines maintain ahead dead slow. Pass buoy number one close aboard to port."

Creeping forward against the ebb tide while continually in the bare minimum of sixteen feet of water, we passed the green buoy, the red mark opposite it, then Egmont Key over on the port side. Finally, green buoy number three slid by to port as we steamed northeast into Tampa Bay itself, our ship a black form moving through the black night, away from our pursuers.

Behind us, two ship's searchlights stabbed out into the inky dark. But we weren't in their line of sight, for they were looking to the northwest for the outer markers of the main ship channel near Palatine Shoal. They never traversed the lights to the northeast, where we used to be, or farther to the east, where we presently were.

"What is the range and bearing of those ships, Mr. Lambert?"

He answered, "Bearing is due west, sir. Range has increased to just over three miles. They are steaming northwest out into the Gulf at about sixteen knots."

As we passed the lookout tower of the channel pilot station on Egmont Key, I told Yeats, "Send the message on the hooded lamp." The hooded lamp was aimed directly at the tower, and could not be seen by any other direction. The message in Morse was simple: USS BENNINGTON FOR PORT TAMPA— NO PILOT NEEDED—FOREIGN WARSHIPS IN MAIN CHANNEL—SEND THEM TO TAMPA ANCHORAGE.

Yeats allowed himself a mischievous chuckle as he replied, "Aye, aye, sir."

Once we were past the shallow area east of Egmont Key, it was time to increase our speed. "Mr. Lambert, please make turns for ten knots on this course, and also continue constant soundings. The depths will be close to four or five fathoms for the next several miles, until we reach a pair of buoys, numbers one and three. Once through them we will turn north-northwestward to the channel for Port Tampa.

"And kindly remind Mr. Angles to be vigilant against stack sparks and embers as we increase speed. We do not want to be seen by the . . ." I almost said *enemy*, but altered it to, "other warships."

"No stack sparks or embers. Aye, aye, sir," came the reply.

Warfield walked over to me. "Captain, I've been studying the chart. Looks like we'll have to slow down once we enter the upper channel, so I'm figuring another two hours to the docks at Port Tampa. Three-thirty a.m. estimated time of arrival."

"Yes, that sounds about right to me."

I saw several quizzical glances among the officers and men. They still had no idea why we were going to Port Tampa, what would happen there, and when we would leave. An addendum was needed, for general consumption of the crew.

"With any luck, Commander Warfield, we'll have this assignment completed by the afternoon and can get back to Key West in time for the squadron gunnery qualifications. That way Mr. Lambert and his people can show off their considerable skills to the admiral. Not to mention a quick liberty ashore on the island, and then another one at Pensacola for Christmas!"

I was pleased to see it cheered up the mood significantly.

Behind us, both foreign warships continued on their course and were lost to view, being masked by the shadowy outline of Egmont Key.

Yes, things were looking up. Finally.

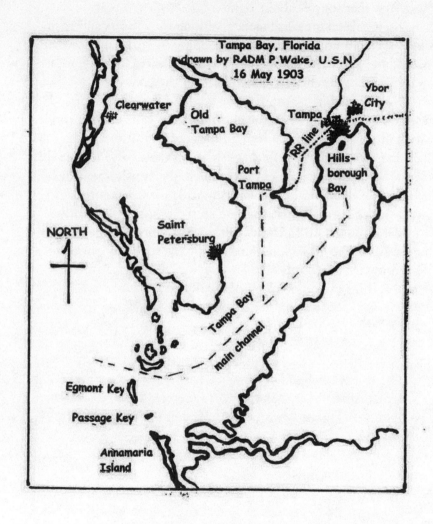

38

The Necessary Accoutrements

Tampa Bay, Florida
Before dawn Friday
16 December 1892

"Sir, only one of the warships is transiting the main channel back there," stated Lieutenant Manning, who was again the officer of the watch. "I can't tell which one she ls, though. Too far away."

I could hear the weariness in my words as I replied, "Very well, Mr. Manning. Thank you."

Warfield and I had been on the bridge throughout the night. I'd just sent him below for an hour of rest as we passed the new town of St. Petersburg to port. He wanted to stay topside, but I insisted. He'd be in command when I went ashore, and I wanted him alert and ready for anything.

I scanned astern of us. Barely visible on the southern horizon, only one set of navigation lights, glowing reptilian red and celestial white, showed in the main channel to downtown Tampa. Earlier, our darkened *Bennington* had altered course to port from the main channel and was now heading north into the narrows between the Pinellas Peninsula and the Tampa Peninsula, which opens onto Old Tampa Bay. Ahead on our starboard bow was Port Tampa.

Six miles dead astern, the other ship was heading northeast up the main channel toward Hillsborough Bay and the anchorage well off the city of Tampa. We would be at our dock in an hour. They still had several hours to go to get to their anchorage.

This new development, however, brought troubling new questions to my tired mind. Which warship was the one in sight—Spanish or German? Where was the other? Did the other one continue steaming up the coast? Or did they douse all their lights also, and somehow make it through the same shoals we did? If they did, where were they now? Somewhere in the darkness, heading to Port Tampa too? I had no answers for any of them.

Manning pointed off our port bow. "Papy's Point now bearing northwest, sir, at one mile. Red light number ten is dead ahead at due north, at one mile. We are right in the center of the deepest water available right now. Bosun reports thirty feet. The channel up ahead will be twenty-two feet at this tide."

We were at the narrowest, and shallowest, stretch of the final approach. Henry Plant, the rail and hotel tycoon who had been building Port Tampa into a major ship wharf facility for the last five years, had gotten the channel dredged and marked, eliminating dangers for those who used common sense. Having known that tortuous channel in earlier years, I greatly appreciated his expensive efforts right about then.

The foremast lookout reported electric lights on shore ahead, then corrected himself and explained they were on a large wharf, two miles on the starboard bow. Manning stared through the night glasses and confirmed it was a wharf, with several ships alongside and one anchored nearby.

Plant, a determined man in his seventies, owned a sizeable area of the west coast of Florida, from Tampa down to Punta Gorda, and east to Orlando. His commercial empire was growing exponentially by the day. It included railroads, hotels, real estate, mining, and steamers. Quite a few people worked for him directly and indirectly.

The crown jewel of his hotel network was the five-hundred-room Tampa Bay Hotel, a magnificent resort, the largest in Florida, built across the river from the town of Tampa and opened in 1891. Its architecture was in the Oriental-Arabesque motif, evoking a fantasy escape from the fast-paced world of bustling northern cities. It was predicted to be the premier resort in America in the next decade, and everyone who was anyone was a guest during its season, from December to May.

The commercial hub of his transportation network was at Port Tampa, and was headquartered inside his roving private railcar, in which he made constant inspection tours. His power wasn't only financial. Henry Plant had considerable political influence from Tallahassee to Washington and New York. He got what he wanted.

Over the previous four years, Plant's people had accomplished an incredible amount at the forgotten mud flat swamp called Little Mangrove Point. It had been turned into a modern deep-water port with two parallel quarter-mile long wharves, complete with warehouses, supply and repair depots, a rail yard, and a rail line out to the end of the southern wharf. More buildings were being erected at a pace unheard of in the sleepy South, for Plant had an old man's urgency to get things accomplished before he died.

There were even two over-the-water hotels, in addition to the commercial structures. Lit up with electric lights, like luxury steamers at anchor, they perched on pilings next to the southernmost of the wharves. Their unique setting made them sought after by veteran travelers wanting a new tourist experience with which to regale their cocktail companions back in New York City.

The largest was the eighty-five-room Port Tampa Inn. It was a full resort, with a fine-dining restaurant with stunning sunset, boats for fishing and sailing, and a dance hall for moonlight soirees. Its small neighbor was the St. Elmo Inn, equally comfortable for Plant's well-to-do train passengers waiting for his plush steamers to come and take them away to exotic Havana.

As we approached I wondered if one of them was Maria. The timing would be about right. As soon as I was done with warning Martí, I intended to look in at the hotels and see if she was there, waiting for passage to Cuba. The thought of seeing her filled me with anticipation of holding her, breathing in her perfume, tasting her delicious kiss. Norton Gardiner faded from my mind, for I was in a room with Maria, looking out over the bay at sunset . . .

"Sir?" Lieutenant Manning was trying to get my attention. Others were staring, too.

"Sorry, Mr. Manning. My mind was occupied with something else. What did you say?"

"Mooring and anchor details are at their stations, sir. But there's no space for us at the wharf. And no harbor boat to tell us where to anchor."

"Very well, Mr. Manning, we'll anchor just northwest of the northern wharf. Ready both anchors and stop all engines. We will drift to a spot to windward of the anchor point and then let go the port anchor and let her fall back on the hook."

"Aye, aye, sir. Both anchors are reported readied and uncatted, donkey engine is powered, and the capstan is ready, sir."

"Very well. Stop engines."

For a full minute I gauged the slowing momentum of the ship, the relative bearings of the wharves, the distance to a faintly outlined buoy, and then, when *Bennington* had stopped her forward movement, I gave the order, "Let go the port anchor

and veer half of one cable of chain. Back starboard engine, dead
astern slow for ten seconds, then stop all engines."

Manning repeated the order and passed it along to the
respective petty officers to carry out. In seconds, the ship was
moving stern-first to the west, away from the wharves, and finally
came to a stop six hundred feet from where we had dropped the
hook. To the east and the west were shoals, with our ship in the
tidal fairway in between.

"Thank you, Mr. Manning. That was well done. Secure
the ship, set the anchor watch, keep minimum steam up in
two boilers for quick maneuvering if needed, and have the
quartermasters log position bearings every ten minutes. This
area has a considerable current when it gets running and the
tide should turn soon, so I want particular attention to looking
out for any dragging. Pass the word for Lieutenant Commander
Warfield to see me in my cabin immediately."

After all that was acknowledged, and with the renewed
energy that impending action brings, I added one more order.
"And call away my gig, if you would please. I'm going ashore.
Commander Gardiner, Bosun Rork, and Dr. Cano will be going
with me. Tell Rork to bring along the necessary accoutrements—
he'll know what I mean. Please have those three gentlemen
notified we will be disembarking in fifteen minutes."

In my cabin, Warfield got his orders while I changed into a
fresh uniform and loaded a small bag with some items that might
be needed ashore. They were my personal counterparts to the
"accoutrements" Rork would be bringing.

"All right, John, here are your orders. Maintain the ship in a
state of readiness to be able to weigh anchor and get under way
immediately. Minimal people ashore. When the port officials
show up, let them know we'll be here only for the day, at the
most for overnight and departing on Saturday morning. We'll
need no port services from them other than a hundred tons of
coal, and we prefer to go alongside rather than lighter it out
in barges. Tell the officers the following: this is an official visit

for me, Gardiner is headed for Washington, Cano is headed for a meeting in Tampa, and Rork is going as my servant. Understood?"

"Aye, sir."

Warfield noticed me slipping my six-shot Merwin-Hulbert .44 revolver with the "skull-crusher" grip into a trouser pocket. His face clouded in concern.

"Expecting trouble, sir? Maybe I should send along a few more men."

"Don't worry, Rork and I'll handle any trouble which might come up. I learned long ago to be prepared, especially when dealing with Colonel Isidro Marrón's thugs."

39

The Goat Locker's Retribution

Port Tampa, Florida
Before dawn Friday
16 December 1892

The row to the wharf was short, but because of one passenger, quite unpleasant. Norton Gardiner, feeling in high form due to the proximity of his freedom from me, unloaded a constant stream of muttered criticism about the coxswain's handling of the gig, the appearance of Rork's uniform, Cano's drunken stupor in the wardroom, the general lack of discipline in the crew since his departure of executive officer and, finally, the filthy condition of the wharf when we came alongside the ladder descending its giant timbers. Cano, who by this time had had enough of Gardiner's abuse, began a retort until Rork silently shook his head. The Cuban lawyer took the hint and stopped in midsentence.

Though I was disgusted by his conduct, I decided not to

"brace up" Gardiner in front of enlisted men, but rather to do it once we were ashore and out of their sight and hearing. It is contrary to sound naval discipline to have them see an officer being reprimanded in public.

Senior petty officers, however, have their own ways to deal with such personalities. I knew something was up when Rork, displaying the very picture of subservience itself, quietly motioned to the bowman that he would handle the sailor's duties instead when we got close to the wharf. This alerted me, for Rork seldom interfered with a boat crew's work, and only when an unsafe situation was unfolding. This was not in that category.

The precedence is the senior officer gets in last and gets out first. Thus, I was the first out when we arrived at the wharf. As I ascended the ladder in the dim light, I caught only a brief glimpse of what happened when the next senior officer, Commander Gardiner, stood up in the boat to disembark.

Rork said to Gardiner, "Ooh, take care, sir. That gunwale's slippery."

He then surreptitiously pushed the gunwale down just as Gardiner, who had ignored the warning with an indignant harrumph, was stepping up to it. The commander's foot missed its intended placement and he stepped right overboard into the slimy black water. Cano laughed out loud.

But my bosun friend wasn't done, for at the same time Gardiner was falling overboard, with a decidedly un-naval shriek, Rork had taken possession of the commander's two personal bags and was handing them up to a bystander on the wharf above him. Alas, in all the commotion when Gardiner went over, the bystander apparently lost his grip, dropping the bags in the water. They landed right next to their owner and began to sink, rescued only by Rork employing a boat hook to spear right through them and drag them back, directly across the flailing form of *Bennington*'s former executive officer.

Commander Gardiner uttered an unprintable oath—one which I am quite sure he did *not* learn in the cultured salons of

Boston—while he grasped the nearest steady object. It turned out to be a wharf timber covered with sharp barnacles, for the boat had somehow drifted away from his reach. The ensuing cuts led to more impolite language, ending with an order to, "Get me out of here, you damned scoundrel!"

Rork looked up at me standing above him on the wharf. With a commendably straight face, he reported, "Sir, Commander Gardiner an' his baggage is gone overboard. Baggage's recovered, sir, but methinks the commander's in a bit o' trouble. Should the lads jump in an' save him?"

At this moment in the action, the bystander, a wrinkled old man reeking of rum, chimed in with a belch, "That officer down there's not much of a seaman, is he?" Someone in the boat crew chuckled and was shushed by the coxswain.

"No, Rork," I called down, "one man in the water is enough for the night. Just bring the boat over and pull Commander Gardiner out. Then help him get up the ladder."

"Aye, aye, sir," came the chorus from the boat as all hands relished the rare opportunity to lay a finger on an officer. Manhandled roughly back over the gunwale and draped over a thwart, Gardiner was then put over Rork's shoulder and carried up the ladder to the deck of the wharf like a sack of potatoes.

Gardiner and his bags collapsed in a soggy heap at my feet. His sea trunk, which had not gone for swim, was hauled up by rope and put next to him.

"Yes, siree," said the drunk bystander to no one in particular. "I've seen little girls do better than that at gettin' off a boat."

Cano, in contrast, climbed up quite easily while carrying his own valise and bag. He smiled down at Gardiner while walking past him.

"Commander Gardiner had been saved, sir!" Rork announced without a trace of sarcasm or satisfaction.

It was all done quite neatly, and completely unattributable. The Goat Locker had gained retribution for the crew against Gardiner. Early in his career, a young officer learns to never be on the wrong side of the Goat Locker—a lesson obviously lost on Gardiner.

"Well done, Rork."

I let that comment float for several seconds, then said, "Now, kindly go see about getting the four of us passage on the railway to Tampa."

Rork lost no time in heading off on his mission. Gardiner spent the time changing into a clean dry uniform from his trunk, after ordering the drunk to, "Go away and die somewhere else." Cano sat on a bollard and waited for what came next.

I succumbed to the temptation born of my daydreams and headed over to the two hotels at the wharf to see if Maria was at one of them. The first visited was the St. Elmo, the smaller of the two.

The drowsy night clerk, roused at half past three in the morning by a naval officer searching for a woman lodger, looked askance at my inquiry and immediately said no lady of that name or description was at either hotel, and he was familiar with the guest registry of both. His tone wasn't respectful of the lady or of me, but I judged it not worth contesting and subsequently returned to Gardiner near the boat ladder. And besides, it made sense Maria might be at the more elegant Tampa Bay Hotel anyway.

When I returned, Gardiner was once again presentable and feeling like an officer and gentleman, now he was decked out in perfectly tailored dress whites.

"Will you be getting a room at the hotels here on the wharf?" I pleasantly asked, hoping I could sow the idea in his mind. That way Rork and I would be rid of him early. "They have some rooms available."

He waved a dismissive hand. "No, of course not. Those places are for the common tourists. I require more appropriate accommodations, so I'll stay in my family's usual third-floor corner suite downtown at the Tampa Bay Hotel."

"Well, my goodness, you mean the big fancy hotel in

downtown Tampa? You've actually stayed there? I thought it
opened just last year."

Norton Gardiner, oblivious to my veiled acerbity, was
thrilled to show off for a lesser being than he, even though it was
only me.

"Yes, it did open last year, at the beginning of the season.
I've been there twice, in fact, including a special invitation to
the grand opening, which Mr. Plant orchestrated magnificently
in proper style—as one would expect from a gentleman of his
status. My parents and I were quite impressed with the quality
of the décor, the cuisine, and the servants." He looked at me
and wrinkled his nose. "But then someone like you can't even
understand what I'm talking about, can you?"

No, I couldn't. And I didn't want to.

40

The Train

Port Tampa, Florida
Dawn Friday
16 December 1892

"Scaring up" the transport—a term possibly more literal
than figurative—took Rork about thirty minutes. When
he returned to us, he jauntily announced, "Got us transport, sir.
Ain't posh, but it'll do. 'Tis an empty phosphate train that'll pull
out in an hour an' a half, at five. On their way to Bartow, they'll
stop in Tampa for us to get off."

"How fortunate to find transport at this time of the
morning," said Cano affably, clearly trying to impress his
future father-in-law with a positive attitude after his dismal
performance the previous night.

Rork shrugged and slapped him on the back. "Oh, 'tis
nothin' to crow about, laddee. Why, once we had to scare up a
whole ship! Remember that one, sir?"

"Yes I do, Rork. And a damned close-run thing it was."

"Phosphate train?" grumbled Gardiner, ignoring our banter.

"What is that? I'm hungry. Is there a club car? Where will we sit on this train?"

"Ooh nay, sir. 'Tis a workin' train with no passengers an' nary a seat. We'll be standin' in the locomotive cab with the crew. No worries, though. 'Tis only ten miles or so. The chap at the yard says about forty-five minutes to Tampa."

To preclude any more of Gardiner's bellyaching, I said, "The train will be fine, Rork. Thank you. Please get Commander Gardiner's trunk over to the train for him. After that's done, you and I will tour this wharf. It's a good opportunity to see how they're doing here. Might come in handy someday."

"Aye, sir." He bestowed an insincere smile on Gardiner and said, "'Tis an honor to help the commander."

With his one real hand he lifted the heavy trunk and slung it onto his shoulder, something few men could do. All the while he was looking at Gardiner. I noticed it wasn't an amiable look. Gardiner never noticed anything.

"I guess I'll go along with Commander Gardiner," said Cano, rather hesitantly.

"Good idea, Dr. Cano," I replied.

After shepherding them to the train, Rork left the two of them sitting dejectedly on their baggage next to a locomotive in the dark, then joined me at the end of the wharf. Our walk about the place showed that Mr. Plant had further improvements in mind for the wharves, for huge phosphate elevators and conveyor belts were being constructed to speed up the loading process. The smell of money was in the dusty air, along with the smell of rain in the southwest wind.

The train got under way exactly when the engineer, a crotchety old Italian-Cuban immigrant named Buttari, had predicted, at 5 a.m. It was crowded in the cab with six men—the four of us and two crewmen—and our baggage inside. Buttari wasn't talking, so we navy men and Cano stood there mutely swaying with the train over the uneven rails as it chugged through a swamp.

I estimated we'd arrive in Tampa just before dawn, which suited my plan fine. The other warship would be arriving at the anchorage in Hillsborough Bay about then, but it would take a while for them to sway out a boat and row the couple miles up to the city. The most important thing was that we'd won the race. Martí and Cuba's future would be safe, and the United States would be spared an international assassination inside her borders.

My plan had the incentive of a pleasurable victory phase. On my return to the ship after notifying Martí or his people of the Spanish plot, I would stop by Plant's fancy hotel and look for Maria. With any luck, she'd be there and we could have breakfast together, perhaps a romantic repast in her room.

Jerking and swaying, the train picked up velocity. I was congratulating myself for being almost done with my mission and soon in my lover's arms. After that beautiful but brief respite from my naval responsibilities, I'd take *Bennington* back to Key West and the squadron. Then I'd be at sea, living my life as I should be, and at last free of Gardiner, the damned Orden Público, coded messages, and the sordid world of espionage.

We'd run at least a mile toward Tampa when a thud sounded, the train lurched faster, and a curse suddenly roared from the after end, some fifteen cars back. This elicited a reciprocal curse in Italian from the engineer. He quickly spun a valve and pulled a lever, allowing a cloud of steam to envelope the locomotive. We slowed quickly to a stop. My companions' eyes looked to me, for there we were, in the dark, in the middle of swamp, nine miles from the city each of us wanted to reach.

"Problems . . ." Buttari said to Rork as he hopped down out of the cab and walked aft along the track bed, swearing all the way.

"Gonna be a long day today," drawled the mulatto boiler-fireman, as he leaned on his shovel.

He then explained what had happened. It turned out the engineer and boiler man had heard in that original curse what had escaped our ears—the coupling for the last two hopper cars had broken. This was the third time that week it had happened. It would need to be fixed and the cars reattached before getting under way again. Maybe an hour, he said with a shrug. Maybe more.

Rork and I exchanged glances. I knew what he was thinking. The date in the message was the sixteenth—today. I tried to remain optimistic. We still had time.

Gardiner huffed something unintelligible and got down out of the cab to pace on the rocky track bed. Cano got down and stretched his arms.

The wind had gotten stronger from the west southwest. Now the rain I'd smelled in the air began to fall. Lightly at first, then building steadily into a solid downpour.

Dawn arrived in an unsettling amber half-light. Our environs were bleak—a swamp as far as we could see. Buttari and the brakeman called for the mulatto to come aft and help. Rork offered to lend a hand, but the mulatto said no, he would just get in the way.

So the four of us remained on our feet and waited. At seven o'clock the crew returned to the cab and reported the repairs were complete. Backing up to the errant cars, they reattached them and headed off once again for Tampa.

The rain had stopped but the sky was filled with racing dark clouds sailing in rapidly from the southwest and west, and I knew it would be a nor'wester by the next day. Two nor'westers so close together? I had a worrying thought. *Bennington* was secure for the moment, but for how long? I was glad Warfield was in charge in my absence, for he knew what to do.

The transit to Tampa was made at reduced speed, due to the jury-rigged coupling. Buttari explained he would stop the train *near* the Tampa Bay Hotel only for two minutes to let Gardiner and his baggage off, but it couldn't be right *at* the hotel, for phosphate trains weren't allowed to go onto that spur—the guests didn't want a dirty cargo train disturbing their relaxation. Gardiner would have to walk a quarter-mile with his hand bags to the hotel and engage a porter go back and retrieve his trunk. He didn't take the news happily. Nobody, including the train crew, cared.

When he departed, there was no goodbye or words of any kind among us, just low grumbling on his part and disinterest on ours. Above the pine tree tops, I could see the minarets and towers of the hotel in the distance. It would be a long walk in the rain. Buttari opened the steam valve and we started moving again.

We crossed the railroad bridge over the Hillsborough River north of the hotel and entered the city of Tampa on Polk Street. Looking south, down the river and out into Hillsborough Bay, I saw the foreign cruiser anchored. Smoke was funneling out of her stack so she had probably just arrived and let go her hook. Even at four miles distance, I recognized her—*Reina Regente*.

The official reason for her port visit would be something benign like "a courtesy visit to our fellow countrymen of Spain, including our dear citizens from Cuba, in Tampa's Spanish Quarter of Ybor City." Few Cubans in Ybor would be fooled.

Buttari slowed the train for a moment in front of the main passenger depot at Polk and Ashley streets so we could disembark. It was evidently against regulations, for he only slowed and was picking up speed again even as Rork, Cano, and I stepped off.

The depot was mostly deserted at that hour, but the telegraph office in the main lobby was manned, so we went there first. I banged on the counter to wake a young fellow lounging in a rocker.

"Is the line to Key West open yet?" I asked.

He jumped awake and quickly looked me over. "Yes, sir. It finally opened this morning. They got the cable routed around the sinkhole easy enough, but had a devil of a time finding that break underwater south of Sanibel Island. Say, are you named Wake? I have a cable here for a navy man named Wake."

I assured him I was and opened the proffered envelope.

It was from Rear Admiral Walker, predictably terse, and unpredictably in clear language.

    XX—ONI CONFIRMS MSG INFO BUT CAN GIVE NO ORIGIN—X—SEND TAMPA SITREP—X—RETURN TO SQDN OPS AT KW WHEN DONE THERE—XX

I wrote a "SitRep"—Situation Report—reply in the clear on a cable form straight away, telling the clerk to send it priority traffic.

    XX—JUST ARVD—X—GERM-SPAN CRUZRS FOLWD US UP COAST—SPAN CRUZR HERE—X—GERM LOCAT NOW UNK—X—RETURNING TO KW WHEN DONE—XX

There was a new steam-powered street car service in the town, which might be faster, so I inquired, "When does the next street steam train leave for Ybor City?"

"Morning train left ten minutes ago, sir. Next one leaves at eleven a.m."

"How about the electric street cars?"

"Afraid you're out of luck, sir. Just got word the electric car line on Maryland Avenue is out this morning cause of the rain making hell with the wiring, or something like that. They say they're working on it, but it's what they always say."

"Any hackneys available?"

"No hackneys neither, not this early in the morning when there's no passenger train from up north. Maybe later on in the morning you can find one over at one of the hotels around here. Let's see . . . there's the Franklin. They're nearby, but no, come to think of it they won't have nothing like that there this time of the morning. And there's the Palmetto and the Orange Grove, but they're a long walk. No hire carriages there either, probably."

He snapped his fingers. "Now the big one across the river, Mr. Plant's Tampa Bay Hotel, that'll have a hire for you! It's the finest and fanciest hotel in all the Southland, sir. You could find one there, even this time of morning. They keep one ready twenty-four hours a day. Just a couple minutes' walk four streets down to Lafayette Street, turn right and cross the bridge, and you can't miss it."

Damn. I hadn't counted on that. It was raining hard again and I didn't relish a two mile walk out the muddy road through the scrub land to Ybor City—at least half an hour, probably longer. A hackney could get us there in ten minutes, make us independent of train schedules, and take us all the way back to Port Tampa afterward.

Cano, who was still unaware my mission was similar to his, piped up in a nervous staccato, "Today is the day of his evening speech and I need to get to Martí without delay by whatever means. Why are we waiting here?"

"All right, let's go, gentlemen," I said. "A walk in the rain to the fancy hotel it is."

"Aye, aye, sir," replied Rork, before he thickened his brogue and added, "Nary's the worry, lads. 'Tis just like a misty day back in the Sainted Emerald Isle. Ooh, an' here's a bright spot— maybe we'll be honored by seein' Commander Gardiner again! Aye, methinks His Highness'll already be livin' the grand life there, amongst all those quality swells. Like a big hog in deep slop, he'll be. Just his cuppa tea."

Cano hoisted his valise and declared, "*Vamonos, caballeros,*" and we all headed out into the rain.

41

The Tampa Bay Hotel

Tampa, Florida
Friday morning
16 December 1892

Rork, as he has done many times before in our misadventures around the world, proved annoyingly prophetic. When we three sodden and exhausted souls at last trudged up onto the four-hundred-foot-long verandah of the magnificent Tampa Bay Hotel, we were greeted by a sight that brought out the worst in me in both mood and word.

"That friggin' sonofabitch," I blurted out.

"Uh, oh. Not good," moaned the bosun, who belatedly registered what I'd seen. "Not good at all . . ."

Cano asked, "What is wrong?" He didn't get an answer.

The enormous verandah around us was crowded with high society matrons and patrons beautifully attired in their morning best, clearly reveling in their tropical Florida escape from the cold north, even on a gray morning. Sheltered from the rain, they were enjoying a sumptuous breakfast feast, the aromas of which were like a beckoning narcotic in my starved condition. Attentive waiters in immaculate tie and tail, potted palms and bougainvillea flowers, and exotic foreign tunes by a lively string quartet completed the atmosphere of total decadent leisure.

My eye wasn't on the crowd. It was on the far corner, a romantic alcove of areca palms around a table for four. Two couples sat there. One was a well-dressed couple with a stunning blond woman in yellow and a tall distinguished-looking gentleman in a gray suit and fedora. They were listening intently to the man of the other couple. He was resplendent in the dress white uniform of a naval officer and, by his animated face and gestures, apparently telling a funny story. It didn't surprise me Gardiner had already made his social mark after only an hour there. What did shock me was the beautiful dark-haired lady sitting next to him, laughing.

Maria.

"Ooh, now me boyo," counseled Rork in a low tone while laying his false left hand heavily on my shoulder. "Don't ya be goin' off an' doin' something bloody stupid. That bugger ain't worth it, so let's be smart about this."

"What is wrong?" Cano asked again. "We need to find a hackney to Ybor.

This time, Rork answered him. "Commander Gardiner's over there with Commander Wake's lady."

"Oh . . ." said Cano, without further comment.

I was astounded. Of all the hundreds of guests at the hotel, how the hell did she end up with Gardiner? I'd never told her about him, nor him about her. In fact, only Rork knew all the details about my relationship with Maria.

But damned if Norton Gardiner didn't have an unerring instinct to find and engage beautiful women in conversation. I'd seen him do it repeatedly at social events in the West Indies. He also had the ability to bore them within five minutes.

As I sloshed my way toward them through the maze of tables, my companions followed, forming a less than impressive parade.

In an irksome reversal of our usual dynamics in confrontational situations, Rork kept whispering for me to keep calm.

I finally stopped and said in a voice a bit louder than I'd intended, "Of course I'll be calm, Rork. I won't hurt the sonofabitch, I'll be calm as hell and just tell him to shove off."

That got the gasping attention of the guests and the management. The latter, in the form of an imperious-looking gent with a long indignant face, was headed on a collision course for me, with a waiter tagging along for his reinforcement. I was faster, however, and was going to make it to the table first.

The other couple at the table hadn't noticed me. Likewise Gardiner, who had his back to me. Maria had noticed, though, since she sat facing my direction. She looked like one of those new Gibson dream girls, her hair swept up in the French fashion, a blue taffeta dress with embroidered flowers perfectly complimenting those sapphire eyes. I could gaze into those eyes for hours. Her face widened into a beautiful smile and melted my heart right then and there. I decided not to hit Gardiner when I saw that smile.

"Good morning, Doña Maria. You are absolutely radiant on this damp morning," I said with a bow. Maria's smile turned into a sly, impish expression. I knew exactly what she was thinking, for I was thinking the same thing.

Before Maria could reply, I said to the other couple, "Please allow me to introduce myself. I'm Peter Wake, obviously of the Navy, and an acquaintance of Doña Maria. I apologize for my rather soggy appearance, but my friends and I just had to walk here from downtown. There are no cabs or hackneys in town, and we were told we might find one here. We need to get to Ybor City."

I introduced Rork as my assistant, and Cano as my acquaintance, with no further details. Maria said a warm hello to Rork, whom she met in Washington and had instantly liked. All women love Rork, for some reason. To Cano she offered a polite greeting, and he replied ornately in Spanish, telling her only that he was a lawyer from Havana.

Maria introduced the couple as Dr. William Welch, a surgeon in Tampa, and his wife Sherry, and said they had invited her to have breakfast at their table. They enjoyed breakfast at the hotel once a week.

Until this point, I and everyone else had ignored Gardiner, who just sat there wide-eyed and speechless, staring at me. Maria raised an eyebrow and glanced at Gardiner.

Then, in a neutral tone which confirmed her opinion of him, she said, "Gentlemen, this is Commander Norton Peabody Gardiner. He came in on his warship this morning and appeared lonely, so we asked him to join us. He has been entertaining us with anecdotes of his life upon the sea and what it's like to be in charge of a big ship. What was the name of your ship, Norton? I cannot remember. Maybe Peter will know it."

His warship? I looked at Gardiner. Rork put his boot on my shoe, cleared his throat, and murmured, "Steady on, sir."

"*Bennington*, right? Yes, that's it," said Dr. Welch. "And what ship are *you* on, Commander Wake?"

"Why, the very same ship," said I in faux surprise. Leaning down toward Gardiner, I exclaimed, "Hello there, Norton! My goodness gracious, spreading more lies about how important you are? Isn't that conduct unbecoming a United States naval officer and gentleman?"

"Ah . . . I was just telling them . . ."

The manager arrived in time to divert everyone's attention from Gardiner's rapidly reddening face and deflating form. Behind the manager, the waiter cast a nervous look at Rork and backed up a step.

"May I help you, sir?" the manager asked as he inspected me. "I'm afraid I don't know you. Are you one of our guests, sir?"

"Commander Peter Wake, captain of the U.S.S. *Bennington*. No, I'm not a guest, but I am a friend of Doña Maria, and am delighted to find her here at this fine hotel. I must be off though, and wonder if perhaps you can help. My friends and I need a hackney right away to get to Ybor City. Can you arrange that?"

Dr. Welch, who had heretofore been bemusedly watching the show, suddenly spoke up. "Commander Wake, I absolutely insist we take you there in our landau. It would be no imposition at all. We've enjoyed a wonderful breakfast with this gracious lady, our new friend from Spain, and were about to invite her to enjoy a drive with us around the city. It is a convertible and our driver has the folding top up already set up for the rain."

He glared disgustedly at Gardiner for a second. "I'm sure Mr. Gardiner is very busy and can't come. What a pity."

"We very much appreciate your offer, Doctor," I replied quickly. "We gratefully accept."

Gardiner was left in the conversational dust as Welch added, "Excellent! I am a naval enthusiast and it would be an excellent opportunity to hear all about *your* ship. Maria, please say you will come along."

"It sounds delightful," she said softly, looking into my eyes.

And thus I was rid of Norton Gardiner, for the third time in as many days. I fervently hoped it would be the final time.

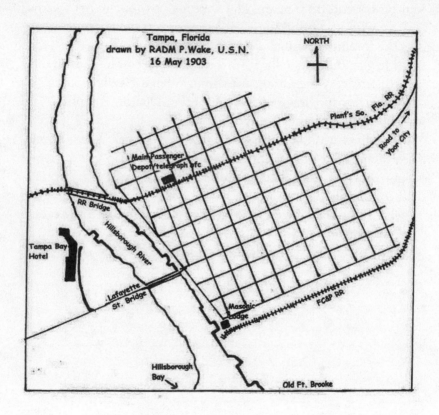

Tampa, Florida
drawn by RADM P.Wake, U.S.N.
16 May 1903

NORTH

Plant's So. Fla. RR.

Road to Ybor City

Main Passenger
Depot/telegraph ofc

RR Bridge

Hillsborough River

Tampa Bay Hotel

Lafayette St. Bridge

Masonic Lodge

FC&P RR

Hillsborough Bay

Old Ft. Brooke

42

Wonderful Potholes

Tampa, Florida
Friday morning
16 December 1892

Dr. Welch's driver shared his outside bench with Rork. It had a canvas awning affair, which gave partial shelter from the rain, so I didn't feel too guilty for leaving my friend outside. Inside the snug interior compartment, the good doctor's wife sat between Cano and her husband in the back seat, the arrangement allowing Maria and I to have the forward seat.

I am sure our furtive mutual glances and closeness did not go unnoticed, but the others made no comment and instead spoke of the hotel, the weather, and the local politics. I learned the newly elected governor of Florida—a Mr. Mitchell, who was from Tampa and a friend of Dr. Welch—was due to be inaugurated in two weeks up at the state capital. Dr. Welch would be in attendance. Clearly, William Welch was a man of repute and influence and I made a mental note to maintain our acquaintance. One never knows when friends such as he could come in handy.

Dr. Welch was also well versed on the history of the community, in which he had lived for many years. He provided a running commentary on the sights as we crossed the iron-trussed Lafayette Street swing bridge, recently built by the city of Tampa to serve Mr. Plant's hotel guests. The rain had diminished to a sprinkle and as we clattered across the bridge, I looked to the south, down the river and out over Hillsborough Bay.

Reina Regente was still at anchor, the funnel smoke a mere wisp now as her boilers cooled and machinery slowed down. A steam launch was departing her, heading for the mouth of the river. I didn't think she had one, so they must have hired a harbor launch. The Spanish were certainly wasting no time in getting someone ashore.

We continued east on Lafayette Street through the city's center at Franklin Street, which featured an opera house, the county courthouse, and the city hall, with Welch giving the history of each. By the time we'd veered left to go four blocks north and turned eastbound on Polk, the doctor ran out of interesting anecdotes.

Cano took up the slack and began conversing about his life in Havana and his law studies in Madrid, with Maria asking supportive questions. He told the story in a very self-deprecating style and soon had everyone charmed by his wit and candor, including, I must admit, me. He had already shown his determination and innovation the night prior, now I was seeing his humility. Perhaps, I began to think, he would be a good husband for my daughter after all. If only I could be sure of his distance from the world of revolutionary intrigue, for it worried me. She had already lost a love to that.

The rest of them plunged into discussions of Havana culture, a long-winded subject, allowing Maria and me a moment to talk in semi-privacy. Conspiratorially, she whispered, "Peter, I am so thrilled we are together—my dreams actually came true. The train to Tampa was slowed by a storm, which got me here later than I anticipated, so it must be kismet."

She leaned closer and it was all I could do not to kiss her right there. Breathing in her delicious scent, I closed my eyes, wanting it to fill my lungs and stay there forever. She chuckled at my expression and asked, "But really, darling, why are you in Tampa? I hoped to see you on my way to Cuba, but thought it might be at Key West."

Holding her hand, I whispered back, "Your last letter, dear. You mentioned something in it which was the answer to an issue I'd been working on. That is what's led me to Tampa, to warn José Martí."

"Martí, the writer? Then *he* is the man they spoke about in the embassy? I thought it might be Gomez or Maceo. Is the threat imminent?"

I shrugged rather than answer.

"What madness, to hurt a peaceful man like that," she said. "I love his prose. Do you know him personally?"

"Yes, José is my friend. He is more than a writer these days. He's been elevated into a leadership role now, and has brought the various factions together into a united front for the independence of Cuba."

"Peter, when I arrived yesterday, I read in the local paper that Martí is arriving from Ocala this evening and speaking at a big gathering in Ybor. Will he stay at the Tampa Bay Hotel? I would be honored to meet him."

"No, he usually stays with friends in Ybor City."

"Will you be here for the event? We could go together."

"No, dear. I'm only here long enough to warn him. I have to get under way to get my ship back to Key West."

All polite social etiquette had evaporated by then and, blissfully ignoring our fellow passengers, we held each other's hand tightly. Her words came out sensually, igniting my passion even further. "That still gives us some time . . ."

Using all my willpower, I forced myself to say, "No, I can't, dear. I need to get back to my ship today. There's a storm brewing to the northwest."

Her eyes were filling with tears. "This afternoon then, after you deliver your message. Just a little time. I have to be with you, Peter. I dream of nothing else."

That was what ended my meager resistance. "Hmm . . . well, yes, I think I could stop by later for a little while."

"Excuse me, Commander Wake. Commander Wake?"

It was Welch, trying to get my attention. I looked at our companions in the back seat. All three regarded Maria and me with perceptive smiles. Embarrassment must have blushed my cheeks, for they laughed, including Maria.

Welch repeated himself. "Captain, we're now on Maryland Avenue and leaving Tampa on the way to Ybor City. Where exactly do you want to go in Ybor City?"

"Don Vicente Martinez Ybor's office. Do you know it?"

"Yes, of course. Everyone does. I've known Don Vicente since he arrived six years ago. A good man who has done wonders out there with his town."

The doctor leaned out the window, calling up to his driver to take us to the corner of Ninth and Fourteenth streets. The landau hit a pothole and jolted, eliciting a curse from Rork topside and bouncing the passengers below into each other. Maria ended up partially on my lap, a very agreeable location in my opinion. She favored me with a caress as she disentangled herself in the name of propriety, making me yearn for more of those potholes.

I took stock of the situation. We were on the final two miles of my five-hundred-mile journey. In spite of mistakes and obstacles, we'd arrived in time to save my friend Martí, help the Cuban cause for freedom, and prevent a war for our country. I was reunited with my love and beginning to bond with my daughter's love.

We hit another pothole, with the same wonderful result. And all was well with the world.

43

The Enemy Around Us

Ybor City, near Tampa, Florida
Friday morning
16 December 1892

Because of the heavy rain earlier, and the road becoming more of an extension of the swamp beside it, another twenty minutes passed, along with several more of those wonderful potholes, before we arrived at the headquarters of the V. Martinez Ybor Cigar Company, a substantial three-story, block-long brick building.

Ybor City was the brainchild of tobacco baron Vicente Martinez Ybor in 1886. The completely planned community featured homes, schools, clinics, parks, swimming pools, churches, and social clubs, all provided at low cost to tobacco workers. Ybor was the grand patron of the operation, even though other employers soon started up, and wielded enormous influence.

I hoped Ybor was at his office, for I knew he could help me. He had years before, when Marrón's killers came after me in this very town. It was Ybor who, with quick thinking, laid an effective false trail using false information, decoying them off to the other side of the state. He knew quite a bit about that sort of thing from his own history.

In 1869, the twenty-one-year-old fled the Spanish authorities in Cuba in the middle of the night as they were coming to arrest him. His crime? He had given money to dear friends who were fighting for Cuba's independence. After making it to Key West, he opened and ran a cigar factory there, before moving the entire operation to an uninhabited pine woods outside Tampa in '86.

The rain had slowed to a sprinkle when we finally arrived at Ybor's building. My senses were overwhelmed the instant I stepped out of the landau, bringing pleasant memories of good times I've enjoyed in Havana. A fast-talking street vendor was selling chances at the *bolita* gambling game, with an old man insisting on number three, the traditional number of sailors. Aromas of rice and beans and tobacco leaf wafted through the rain-laden air. From inside the factory came the sounds of *lectores* reading newspapers and magazines aloud to the cigar workers, and the little thuds of cleavers on their tables cutting the wrapper leaf. From the café across Fourteenth Street, I heard the staccato smack of dominoes being slammed down on a table, to the glee of the players.

The Welches were heading to their home at Spanish Creek, after dropping off Cano two blocks away at the Las Nuevitas Hotel, and Maria back at the Tampa Bay Hotel. Dr. Welch gave me his two-digit telephone number, saying, "Please call me if I can assist you while you're visiting Tampa, Commander. I'd be glad to have the opportunity to serve our navy!"

"Thank you, Doctor, but I won't be here long."

Shaking hands with Cano, I told him, "I'm looking forward to seeing you again soon. We'll sit down and have a private talk about Useppa's future. What're your plans here?"

This was as far as I could go right then—my permission and blessing for a marriage would have to come later, after that talk.

To his credit, Cano didn't argue or continue to plead his case for marrying my daughter, but instead told me he was going to see some people he knew to pass his warning on to Martí. I wished him well on that and meant it. It would be a secondary insurance for success for my mission. Of course, I never told him my mission or plans.

With a wink and a kiss, I suggested to Maria we meet at one o'clock at the Tampa Bay Hotel's boathouse on the Hillsborough River, assuring her my duties would be completed by then and we could spend an hour together. Then I kissed her again and they were gone.

Inside Ybor's factory, a clock struck 10 a.m. as Rork and I climbed the iron steps at the front. The light patter of rain had ended and the clouds thinned enough for the sun to come out. The wind had veered more northwesterly and the worst of the squalls were done.

Rork was in a good mood. "Well sir, methinks we've finally made it, an' nary too soon. Can't wait 'til this whole mess'll be nothin' more than a laugh over a pint o' suds. Ooh, an' speakin' o' pints, me gullet would fancy one with a bite o' lunch today, afore we head back to *Benny* an' Uncle Sam's Navy hardtack an' salt horse."

I was feeling pretty good right about then too. "Capital idea, Rork! We'll do that right after speaking with Don Vicente. Hey, since we're in Ybor, I bet we can find some Cerveza Tropical de Cuba and decent *arroz con pollo*."

Even as I made the cheery comment, instinct reminded my brain all was *not* well. I suddenly realized the old man buying the number three chance at *bolita* had been watching us intently for the last several minutes, with cautious glances toward an alley off Fourteenth, next to the café. What really alerted me originally was that the old man had just nodded to someone in the alley. Now I saw who he was nodding to—a man looking at us through a pocket telescope.

Turning around so the telescope couldn't focus on my lips, I said quietly, "Rork, do not look around right now, but we are being watched. By professionals. Two men at least. The old fellow buying *bolita* is one. The other is a younger, bigger man in the alleyway, just north of the coffee house. Number two man is using a telescope. Follow along with my ploy so we can get close enough to the man in the alley to intercept him and find out what's what. Ready?"

He nodded. I slapped him on the shoulder and, raising my voice to be heard, declared, "Great idea, Rork! Old Garcia can wait. I think a touch of rum would go down my throat just fine this morning. Hell, it's almost noon." Another slap to my friend. "Yessir, nothing like the hair of the dog that bit you! Maybe they have some rum at the café over yonder. Let's go see."

We wandered across the street, the telescope man shifting his position to behind some lumber piled in the alley. He was fairly large, light skinned and clean shaven, and dressed like a typical Cuban merchant in faded blue cotton suit with a floppy straw hat. The *bolita* man was far spryer than my first appraisal indicated, and he made his way across the street to our rear, by the cigar company's iron steps. Meanwhile, Rork and I kept up a good-natured banter about our thirst all the way over to the alley's entrance.

"See him?" I inserted into our banter.

Rork nodded yes.

"Let's get him now!"

We ran the eighty feet to the lumber pile. At fifty-three I couldn't run as fast as I used to, and at sixty-one Rork couldn't run as fast as me. Our target was obviously much younger and more agile, for he was out of there like a buck in full flight, leaping over some barrels and dashing around the back corner of the café. I continued after him south bound through a narrower alley. Rork altered course to starboard and ran south down Fourteenth Street, parallel to the alley, in case our prey should cut to the west.

Whilst running toward the lumber pile I glanced back, but the old man was gone. By the time I emerged from the alley onto

Eighth Avenue, our buck was nowhere in sight. Rork crossed
Eighth and pointed to the front of a saloon on that corner, then
to me. Next he pointed to the back of the salon and to himself. It
seemed logical to me.

I walked through the front door of the saloon and into a
darkened barroom. It was still early in the day for drinking
and only a few men were sitting there, chatting in Spanish.
That stopped instantly and everyone stared at me, a lone Anglo
intruder in a blue uniform. None of the patrons wore our man's
clothing, so I presumed he'd gone out the back and headed
cautiously in that direction. The lone bartender glowered at me,
one hand kept under the bar.

I heard a chair scratch across the floor behind me and turned.
At a table with four men, one of them stood and asked, "Who
you are? What you want here?"

He was a roughest of the rough-looking crew, so I judged it
time to get official.

"Commander Wake, U.S. Navy, looking for the man who
just ran in here. He has information on a sailor who deserted and
I want to talk to him. Who are you?"

"Don Manuel Saurez," he said, in a way which was meant
to impress me. It did, for I knew the name and the reputation.
Saurez was the *bolita* king of Ybor City, and kept tight control
over the illegal gambling operation. His nickname was derived
from his homeland of Galicia In northwest Spain, a place many
Cubans came from originally.

"The famous El Gallego?" I said, pulling out a dollar. I
walked over and slapped it down on the table. "In that case,
please put me down for a dollar on ball number three, for my
missing sailor."

It got the response I wanted: a roar of laughter from
everyone in the place and a complete change of atmosphere.
Saurez snatched the dollar and said, "In honor of the sailor who
deserted, I accept your wager. I hope you win when the balls are
chosen tonight."

He cast a look at the bartender. That nasty character withdrew his hand from under the bar and gestured toward a back room door, then began polishing bar glasses. Saurez sat down, the noisy talk started up again, everyone studiously ignoring what was about to happen while at the same time keeping the corner of one eye on the back room door.

I opened the door, revolver in my right hand. The instant the door opened, out he came, right into my torso with a punch which stunned me. I never got off a shot. He ran around a corner and down a hallway. No one helped me as I, more than slightly embarrassed, went down the hallway after him, right hand holding the revolver and left holding my aching abdomen.

I am pleased to report poetic justice made an appearance three seconds later, for the exact same thing happened to my assailant. Just as he was about to open the rear exit of the saloon and make his getaway, the door flung open and Rork swung his right arm around at stomach height.

Rork may be sixty-one, but he still knows a thing or two about throwing a punch. It doubled our adversary over and knocked him on his back, his head hitting the plank floor with a loud thump. Rork had also removed his false left hand, exposing the wicked marlinspike beneath. His face frightfully masked in maniacal rage, he then straddled the man and placed the spike between his panicked eyes.

Rork got close and whispered in his ear, "Do . . . not . . . move. *¿Comprende?*"

A terrified affirmative sound emerged.

"He's all yours, sir," Rork informed me.

"Thank you, Rork. Good timing." I knelt down next to the man. "Orden Público?"

A vigorous shake of his head was his reply. The wide-open eyes shifted my way, then looked away to the main bar for help against these two crazed gringos, but everyone there was having a wonderful time playing dominoes, ostensibly ignoring us.

"I'll search him, Rork."

The telescope was a German Ziess model, the short kind used by militaries in Europe, including the Spanish army. I found no weapons, no identity document, nothing that would show his nationality or profession. I searched him again, head to toe, and found something inside the top of his left sock. When I pulled it out, the man whimpered.

My discovery was a simple brass button. The back showed it was made by the Durant Company of New York. The front had an oval shield divided into quadrants. The upper right and lower left had a fighting lion, the upper left and lower right had a castle. Topped by a crown, the shield was the ancient crest of the kingdoms of Leon and Castile—of Spain. But the most important part of the button for me were the two large letters embossed on it, one on each side of the crest. An *O* and a *P*.

Orden Público.

"You are with *El Cuerpo Militar de Orden Público. ¿Y cómo está mi buen amigo, Coronel Isidro Marrón?*" That made him squirm and moan.

Not many Americans knew of this infamous Spanish battalion that terrorized the Cuban people in the area of Havana. The button was from their uniform.

Fewer still knew of the battalion's clandestine unit run by Colonel Isidro Marrón. It specialized in penetrating Cuban insurgent groups and in conducting assassinations. The button was a way their agents confirmed the identity of other members of the unit.

Rork growled, "I *hate* the Orden Público and what it does to the Cuban people."

Thus encouraged, our man finally spoke. "Please, I leave Florida, go Cuba."

I replied with a sick chuckle. He glanced desperately at the domino players.

"No one will help you. These Galicians've always hated Madrid, so they won't care. In fact, they would enjoy watching you die, once I tell them who you work for."

Tears began to form. "What . . . you . . . want?"

"The truth. *La verdad.* If you tell the truth to me, I will let you live and take a message to Marrón. But if you lie, I will know it and walk away. Then the men in this place will kill you slowly, for their enjoyment. Do you understand me?"

"Yes."

"Your name, age, work location, and place of birth?"

"Francisco Sanchez, two-seven years, work Key West, from Matanzas."

No wonder he outran me. "What is your mission here?"

"I see where you go."

"Correct answer. The old man is too old to be in Orden Público. He is an informant here in Ybor? His name?"

"Yes, he live here. Name Torito."

Little bull, a common nickname. "How did you know I was here in Ybor?"

"*Jefe* tell me this morning."

"Your *jefe*—what is his name, rank, and work location?"

He was hesitant, until Rork leaned even closer and grunted a Gaelic curse.

"*Teniente* Roldan, work Key West, but he here now."

I'd heard of Lieutenant Narciso Roldan. He'd been operating in Key West for several years, the replacement for Lieutenant Julio Boreau, whom I killed in New York in '86, and whose son tried to kill me in Havana in '88. A tangled web of façades and death.

"Correct answer. And what is Roldan's mission here in Ybor?"

"He no tell me."

"How did Roldan know I am here?"

"He no tell me."

"When and where will you kill Martí?"

"*Jefe* no tell me about kill Martí."

Sanchez wasn't showing signs of deceit. I believed him. He was only a minor cog in the machine, not privy to operational plans or personnel outside of his own small area.

"Tell Marrón this: I know everything. So does Washington. Understand?"

Sanchez nodded, obviously still unsure if he was about to die.

"Let him go, Rork."

Rork pulled him up and pointed to the back door. Sanchez didn't wait around and darted out the door. We went out the front. On our way, I dropped another dollar on Saurez's table. "*Un poco más, señor. Muchas gracias por los buenos tiempos.*"

44

A Time for Blessings

Ybor City, Florida
Friday morning
16 December 1892

Rork and I steered for the cigar factory again, this time in an uneasy state of mind. Would they come after us now? We watched everything and everyone on the streets.

At the offices, we met Ybor's private secretary. He informed us Don Vicente was out of town, but expected back later that evening. We also discovered Martí was arriving on the seven o'clock train from the new Cuban tobacco town of Martí City, near Ocala.

His Ybor City gathering would be right there, on the front steps of the factory, where he would give a speech at 8 p.m. The subject matter would be supporting the independence movement of Cuba with their time, effort, and donations; and explaining what the Cuban Revolutionary Party was planning to do to make the island free.

Ybor's secretary wasn't sure of Martí's itinerary after his

speaking engagement, but thought he'd be in town until Monday morning at least. Then he would either take the train back north to New York City or the steamer south to Key West.

Unfortunately, other than Ybor himself, I knew no one else in the company to whom I could entrust such important and secret information. The secretary, a cold and calculating type, did not inspire my confidence. I found that odd, for his boss, Don Vicente, was known to be openly pro-revolutionary and a friend of Martí. Still, my instinct said no, so we thanked the secretary and left, never giving the true reason for our intrusion.

One of the first rules in espionage is to always plan for those things you can't anticipate. In other words, have redundancy built in for when the first option doesn't work due to unforeseen circumstances, like Mr. Ybor not being available. In my experience, the first preference seldom works smoothly. Accordingly, I had two other options ready.

One was to contact the Pedrosos, Paulina and Ruperto, black Cuban tobacco workers who lived at Thirteenth Street and Eighth Avenue. Martí considered them dear friends—Paulina was like a mother to him—and he usually stayed at their home when in the Tampa area. Several times over dinner and wine in New York, I'd heard Martí speak of them in affectionate terms, but had never met them myself. I knew I could trust them, but would they trust me?

It was little more than a block away, so Rork and I started walking. In low tones, we discussed how the assassination would be carried out.

"Rork, I think they'll poison him tonight."

"Why not just shoot him?"

"Well, there's another factor here—anonymity. The assassin arrived in Ybor City within the last hours or days. Agreed?"

"Aye, sir. Either with Roldan a few days ago, or with *Reina Regente* today."

"Exactly. We know Martí won't arrive on the train from Ocala tonight until seven p.m., just before the speech at eight.

Like most Cubans, he doesn't eat dinner early. He'll eat after the speech, and after he deals with the post-speech crowd of admirers. That means it will be late, around eleven or midnight. He'll be very tired and go to bed right after eating. Tomorrow morning, he'll be found dead in his bed. That works out very well for the Spanish."

"Killed anonymously. Like Drake was. So it can't be tied to *Reina Regente* an' the Spanish government. No international complications."

"Exactly. Martí is known to have frail health, and there will be no reports of a commotion, no wounds, no sign of struggle, no suicide note. Death by natural causes will be assumed. Cuban rebel unification ends and they return to their internecine conflicts to determine the new leader of the movement. The Spanish aren't even blamed for Martí's death and celebrate the sixteenth of December as the day their most effective foe to the colonial occupation of Cuba ceased to be a problem. Marrón gets a quiet accolade from Madrid and becomes the most powerful man in Cuba, unseen by the masses, but feared by those in authority, even the royal governor."

"Sounds logical. Methinks the bastards'll put the arsenic in his rice an' beans at that late dinner," said Rork. "Martí an' his lads'll eat at one o' these restaurants 'round here. The assassin'll be one o' the kitchen help an' slip it in his food nice an' easy."

"I agree. But if the assassin is newly arrived on the Spanish cruiser, he'll have to get a job there right away. That's too unpredictable, though, so it would have to somehow be pre-arranged."

"Aye, good point. So the restaurant owner would be in the employ o' Roldan, an' have the kitchen job waitin' for when the killer gets there tonight."

"Which restaurant, though? Perhaps Señora Pedroso will know."

The Pedroso home at 1805 Thirteenth Street was like many others recently constructed in Ybor's town. A simple frame affair, the second story was little more than an attic with a window. It was normally the couple's bedroom. When Martí visited, it was his room.

No one answered my knock on the door. The neighbor ladies, rocking on their porches while sewing or shucking, studied our every move. The woman across the street feigned not to understand my English, or even my Spanish, when I asked when the Pedrosos would be home.

"Well, that didn't work," I grumbled to Rork as we stood in front of the house.

"Can't blame the neighbors for not talkin'—we're strangers in uniform an' they don't trust us. 'Tis just like back in Wexford, it is. When those damned Limey overseers came sniffin' 'round the croppers' places, lookin' for taxes an' such, nobody'd tell the buggers so much as a how d'ye do."

Once Rork got started on the Irish situation he couldn't stop, so I steered him back to our mission. "Maybe Cano can make some headway here. Nuevitas Hotel is over on Seventh, so let's ask him to help."

"Ooh, so now you're trustin' the lad, are ya?"

"Yes, I suppose I am," I admitted. "He's passed muster—so far."

Las Nuevitas Hotel was a moderately priced frame place, completely unlike Plant's exotic palace on the other side of the river. Of course, rich tourists didn't visit Ybor City, so opulence wasn't needed. Across the street from Nuevitas was Ybor City's theater, an equally moderate cultural center for the Cuban community. I noted the alley behind the theater separated it from the Pedroso house. I also saw that the marquee showed a performance scheduled for the evening, and predicted to Rork they'd have a sparse attendance. Everyone in town would be over at the cigar factory listening to Martí.

Cano was sipping coffee in the lobby. We joined him and I inquired if he had been successful in alerting Martí's colleagues to the threat on their leader's life. He said he had been to the local office of the Cuban Revolutionary Party, but the leaders were gone. He set up a meeting with them before Martí returned to Ybor City, which he'd also heard wasn't until seven that evening.

Not explaining what Rork and I had been through with Roldan's men, I told Cano I needed two favors. The first was that everything I was about to tell him would be completely confidential, for lives depended on it. The second was the message I had alluded to when meeting him in Key West was also about an assassination of Martí, and I needed Cano to pass it to the Pedrosos. I then told him the murder would likely be by arsenic poisoning in his food, probably tonight at dinner after the big speech. I added my conjecture that Martí would then be discovered dead in his bed tomorrow morning, with no signs of traumatic wounds pointing to the Spanish.

He was visibly stunned. "So that's how they will do the murder? I thought they would try to shoot him at the train station or at the speech, but this . . . this unspeakable deed . . . is even more evil-minded than I had imagined."

"Remember, please impress upon your friends neither of our warnings can be made public, Dr. Cano. The press would seize on this to sell papers by printing the most sensational rumors as facts, creating a storm of indignation that will lead in unforeseen directions, most of which culminate in a lot of innocent people dying. This information needs to be kept under control, for both Cuban and American purposes."

"Yes, I can understand that. It will ultimately be up to Martí, though."

"I know," I reluctantly agreed. Martí was unpredictable.

Cano then gave us some welcome news. "I was introduced to Paulina and Ruperto Pedroso by Martí himself two years ago, and will remind them of it when I see them, Commander. It will establish my creditability. I am sure they will listen and understand the gravity of this development. Paulina will insist on cooking the dinner personally, which will neutralize the Spanish plot."

"Excellent. That is the best thing that could happen."

Cano rose from his chair with a determined set to his expression. "But we do not have much time, do we, Commander? Those closest to Martí must know this intelligence as soon as possible. I will speak to the neighbors to learn where the Pedrosos work, then go and give them the message. I think they may work at Barreto's factory, it is on Eighth Avenue by Fire Station Number Two, just around the corner from their house."

"Thank you, Dr. Cano. While you are doing that, Rork and I will be over in Tampa notifying another group to get the word to Martí through a separate stealthy method. I want redundancy to ensure success."

I could tell he wanted to ask who the group was, but he held back. "Good luck, sir. Our multiple efforts should be effective."

"Yes, well, the alternative is catastrophic. Look, we won't be able to come back here afterward, since we have to return to the ship," I put out my hand, "so this is goodbye, once again."

Something else was on my mind, or actually, my heart. "Dr. Cano, I think after all we've been through together, and since you're about to be my daughter's husband, we can dispense with ranks and formality. How about if you call me Peter?"

"Thank you, sir, I mean Peter. I am honored and certainly will. And please, my name is Mario. And now, I too must be going. I have a lot to do."

He turned to go, but I stopped him, for I hadn't said all I needed to say.

"There's one more very important thing, Mario, which I need to say. When Useppa's mother and I got married at Key West in 1864, we didn't have her family's support at all. They were committed Confederates and I was a Yankee occupier—and in the view of my navy and of her family, we were both consorting with the enemy. It was so bad I had to move Linda away from Key West to Useppa Island, where our lovely daughter was born."

Those memories nearly overwhelmed me at that point, and my eyes filled with tears. But I had an important thing to say to this man, and was determined to say it.

"It is quite apparent you and Useppa love each other, and the fact she has found you to be a good and decent man is all I need to know. So, in addition to my permission, you have my sincere blessings for a long and loving marriage with Useppa."

Cano shook my hand again. "Thank you, Peter. That means so much to us."

Rork gently put his hand, the real one, on my shoulder. "Well, done, me friend."

45

The Brotherhood

Tampa, Florida
Friday morning
16 December 1892

T ime was still of the essence, for I wanted more than the hope Cano could reach the Pedrosos to ensure Martí's safety. So Rork and I marched down Sixth Avenue to the Ybor City railroad depot and caught the eleven thirty steam street train to Tampa. Our destination was one I knew only vaguely, and the people there I knew not at all. But I was certain if I could impress them with my validity, they would help me in the most effective, and quiet, way possible.

Allow me to present some necessary background. In 1869, at the tender age of sixteen, José Martí was arrested in Havana for daring to question Spain's methods in the occupation of Cuba. Sentenced to hard labor in a remote rock quarry prison, his health quickly deteriorated to the point of near death. After a couple years in the pits, his sentence was changed to exile to Spain. Because of his time in the Spanish rock pits, he would endure respiratory infections for the rest of his life.

In Madrid, he studied at the university to be a lawyer and tried to begin life again. But the rebel in him was never far below the surface, and he joined an underground fraternity forbidden in Spain by order of the Church and the government, which are intertwined in that country. Moreover, through a special exemption due to his maturity and intellect, he became one of the youngest applicants to ever become a brother in the fraternity.

The fraternity is Freemasonry, and Martí quickly rose to the level of Master Mason. Respected among his Masonic peers, he developed close relationships with them during his travels around the world. Among those who were fighting for Cuba's liberty, many of whom are Freemasons, Martí was highly esteemed.

This association became important to me while on a covert mission inside Cuba against the Spanish in 1888. I was to find and rescue several Cubans imprisoned by Marrón's section of the Orden Público—a nearly impossible task. Martí, a genius in secret communications, used his skills and connections in Cuba to arrange assistance there for me. It was perilous, but ultimately productive. I emerged from the mission with a profound respect for Masonic integrity and strength.

I am not a Mason, but am proud to have been designated by Martí as a "friend of Masonry." My intention was to use that status to request that the Masons employ their considerable abilities to warn their brother José of his impending doom.

Of course, in the United States we don't forbid Freemasonry. Many of our Founding Fathers, including Washington, were Masons. We value the separation of the Church and the State. Therefore, unlike in Spain and in Cuba, Masonic lodges are not underground and not subject to official or cultural ostracism. The one in Tampa is known as the Hillsborough Lodge, formed in 1850, and it was there we now headed.

Staying on the train past its stop at Henry Plant's sophisticated Polk Street depot, we arrived at the much less refined Florida, Central and Peninsula depot on Whiting Street at the lower end of Tampa, the industrial area near the mouth of the Hillsborough River.

The faded remains of Fort Brooke, abandoned by the army seven years earlier, spread out under the oak trees just to the south, along the shoreline of Hillsborough Bay. Far out in the bay, well beyond Depot Key *Reina Regente* was still at anchor, waiting for what, I did not know. For the assassin to return from his deed for a quick escape out to sea, perhaps?

My uncertain memory served me correctly and we found the Masonic lodge a mere two hundred feet to the west of the depot. The nondescript two-story frame affair was built forty years earlier, and it showed its age. The front room of the first floor was still a school classroom, and had served as the office of a two-page newspaper many years earlier.

I knew the editor of that paper during the war. Henry Crane was a pro-Union Floridian who moved to Useppa Island as leader of the loyalist refugee community there. He helped the U.S. Navy considerably with his knowledge of the coastal shoals and channels, and later commanded the Union militia unit formed at the island.

The Masonic lodge occupied the second floor. We climbed the outside stairs at the back of the building and knocked on the door.

After a long wait, a small, thin, older man opened the door. He looked up at us, his visage neither welcoming nor rejecting, but simply evaluating. It reminded me of the scrutiny I had often felt when on missions in the Orient.

"You need help?" he said, in a way that could be either a question or a statement.

For some reason, his enigmatic demeanor took me aback for a moment and I stammered an inane preamble to my message. "Well, first off, I am not a Freemason."

"Of that, I am already aware," he stated flatly.

My wits recovered and my temper rising, I explained to

him, "Yes, well, I'm Commander Peter Wake, captain of the U.S.S. *Bennington.* I arrived today in Port Tampa to deliver a confidential message of mortal urgency to one of your brethren, José Martí, who will be visiting the city tonight. He designated me a special friend of Freemasonry years ago. I know you have ways to get things done quickly, quietly, and effectively, so I came here. Should I talk to someone in charge or can you convey the message?"

"Everyone else is gone right now. You can give it to me."

He saw my reaction. With a tinge of humor lightening his expression for the first time, he said, "Don't worry, Commander. We know how to keep a secret."

I had written down the message on the way to the Masonic Lodge. It was in plain language, for I wanted the Masons to understand the import and trusted them not to abuse the confidentiality.

To José Martí, from Peter Wake
Noon, Friday, 16 December 1892
Dear José,
I have good information Marrón's men, under Roldan, will try to poison you with arsenic tonight. Roldan is in Ybor now and knows I am here to warn you. Be careful of everyone and everything. I will be in my ship at Port Tampa until late this afternoon, when I have to get under way for Key West.
Peter

I gave it to the man. He studied it carefully, showing no reaction.

"Brother Martí is in Ocala at this moment and will be given this within the hour. If he has a reply, where should I send it?"

Within the hour? I found that interesting. Ocala was a hundred miles away. He wasn't at a hotel, for he seldom stayed at one, preferring private homes. Assuming they could claim priority traffic over everything else and telegraph him, they would have to know to which house to deliver the cablegram. Did Martí keep in constant contact with Masons where ever he went?

"I'll be at the Tampa Bay Hotel until three p.m. Then I'll head over to my ship at Port Tampa. We'll get under way at five."

"Very well," he said. "Is there anything else, Commander?"

"No. The message is everything. Thank you."

"Thank you for alerting us to the peril of a brother." He paused, then said, "We will meet again, of that I am sure, Commander."

We shook hands. His grip was surprisingly strong and his glare more intense than ever. The entire episode produced an eerie feeling in me. If it had been anyone other than a Mason, I would have been alarmed.

As Rork and I walked away from the building, I gave Rork the plans for the rest of the day.

"Now we'll walk up to the telegraph office on Polk to see if there are any replies from the admiral and to report the assignment done. After that, it's off to the Tampa Bay Hotel by one o'clock, where I'll spend a little time with Maria and you can nose around the scullery maids and find out what Gardiner is doing."

I didn't really expect Rork to obtain any usable intelligence from the hotel servants, but thought it sounded better than what I knew his actual intent with the scullery maids would be.

Rork was distracted, however, looking around and not listening as I continued with our program for the day. "We'll leave the hotel no later than three, engaging a hackney to take us back to Port Tampa. Weigh anchor by five, and we should clear Egmont Key by seven thirty, bound for Key West and the squadron. That means we'll arrive by tomorrow night, have time to get the ship squared away, with some time ashore for a few of the men. We'll make the gunnery exercises on Monday. Questions?"

"Nary a question, but do have a wee suggestion, sir," he said with a boyish glint in his eye. "There's a fine establishment just down Franklin Street from that telegraph office."

I knew exactly where he was headed with the comment. "No

time for that, Rork."

"Well, now, you now we've had a bit o' stress here this morn, sir. An' we ain't young lads anymore, are we? Ooh, nay. The fact o' the matter is that at our age, if ye let this sort o' stress an' such build up, why, it can kill you just as much as a bullet." His rubber hand went up for emphasis. "An' that, sir, is a known scientific fact. Read it in a quality newspaper from New York."

"No, Rork."

Rork displayed a suitably furrowed brow and sad expression. There is nothing sadder in the world than a forlorn Irishman. Or more aggravating, for he wasn't done.

"An' in addition, sir, there's a wee point o' honor involved too. Aye, methinks quite clearly you promised us a pint back there in Ybor afore we had to deal with Roldan's thugs. Well, o' course, it goes without sayin' that promisin' one o' Uncle Sam's bluejackets a pint o' suds, 'tis a solemn vow for a commissioned officer an' gentleman such as your ownself. Aye, a solemn vow an' a matter o' honor, sir."

There were times when I felt like I was the old coot's father.

"Good Lord, Rork, you sound like some old rummy jack tar whining for his tot," I countered.

Without embarrassment, he replied, "Well, sir, 'tis the honor o' the thing."

"I'll think about it," I temporized, and began walking north on Ashley Street.

Upon arrival at the cable office, we found a different clerk, equally as dim-witted as the previous, staring at his keyboard. After much rummaging around in pigeon-hole files, he informed me there were no cables for me.

I kept mine to the admiral concise:

XX—HAD CONFRTN W ORD PBLCO HERE—X— NO DAMAG—X—WRNG SENT TO TARG—X—DONE HERE—X—LVG TONITE—X—ARVG KW SAT NITE—XX

There was no electric or steam car to the Tampa Bay Hotel right then, so we walked out and down Franklin Street, en route to the bridge over the river. The day had turned cool, such a change from Jamaica a mere week earlier. Strolling at a more relaxed pace now, I dreamed of my imminent warm embrace with Maria. I could tell Rork was dreaming of embracing a cool beer.

Coming to Lafayette Street, I turned west toward the bridge, but found myself alone, for Rork had stopped and presented his poor-me face again. Then he gestured south down Franklin Street and said, "Oh, we've come so close me nose can whiff it. Just a wee bit further, sir, an' all will be right with the world."

46

A Delicate Subject

Tampa, Florida
Friday afternoon
16 December 1892

Ahundred feet south and across Franklin was a row of brick saloons serving the courthouse crowd of lawyers, judges, politicians, and policemen—not the sort of places I enjoy. But Rork being Rork, and in serious need of a brew, that's where we steered.

Once we walked into the largest of the bars, the aptly named Final Appeal Tavern, and sat down at a back corner table, I made an unpleasant discovery. Rork had lied to me. He didn't want beer. He wanted rum, and only the best, Matusalem.

Once I paid for it and he'd had his first sip, he said he wanted to talk. Well, that wasn't an unusual cause and effect. The topic, however, was unusual.

With a grimly determined look, he said, "We need to speak on a delicate an' heartbreakin', but necessary, subject."

The list of woes in Rork's life was long, but ordinarily he

didn't dwell on them. In fact, Rork was a pretty cheerful fellow. It must have something to do with one of his women friends, I thought. At any given time, one of them would be giving him trouble.

"I've noticed something's bothering you lately. What is it?"

"Sean to Peter? Man to man? No rank?"

That boded ill. It was something about me, not him. "Yes, of course. Sean to Peter. No rank."

The color faded from his face. "'Tis *you* what's botherin' me, boyo. Your head's befuddled over this fine Spanish lady, an' you're not thinkin' clear an' smart. You're headin' full speed for a nasty reef, Peter. An' not only inside Uncle Sam's Navy, but inside your own heart an' soul as well. This won't turn out well, Peter. Not at all."

It took me aback. "Sean, I thought you liked Maria. I know she likes you."

"Aye, that's true on both accounts. But it's not the point, boyo. She's a fine an' lovely lady, but there's more to the situation. You're not seein' things as they are. You're dreamin' the way you want 'em to be."

"Me, a dreamy-eyed fool? You're always telling me I'm not romantic enough and I need to loosen up. 'Have a little Irish in your soul, Peter,' you say to me."

He smiled at the memory. "Aye, that I did. But it was for fun an' this lady ain't one o' those girls. You're takin' this to another level with a lady whose not o' your kind. There's danger ahead, me friend."

"Oh now, really. I think your Gaelic imagination is getting overworked on this, Sean."

"It ain't me imagination, Peter. Me eyes an' ears're workin' just fine, an' they tell me what you're thinkin' an' gonna do even afore you can fathom it. You're wantin' to marry her an' live happily ever after."

"Yes, I've been considering that. We love each other, Sean. And she's different from the others I've known since Linda died."

"You said the same about Cynda, back in eighty-eight."

He had a point. I'd fallen head over heels for her, a love born of shared danger and desperate loneliness on both our parts. But Cynda had refused my offer of marriage, and died in childbirth of our daughter, now three and being raised by her maternal aunt Mary Alice in Illinois.

"Very well, I admit I was wrong on Cynda, and I learned from that mistake. Now listen well, my friend. Maria's completely different from Cynda. Maria understands me and this profession."

He shook his head. "She'll not be happy, Peter. Not as the wife of a sailor. Not as the wife of an American. Not as the wife of a man without wealth. An' not as a wife to a Protestant. Maria is used to bein' comfortable an' havin' servants, culture, excitement, fine cuisine, an' always surrounded by her fancy lady friends. Can you give her the fancy life? Can you see her alone at Patricio Island while we're at sea, toilin' away on the island to make ends meet?"

"Maria is very strong and intelligent. She's not as frivolous as you think, and yes, she can handle living on the island. Besides, she wouldn't have to live there all year. She—we, when I'm home—could live up north in the summer."

Rork then did a rare thing. He bought us a round. Typically, he considered this the responsibility of the officer, namely me. When he occasionally bought a round, it was either to celebrate a victory, commiserate over a defeat, or mourn a death.

"Peter, you're lonely an' tired an' feelin' your age. She's beautiful an' exotic an' clever, with more brains than most o' the people you know. She makes you feel young and strong and hopeful for the future. 'Tis only natural for you to think the way you are, for any normal *civilian* man surely would."

I didn't like where this was going. "Sean, say your piece and be done with it."

He downed a gulp and nodded. "You're not like any other man, civilian or even naval. A fellow such as you don't have the luxury of gettin' dim-witted by love. Nay, Peter, for you have to think about things most men don't. You know things, secret things, that're valuable to our enemies."

He sipped pensively, his eyes seeing something beyond the barroom. "An' make no mistake about it, me dearest old friend, the Spaniardos're our enemies an' we'll be fightin' 'em someday soon. An' as me an' you damn well know, Marrón's the shrewdest bastard o' the lot. He's the best at infiltratin' his enemies to learn their plans, an' always ten steps ahead o' 'em."

"You think Maria is a spy? For Marrón?"

A hesitant shake of his head. "Don't know rightly whether she is or not. But how do you know for certain she ain't, Peter? How do you know the wily bugger hasn't put a double agent in place well ahead o' the war that's surely comin'? An agent who'll be able to hear an' deduce confidential things from the one *yanqui* naval officer who knows more about the Spanish military in Cuba than any other. Aye, that'd be a valuable agent to have, now, wouldn't it?"

It suddenly dawned on me the reason his words sounded familiar—Rork's private interview with Admiral Walker when we first were summoned to Key West.

"Sean, you're using the same language Admiral Walker used with me. Did you two talk about Maria and me? Did he put you up to this?"

He exhaled sadly, not answering. He didn't have to, for I could read his thoughts too. The admiral had certainly put him up to this, but Rork was more than willing because he had his own doubts about Maria.

After another gulp of liquid courage, he admitted it. "Oh Peter, o' course Walker asked me about the lady, an' how serious this thing was becomin'. Hell's bells lad, he's covered your scrawny arse for years against the ring-knockers and brown-nosers up at the palace. An' now that he's on his way out in a couple o' years, he wants to make sure you're not gonna do somethin' stupid to ruin all his efforts when he's retired."

"All right, let's get this straight. I'm not going to ruin my career. I'm taking care of my own personal happiness, Sean. Yes, I was feeling old and tired and worried. And now, for the first time since eighteen-eighty-one, I feel alive and happy and hopeful for the future. So I'd be a fool not to seize this chance for love. Why the hell can't I be happy?"

I interrupted his reply by declaring, "And Maria is not a spy! The damned paranoia of you and Walker is astounding—and not a little aggravating!"

He waved to the barman for yet another round, then leaned closer to me.

"Peter, nobody, least o' all me, wants you to be without the love o' a good lady. Just please, slow it down a bit. Get to know her better. You've lots o' time, so don't make fancy promises out o' pipedreams."

My resentment at all this meddling boiled over. "Why is it you haven't used her name, Sean? Do you despise her that much?"

He held up his hands in surrender. "Run your guns back in, Peter. Maria is a lovely name an no offense is intended by me omission. An' no, there's no despisin' o' her by me. Just bein' careful is all, for you've only known her for five months, an' you're actin' like you've known her for years."

"Yes, and you've known me for twenty-nine long friggin' years, so I would think you've got a higher opinion of me than as some fool who's swayed by a pretty face and curves."

Rork's temper was rising too. "Aye, Peter, o' course me opinion o' you is higher than that. If you think otherwise, than you *are* actin' like a friggin' fool an' ought to damn well stop it right now."

It was time to stop this useless prattle. "Yes, well, you've had your say, and helped me cement my decision. So drink up, Rork, it's time to get the hell out of here. I've got an important engagement with my love at the hotel."

"Aye, aye, sir," muttered Rork as he called for the waiter and

put coins on the table. I sure as hell wasn't going to pay for that
third round.

47

Ambrosia, Anticipation and Decision

Tampa Bay Hotel
Tampa, Florida
Friday afternoon
16 December 1892

The riverfront was delightful in the cool breezy air. In the gardens around us, hundreds of green bushes and trees were trimmed in yellow, red, pink, and blue flowers. The opulent hotel spread along the western horizon, its towers and domes and spires reaching high into powder blue sky puffed with white. The green river itself was a hive of action as the fishing smacks and trading schooners sailed in and off the docks of Tampa across the way. In a gazebo nearby, a string quartet began a soothing Spanish melody.

All of it was the backdrop for the main entrée of the scene, the lady in white strolling beside me. I'd never seen Maria in white and the effect, from parasol to hemline, was marvelously angelic in the sunlight.

"Peter, I have wonderful news I learned today in the newspaper. As of the eleventh of this month, Sagasta and the liberals are now back in charge in Madrid. My cousin-in-law Antonio Maura has been named the Minister of Overseas Colonies. None of these men want war with the Cubans or the Americans. I am hoping sanity will return to my country's policies. This must end the threat against your friend Martí, do you not agree?"

I wasn't sure of that at all. Havana was a long way from Madrid, and I was convinced the decision to kill Martí was made in Havana. Sagasta was despised by the conservatives, royalists, and army. This was his fifth term as prime minister and I wondered how long this one would last. No, I decided, Marrón would go ahead with the plan.

"We shall see, dear. I hope you are right about Spain and Cuba." Taking her in my arms, I whispered, "But why are we talking politics? I have less than two hours now, so let's enjoy it somewhere more secluded."

I guided her back toward the hotel. She rewarded my effort with that deliciously wicked smile of hers.

"Peter, neither of us have had our lunch yet. Would you like to share it in my room? It is very comfortable and there is a magnificent view of the river and gardens."

"I thought you'd never ask."

Passing through the main lobby arm in arm, the naval officer and his lady, we engendered envious glances from the patrons, an experience I could tell she enjoyed. Using the elevator, a new experience for many Floridians, we ascended to the third floor and strolled to her spacious corner apartment.

Comfortable was an understatement—the place was luxurious. As we sat down at a table for two in the bay window alcove, my attention was diverted to the large soft bed in the center of the suite. My mind reminded me how long it had been since I'd had any real sleep, in addition to more amorous uses for a bed.

Maria feigned to ignore my gaze, and concentrated on the matter at hand, ordering lunch from the stoic waiter. She was delighted with the en suite luncheon selections the hotel offered, selecting *vivaneau rouge* (which I learned was red snapper), *haricot verts tarragon* (green beans), and a mango *tarte* (pie).

It took only twenty-five minutes to arrive, which I found quite amazing. From the hotel's *Carte des Vins du Sommelier en Chef* came an accompanying bottle of Château Olivier *Sémillon* white wine. The entire repast was the perfect ambrosial therapy, just what I needed to alleviate my Rork-instigated headache.

Encouraged thus by the lady, the luncheon, and the plush boudoir, my disposition improved so much that, for the first time in our courtship, I boldly made a risqué suggestion. "There's not much time left, my dear. Might we retire to this beautiful bed? Do you know the English word *snuggle,* my dear?"

Maria did indeed understand both the concept and my intent and, relaxed herself from the luncheon wine, acceded to my request postehaste. Within seconds she had locked the door and joined me on that soft expanse.

Well, I must admit I had never had a lady take care of me in such an elegant and expensive fashion, and thought the entire experience absolutely grand and one to which I could easily become accustomed. As any gentleman can readily understand, by then my mind was swiftly transitioning to anticipation of consummating even grander experiences in that bed.

Anticipation, however, is not always an accurate harbinger of things to come. In this particular instance, that most misleading of human emotions played second fiddle to the physiology of age and exhaustion. Half a minute after I stretched out on the blissful bed, I seemed to somehow have lost consciousness.

I regained consciousness almost two hours later, when Maria nudged me and asked, "Peter, weren't you and Mr. Rork supposed to go to your ship now?"

A quick glance at the bedside clock showed the time to be almost four in the afternoon, an hour after I'd planned to leave.

Disaster! I fairly leaped off the bed and went over what had happened. I clearly recalled the feast and my plan of action, but nothing else. When awakening, both Maria and I were fully clothed and atop the covers. Could it actually be that when in bed with a beautiful woman I'd fallen asleep?

To say I was embarrassed is far too lightweight a description. Maria, seeing my mental evaluations and realization, came over and cupped my face in her hands, then kissed me. With maternal gentleness and a wisp of a smile, she murmured, "Peter, you were *very* tired, my love. Do not worry. There is no time now, but there will be other opportunities for us."

My response was rather lame. "Thank you, dear. I guess I was pretty tired."

"I do not want you to go, but should you not be finding Mr. Rork?"

She was right, I had no time left for small talk. "Yes, I've got to be going. I suppose this is it, dear."

My right hand was on the door knob and my left around her waist when my mind was struck with yet another realization—I wouldn't see Maria again until possibly at Spain in late January, and if not then, until the spring. A decision needed to be made and the time was now or never. Rork and the United States Navy would have to wait another five minutes.

"Maria, there's something I need to ask you. Will you marry me?"

She frowned. "Your American humor is sometimes beyond my comprehension, Peter. Is this a joke of some kind?"

I held her close to me. "No. I'm very serious, Maria. We love each other. We need each other. We should be together, not in periodic rendezvous, but in marriage."

Maria looked out the window for an instant, then back to me, trying to hold back tears. "Peter, you are the strongest, finest, and most decent man I have ever known, but our two cultures are completely different. Many people on both sides would scorn our marriage and make our lives miserable."

"I understand exactly what you are saying, and you are right, up to a point. There will be some people who will try to make our lives miserable. Whether they do or not will be up to us. They can't make us miserable, Maria, unless we let them. And if we stay together, we're stronger than all of them on both sides."

She pulled away and walked to the window. Sensing she wanted to be alone, I stayed at the door and waited. After looking out at the gardens and river, Maria turned around and answered me.

"My family has known over five hundred years of turmoil and fear directed at us because of our beliefs and our Jewish history. I am not afraid of the small-minded men who speak Spanish or English, for they are without honor or history. And I will not let them, or anyone else, keep me from the man I love. My answer is yes, Peter. I would be very happy to be your wife."

I fairly ran to the window and took her into my arms tighter than I'd ever held her before. I held her like I'd never let go. Our lips met and I knew I would remember that kiss forever.

But the thing that worried me was still lurking in my mind, and I had to bring it up, especially now. "Maria, there is something else we need to remember. In our happiness, we can't be blind to reality, and we have to take a few precautions at the outset."

"Such as?"

It was not without realizing the irony of using Rork's words that I said, "I know you aren't afraid of the small-minded men around us, but we need to be smart. I might be the target for gossip, but would not be in danger. Your situation is different. Our engagement can be told only to a few of your trusted friends, for your position and physical well-being could be in danger. There are elements in the Spanish government that would see you at least as an obstacle, or possibly even as a traitor. So please, for now, be circumspect about who you confide this in."

"I understand."

"Marriage ceremony in the spring?"

"Oh, Peter, that would be delightful. A small Christian ceremony, with just close friends. Away from Spain and Cuba and Washington. Can we have it at your island?"

"I love the idea."

"And I love you, Peter." She saw me glancing at the clock. "I know you must go."

"Maria, I love you so much. You've made me the happiest and luckiest man in the world. And I promise next time I won't fall asleep on you."

"I will not let you!"

That got us laughing, and still entwined, we walked to the door. A final kiss was our goodbye and I was gone from my fiancée.

The bustle and noise of the hotel formed but a distant background as I made my way through the lobby. Rork was on a settee near the front doors, talking to a man in a suit. They stood as I approached and, after our earlier contretemps, I was glad to see Rork smiling at me.

He then cocked his head toward the other man and said, "I am sure you remember the gentleman from the Masonic lodge, sir. He has a message for you."

48

Messages Received and Sent

Tampa, Florida
Friday afternoon
16 December 1892

It was the same Mason. He handed me a sealed plain envelope. Inside was one sheet of note paper.

Before I could read it, he explained, "I received an immediate reply from Brother José in Ocala, Commander. No one else has seen it or will ever know its contents. After you are done reading it, I will destroy it."

Martí was a master at surreptitious communication, and many lives depended on those abilities. Frequently in the past, he had employed several layers, as well as various types, of protection in his messages to me. Anyone in the Spanish counterrevolutionary forces trying to decipher them would have to penetrate his different methods, from invisible ink and pictograms to code substitutions, complex ciphers, and innuendo. And even if they ever did get to actual message, his intentional use of atrocious Spanish grammar disguised the identity of the sender, for no one would think it had been sent by one of the most acclaimed writers in that language.

I had no doubt it was from Martí, for I knew his hurried cursive style, but I was surprised at its quick arrival. Somehow, from a hundred miles away in Ocala, he had gotten a handwritten note to me through his Masonic brethren in only four hours. Unlike most of his letters to me, even within the United States, it was short and in plain English. Obviously, he trusted the courier.

Peter,

Ocala, Noon, 16 December1892
Thank you for the warning. We need to talk. I know your ship is leaving, but please meet me at Paulina's at midnight. It is important. You can trust the man who gives you this. He can arrange everything.
José

Rork looked at it and groaned. "Not good, sir. We've nary the time for it."

"Hmm, I don't know, Rork. We may have to make time. Martí knew from my message to him that we had to leave this evening. For him to make this request means it's more than important, it's vital."

To the man from the lodge, I said, "Thank you for the time and effort, sir. I have three requests of you. First, we need transport to Port Tampa straight away. Second, please get a cable to Key West. Third, we need transport between Port Tampa and Ybor City this evening, picking us up at nine. I want to get there early. Can you handle all that?"

"I can. But his note said to meet at midnight."

"We will, but first I want to see the crowd watching his speech."

I walked to the front desk for some paper and wrote out the

telegram. To the Mason I said, "Here, please send this cable to Admiral Walker in Key West as soon as you can after taking us to the ship."

XX—DELAYD IN TAMPA—X—ARVG KW LATE SAT NITE OR SUN MORN—XX

He nodded. "I have a carriage standing by and we can leave immediately for the wharf at Port Tampa. Then I'll return here and have the cable sent. At nine tonight, I will return to the wharf and take you to Ybor City, remaining there until you are ready to return to Port Tampa."

He sounded like a petty officer in his deadpan acknowledgement and I wondered this cryptic man's background. He didn't *look* like a former petty officer, or seaman of any type. No sun crinkles around his eyes, no tan, no roll to his walk. Maybe he was a former army sergeant?

I was tempted to ask his name, but a perverse streak of pride stopped me. It wasn't important. I knew I could trust him, and that was all I needed to know.

"Thank you, sir, for all of your help on this," I said.

His answer was as matter-of-fact as all his other speech. "It is done for a brother in peril, Commander. The carriage is out front. Please follow me."

As we walked through the open double doors onto the verandah, Rork growled in a low tone to me, "Ooh, now there's trouble brewin'. Broad on the starboard beam, sir."

I looked to the right. A hundred fifty feet away, at the far south end of the verandah, was a group of men in crisp white uniforms. Four naval officers. Three were Spanish. I couldn't tell their rank. One was American. Another man in a gray suit was with them. They were all talking amiably and hadn't noticed us. Rork and I were in working blues, considerably crumpled by this time, and didn't stand out as much.

"Spaniardos," observed Rork, somewhat unnecessarily. "Oh,

an' who would that be with the blighters? Why, 'tis none other than Commander Norton Gardiner."

We stopped. The Mason, visibly perplexed, halted also.

"I know we're in a hurry, sir," I explained to our Masonic benefactor, "but I need to talk to one of those men over there. I'll be back in a moment."

He was no fool. Surveying the Spanish officers, he assessed the situation instantly and nodded. "Do what you must, Commander. I'll go get the carriage and meet you back here at the front drive."

Meanwhile, I called over a waiter and, in my sternest command voice which brooked no dissent, told him to go to the tallest of the naval officers and pass my wish for him to meet Commander Wake immediately inside the hotel at the front desk.

To Rork, I said, "If the others try to come with him, divert them somehow. I want a private talk with the commander."

This was just the sort of thing Rork reveled in, his mind being a veritable hothouse of ideas on how to divert, decoy, and dissuade people from doing things they intended, and he enthusiastically complied.

Norton arrived at the front desk alone, clearly perturbed by having a further experience with his archenemy, the low-class pretender who had kicked him off his ship.

"Wake, what now?" he scoffed. "We aren't on the ship anymore and since we're the same rank, I don't have to put up with your sophomoric stunts. Shouldn't you be on the ship, trying to be a real captain, instead of playing at being a patron of a quality resort hotel?"

I ignored that and pulled him into an adjacent office, which providentially was empty. After closing the door, I asked, "Four questions. Who are those Spanish naval officers? Who is the civilian with them? Why are they all here? Why are you with them?"

His response was unsurprising. "This is yet another charge,

Wake! Dragging me in here by unlawful touching is criminal assault and battery! And another interrogation? How dare you treat a fellow officer this way? Are you completely devoid of any sense of propriety?"

"Battery? No, Norton, not at all. Battery is when I pick up the paperweight on the desk by my right hand and smash it into your snide face to end all possibility of ever having to listen to you whine again. That *will* be battery, and it'll be well worth it."

I was seconds from giving in to my fantasy. It would be worth it. Walker might not condone it, but would certainly understand. Gardiner saw my hand moving toward the paperweight.

"Well, if you must know," he began, in a much reduced tone, "I met a British gentleman of the press at tea just now. He came down by train from New York, having crossed over on the *Umbria*. He is headed to Cuba to write about the Spanish governance there. The Spanish officers are from *Reina Regente* and they are here in Tampa to provide transport for him as a guest of the Spanish Navy. The journalist invited me to meet them, and I found Captain Boreau to be very impressive, clearly of the highest refinement—unlike you."

"Did you say *Boreau?*"

"Yes, he is a commander by rank, and took command a few months ago. He speaks impeccable English, much better than yours. I do not understand this ridiculous attitude you have against the Spanish in Cuba. They are the civilizing force there. Without them, the place would descend into another version of Haiti."

When I didn't comment, for I was assessing the news that my old adversary Boreau was in Tampa, Gardiner got plucky again. "And let me tell you something, Wake, if you still think the Spanish are in the least bit involved in some murder plot, you are letting your animosity make you delusional. These are naval *gentlemen* and they don't think and act like you. I don't think our naval leaders understand just how out of touch with reality you are, but I can assure you, they will. Far more than an embarrassment to our country, you are a danger."

"When is the Spanish ship leaving Tampa?"

"You haven't heard anything I've said, have you?"

"When are they leaving?"

"You are hopeless—"

His opinion of me was cut short when I grabbed his lapel with my left hand and got close to his little piggy eyes. I repeated my question very slowly. "When are they *leaving?*"

"Later tonight sometime. They're going out to the ship now and invited me to see her."

"You aren't going to be able to do that, Norton. You are not returning to the verandah at all. They will be given your regrets, with the explanation you were called away on an urgent matter and will be unable to join them. You will go to your room and stay there for the evening. Tomorrow, you can do whatever the hell you want. Understood?"

"Yes . . ." he said shakily.

"Good. I hope you do, Norton. I want you to live."

And with that said and done, I left Gardiner in the office and rejoined my companions, pausing only to flag down the same waiter and give him the new message for those distinguished naval gentlemen on the verandah.

As we walked out to the carriage, the Mason went off to the carriage park to bring back our transport. I took the private moment to share the latest news with Rork, who showed his surprise, "So Boreau got promoted? An' now the bloody bastard's here. Roldan an' Boreau, the hounds o' hell've gathered in Tampa, sir. Methinks they'll fancy killin' you too, you know."

"Maybe," I admitted. "That would make Colonel Marrón happy, would it?"

"Gonna add this Boreau business to the cable to the admiral?"

"No. It'd just get him more nervous than he already is. This is just another complication, that's all."

"A bloody big complication, if ya ask me, sir. Ooh, me bones're achin' somethin' fierce, an' especially me right foot. An' as you know, that's not a good sign."

I was a bit too preoccupied right about then to converse about his legendary prognostic ailments, so I to placate the old boy I muttered, "Put it on the list of bad signs, Rork."

"How're we gonna stop Boreau and that friggin' ship o' his? Got no ideas in me noggin. Do you, sir?"

I didn't have a clue what to do. "Don't worry, I'll come up with something, Rork."

He grinned. "Aye, you always do, sir. Sometimes those ideas o' yours're a wee touch harebrained," he said while shaking his head in wonder, "but damned if they don't usually work out fine. No disrespect intended, o' course, sir."

I laughed. "Harebrained? I prefer *unconventional,* Rork. It sounds far more professional, especially when explaining our actions later on."

When it arrived at the driveway, the carriage wasn't what I expected. It was a lightweight and speedy phaeton with a pair of big roans. The accommodation was a single, crowded bench seat, and our unnamed benefactor was the driver. By this time, it didn't surprise me to find he wasn't a timid one, either. The large wheels proved efficient on the still-wet sandy road southwest to Port Tampa as he pushed the roans without let up and we covered the route through pine woods and swamps in forty-five minutes.

By the time we arrived, the sky to the west was cast in an ominous yellow hue as the lowering sun filtered through the clouds racing down from the north. Looking at the scene, another of those harebrained schemes hatched in my head. This one had very little chance of working out, but it was all I could come up with.

After exiting the phaeton, I quietly asked Rork, "Say, did that youngest Spanish officer, the one talking with the reporter, seem a little under the weather to you?"

He stopped and looked at me. I stared back at him.

It took a while before he got my meaning. "Ooh, aye, sir. Now you mention it, methinks the bugger did seem a bit sickly."

"Hmm, that makes two of us who got the same impression, Rork." I tsk-tsk'd in anxious contemplation. "Sickness can be so contagious in the confines of a ship. Can't let it get out of hand and get ashore, can we? And can't let anyone from shore go aboard the ship."

"Nay, indeed, sir. Especially not with those Cuban fevers. Got to nip this sort o' thing in the bud straightaway."

"Total quarantine on that ship is called for, isn't it, Rork?"

"Aye, sir. Regretful but necessary. 'Tis a good thing we spotted that sickly lad."

49

An Idea on the Edge of Propriety

U.S.S. Bennington
Port Tampa, Florida
Friday afternoon
16 December 1892

I briefed Warfield on what had happened ashore. He shook his head in wonder when I described Gardiner's breakfast show, laughed at how we dealt with Roldan's thug, and nodded reluctantly when I passed on Martí's request for a meeting that night and our revised plan for departure at two a.m. He said the departure time would still give us time to reach Key West for qualifications, if we had no major mechanical problems.

Needless to say, I omitted mentioning Maria as well as my last tête-à-tête with Gardiner. When I was done, Warfield had a list of things to go over. Most were routine notifications of his decisions and actions. The executive officer of a warship has charge of the daily operation, but the commanding officer is

282

responsible for everything that happens. And I always insisted on knowing everything happening in the ship.

Condition of the engine and steam plant was my primary concern, and the report was neutral—there were no problems, but an overhaul was well past due and problems could be expected. Fuel was somewhat in good shape, a collier barge having come alongside and added to the bunkers. No injuries or equipment failures were reported. No signals or cables, no problems with the Port Tampa harbormaster, no spats with locals involving the crew working parties ashore, and no major discipline violations.

"Could *Reina Regente* really be here only to take a Brit reporter to Cuba, sir?"

"No, too many coincidences. But I'll give them credit—it's a damned good cover story."

"I would think their man already went ashore on the first boat you saw. Damned clever fellows, aren't they? We can't touch them or even hinder them."

"Yes, you're right, but only if we wait for good luck to arrive on its own, John. I don't have enough patience for that, though. I like to make my own luck."

"Aye, sir, it's the American Navy way. You sound like you're cooking up something."

"I was too late to figure out a way to stop their people from going ashore earlier, but I do have an idea on how to shut Boreau and his ship out of this equation from this point onward."

"How's that, sir?"

Remembering what Gardiner had said to me in our last encounter, I pleasantly said, "Well, it not entirely within the realm of accepted propriety."

Warfield's brow darkened as I continued and I carefully gauged his reaction, for it would be an indicator of what I could expect ashore during the execution of my plan.

"I believe there may possibly be sickness in *Reina Regente*. One of the Spanish officers we saw appeared seriously ill. Given

Florida's recent yellow fever outbreaks, I think the proper authorities might want to investigate."

He wasn't impressed. "It's rather late in the season for yellow fever, sir."

"Not in Cuba. The season runs later down there, and it's been an exceptionally hot, wet season in the West Indies, just like it was four years ago in eighty-eight."

I invoked the year hundreds died along the coasts of Florida from yellow fever. Since then, no chances were taken by authorities, especially with ships coming from Cuba or Haiti, where the disease was seasonally rampant.

"I dunno, sir. They just came from a U.S. port, where the quarantine doctor examined the ship upon entry into the country."

He didn't add that we had not cleared the quarantine doctor in Key West upon returning from Mexico—a flagrant breach of regulations. I'd had other priorities at the time.

"Well, I've had the damned thing and know Yellow Jack doesn't usually show until around six days into it. Which would be right about now for the *Reina Regente,* since they left Cuba earlier this week. Always better to be safe than sorry, John."

He still looked dubious. "So you'll notify the port's quarantine doctor tomorrow? That'll be too late, sir. The Spanish won't be deterred and the assassin will get away."

"I can't notify the port doctor. It would appear contrived, given the animosity between our two navies. No, I think I'll suggest that another local doctor do it—colleague to colleague, so to speak. It'll carry more weight."

"That might work, sir. But when could you find a local doctor?"

"Right now. Please have my gig called away. I'm going ashore to the St. Elmo Hotel. I need to use their telephone."

50

Victory at Dinner

U.S.S. Bennington
Port Tampa, Florida
Friday evening
16 December 1892

My task didn't take long to conclude and, still unsure if the plan would be successful, I made my way back to the ship, but not to my cabin.

Instead, I busied myself with some of the leadership duties incumbent upon the captain of a United States warship. During the tumult of the previous week, I had been remiss in attending to them.

It was already dark below decks. Walking forward on the berth deck to where one of the two smoking lamps hung near the passage to the senior petty officer's "Goat Locker," I found two bosun's mates igniting their pipes and yarning about grog shops in Cartagena with the master-at-arms.

Greatly startled to see their captain suddenly appear, they all instantly straightened and stood mute, waiting for me to pass

285

from their domain and become somebody else's problem. But it was not to be. From my younger days, I knew a thing or two on their subject myself. So, rather than continue my stroll and end their nervousness, I surprised them with my opinion on Cartagena's watering holes.

This resulted in a polite but gradually spirited debate on prices, quality, and quantity of the concoctions served in the taverns of that most notorious of Cartagena's districts, the sadly misnamed Getsemani. In the end, I freely surrendered to their wisdom on the matter, and left the compartment knowing my story would be around the ship in minutes.

Next, I visited the crew galley, where I could tell the cooks had already gotten word of my lower deck perambulation, for all cursing and commotion had vanished. The crew was lined up for dinner and I broke in among them to sample some of the food, a weekly ritual of mine. The current fare was creamed fish chowder, boiled cabbage, bean soup, and brown bread, doused with a cup of steaming navy coffee. It wasn't bad and I said so, which spurred looks among the cooking crew ranging from smugness to relief, depending on their seniority.

Next on my itinerary was a descent into the bowels of the ship, the hellish dominion of the Black Gang, so called for their skin hopelessly impregnated by soot and grease. The senior artificer greeted me on my entry into the after engine room. He was not on duty, explaining with remarkable skill in prevarication that he made a habit of daily off-watch inspection tours, just to make sure things were efficient and safe.

Seconds after the petty officer had finished trying to impress me, Lt. Angles dropped down the ladder with a thud, still buttoning his coat and appearing quite worried.

I assured him all was well and inquired about our boilers' pressure.

"Pressure's holding steady under load, sir. I think our repairs will last through the squadron gunnery exercises and the transit to Pensacola. But she really needs a real overhaul in all four boilers' tubes as soon as you can arrange it."

I agreed and moved on, inspecting the boiler and engine rooms, coal bunkers, shaft alleys, and steering quadrants. The next arrival was Lt. Commander Warfield, who apologized for not being at the quarterdeck for my return.

"Not a problem at all, Commander. All looks well so far."

Knowing some of what was to come that evening, I floated an idea. "Say, I've just been up at the crew mess and it reminded me I'm rather hungry. Have you eaten?"

He took the cue, as a good executive officer would. "Not yet, sir. May I have the honor to invite you to the wardroom? We're having fried fish with some vegetables—and our bull ensign's promised, on pain of severe disrepute, nothing less than plum duff and some decent port for dessert."

I laughed, for the bull ensign—the senior ensign aboard, and in our ship's case, responsible for the wardroom provisions—was the very capable signal officer, Mr. Yeats.

"Thank you for the invitation," I said, as if it had been a spontaneous thought on his part. "Sounds perfect, and I accept with total confidence in Mr. Yeats's success. Now, would you care to join me for a look at the magazines and ready lockers?"

An hour and a half later, I arrived at the wardroom precisely at the appointed time, one bell in the first dog watch, in my winter blues, for an invitation to the captain to join the wardroom for dinner was a special occasion. Eleven of our thirteen officers, two being on watch, were waiting at the table and stood as I entered. The executive officer being my official host, I thanked him for the kind invitation.

After we sat, he graciously inquired, "Sir, do you have anything of a general nature to say to the wardroom before we begin dinner?"

"I do, indeed, Commander Warfield, and request the stewards not remove themselves, for no privacy is necessary. In fact, I want all in the ship to understand my opinion on the matter."

Well, that got their attention. All heads swiveled toward me. Even the wardroom cook peeked around the pantry window to hear me.

"Gentlemen, thank you for having me tonight. I know our actions over the last week have been odd, to say the very least. Since we unexpectedly departed Jamaica on the eighth, *Bennington* has steamed over fifteen hundred miles, which in itself is impressive. That we have done this through two major storms, with faltering boilers, and have sustained no major casualties or damage, no long-term loss of efficiency, and no deterioration of discipline, is nothing less than extraordinary. This is entirely due to the leadership of the officers and petty officers of this ship, and of the stalwart men we are privileged to lead."

Warfield led the predictable round of obligatory applause, which I let linger before going on. "The reason for this long and winding itinerary of ours, from Jamaica to Key West, to Mexico and back to Key West, and then here to Tampa, is complicated, with many nuances. I am regretfully not at liberty to share all of it with you. But I can share this . . ."

I had to do this next part very adroitly. I dare not look at Lt. Lambert too long, lest I betray his role. My words, with the predictable exaggeration, would be known and dissected throughout the ship within minutes.

"We have been on a confidential mission since Jamaica. It is a mission involving life and death, and the prevention of a possible war in this hemisphere. If it is concluded successfully, no one will die, there will be no war, and the average person in our nation will never know what we accomplished.

"Only in failure will the negative consequences be ultimately known. Such is the nature of this rare type of assignment. Each of you here has, along with every man aboard, been an integral part of this mission. I thank you for your skill and your attention to details, even though you did not know the purpose. That is the sign of true professionals."

I paused, but there was no applause, only pensive expressions as each officer busily attempted to deduce what the hell I was speaking about, and his own role in it.

"Gentlemen, I believe this mission will close later tonight, in quiet and anonymous success. Once it is accomplished, we will weigh anchor and head for Key West. While in transit to the south, we will do continuous gunnery drills, both static and live fire. Our guns, and their effective use, are the paramount reason for this ship and our navy. And come Monday morning, *Bennington* will show the squadron, the navy, the nation, and the world, exactly what it means to be a modern American warship!"

The applause wasn't obligatory, it was heartfelt, for I had touched on the old theme familiar to all sailors: "Our Ship—against all others."

The assembled gentlemen leaped up and actually cheered, joined by the stewards and a pot-banging cook. Warfield cast me a fleeting appreciative grin.

I waited until the ovation subsided then, with the intent to end my speech with some levity, I gestured to the table. "And now, gentlemen, I suggest we do justice to our chef's considerable exertions. For, as every sea cook in Uncle Sam's Navy will readily tell you, victory in battle begins at the dinner table the night before."

The wardroom's morale having been thus stoked, dinner was consumed with gusto. The conversation soon centered on a boisterous debate over the various gunnery and engineering characteristics of our competitors in the squadron, accompanied by several of the officers offering their plans for holiday leave. It ended with the traditional Friday evening toast with port: "A willing foe and the sea room to fight him!"

A pleasant evening it was. Just the thing to relieve the disquiet which had been building within me from the anticipation of what was to come, for I knew not what I might find in Ybor City later that night.

The ship's bell struck once in the first watch—eight-thirty

in the evening—as I fell on my bunk for a quick cat nap. It was fully twenty minutes long, but seemed twenty seconds when the alarm clock bell jangled me awake and summoned me back to reality.

And thus it was I left the neat and reassuringly structured world of the real sea-going navy and descended back into the unclean and unpredictable world of espionage ashore.

51

¡Viva Martí!

Ybor City, Florida
Friday evening
16 December 1892

Rork and I were in simple civilian coat and tie for the
evening's shore excursion. Rork toted our "accoutrements,"
since we expected Roldan, et al, might well be after us, in
addition to Martí. Our ellmination would be a bonus for them,
so to speak, to curry favor with their colonel in Havana.

The night air was cold, with air brought down from the far
north. The ship's log listed it as forty nine degrees, and the breeze
made it seem even lower, especially to my tropically thin blood.
We were pleased to note our nameless driver was as punctual as
he was peculiar and was driving the same fast rig.

At a little after ten o'clock, we arrived at the corner of Eighth
and Twelfth and I asked our Masonic facilitator to let us off
there, explaining that we would be thankful to meet him at that
very same place later, at one o'clock in the morning. He wished
us good luck in his perfunctory manner and drove away down

the side street, headed back for the downtown area of Tampa proper.

"That old sod is a queer bloke, if ever there was one," opined Rork while shouldering his bag. "Nary a drop o' red blood in his veins."

"Can't argue that, Rork," I agreed as we headed north on Twelfth. "But at least he's on our side."

"We'll see when it's time to get out o' here," was his grumbled reply.

To confuse Roldan's lookouts, our route was not the direct one from that location to Martí's speaking venue at Ybor's factory. This was intentional, for I wanted to approach my friend's speech from the opposite direction expected from someone coming from Tampa, which lies to the southwest. We would approach from the east.

This goal involved a circuitous march to the north to Eleventh Avenue, thence east to Sixteenth Street, and finally south to Ninth Avenue, where we walked west. And so we walked four times farther to get there.

"The scenic route," I told an unhappy Rork, whose arthritis was making itself felt. After our jaunt, we spied ahead of us at the intersection of Ninth Avenue and Fourteenth Street a vast crowd. The mass was abuzz in excited whispered Spanish opinions regarding what they were hearing from the great orator. Entering the crowd, Rork and I put a distance of fifty or sixty feet between us, keeping each other in peripheral vision. This was close enough for mutual reinforcement if needed, but far enough away to not be immediately assumed to be together.

During this entire time, we scanned everywhere and everyone for a sign of surveillance. We particularly were on the lookout for our previous acquaintance with the binoculars and more generally for any man or woman eyeing us closely. We perceived none so far, so I allowed myself the pleasant thought that perhaps our anonymity was preserved.

By the time we arrived to a place where we could hear

our friend speak, ironically at the same alley's entrance where the telescope man had been stationed earlier in the day, it was 10:35 p.m. Around us were people of every age and color; some standing on boxes, perched on wire poles, hanging out windows. This close to the great man himself, there were no conversations in the audience. All were focused on the rhythmic oration emanating from front steps of the factory. His voice was the only sound at the scene.

The imagery was the same as at other Cuban revolutionary gatherings I'd attended, from New York City to Key West. The flags of America and Free Cuba were displayed everywhere, along with posters of Martí, old General Gómez, and the virile "Bronze Titan," General Antonio Maceo.

Illuminated by the factory's gas lights, Martí was at his best, despite having been at it for over two hours. At his performances before, I had been consistently amazed at his demonstration of endurance, not to mention vocal projection, for the man was of slight stature and his respiratory ailment was well known. He had a lot to say, however, and his passion never diminished. He was a force to be reckoned with, either as friend or foe.

It was while standing amongst this enthralled assembly, their shining faces uplifted toward the factory's front steps in almost religious reverence, that I did finally notice something out of place. Or rather, I should say *someone.*

Maria was across the street, her close position indicating she'd secured it early on. A mere forty feet from Martí, her countenance matched the others around her. But there the similarity ended. She was dressed far too well to blend in with the locals, as if she had a soiree to attend after the speech. In fact, it was the dress I spotted first, a yellow satin affair with white jacket which stood out from the drab multitude. I wasn't the only one who'd noticed. Though surrounded by people, none stood close to Maria, and several women of lesser means were openly inspecting her. Rork saw her too, and glanced at me, then her. I nodded my acknowledgment.

Her presence complicated things considerably, and it angered me.

During our stroll in the hotel's park that afternoon, she had twice said she wanted to "hear the distinguished Martí," the better to tell her friends in Cuba and Spain about him. Knowing of the physical danger lurking in Ybor, and certain the emotions of the crowd would be heightened against anything or anyone from Spain, I suggested it would be safer for all concerned if she wait until another time and place to meet my Cuban friend, well out of the public eye and minus any inflammatory rhetoric by unthinking hotheads or intentional agitators.

Perhaps a dinner for the three of us when Martí next visited Washington, was my idea. At the time, I thought she saw the merit of my point and had acquiesced. Now I knew otherwise. So, knowing of my disapproval and the reasons for it, why was she there? That question had several potential answers, most of them disturbing.

Martí was nearing the end of his story, invoking with rising voice his vision of a free Cuba's future, where true equality among the islanders was matched by the country's equality among the international community, where the individual rights and freedoms of each man were complemented by their responsibilities to the community and compassion for those fellow human beings in need, and where fear would be surpassed by confidence and pride.

He concluded his sermon with a loud, "*¡Viva La Libertad para nuestro pueblo! ¡Y viva La Cuba Libre!*"

Everyone went wild, echoing the cries with a deafening roar. Rork and I shouted along with the others, as did Maria, waving her folded yellow parasol high in the air, and fairly jumping in her joy. The reverberations continued until a new cry arose. It started as Martí descended the steps and headed to a carriage parked along the street.

The carriage slowly made its way through the crowd, turning west on Eighth and disappearing from view. But no one went home. They were too excited to leave. Soon the entire mass was chanting in unison two words, louder and louder each time. Feet began stamping as the cry was repeated. I noted the time—eleven o'clock.

"*¡Viva Martí!*"

Maria was as enthused as the rest. I could hear her shouts, the accent quite distinctive among the Cuban Creole accents around her. Her Spanish was a mixture of Castilian, the dialect of the ruling elite in Madrid, and Ladino, the dialect of the Iberian Jews known as the Sephardim. Though her family spoke Ladino among themselves, Maria had received her education in Madrid and her voice had taken on its sounds as well.

And then the inevitable happened.

Someone yelled, "*¡Abajo con España! ¡Abajo con los peninsulares!*"

Down with Spain. Down with the peninsulars.

"Peninsulars" was the term for the people in Spain, and in Cuba it referred to those who ruled over the Cubans. Martí never used that kind of divisive language; he abhorred it and urged just the opposite. He believed all the people of Spanish heritage should be brothers and stop shedding fraternal blood. But Martí wasn't atop the steps and in control anymore. No one was. The officials, including Ybor, had left in carriages also. The factory lights were dimmed. There were no policemen in sight. It was late and the crowd was thinning.

Most didn't echo the shout, and looked with contempt at the rabble-rousers. But there were a few, perhaps half a dozen, who did echo the shout, and began looking around for cohorts. It was only a matter of seconds before they would start looking for targets.

I glanced at Rork, who had moved in closer, and said, "We need to get her out of here, right now!"

We threaded our way across the jammed street, stemming the flow heading south on Fourteenth. I called out to Maria and saw her look around. Just then, an older woman near Maria asked brashly in Cuban Creole why she was there, since she was obviously a rich lady from Madrid. Maria hesitated. The old woman called out to her friends a Spanish spy was in their midst, pointing to Maria.

One of the toughs started running toward Maria. He was three paces from her when I dropped him by turning to the right with an elbow to his throat. As he clutched his crushed windpipe, I completed the turn, putting my left index and middle fingers in both his eyes, pushing his head down into the street, then walked to Maria. It took seven seconds, unregistered by most around us, but the old woman noticed and screamed a threat.

52

A Most Incongruous
Turn of Events

Ybor City, Florida
Friday evening
16 December 1892

Rork was not idle during this. He grasped Maria's arm and pulled her into the candy shop ten feet away. The owner was in the process of closing up and was visibly alarmed when they burst open the door, followed by me. I closed and locked the door behind me as Rork propelled Maria past the shopkeeper and out the back of the store. Not a word was exchanged with the dumbfounded man the entire time.

We emerged in the open lot in back and headed diagonally across the lot to Eighth Avenue. Seeing no pursuers, I told my companions we could walk easy for a while down Eighth until we got to the Pedrosos' house. Two seconds after saying that, I heard the old woman's raucous squawk, shrieking that the

Spanish murderers were getting away on Eighth.

When Rork heard the word *asesinos* he shot me a questioning look.

"He's not dead, Rork. He's blinded and choking, but not dead," I explained.

Some of the tough's chums rounded the corner behind us at a run.

Seeing a fire station across the avenue, I told Maria and Rork, "Get in there!"

The main fire engine barn doors were closed but the pedestrian door was unlocked and we rushed inside.

"Rork, lock the door!" I commanded.

A measured voice behind us said accented English, "We do not lock that door. I am Captain Puglisi and in command of Company Two. Can I help you?"

A stern-looking man stepped forward from the shadows, tall and muscular in light blue trousers and dark blue shirt, and the bonneted helmet of the fire brigade. He had crossed brass nozzles on his lapels.

"Captain, there is a mob outside after this lady because she is from Spain. We need to lock the door immediately."

Captain Puglisi didn't reply at first, but strode to the door and locked it. Then he asked in a guarded tone, "Who are you and why are you in Ybor tonight?"

"I am Peter Wake, this is Maria Maura, and Sean Rork. We are friends of José Martí and we went to hear him speak at the cigar factory."

The lock was being tried from outside, to no avail, followed by pounding on the door.

I ignored it. The pounding got louder. The captain, still standing by the door, shook his head at me. "That was over a while ago. Where were you going just now?"

"Martí asked me to meet him after his speech at the Pedroso home."

Puglisi still doubted us. His hand was near the lock. I heard other firemen coming down a stairway cursing in Spanish about the drunks outside ruining their sleep.

The captain tilted his head to the left, a sign of disbelief, and asked, "And do you know where that is?"

"Yes, sir. Thirteenth Street, just south of Eighth, on the east side of the street."

The men outside began arguing with each other, and I heard something about the back door.

"And their first names?" asked Puglisi.

"Paulina and Ruperto. Look, can you help us, Captain? We need to get out of here," I said, understanding his hesitancy, but getting exasperated by the delay. "This lady has done nothing wrong, but those thugs outside your door threatened her just because she is from Spain. And I know for a fact José Martí does not condone that sort of thing."

He didn't respond to me, however, to one of the firemen, the captain said, "Lock the back door and do not open it until we leave in the engine." He instructed another, "Rig the team and turn the engine around. We're going out the back to the alley."

After that he turned back to me, his tone still dubious. "Mr. Wake, the Fire Department will give you a ride down the alley behind us to the Pedroso house, and if Ruperto agrees to let you enter his home, then we'll leave you there. Otherwise, we will take you to the police station."

I heard pounding on the back door. A fireman yelled for them to go home and sleep it off.

The captain handed me a heavy coat. "You all will wear a coat and helmet." He paused, frowning at Maria's yellow and white dress and jacket. "That is the best I can do as far as making you look like one of us. Now get on the back of the engine."

The engine wagon had been turned around and faced the rear door of the main barn room. Sensing action, the pair of gray horses was snorting and pawing the floor. One of the firemen looked askance at us, then questioningly at his captain.

Puglisi told him, "Consider this a drill run. These people will ride on the back."

We three climbed up onto the back platform behind the steam pump engine and held on to the handgrips. Captain Puglisi climbed up in front beside the driver and calmly said to a firemen near the double barn doors, "Open up!"

In a flash, the brass bell of the engine began clanging, the doors were flung open, the horses leaped to their work, and we were lurching out of the brightly lit station and turning right into the dark alley. The three of us hung on for dear life as the wagon leaned over in the turn, then straightened into a westbound course.

Three young men near the back door stood there silently as we galloped past them. My final glimpse showed them walking toward the front of the station.

Seconds later we were hurtling past the Teatro Ybor and approaching the end of the alley, where it met Thirteenth Street. The driver swung the entire rig into a hard right turn and screeching stop in front of the house where I'd tried to get someone to answer the door twelve hours before.

Inside the house, every window showed light with human shadows. Several men were seated on the porch, more standing in the yard. In each group red dots pulsated as cigar smoke and serious toned discussions filled the air. Other men by the street stood with arms akimbo, obviously on guard duty. The three-quarter moon overpowered the racing clouds to show me that all the men at the house watched our arrival with concern. This was a serious place, and I had no doubt that many were armed as well as Rork and I.

Captain Puglisi jumped down and spoke to the men in Spanish while pointing at me. His Spanish had an Italian flavor to it, as his name would imply. "Any of you know a Mr. Peter Wake? He is the one on the left there, in the back of the wagon. Does he have permission to see Señor Martí?"

A chorus of "No's" came back from yard and porch. Puglisi cast me an I-warned-you look as he climbed back aboard. Rork grimaced and glanced at me for guidance. I had no bright ideas right then, but Maria, who had been quiet for some time, tried to help.

Presumably to hide her *Madrileo* accent, she spoke in English to the men surrounding us. "Gentlemen, Peter is an old friend of Señor Martí from Washington and New York."

Her attempt lost a lot of its validity because of our ridiculous appearance, especially hers. She seemed to suddenly realize that and unburdened herself of the heavy fireman's coat and helmet, then repeated herself, this time in her Castilian Spanish. This got attention—she was the only woman in view—but no action. The standoff remained for several awkward seconds more.

Just as Puglisi told his driver to head for the police station, the front door of the house opened and a man stood there, silhouetted against the light inside. His spectacles glinted in the reflection as he emerged. Without a word he quickly crossed the porch and stood in the yard, staring at us with incredulity.

I had to laugh. We did present quite a sight. It was Mario Cano.

Rork and I took off our firemen coats and helmets and I said, "Mario, would you please explain to Captain Puglisi here that I am welcome at this home and with Martí?"

"This is a most incongruous turn of events, indeed. Why are you all firemen tonight, Peter?"

"It's a long, stupid story, Mario. Just tell the captain our names and I am a legitimate friend."

To Puglisi he said, "They are Mr. Peter Wake and Mr. Sean Rork and Doña Maria Maura y Abad. All three are friends of mine, and the two gentlemen are longtime friends of José Martí. They are all very welcome here, Captain. Thank you for bringing them. I will let Señor Martí know of your kind assistance."

Puglisi evidently knew Cano—which surprised me and indicated the lawyer was far closer to Martí and the Ybor community than I had known—for the captain immediately changed his attitude and helped us down off the wagon, smiling the whole time.

Cano shook our hands heartily and bade us come inside and relax, saying José Martí would be free to see us soon.

53

Drinking with an Apostle

Ybor City, Florida
Late Friday evening
16 December 1892

Inside the tiny parlor, we met the owners of the house. Paulina Pedroso was a short, dignified black woman in her late forties with a no-nonsense manner who was clearly in charge of the scene and everyone within it. In that respect, she reminded me very much of my mother. Ruperto was an older black man who looked us over in silent scrutiny. He invited us to sit on the tattered divan, a tight fit for the three of us, and brought coffee once we did so. The room had three other men in dark suits sitting there on well-used bent-cane chairs, none of whom spoke or were introduced. They sat there staring at us, particularly Maria, as we sat there gazing at each other.

I wanted to ask Maria why on the world she had attended the speech, but that was not the time nor place. Since Cano had disappeared somewhere out of the room, there was nothing to say or do but sit there, with the absurd sensation in my mind of waiting to see the headmaster. I could not see or hear Martí, and presumed him to be upstairs, an appropriate location both literally and figuratively.

We sat in the increasingly stuffy room for fifteen long minutes. I noted the time was 11:40 p.m. when Cano reappeared and invited us up to see the great man himself, whom I heard several in the house refer to as "the apostle." I thought that a bit much.

Our disengagement from the divan was less than graceful, with Rork thunking his weapon-laden sea bag around and me accidently snagged on Maria's voluminous dress, but we made it, ascending the narrow stairs in a solemn pilgrimage to the mount. Cano excused himself and exited the front door, saying he would return shortly.

When we reached the room at the top of the stairwell, Martí stood up from a crude desk. Fourteen years younger than me at thirty-nine, he seemed far older than his age. With his hairline receding ever more, his eyes bloodshot, and his movements slowed, he presented an image of a tired grandfather at the end of his work day: the red tie undone, the coat draped over the chair, both shirt sleeves rolled up, soon to be slumbering in bed. I knew the reality was different, however, for Martí was renowned for his determination to finish his tasks even when sick or exhausted. He would be "on duty" for at least another two hours and up again by six o'clock in the morning.

In spite of all that, he was nonetheless in a very good frame of mind. Greeting me with an *abrazo*—the Cuban version of a bear hug—his face split into a big silly grin, that enormous mustache of his accentuating his delight.

Holding my shoulders in his hands, Martí used his nickname for me. "My Neptune is here at last! It has been far too long, Peter."

"Neptune?" inquired Maria in a whisper.

With a laugh, he explained, "Well, madam, if Abraham Lincoln could have Gideon Welles be his Neptune, then I insist upon having Peter Wake be mine!"

Martí then hugged Rork. "And the Gaelic Titan, too! My cup truly runneth over. How are you, my friend?"

Rork has never been shy, especially when thirsty. "Ooh, boyo, since you asked, listenin' to all your talkin' made me throat dry as a bone, José."

"Well, I cannot let that wretched condition continue, can I?" He called down the stairs, "Paulina! *Una copa de buen ron, por favor!*"

I introduced Maria. "José, this is Doña Maria Ana Maura y Abad, of Spain. She is an admirer of your efforts and wanted to meet you. Maria, this is José Julián Martí Pérez, the writer, teacher, and patriot."

Martí could be very charming when the moment called for it, and he rose to the occasion. Turning to Maria, he smiled and took her hand, lightly kissing it. Apparently for my benefit, he spoke to her in his fluent English. "I am enchanted, madam. Mario said there was a beautiful woman from Spain with Peter, but I now find that description to be a sadly misleading understatement. I recall seeing you at my little speech tonight. Thank you for listening to my simple ideas with such kind attention."

After decades of diplomatic soirees, Maria was rather quick-witted herself. She favored us with the angelic version of her smile and turned those deep blue eyes on my Cuban friend. "Thank *you*, Señor Martí, for expressing them so wonderfully. As for me, I was merely one of the many people who were entranced by your brilliant oration."

"Your modesty becomes you, madam. You are, without the slightest doubt, the loveliest daughter Spain has in the New World, and I am very fortunate to have the honor and pleasure of meeting you. Thank you so much for coming to visit me this evening, for your radiance has brightened my life and given me added vivacity. Please be assured our humble home and myself are completely at your service."

He led the way into another, smaller room, where chairs had been set up around a table. Gesturing to the table, he suggested to Rork, "Perhaps you and Doña Maria will enjoy your refreshments here while Peter and I adjourn for a moment. I promise it will not be longer than that," he looked at Maria, "for I would be a fool to deprive myself of such wonderful company."

Rork grunted his agreement and Maria made a little curtsy. Paulina arrived with a glass of rum for Rork, a stemmed glass of red wine for Maria, and a plate of sliced pineapple and banana.

When Martí and I were seated in swivel chairs at his desk in the first room, his face hardened. Charm time was over, for he had serious things to discuss.

"Thank you for coming, Peter. I know I have imposed upon your schedule. First, let me say thank you for your warnings about Orden Público's intentions to poison me, rendered in quadruplicate, no less. I received them today from Mario, courtesy of you getting him to Tampa; from my brother Masons, because of your informing their local lodge of the situation; from Don Vicente Ybor's office, due to you alerting them; and from your personal note."

He shrugged, with a slyly cocked eyebrow. "As you can see, my friend, I am untouched and well. After your warnings, I have eaten only food and drink which Paulina has personally prepared. On a brighter note, my events recently have brought in a considerable amount of donations for the cause. And now, will it be rum or wine for you?"

"José, as far as the warnings are concerned, I owe you several times over for helping me, and saving *my* life, in Cuba. As far as a drink, I'm getting older and less resilient, and will be taking the ship to sea later, so no rum. A glass of wine would do well, thank you."

The reader will note I didn't tell Martí the entire story of my huge waste of time and effort by initially assuming the Germans were killing the Mayan rebel leader; how I realized the plot was actually to kill Martí; how close he'd come to not getting a warning and dying; or about my official, albeit confidential, assignment to get warning to him. In the business of secret information, one never tells *all* one knows.

"Ah, then a Bordeaux to celebrate," said Martí, an aficionado of French cuisine and wine. Paulina was asked to bring a bottle up and went off. He returned to our discussion.

"There is something else I wish to speak about, Peter. A very important matter."

"What is it?"

"The new presidential administration here, which will take office in March. Grover Cleveland has strong views about maintaining U.S. neutrality in the Cuban situation. Since this will be his second term, admittedly with an interruption of four years, he knows how to wield power and implement his policies from the start. Therefore, the next four years will be a different environment for Cuban independence."

He was being circumspect, so I cut to the chase. "President Harrison and the Republicans are supporters of your cause, but in four months they will be out of executive power, and until then he is a lame duck president. I know President-elect Cleveland. He wants to avoid any kind of war with anyone. You are worried your movement's building up of arms, supplies, and men will be affected by that attitude, because the Florida coast may be patrolled by naval and revenue vessels and neutrality strictly enforced. Correct?"

He sighed. "Yes. We are not ready yet to liberate our island by force of arms. Our previous attempts have shown the folly of half measures. But our momentum is gaining, and when we are ready, we will need to strike quickly and with coordination. Everything depends upon our armies getting what they need."

Paulina padded quietly into the room and poured the bottle of Bordeaux. There was only enough for our two glasses and she informed him it was all in her possession.

A fleeting look of disappointment showed on his face. He told Paulina in Spanish, "Then please bring us the bottle of Vin Mariani." She hurried off.

Vin Mariani, a Bordeaux infused with the extract from coca leaves, was not only Martí's favorite late nightcap, it was the choice of many famous people, from Queen Victoria to Pope Pius to my friend Thomas Edison, who once told me it helped him stay awake and work longer hours. Cocaine is popular in drinks these days, but not for me, and I prefer my wine unadulterated. I kept my opinion to myself, though, as Martí continued, "Is there any legal method, precedent, or ploy you know of that would enable us to continue our sending of supplies to Cuba?"

"No, none within the existing laws and regulations. In fact, there are laws specifically against running guns and rebels out of our country into another. And Congress is in no hurry to change them because Cleveland won the election pretty convincingly."

He nodded grudgingly and was about to say something when an embarrassed Paulina returned without a bottle, explaining they had none. The last bottle went to Ocala with him and they couldn't find it. She said not to worry though, for she had ordered more and it was on its way. Seeing her anxiety, Martí kissed her cheek and thanked her.

He watched her depart and softly said to me, "She is such a dear, my black mother. I dislike being such a bother to her and Ruperto. They work so hard in the cigar factory. And now, Peter, I think we should rejoin our other friends."

We took our wine into the other room and sat down at the table, joined by Mario Cano. Soon a general conversation in English about books and plays and music had consumed our attention. Martí was at his charismatic best, utterly captivating Maria. Sean and I laughed uproariously at his acerbic depictions of New York's grand littérateurs and thespians, including himself.

Maria enjoyed herself immensely, using Martí's public sobriquet in a whisper to me, "Oh Peter, here I am laughing and drinking with the apostle of freedom. Amazing!"

Our glasses were empty when Paulina returned yet again, this time with a bottle of the Vin Mariani. She poured for everyone and in the spirit of the moment I did not demur. I would have one polite sip.

Martí, happier than I'd seen him in years, abruptly stopped in mid-sentence and suggested with raised finger, "*Carpe diem, my friends!* We must toast my young friend and fellow seeker of justice, Dr. Mario Cano. Mario, may you and dear Useppa know health, wealth, and happiness, and all the time to enjoy them . . ."

In his enthusiasm, he drank his Vin Mariani before the rest of us even raised our glasses. We were in the midst of doing just that when Martí's eyes grew wide in fright.

"Stop—do not drink it!" he blurted out, gasping for air to get out, "*Poison!*"

Then he clasped his throat, doubled over, and began choking to death.

54

Discipline in the Face of Evil

Ybor City, Florida
Midnight Friday
16 December 1892

The instantaneous transition from complete joy to abject horror stunned the rest of us at the table, but in a flash my training and instinct took over.

"Get a doctor!" I ordered Maria, who dashed down the stairs.

Rork already had his Navy Colt .44 in the good right hand and the marlinspike exposed on his left stump. I said, "Check the street from the window and cover the door to this room."

To my future son-in-law I said, "Mario, help me with his collar and tie."

Cano and I ripped Martí's collar away. It became clear to me his choking was not due to an obstruction, he was gagging due to the ingestion of the poison.

His voice was hoarse and weak. "They did it . . ."

The initial shock was over and he was no longer choking, but he was still doubled over, clutching his stomach. There wasn't anything I could do.

"The doctor is on the way," I said. "You'll make it through this, José."

Martí grasped my arm, his fingers digging into my flesh, as he forced out his next words, "No one must know! If I live, no one must know of this. Do you understand?"

He was so close I smelled the garlic on his breath. His face was contorted and those famous eyes bored into me. There was only one answer I could make.

"I understand, José. I will tell no one outside of this house."

Ruperto and Cano carried Martí to a bed along the wall, where he lay on his side, groaning with the pain and saying nothing. Paulina ordered everyone out and we trooped down the stairs as Ruperto, a revolver in his hand stood on the first step of the stairs and glared at everyone.

The parlor was packed with distraught and angry people, a dangerous situation for us. By then, Rork had returned his Colt inside his jacket, but kept his hand near it. I did likewise, for I did not know these men, one of whom might be a spy or assassin of Roldan's, or might think *we* were. Cano did know several and tried to calm them, to no avail. He motioned for us to follow him out to the porch.

One of the men outside was admonishing the others to stay silent and tell no one what had happened, that discipline was needed for the apostle had ordered it so. None argued. All remained nervous. Several kept glancing at Maria, Rork, and I— strangers to them and the last to be with Martí. They were not friendly glances.

A moment later a distinguished gentleman carrying a large valise strode through the porch, having been passed through by the outer guards. Cano recognized him and told me he was Dr. Miguel Barbarossa, Martí's friend and local physician who cared

311

for the leader when he visited the Tampa area.

Rork nodded his head away from the others and walked toward the side of the house, his gray sea bag showing white in the half-moonlight. He had a grim look when I met him there.

"How the hell did Roldan do it?" he asked, slowly shaking his head in contemplation. "Our friend's request for the coca wine was last minute. It couldn't have been anticipated an' set up ahead o' time."

I'd been cogitating on that very issue. "The only thing I can come up with is Roldan guessed Martí probably would send for more Vin Mariani because he had none with him, and because he usually has a little every night after dinner, especially when he has a lot of writing work to do."

"Or one o' these fellows standin' around here is an informant for Roldan and Marrón, an' told 'em Martí'd run out," he growled as his head swiveled around to scan the area. "An' how is it they ran out o' the stuff in the first place? Or did that bottle just up an' disappear in Ocala? Aye, any damn thing is possible with these tricky Orden Público bastards, sir, an' methinks we best keep a sharp lookout now for ourselves, as well as poor José."

He was right. "Agreed, Rork. And remember this—these men don't trust *us*, either. To them, we're the interlopers, so let's take care not to give offense or feed their suspicions."

We returned to where Maria and Cano were speaking in Spanish about Martí's writing. I was surprised and pleased to hear she had read quite a lot of it.

Half an hour later, Cano was summoned to the bedroom. He returned afterward with a detailed report of the state of affairs thus far, which Martí had authorized him to share with us.

Dr. Barbarossa had quickly determined from smelling the Vin Mariani that a large amount of arsenic had been mixed with it. He was in possession of the bottle and would conduct something called a Hahnemann test later at his office to confirm that opinion. Martí had consumed half a small glass before

realizing something was wrong, which the doctor considered
a moderate amount and probably survivable, though with a
lengthy and painful recuperation period, estimated to be at least
five weeks.

The doctor had immediately given his patient a blend of
ipecacuanha and opium to induce the regurgitation of the
poison, which had produced much of it, but not all. His overall
condition was weak, his pressure elevated, his breathing regular.
Pain from stomach cramps and severe headache was being
addressed with opium.

Cano reported something else—the two men who had
delivered the poisoned wine to the house were Cubans, one black
and the other white. A covert search by the few in the know had
begun, but the two men had fled the area. Since tempers were
well past the boiling point, the assassins' lives would be forfeit
upon apprehension. Martí had specifically ordered against killing
them, but Cano doubted whether the command would be
adhered to when the time came.

As far as Roldan and his men were concerned, no one had
seen them. A telephone call to Tampa revealed the *Reina Regente*
had slipped away in the night, well before the end of Martí's
speech. That, of course, was her legal right, the quarantine
prohibition only applying to transportation with the shore.

Concerned foremost about the effect on his years of work
to unify and strengthen the Cuban cause, Martí had strongly
reiterated he did not want word of the poisoning to get out to
the public and press. If there were inquiries, the story told would
simply be a case of indigestion had inconvenienced the man.
Nothing more.

Cano chuckled softly as he explained the cover story
was Martí's idea. It was pretty smart, the lawyer concluded,
because technically it wasn't really a lie. Martí certainly was
inconvenienced by something he'd ingested.

Finally, Cano said that Martí wanted me to come up to his

room for a moment. The doctor had consented, but limited my time to one minute.

Every eye in the house followed me as I reentered and made my way up the stairwell. Their unspoken thoughts showed clearly on their faces: exactly who is this unknown Anglo who suddenly appears the night our leader is poisoned, and then is granted special admittance when we are not? And who are the Spanish woman and Irish giant with him?

Dr. Barbarossa tapped his pocket watch and held up one finger when I arrived in the room. Paulina sat next to her adopted son, caressing his forehead with a damp towel. She rose and gestured for me to sit in her chair. I nodded my submission to the doctor's orders and sat down. The bed was stained and stank of vomit. Martí lay there unclothed, only a light sheet covering him.

He looked worse than before, his normally thin face even more drawn as he grimaced when the spasms erupted within him. He held out a hand and I took it. I did not speak, for he was trying to say something.

He pulled me nearer in desperation. I leaned in until my ear was at his mouth.

"Not . . . your . . . fault . . . Peter. You . . . tried. Thank . . . you."

I didn't know what to say or do, but he wasn't done. There was something else.

"Disci . . . pline . . . important . . . now. *Evil . . . can . . . not . . . be . . . allowed . . . to . . . win.*"

I felt the doctor's hand on my shoulder as tears filled my eyes. The slightly built man before me was not some bemedaled leader of feared warriors, but he had accomplished more with his pen and his voice than all the triumphant soldiers who had come before him in the fight for Cuban independence. Since his sixteenth year, Martí's lonely life had been lived for one purpose—true freedom for his people, and by extension, for all

314

the downtrodden of the world.

There was only one thing I knew to say to help alleviate my friend's misery.

"Cuba *will* be free, José. And you and I will be there to see it."

He squeezed my hand and smiled.

Then he let go.

55

Bloodlust

Ybor City, Florida
Saturday morning
17 December 1892

Rork's snoring penetrated my unconsciousness just as the sun's first ray came through the window. We had gotten the last available room in Cano's Las Nuevitas Hotel at 1:15 in the morning. I laid down a few minutes later, but four and a half hours wasn't enough sleep for me, for the intense emotions of the preceding days—especially what happened six hours earlier—had drained utterly me of any vigor.

Since Wednesday I'd had only a few fitful periods of sleep, snatched here and there, when my mind and body required far more. Laying there in the bed, with sunrise announcing another day and yet more ordeals, I had to admit my limitations, if only to myself. The inevitable process of aging had caught up. That fact was indisputable.

The evening hadn't ended according to plan, except that our Masonic friend did arrive promptly at 1 a.m. as promised.

He immediately sensed the atmospheric change in our behavior and became wary but, honoring Martí's wishes, I did not share the terrible information with his fraternity brother. Rather, I hurriedly requested that he deliver Maria back to the Tampa Bay Hotel. I did not tell him why Rork and I would stay in Ybor.

We needed to be close to the action. This decision was not made lightly, for it meant *Bennington* would be getting under way for Key West much later, with a much tighter chance of making it on time for the gunnery qualifications. Nevertheless, I felt compelled to make the gamble, and the potential costs weighed heavily on my mind.

Besides transporting Maria, the Mason was given two messages to deliver. The first was to be taken to the wharf at Port Tampa and hence by *Bennington's* boat out to the ship.

> *Lt. Commander Warfield,*
>   *1 a.m., Saturday, 17 December 1892*
> *Everyone safe but problems have arisen. Need to stay ashore at Las Nuevitas Hotel in Ybor City tonight. Will return to ship midafternoon. Cable explanation to Key West is being sent when office opens later in morn.*
> *Wake*

The other was a cable to Admiral Walker. It took me a moment to compose, having to do so in plain language because I had no code book with me to hide my highly sensitive information.

> XX—DELAYD HERE—X—RIVAL SEMI SUCCESSFUL—X—FRND STILL HERE—X—SPN CZR GONE—X—SITREP LATER—XX

After the Mason departed to take Maria to her hotel and deliver the messages, Rork, Cano, and I walked south a block to the Nuevitas Hotel.

By the time I was fully awake Saturday morning, the sun had ascended high enough to fully flood the room with light. Sleeping late was an indulgence I could ill afford. There were things to be done. So, with a grunt and a groan, I made myself get out of the bed. Standing by the window, I called over to Rork's bed with a time-honored salty phrase I thought might infiltrate his enviable dormancy. "Shake a leg, you slimy old son of a gun. Time for all hands to get under way."

It worked. He grumbled something uncomplimentary, rolled out of bed as if it was a hammock, and even before waking completely, began installing his left-hand appliance right away. This was a three-part operation, starting with the leather stump cover, then the marlinspike, then the India-rubber false hand. Rork normally didn't sleep with his false apparatus on, his arm stump needing a rest from the strain of carrying the thing. Reattaching it was the initial task of his day, before anything else, including realizing where in the world he was.

I once asked him why he did this. His answer was a lamentable illustration of his lifestyle. "Ooh, well, 'tis simple, really. You see, boyo, when wakin' in a strange bed, me mind just never knows if the first person in me sight'll be a happy lady or her irate husband."

We cleaned up, stopped by Cano's room to get him, and all went down for breakfast. The events of the night before made the meal a quiet one, for each of us was weighed down by the enormity of what had happened to our friend Martí. But I had another issue to discuss, one far more uplifting.

My intention had been to tell Rork of my secret engagement to Maria when we were traveling from the hotel back to the ship the previous afternoon but, as the reader can fully understand by this point in my chronicle, more important things intervened and dominated our time. The present moment, however tardy, I judged to be the right time to tell both men. Through Mario Cano, my daughter Useppa would also be notified. Of course, she and my son Sean would receive detailed letters from me later.

My friends' reaction was far better than I expected, especially considering previous discussion between Rork and me. With Irish drama, he pledged his undying friendship to Maria, then gaily declared, "An' now she'll be me sister!"

Cano suggested we have a double wedding for the couples, saying he was certain it was what Useppa would want.

Rork wasn't done, though. He launched into planning the wedding celebration, which he decided should be on Patricio Island, and paid particular attention to the libation and musical components. Useppa would be aghast at his proposals, but her fiancé was amused. "Capital idea, Rork. What about accommodations on your island? Useppa says it's small."

Before Rork went any further and had wedding guests living in tents at Patricio, I nipped the whole fantasy in the bud. You had to do that with him, or before you knew it, things would be out of control and take on a life on their own, usually costing me money and annoyance.

"No double wedding, Mario. It should be *her* special day and Useppa deserves a proper wedding at the Methodist church in Key West, shared with no other couple. And no big party for Maria and me, Rork. Our wedding will be a small affair, at a location of her choice, with you as my best man—without a lot of hoopla or a big party. We're too old for that sort of thing."

It dampened their enthusiasm, and after a brief discussion recapping the Martí situation, we adjourned to walk the short distance to the Pedrosos' home.

There was still a crowd around the house. A man passed our way coming from the house and I inquired about the latest news. Contrary to the policy of keeping the poisoning confidential, he confirmed to us Martí was still expected to live.

As we passed the alleyway near the theater, the same backstreet we had sped along on the fire engine, I spotted a distraught, average-looking fellow also heading for the house. Tears streamed down his reddened contorted face and his gait was hesitant. A continuous mumbling came from him. I assumed he was a Martí devotee who had heard the news and come to offer help.

With such a countenance on his part and assumption on my part, one can well imagine my surprise when we all got closer to the house and one of the hangers-on pointed to the fellow and shouted, "*¡El asesino! El hombre blanco que entregó el vino venenoso. ¡Captúralo!*"

My Spanish was good enough to understand the meaning: *The assassin! The white one who delivered the poison wine. Capture him!*

Someone else yelled, "*¡Matarlo ahora!*" I knew the phrase from when it was used against me in Peru a decade earlier: *Kill him now!*

I happened to be closest to the man and grabbed his right arm. Jerking it around and behind, I forced him to bend over, precluding any resistance. Rork brushed Cano out of the way and seized the left arm. Our efforts weren't needed, though, for the man didn't resist at all as we headed for the house. He only continued his mumbling, which I now could make out to be repeated apologies in Spanish for what he had done.

Cano's legal mindset came to the front and he took over, trying to interview the assassin for the details of his name and home, involvement in the crime, and location of his black partner. But the man continued blubbering, as if he was catatonically unaware of the tumult around him or questions posed to him.

The commotion had built considerably since the first shouts. Within seconds, there were twenty or thirty enraged men around us, trying to elbow their way to the assassin. Several had pistols, one had a rope. Their faces were inflamed by bloodlust, making them almost demented in appearance. There were no more frantic shouts. The crowd had become more sinister, snarling deep-pitched demands for instantaneous vengeance.

It was at this rather dicey juncture that our prisoner broke his monotone mantra and made a bizarre request—he wanted to apologize to Martí personally.

Cano was the quickest to respond. He told Rork and me to walk the man to the front porch. He told the surrounding vigilantes none of them would touch the prisoner because he would inform Martí of the situation. Their leader would decide the issue. The invocation of that magic name was a smart move, for no Cuban dared to contradict or obstruct Martí, and the men parted to let us by.

Accordingly, Rork and I deposited our charge into a chair in the parlor and stood guard over him. Cano and Ruperto Pedroso had cleared most of the entourage out of the parlor, so we had some room to breathe and maneuver. Another trusted man was put at the front door to keep out the swelling mob.

Ruperto, still guarding entry to the stairwell, was the most crazed of them all. His pistol was held in the open as he glared at the prisoner and fidgeted to the point where I feared it would go off accidently. Quite reluctantly, I moved to stand in front of the prisoner, hoping my presence might calm Ruperto down a bit by removing his target from sight. It didn't work. Martí's surrogate father figure still kept the pistol aimed at a spot on the floor six feet in front of me, his maniacal gaze going right through me to the target behind.

Cano had left Rork and me alone to face this standoff, for he was upstairs explaining the matter to Martí—academic to academic, so to speak. After what seemed like a very long time, he returned and told me the doctor said Martí had a good chance to recover, if he rested. Then Cano calmly told Ruperto that Rork and I were bringing the man upstairs, and Ruperto was to remain at his guard post—all this being the wishes of Martí.

With Rork's help, I gingerly steered the prisoner around Ruperto and his revolver, and started up the stairs, Cano preceding us. At the entrance of the bedroom, Dr. Barbarossa shook his head in protest, but waved us through.

The scene had changed. Martí was still in bed, but now was clothed and had clean sheets. Flowers scented the air. Bottles of water, wine, and gin were arranged on a nearby table, along with an assortment of medical vials, ampules, and powder boxes.

The great man himself still looked to be on death's doorstep. He raised a weak arm and beckoned me over. His voice was yet hoarse, but a bit stronger. And the dry wit was still strong. "My dear Neptune . . . I see . . . you have been . . . fishing on the street. What did you . . . catch?"

"This one jumped in my hands, José. He wants to apologize and appears sincere."

He smiled. "You have always been a . . . good judge of . . . character, Peter. And now, I will ask . . . everyone to leave me . . . alone . . . with this man. He and I need to . . . talk, privately."

"What if I am wrong, José? I was terribly wrong before. How about if I remain?"

Paulina arrived in the room with a damp towel for Martí's forehead. She refused to look anywhere near the assassin. Her patient said thank you and bade her return downstairs. Then he repeated his statement to me, this time making it an order, and saying he wanted the door closed too.

No one argued.

56

The Curious Redemption
of Honor

Ybor City, Florida
Saturday morning
17 December 1892

Outside the door, we strained to listen through the wood.
I could hear the assassin's tearful apologies at first, then
Martí asking his reasoning for doing the deed. Infuriatingly, after
that the conversation became muted. We eavesdroppers were
joined by Ruperto, who had fortunately jammed the revolver
into his belt, his temper still barely held in check as he placed his
ear to the door.

Below, the parlor filled again. Ominous grumbling emanated
upward, making me even more nervous. Rork and I were in an
impossible position, tactically, if things went the way I feared
they might. The assassin's safety was expendable, as far as I was
concerned. I was worried about *us*, since we were the only Anglos

in sight, and had been the killer's escorts. In my experience, crazed mobs seldom listen to logic.

An hour went by, with ever-heightening tension. The crowd below grew louder in their debate, which centered on not if, but when, the assassin was released to their clutches, and the best method of execution for the perpetrator. I heard no one counsel a legal remedy through the courts. No police had been called yet in this whole affair, and it appeared to me they never would be. I could tell Cano, himself a foreigner in a *yanqui* land, was worried as well.

By my pocket watch, the door opened one hour and twenty-two minutes after we'd let the assassin have a private interview with his victim. Martí himself stood there, holding up a hand to stop the rush into the room of men wanting to carry out the wish of every Cuban in the house.

"Do not harm this man," Martí raspingly commanded us in Spanish, looking directly at Ruperto and Paulina. "He has made amends. He is now one of us, a brother Cuban, who has pledged to fight for our cause of liberty. This man will be there helping to lead the forces of freedom, when we rise up in the island for our independence. Let no one, Cuban or North American, doubt him or harass him in any way. The validity of our cause is at stake."

Martí reached out for me and I took his hand. His sunken eyes were sad, pleading. With a frail voice, he spoke to me in English, "Peter, I must ask you a great favor. Please see this man is given safe passage away from Ybor City and Tampa. Get him to Key West. Once there, your responsibility will end. I have given him the name of a man there he can trust to get him to Cuba."

He was running out of steam quickly, but he had more. "I have told him . . . to keep his . . . previous name unknown, for his life has . . . started anew. If somehow you do discover his . . . name, it is . . . crucial . . . you do not . . . reveal it to anyone. More . . . than most, Peter, you . . . understand the . . . necessity

. . . for this. I trust you. Will . . . you . . . do this . . . for me?"

There was no time to discuss the finer points of his request, or the consequences of saying yes, or how the hell I would actually accomplish the job. When news of the door opening was learned down below, the stairwell promptly jammed with men, every one of them vocally demanding to lay a hand on the prisoner. None of them heard Martí's conciliatory words.

"Yes, José," I answered. "I will take him with me."

His shoulders slumped as if all the air left his body. "Ah . . . then I . . . can . . . rest easier . . . now. Thank you . . . my friend."

"The worm deserves death," someone said from below, an opinion endorsed by several others. The mob pushed higher on the stairs.

"No!" shouted Martí, startling me. Using his last degree of stamina to make his words heard, the great orator told the men in the stairwell, "For me, this man's honor is redeemed! He deserves the . . . opportunity to prove himself . . . worthy of our cause. Yes, he was weak . . . and made . . . a bad error. Who among you . . . have not made . . . an error, by omission . . . or by commission? Who among . . . you . . . is . . . perfect?"

Dr. Barbarossa, his face red with anger, ended the argument. "Just do what our country's leader says and stop aggravating his condition!"

The doctor took Martí by the arm back inside the room to his bed. The assassin stood in the middle of the room, his face a study in misery. I walked in and asked him if he spoke English, to which he replied yes.

To Cano and Rork, I murmured, "Mario, please clear the way out of the house for us. Rork and I will escort this man out. When we get on the street, get the first wagon you can and we'll use it to get out of Ybor City."

Both nodded curtly and Cano started down the stairs, ordering the men to clear a way. I brought my Merwin-Hulbert "skull-crusher" revolver out into plain sight and Rork did the same with his 10-gauge pump shotgun, retrieved from the sea bag still slung on his shoulder. With me ahead of the pardoned man and Rork astern, we pushed our way down to the parlor and out to the street.

The day was getting surprisingly warm. Dust from the dry sandy street floated in the air. Cano met us in the middle of the street, saying in exasperation there were no wagons or carriages in sight, and he couldn't get anyone to bring us one. The mob had spread out on our flanks by then, but stayed several paces away, discouraged by Rork's leveled shotgun and grimly set jaw. Cano admitted to being at a loss for an idea of how to escape with our charge. The man in question just stood there, saying and doing nothing, staring listlessly at the ground, waiting to be killed.

Not anticipating any of these developments, much less Martí's request, I didn't have a plan either. I went down the list. Señor Ybor himself was a moot point, for his secretary told us the day before that Don Vicente was leaving town after Martí's speech. The Masonic lodge had no telephone, so I couldn't call our friend there. The Pedrosos had no telephone either, so I couldn't call out for a carriage from Tampa.

Our continuing inaction was noticed by the vigilantes, who began sneering at us. Then came the jeering, with references to "*los gringos.*"

"An' what would be our orders, sir?" inquired Rork in a deliberately nonchalant way, not wanting to show indecision or concern in front of our adversaries.

Then it hit me. I *did* have an acquaintance in Ybor—just the kind of man who could get people out of town efficiently and quietly.

"Follow me, men," I muttered and started walking east on Eighth Avenue.

They stayed close as we quick marched down the avenue a block to where Fourteenth crossed it. With crossed fingers, I entered the same saloon we'd chased Roldan's binocular man into.

And there he was, my new best friend in Ybor City.

"Ah, the navy man with the missing sailor! I have something

for you, *amigo*," said Manuel Saurez, El Gallego, the king of *bolita,* with an evil sort of laugh. He was sitting at the same table with the same men, this time including the bartender. They chuckled too. Everyone stopped laughing, however, when they saw Rork walk through the door with a shotgun.

I held up a hand for patience from the *bolita* gangsters, then turned to Rork, pointed to the front doors, and made a twisting motion. He locked them. Afterward, he stood menacingly examining each man at the table of cutthroats.

All of them slowly moved their hands onto the table and kept them in plain sight. El Gallego's face went from sly mirth to concern. "I have your winning's, *amigo.* No need for guns."

Ignoring him, I walked to the bar, put a glass under the tap, and pulled a beer, then drained it down in one long draught. I pulled another, then four more. Putting them on a tray, I took them to the table and put a ten-dollar gold piece with them.

El Gallego and his cohorts still weren't sure of what was going on. There was pounding outside on the front doors, but no one at the table moved.

With a smile, I said, "El Gallego, I apologize for my rude entry, but there are some men outside who are less than friendly. I am sure you have been in similar situations and can understand. Please, keep my winnings, and this ten-dollar coin, as a token of my appreciation for allowing us to rest for a minute. I also have a request, one I am sure you have the ability to make happen. But first, may I propose a toast?"

More pounding on the door, but El Gallego and his cutthroats never took their shrewd eyes off me, raising their glasses cautiously as I offered, "To free enterprise!"

After the toast was drunk, I made my request. "I want you, El Gallego, to arrange immediate passage for my three friends and I out of Ybor City to a place about ten miles from here. You will go with us. For this favor, I will pay you the rest of the money in my pocket, twenty-two dollars in gold pieces."

He made no reply, but the sly smile returned.

Mine, however, disappeared. "El Gallego, you know this is an easy request to fulfill and the payment is more than fair. But I must tell you this—if I get even an idea something is wrong, my men will kill you. Do you understand my English exactly?"

El Gallego's calculating expression never altered as he quietly replied, "Yes, I understand you and will do the deal. There is a box wagon behind the *taverna*. Let us go now, before your enemies in front become smart enough to come in through the back door."

El Gallego was a good teamster and backed the box wagon right up to the rear door just as the vigilantes rounded the corner. As we pulled away, they invaded the bar.

Inside, the wagon was partially filled with ladies' goods, but there was enough room for us, and equally important, an opening port in the front wall, which allowed me keep an eye on our less-than-trustworthy driver. I made sure he saw my .44 in the porthole, and off we went, with him driving and me navigating. Behind us, the mob had returned outside, They milled about perplexed, not wanting to take on the notorious El Gallego but clearly wondering about the timing of the wagon's departure.

As we crossed the Lafayette Street bridge en route to Port Tampa, I made a change in itinerary. Once on the west side of the river, I told El Gallego to turn right and enter the drive for the Tampa Bay Hotel.

There was one more important thing for me to do before leaving Tampa.

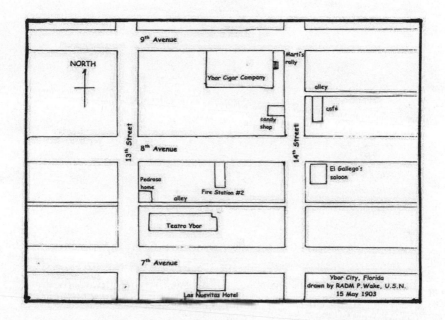

9th Avenue

NORTH

13th Street

Ybor Cigar Company

Marti's rally

alley

café

candy shop

8th Avenue

14th Street

Pedrosa home

alley

Fire Station #2

El Gallego's saloon

Teatro Ybor

7th Avenue

Las Nuevitas Hotel

Ybor City, Florida
drawn by RADM P. Wake, U.S.N.
15 May 1903

57

A Service to Humanity

Tampa, Florida
Saturday morning
17 December 1892

I dashed through the verandah and into the lobby, which was swarming with guests, for the train to Port Tampa and the Plant Line steamer was leaving in twenty minutes from the train siding on the west side of the hotel. Piles of trunks, portmanteaus, and suitcases were everywhere, with harried porters straining to load everything onto carts.

I found her at another doorway to the verandah. She was in my arms in an instant and I felt the strain evaporate away. People stared disapprovingly at this most unseemly behavior, but neither of us cared.

In the carriage park nearby, the three men inside the box wagon emerged to stretch their legs and she saw them. Waving to Rork and Cano, she asked me who the third man was. I told her he was a friend of Martí, who was recovering better from the poisoning. Then I got to the heart of the matter. "Maria, I have only time to ask you this: please stay in Key West for a week, before going on to your friends in Havana. The squadron will be done with our exercises by Wednesday and I'll have a night off before we head north to Pensacola. I want you to meet my daughter, and I think my son will be in port too, so we can have a nice pre-Christmas dinner together. It's important to me. Will you?"

I loved it when her eyes sparkled. She kissed me again and said, "Of course, my love. I would be delighted to meet Useppa and Sean. I'll stay at the Victoria."

With what willpower I had left, I pulled away. "Thank you, darling. I'll see you in Key West in a week. But we both have to go now."

She blew me a kiss. We parted ways, and she became lost in the crowd.

My euphoria ended when I suddenly sensed danger nearby. Stopping to turn around, it wasn't hard to discern the source.

Norton Gardiner, in dress whites again, was five feet away, scowling at me. Beside him, an elderly Negro porter wearily stood at attention carrying two suitcases and valise in one arm and several paper bags in the other. I wondered if there was a train leaving that morning for the north.

Gardiner's tone matched his face. "I can't believe a lady of quality sees anything in an imposter like you, Wake. I thought she was much better than that and preferred the company of gentlemen."

I immediately felt an overwhelming urge to bludgeon him and end his ability to speak forever, as a service to humanity. Maybe break his legs as well, as a bonus.

Instead, I just stated, "Nice to see you're still consistent in your idiocy, Norton. It makes it so much easier to predict your underachieving behavior. They like sycophants up there, so I imagine an officer like you will do very well during your visit to naval headquarters."

"Well enough to end *your* career."

"I don't have time or patience for you anymore, Norton. I hope your train north leaves soon."

That was when Commander Norton Gardiner, U.S.N., of Beacon Hill, Boston, descendent of the *Mayflower* and scion of wealth and influence, made his big mistake—at ten-thirty-two a.m., on Saturday, the seventeenth day of December, 1892.

"Wake, you pathetic fool, I'm not riding in a cramped stuffy train up north. I'm going by Plant steamer to Key West, then by Ward Line to Philadelphia—*first* class the entire route, I might add. And on the way to Key West, I'll show the Spanish lady what a *true* gentleman is."

That did it. It was time. Someday, the world would thank me.

"I'm going to hit you now, Norton. Just wanted to give you warning, like a *true* gentleman would . . ."

And like a gentleman, I did as promised. It was an uppercut to the wonderful point at the bottom of the chin that ensures the most damage for the effort.

Of course, I did not use a fist. That is the best way to break one's knuckles. No, I used the heel of my opened hand, which resulted in a very satisfying *thwack* sound, and the equally gratifying sight of Gardiner's head snapping backward farther than it was designed to do. The beautifully laid parquet floor provided yet another blow—to the back of his head—when he landed.

Well, as can be imagined, the crowd rapidly thinned out in Gardiner's vicinity, with the attendant female screams and male harrumphs. My target lay there, trying to figure out what happened, as a stain spread on his starched white trousers.

As an alternative to placing my boot on his right knee cap and completing my fantasy, I took the moral high road and merely walked away.

The porter, stalwart man that he was, never moved a

muscle during all this, but maintained custody of Commander Gardiner's baggage unharmed. While exiting the scene, though, I was pleased to see the old fellow flash me a wink and a grin.

Interestingly, not a person in the hotel tried to stop my egress. Evidently Norton Gardiner had worked his magic on everyone there too.

Back in the wagon, Rork gave me a quizzical look.

"Trouble, sir?"

"Not in the least, Rork. Merely doing my bit for humanity."

He knew something was up, but he also knew not to ask any further. I decided the tale was one best told someday at Patricio Island, over some decent rum at sunset.

With no further hindrances, we arrived at Port Tampa's boat landing at long last. I was glad to see my coxswain there to greet us, and even gladder to hear the welcome news that the gig was ready to shove off, the ship had steam up, and all was ready to weigh anchor.

Turning to our driver, I pulled my pocket inside-out and handed over two ten-dollar pieces and two one-dollar coins. El Gallego examined them swiftly, put them in his pocket, and climbed back up to the driver's seat.

"By the way, señor, precisely how much did I win in the *bolita* last night?" I asked.

He called over his shoulder with that wicked laugh of his, "Fifty dollars, señor. You were a very lucky sailor last night, and I am a very lucky wagon driver today!"

"Luck o' the Irish. Never fails . . ." muttered Rork.

Half an hour later, Cano and "Pablo," as I decided to call him—after the Biblical story of Saul's redemptive transformation into Paul—were in a junior officers' cabin. What Pablo's future would hold was beyond my prognosticative abilities, but I was sure of Mario Cano's future, and proud to have him as my son-in-law.

The work of a ship trumps everything else, and so it was

then. Rork was on the foredeck with his men handling the anchor chain as it clanked up from the mud, and I was on *Bennington*'s bridge with Warfield. Ahead of us beckoned the clean air of the sea.

It felt good to be home.

58

A Reunion with Love

Hotel Duval dining room
Key West, Florida
Wednesday evening
21 December 1892

My son, Ensign Sean Wake, Naval Academy Class of 1890,
had been recently assigned as assistant navigator to the
U.S.S. *Yantic,* an ancient, small, fourth-rate cruiser, really a
gunboat, commanded by a good man, Lt. Commander Samuel
Belden. *Yantic* was part of the squadron, cruising off Puerto
Rico and the Danish Virgins on hydrographic duties, when she
returned to Key West for the gunnery qualifications.

Overall, the squadron scored averagely, with *Bennington*
and *Essex* a bit higher. *Atlanta*, whose main guns were having
problems, scored a bit lower. The admiral was not pleased, for he
wanted the highest scores in the fleet. Still, he granted captains
permission to give liberty ashore to those in the crew deserving
such.

Yantic's captain included my son Sean in the liberty ashore, but I did not include his namesake for liberty from *Bennington*. Rork fully understood. He had been ashore far too much and needed to repair his rapport among the petty officers. For myself, I only allowed two hours.

And so it was my children and I met for dinner for the first time in many years, with the added pleasure of our future spouses. Sitting at the head of the table in my whites—Maria loved to see me in them—I memorized the scene.

Maria, in a light blue dress that brought out her eyes, was to my right. Beside her, in his whites, was Sean. To my left was Useppa in a gay pink number, with Mario beside her in a gray suit.

Both young men got along well, as if, as the old saying goes, they were brothers of different mothers. Sean's laughing camaraderie with Mario built over the evening, but his captivation by Maria's charm was instantaneous. He listened with rapt attention as she told the story of her family's history, of her marriage and her son's life in Spain. Her story of her widowhood garnered his sympathetic nod, and Maria's humorous account of my ineptness during our first encounter got him laughing out loud.

That left the toughest nut to crack—Useppa. What would she think of me marrying a well-to-do woman of the world, who was also Roman Catholic, of Jewish heritage?

What gave me hope for a positive reaction was something I'd recognized when seeing Useppa in Key West the night I met Mario. It was a subtle change in demeanor and tone, visible in her eyes also. With all that was swirling in my mind at the time, I couldn't put my finger on it. Now, however, I realized what it was, for I shared the sentiment. It was, in fact, profoundly simple: Useppa was finally *content*. And with that peace in her heart—something sadly elusive since her mother died of cancer eleven years earlier, and her first fiancé had been killed five years after that—came enough confidence to be tolerant of her father's foibles, and his new fiancée's dissimilarity from her mother Linda.

The encounter started out slowly, the two women gauging each other first through sartorial inspection, then by evaluating social skills and poise, then conversational ability. This was not done with overt maliciousness or even veiled sarcasm, such as men employ.

Quite the contrary, it was done with the greatest observance of the expected public graces, with not a glance or word out of line or sharply tinged. Yet, with my life experience I could see the merciless intuition of the female sex at work, for nothing escaped notice.

The issue seemed to me to be still unsettled when the topic of weddings came up. The month was decided easily. It would be early May—five months hence. Concerning the ceremonies themselves, Maria agreed with me about us having a small ceremony, done by a Methodist circuit pastor, perhaps at Patricio Island. But we both said Useppa and Mario deserved a real church wedding at her church in Key West. The youngsters adamantly insisted on a double wedding in Useppa's church.

The impasse appeared irreconcilable until Maria and Useppa returned to the table from visiting the ladies' necessary room. I noted laughter between them as they approached. Then the two ladies stood before the gentlemen and together announced the double-wedding idea was completely worked out and we should listen carefully.

The ladies would be each other's bridesmaids, with Sean Wake serving as the best man for Mario and Sean Rork as best man for me. The ceremony would be held at six o'clock in the evening of Thursday, May fourth, at the Methodist church on Eaton Street. The reception would be held right there at the Duval Hotel, and yes, there would be libations and music.

After the reception, Maria and I would board the small overnight schooner northbound for Punta Gorda and a honeymoon at Patricio Island. Useppa and Mario would depart by sea in the opposite direction, for their honeymoon in Cuba.

Maria then addressed a topic we had already decided between

us, but might still be sensitive to others. She was Catholic, yes. But she had no qualms about being married in a Methodist church, for we were all Christians, whatever building we were in. She was absolutely sure Jesus would be pleased by our marriage, and He counted more than any mortal clergyman.

When they were finished, my two favorite ladies embraced. The sight of their affection was everything I hoped for. My past and my future were right there in front of me, and long-suppressed emotions welled up in my heart.

Thirty years earlier, Useppa's mother and I met on that very island of Key West, amid the tragedy of war. A year later we were married there. Not in a church, for we were shunned by each other's cultures, but on a deserted beach by a slave cemetery. Linda and I overcame that beginning, in spite of the odds. Now I was about to begin another.

Useppa wasn't the only one who felt content.

59

That None Must Know

Delmonico's
214 Fifth Avenue at 26th Street
Madison Square
New York City
Thursday evening
2 March 1893

Mostly, I've respected President Grover Cleveland. Occasionally I've disliked him.

My vote for his opponents in both elections wasn't due to him being crooked, lazy, incompetent, or personally reprehensible. Quite the contrary, by all accounts and by my own personal observations, having been with him professionally several times in my capacity as a senior ONI officer, the man was straight-arrow honest, hard-working, very intelligent, and genuinely charming.

My differences with him centered on foreign policy and national defense, and his lamentable ignorance about them. That sort of ignorance in a citizen is expected and can be excused. In a president, it is tragic, for it gets men in uniform killed needlessly. This wasn't an academic observation on my part, and I carried the wounds to prove it. I shouldn't have expected more, really, for Cleveland hadn't traveled overseas and had never served in the military, even when those around him were. In fact, he was one of the few who bought a surrogate to stand in for him when he was drafted during the War Between the States. Twenty years later he was president of the United States and I was honor bound as a naval officer to obey him.

Now he was back from his four-year hiatus from the highest executive office in the land. He had won election to the presidency again, the first former president to do so. And I had to have dinner with him in New York City, two days before his inauguration in Washington.

A week earlier, *Bennington* came alongside at Brooklyn Naval Yard for a much-needed refit after a two-month assignment to the Mediterranean. That same day, I received an engraved invitation to the dinner. To a serving naval officer, it equated to a command. Why did he want *me*? There were plenty of sycophants lined up who wanted an opportunity to curry favor with the incoming commander in chief. It made me nervous.

Because it was a formal affair in March in New York City, I was in dress blues, complete with bangles and baubles, as the saying goes. My fiancée Maria was not with me, but in Spain, visiting her family. I entered Delmonico's first-floor dining room, where the merely rich gathered, and ascended the stairs to the second-floor private salons, where only the truly exclusive relaxed over dinner and drinks and decided matters of state and commerce.

Ironically, it was in the same mahogany-paneled dining room I first met one of Grover Cleveland's political nemeses, young Theodore Roosevelt, on a frigid January evening in 1886. Initially, I thought Roosevelt, then twenty-seven, a stark raving mad politico, but then I recognized that he was merely passionate about his beliefs, albeit eccentric in his demeanor.

Once I knew him, I actually found him to be hilarious, compassionate, and greatly concerned about the country and her people—all of them, including those marginalized by the social elite. Thus, a deep friendship began with that odd fellow who went on to huge challenges and big things. The bond has lasted to this day.

At the door to the private room, I said my hello to Delmonico's famous French chef, Charles Ranhofer, who gushed as if I was a long-lost friend, but in fact didn't know me from Adam. He did the same with those behind me. My first impression on entering the sanctum sanctorum was of being the sole man in uniform at the room, which contained thirty sophisticated gentlemen of commerce and government. My uneasiness mounted.

Deciding some liquid courage was needed about then, I repaired to the busy bar, where everyone knew everyone else except me. While busy trying to impress each other by ordering and sipping bizarre concoctions, they discussed with great gravitas just how they would use the upcoming administration for the benefit of their bailiwicks.

Something called a Manhattan Cocktail sounded good to me, for it had bourbon, but the head barman sagely shook his head. He was an older Hungarian immigrant, sporting a large moustache and a dry wit. Delmonico Rum Punch was the only thing for me, he suggested, no doubt because of my profession. Explaining it was a secret house specialty, but he knew by my eyes I could be trusted me with such crucial matters of culture, he proceeded to divulge the recipe as he blended the ingredients.

I recall the deliciously deadly brew to this day: two parts St. Croix rum, one part Jamaican rum, three parts pure water, a large lump of sugar, a gill of lemon juice, and a wedge of pineapple, delivered to the restaurant by special iced hold in a fast ship from the Caribbean. I will fully admit it did wonders for my outlook on the evening.

Dinner was announced shortly afterward and all us

swells headed to find our places. The reader can picture my astonishment when I discovered—after fruitlessly wandering at the far ends of the U-shaped table—my lowly name near the head of the left perpendicular, to the right of and only six places from the president-elect himself.

One look at the menu made me heartily wish Maria had been there to help me navigate through the cuisine, for it was even more ornate than my sole previous experience there. That dinner had been of all-American fare, this one was pure French. But alas, like that other gathering, no ladies were present at this one.

Though my tablemates did not deign to converse directly with me, I can report that I maintained my dignity throughout the various courses outlined in the menu, which I kept to show Maria: the Potages, Hors d'oeuvre, Poisson, Relevé, Entrée, Rôt, Froid, and finally, the Entremets de Douceur.

At nine o'clock, I noted gratefully it was time for the *Pièce de Résistance* and an end to the entire farce. Ranhofer himself escorted the dessert to the table, presenting it with Gallic flourishes to the man of honor. "Peach Pudding à la Cleveland!" he proclaimed, describing it as twenty of the finest hand-chosen Georgia peaches fileted into strips, then macerated in powdered sugar and topped with a Madeira sauce.

All in all, the evening was quite the show of decadence. Whoever paid the bill got set back a lot of money. But it was money wasted on me, for I can honestly say, from the beginning course to the "Peaches Cleveland," it all tasted terrible.

As this miserable evening concluded, I finally learned why I was attending. President-elect Cleveland nodded to me and gestured to an alcove. I met him there.

He was even bigger now than he had been when last in the presidency, which meant he had become unhealthily enormous. I wondered how bad his ailments were, and how long this bloated fifty-five-year-old politician would live.

"Good of you to come, Commander Wake," he said. "It's

been a while, and I hope all is well with you."

"I am well, sir. Thank you for the invitation to the dinner."

His face went deadpan. "Yes, well, sorry about the dinner, Wake. I didn't like it either. You what my favorite is? Pickled herring, Swiss cheese, and a chop—with a cold lager or two—over at Louis's place. I can't stand this French stuff."

The president-elect cast an expectant look at me. His culinary preference sounded pretty bad to me too. I wasn't sure what to say, so I gave the standard naval response in these scenarios. "Yes, sir. What is it I can do for you, sir?"

Cleveland belly laughed at my discomfort and deferential change of topic.

"I *like* you, Wake. By God, you're man who can get smack dab into trouble, and then get right back out!"

His face abruptly lost its mirth. In a low voice, he said, "Now to the reason you're here. I want your opinion on the Hawaiian issue."

Ah, so that was it. Cleveland was remembering my 1889 mission to stop a war between Germany and America in the Pacific—which *he* sent me on to save his legacy for another run in four years. Did he also remember the toll in Samoa, to me and hundreds of others?

Hawaii was an adjunct part of the mission then, but was now a hot topic in the national press and political circles. Everyone wanted to know what the new president would do about the place that was about to become our first colony.

Perhaps the rum punch helped, but I suffered no lack of words or passion on the matter. "Rescind the recognition of the rebel government and the U.S. protectorate over the islands, sir. It was against American law, against Hawaiian law, and our navy responded to fraudulent calls for assistance. The white planter and banker elite who staged that coup against Queen Liliuokalani in Honolulu three months ago don't have any support among the real Hawaiians. And why do we need colonies anywhere? They're just a drain of money and manpower and breed resentment toward us by the natives, which only gets worse with time."

I was about to give a recitation of the costs in blood and treasure of maintaining far-flung colonies to the British, French, Spanish, and Dutch empires but, remembering who he was and who I was, I paused to let the president-elect speak.

"My thoughts exactly, Wake. I remembered you knew the Hawaiian royals and situation there, and I wanted your thoughts. I'm thinking of sending Jim Blount from Congress on a fact-finding mission over there to get to the bottom of it and report back to me."

Cleveland lightened the tone. "Now, as for you and the navy, I have some big plans. Hilary Herbert is going to be secretary of the navy and keep the modernizing of our fleet going in the right direction. From all those years in the House Naval Affairs Committee, he knows his stuff, and I think he'll be able to help greatly."

Blount was a Georgia congressman and Herbert was an Alabama congressman—both could be powerful allies or adversaries to a president. I didn't trust either one, but then again, I didn't trust anyone who worked within a block of the Capitol Mall.

"Yes, sir," I said, still wondering why the hell I was there. It surely wasn't for my opinion on Hawaii.

Cleveland's aide came over and whispered something to him. He wasn't pleased, but nodded and waved the man away. "Humph! I've got to go, Wake. Some important people want to start telling me what to do. Well, anyway, I want let you know I'll be asking Herbert to send you to Washington on April third. I have something for you that has been far too long in coming. By the way, it's important to me that none must know what we just discussed. See you in April."

With that Grover Cleveland was gone. I still had no clue of why I'd been there.

60

By Order of the President

Executive Mansion
Washington, D.C.
Monday evening
3 April 1893

"Once again," Rear Admiral Walker had growled when giving Rork and me orders to report to Washington in three days, "you two misfits are in some sort of hot water with the powers that be at Naval Headquarters. Get there by noon on the third of April and do not be late. And this time, I can't help you. You must've really done it, because this has gone way above my pay grade. Evidently, you'll have to explain yourselves to the commander in chief himself."

"What's the reason, sir?" I asked with trepidation.

"They didn't tell me, but with you it's never good. Maybe Norton Gardiner finally did you in when so many others failed—you've given him plenty of ammunition to use. Of course, it could be the list of German complaints, too. The possibilities are always endless with you two."

He had a point. Both Gardiner and the Germans were pretty upset with me.

Gardiner's threatened retribution came in the form of a formal complaint against me, filed with the Bureau of Navigation, the operations branch at Naval Headquarters. The main charges consisted of Assault and Battery, Dereliction of Duty, Failure to Follow Naval Regulations, and Conduct Unbecoming a Commissioned Officer. Other lesser violations were appended.

This information didn't get to me for some time, because Gardiner didn't make the charges for quite a while. He was otherwise occupied, mutely convalescing at the Washington Naval Hospital from a "parasymphyseal fracture of the mandible," according to the report. In mid-February 1893, Gardiner was released and made his charges against me.

In consequence of this delay, the billet at his hometown Boston Navy Yard was filled by another officer. Because he couldn't go to sea in his condition, and because no captain wanted him, Gardiner had to take a billet left open, at Mare Island Naval Station in California, the administrative assistant to the executive officer. He reported for duty in early March and that had been the last news of him I'd heard.

What happened to the charges, I knew not, and never inquired. Sadly, in the bureaucratic labyrinths of the U.S. Navy, forms disappear due to accidental misfiling by our overworked and underappreciated yeomen all the time. Unless someone persists in tracking down such errant documents, they can be lost forever. Apparently, Gardiner had shown no such persistence, busy as he was out west.

The German matter started to unfold rather ominously. With enviable efficiency, Captain Blau's complaints reached Berlin by cablegram three days from his arrival in Mobile, where he found no German émigrés willing to register for the Kaiser's army back in the Fatherland. Within a week after that, the State Department in Washington was trying to figure out what to do with Berlin's indignant demands for my dismissal, the German Navy's reimbursement, and a public formal apology by the United States of America. He alleged I had stolen their coal and violated international law and naval honor by invoking *Force Majeure* under false pretexts during the man overboard episode. My defense to Walker was that they got their coal for free at Key West, and my officer really did fall overboard, with witnesses to prove it.

He wasn't impressed, saying, "That's the best you can come up with? You're slipping, Wake."

I admit this all sounds pretty bad, especially the international law and personal honor violation, but it seems the U.S. Navy isn't the only department in Washington with inertia lubricated by incompetence. Thank goodness.

My acquaintances within the minion class at the State Department—which coincidentally resides in the same building as the Navy Department and my old office at ONI—reported to me in January an impressively large file had been prepared for the usual detailed review up the chain of diplomatic command. A very thorough piece of work it was, too, including a standardized assessment of the validity of the foreigners' claims, potential legal recourses and remuneration costs, potential lingering liability issues, and a detailed timeline of making decisions on the entire matter.

This enormous effort, one of dozens simultaneously engaged in by our country's diplomatic folks, naturally took a long period to create, assemble, organize, and present. That explains its lateness in completion, which effectively negated the included timeline for making a decision. This development necessitated a revision of the assessment and timeline, with the attendant re-ascension up the chain of command. Thus, by mid-March, as Norton Gardiner was reporting in to his new job, nobody at the State Department was sure of exactly what was in the huge file valise lying atop the cabinet in the corner, how long it had been there, or when it would have a decision made on it, for now a new problem arrived. The senior people in the chain of command had changed with the arrival of a new administration. That necessitated another . . . well, I am sure the reader knows the rest by now.

Obviously, a little of Captain Blau's Teutonic efficiency is needed at the State Department. But far be it from me to criticize hard-working federal employees.

A definitely more important factor was the shift of Germany's attention away from poor Captain Blau's humiliation to momentous events unfolding in Europe. The Slavic Russians had joined with the Gallic French to encircle Kaiser Wilhelm and his vaunted Prussian army. Not only that, but the British were proving to be less than helpful friends to Germany. I sincerely promise none of this was any of my doing.

Old Otto von Bismarck, Europe's master at the diplomatic intrigue game, would never have let it get that bad, but rash young Kaiser Wilhelm had dismissed Bismarck two years prior, convinced he knew better. So the problems of a navy sea captain off the coast of Mexico paled in comparison to the very real problems Germany faced—those two allied colossi on her borders, both of which had ample resources and reasons to crush her.

So, though I wasn't too worried about Gardiner or the Germans, Rork and I were still anxiously ignorant as the presidential butler solemnly took us down the hall and announced us. With a deep breath and crease-straightening final self-inspections, we entered and stood at attention in the president's private study.

There were only two men there, President Cleveland and Secretary of the Navy Hilary Herbert, both sitting in leather chairs by the paper-cluttered desk. Herbert was a slow-talking Alabamian with a receding hairline, deceptively sensitive eyes, and a fluffy chin beard. His grandfatherly image belied his political acumen in naval affairs.

Cleveland greeted us formally, as did Herbert.

Then the president said, "Commander Wake and Bosun Rork, I have been meaning to get something done with you two for some time now, and that time has at last arrived. Secretary Herbert, will you please do the honors?"

"A privilege, sir!" answered Herbert as he rose from his chair with a shallow box and long document in hand. Rork and I still stood at attention, for we had not been given permission to do otherwise.

Herbert's drawl was even more pronounced as he read the document aloud. "Let all men know that, by order of the President of the United States of America, in recognition of three decades of faithful and perilous service to the country, the rank of captain, with all its privileges and respects, is hereby conferred upon Commander Peter Wake, of the United States Navy. "Done this third day of April, in the year of our Lord eighteen-hundred ninety-three, in the one-hundred-nineteenth year of our country, by Hilary Abner Herbert, Secretary of the Navy of the United States."

The president ponderously rose from his chair and shook my hand.

"Congratulations, Peter. I told you years ago you would get this because you had earned it."

With the silver eagles of a full captain in his other hand, he turned to my friend and said, "Bosun Rork, would you please affix these insignia upon Captain Wake's collar?"

"Aye, aye, sir!" snapped Rork, unsuccessfully trying to suppress a grin.

"The collar, not his throat, Rork. I don't want the captain bleeding on my new carpet," joked the president.

When Rork was done, the president grinned and said, "And now, Mr. Secretary, you have yet another duty to perform, do you not?"

"I do indeed, sir! A true honor. And a new one in the history of our country!"

He glanced at Rork, then began to read the second document.

"By the authority invested in my office of Secretary of the Navy of the United States, I hereby designate and promote Boatswain's Mate Sean Aloysius Rork, United States Navy, to the rank of Chief Petty Officer. Done this third day of April, in the year of our Lord eighteen-hundred ninety-three, in the one-hundred nineteenth year of our country, by Hilary Abner Herbert, Secretary of the Navy of the United States."

The president pumped Rork's hand. "Congratulations, Sean. This new rank just began two days ago. You are the fourth to receive it in the navy, and the first to receive it in this great house!"

To me, Cleveland said, "Captain Wake, would you please present Chief Petty Officer Rork his new insignia?"

"Aye, aye, sir!"

Rork stood tall and straight, but I couldn't stop the tears from filling my eyes.

The week prior, we'd discussed the navy's new rank, which Rork noted was implemented on April Fool's Day, but my friend didn't think he'd be promoted to it.

"Me bones're too bloomin' old," he grumbled. "The younger lads'll get it."

Herbert had another surprise.

"You're too senior for *Bennington,* now, Captain Wake, so it's back to Washington for you after your annual leave is up in May. I need a special assignment aide, and you are the man to do the job. Rork here can be your assistant."

The president added, "And I want you both close by me for your advice. So I'll see you again in mid-May, ready for work."

He headed for the door, then stopped and looked back at me.

"By the way, Captain Wake, I read the German complaint about you, as well as your rebuttal." He frowned before continuing. "That's the best you could come up with? Your excuses were always more entertaining in the old days . . .

"And someday, I'd like to meet that young officer who

accidently fell overboard, Lambert. But now, I have to depart, gentlemen. Again, congratulations."

61

Tears of Love

First Methodist Episcopalian Church
714 Eaton Street
Key West, Florida
6 p.m., Thursday
4 May 1893

The church was filled to capacity by the entire congregation, all of whom knew and loved Useppa, for she had attended there and lived in the parsonage for many years. In addition, there were the black students and faculty of the Douglass School, where Useppa taught; a large contingent of Cano's family from Havana, led by the matriarch, his charming mother; and several navy acquaintances in white. Resplendent in medals, gold braid, and that intimidating beard, was the commander of the North Atlantic Squadron himself, Rear Admiral John Grimes Walker.

There was even a sprinkling of Rork's pals from the seedier establishments in the town, including the venerable Annie Wenz, primly attired and ignoring the verbal and visual daggers aimed her way by the lady congregants. She probably knew most of

their husbands better than they. Annie was squired by Brian
Travis, former Union army officer and the only member of
the Yard Dogs troubadour band out of jail at the time. I noted
they were seated at the back pew by the door, just in case a fast
getaway was needed.

Next to them was a special guest, whom the wedding party
was overjoyed to greet before the ceremony. José Martí looked
and sounded pretty well recovered from his close call. He was
already in Key West for a meeting about an unauthorized
uprising in Holguín, Cuba, which had failed terribly with the
loss of many lives—the very thing he had warned against.

A musical prelude announced Useppa's arrival at the narthex
of the church and I hurried to meet her there. I had been
repeatedly reminding myself not to fall apart with sentiment in
this emotionally charged moment, but to do my ancient and
solemn duty. Then I saw her and nearly lost my composure.

Useppa was an absolute vision, truly the prettiest girl in the
world.

Gowned in simple white satin with tiny pink wildflowers
in her auburn hair, her grace made the ensemble look elegant.
Taking her arm and putting my hand over hers, I led my beloved
daughter down the aisle to her husband and her future life. The
limp of her left leg, crippled since youth, wasn't even noticeable
as we serenely strolled by the smiling faces.

Next in the procession came Maria, lovely in light blue satin,
escorted by my tense son Sean, trying not to march in his whites.
I had last seen my bride-to-be in February, when *Bennington*
put in at Málaga, Spain, and then only for an evening. The three
months since were an eternity.

The pastor, a large young fellow with a boyish face and easy
smile, did a good job of it, making the invocations of prayers,
the pledging of vows, and exchange of rings a joyous affair, as
opposed to the menacing lectures so many clerics feel compelled
to use. My proper naval stoicism was maintained right up until
the moment when I gave my daughter away.

That's when my heart, filled with memories and joy, nearly overcame me. With faltering voice, I made the proper reply and stepped away to stand at parade rest on the side, next to Rork, who was sniffling too.

He put his hand on my shoulder and whispered, "Oh boyo, our wee little girl's grown up just fine. Aye, Peter, dear Linda would be right proud o' her."

I'd been thinking the same thing, and tears of love flowed down my cheeks.

Other than my blubbering, all went well. My son Sean was Mario's best man and had the ring ready, as did Useppa's dear friend Christine on the other side, and the deed was done without mishap or mayhem. When the pastor pronounced them husband and wife, Mario didn't hold back on the kiss, good man that he is, which gave the crowd a jolly laugh. Then the pastor introduced the beaming couple to the attendees as "Dr. and Mrs. Cano," and the applause was absolutely, wonderfully, thunderous.

Once the ovation faded to an end, it was time for Maria and me to tie the knot. We took the center spots, Rork beside me and Useppa beside Maria. The pastor read the words and asked the questions, and throughout it all I could see Maria was experiencing what I was—a kaleidoscope of past memories and future dreams.

We quietly made our replies and exchanged rings. Looking into each other's life-worn eyes as we made our vows, we both knew exactly what they meant. And we also knew there were two people in heaven who were with us in spirit and wanted us to be happy and at peace.

Then I took Maria into my arms and gave a proper demonstration of how a veteran naval officer kisses his bride. Our married introduction to the guests resulted in an approbation nearly equaling that for the youngsters, which made Maria blush with pride as she clung to my arm.

When the clapping slowed to a stop, Rork's booming voice

filled the sanctuary. "Ladies an' gents! Everyone is now invited to refreshments an' music over at the Duval Hotel. All hands, dismissed!"

The party was quite a shindig. A Cuban duo played love ballads, Rork's brother denizens of the Goat Locker served as barmen, and Useppa's girlfriends served at a seafood and fruit buffet. I was pleased to see the teetotalers studiously ignoring the drinkers, and the drinkers kindly refraining from doing anything too boisterous.

Everyone danced, drank, and sang, even the Methodists—well, most of them. Martí, accompanied by Mario's mother, got up and showed his dancing skills with the classical Cuban *contradanza,* several of the Key Westers played songs with the band, and the hours went by in a flash.

Finally, it came time for the newlyweds to leave and catch their respective ships. With much hoopla and many good wishes the two couples departed under a tunnel of crossed swords, including the admiral's and my son's, and made our way north on Duval Street the three blocks to the steamer wharf. The evening was perfect for a romantic stroll under the moon, with jasmine and gardenia scenting the warm breezes, and honeymoons ahead of us. Ensign Wake bid us a touching goodbye and made his way to the officers' landing, several wharves away. I was so proud of him.

At Tift's Wharf, the *Olivette* was beginning to board for her run to Havana. Useppa and Mario's baggage was already piled on the wharf with the other passengers' belongings, courtesy of her friend the pastor. All that remained was for them to embark. Maria and I would embark on the schooner to Punta Gorda in an hour. Rork, who was still at the party, probably with Annie, was heading for our island also and would meet us aboard.

As we were embracing each other in farewell, my eye caught something that shocked me out of my euphoria. It was Roldan's surveillance man from Ybor City. He was on the main deck at the railing, nodding to an accomplice forward along the deck, who then swung his gaze our way. Then I saw two men in the line of passengers on the wharf eyeing us generally, but focusing on Mario. A chill went through me as I realized I'd seen one of them hours earlier—at our wedding.

"Mario," I said quietly as I grasped his wrist, "do not react openly, but Roldan's men are aboard the steamer and all around us. They're watching us, particularly you."

Both ladies heard me and stopped their conversation in midsentence. Mario was stunned as well, and asked, "Why us, why now?"

"I don't know and it doesn't matter. Do not get on that ship. You'll come to Patricio Island with us. Leave your baggage here, we can go to the Plant Line office and have it delivered to our steamer. Understand?"

He was still stunned. "They are just watching. Really, what could they do to us on a U.S. ship, Peter?"

He wasn't in the know about Drake, or many others Colonel Isidro Marrón's henchmen had killed in the United States.

"Mario, they can and will kill you, like they tried with Martí. Why? Because you are a friend of Martí and it would disrupt his organization. At the very least, you and your wife are kidnapping or blackmail targets. You and your wife are not safe on that ship or in Key West right now, and certainly not in Cuba. Stay at Patricio Island for a while and we can gauge the situation then."

"He's right, Mario," said Useppa. "Listen to him."

"All right, then we go with you. How do you propose getting away from here undetected?"

"Disguise and diversion," I answered. "Everyone follow my lead."

I was the only one on the wharf in navy whites, which were even more prominent in the moonlight, so I ducked down and removed my coat, replacing it with a long black jacket lying conveniently on a passenger's nearby portmanteau. My trousers were still snow white, but it was better than nothing.

Mario smoked cigars, so I asked him for a match. Once that

was in hand, I directed the three of them to slowly move toward the edge of the milling crowd.

I headed to the opposite side. Hidden by one of the support beams of the elevated coal tramway from Tift's coal depot, I searched for something easily combustible and found it. Extracting a ream of Plant Line stationery from a supply crate to be loaded aboard, I took it to the far side of the wharf and lit it. The wind was from the southeast, so I wasn't worried--any tray embers would carry out over the water. Before long, a small but visible pillar of flame and smoke grew and I waited for it to garner attention and alarm.

It didn't take long, for after the great fire of 1886, Key West was very alert for the first sign of trouble. Shouts were followed by alarm bells. Soon the attention of everyone on the wharf and the ship was on that spot. Men began running to help. Within a minute, the clanging of the approaching fire brigade could be heard in the distance.

Meanwhile, the four of us sauntered off into the shadows by Phibrick's ice house. While the others waited, I switched coats again and entered the Plant Line office. There, puffed up in my bemedaled uniform, I informed the manager a family emergency had forced a change in travel plans for the Canos. Their fare was to be refunded and their baggage taken to Lowe's dock Immediately. My imperious manner and a five-dollar coin convinced him to accede.

Back in the shadows again, I made my third costume change, back to the black coat, and soon we were traversing the back alleys to Lowe's schooner dock at the end of Greene Street. I saw no sign of anyone stalking us, and concluded our ruse to elude the Orden Público had worked.

We went right onboard the *Josee* and waited at the transom as her hold was filled and main deck piled with cargo. None of my companions spoke, each lost in contemplation of the sudden change from happiness to terror. Guilt filled me now, for this was all because of my espionage work, which had reached its tentacles even into this special day of joy.

The crew got ready to warp her out from the dock and there was still no Rork, or the baggage. Various scenarios went through my mind but kept returning to one: to wreak revenge on me, the Orden Público had gotten him, either kidnapped or killed.

In a thick Dutch accent, the captain, a no-nonsense sort, notified us the schooner was leaving in ten minutes, with or without the lost bosun and baggage, for the tide waited for no man. Five minutes before the deadline, the baggage arrived and was stowed on deck. Then the deadline came, and as the lines were being cast off and my fear was reaching panic, Rork staggered aboard, said hello, and passed out on the foredeck.

We sailed right past the still-loading *Olivette* and steered north, into the Gulf of Mexico, each couple huddled quietly under the stars.

62

The Honeymoon

Patricio Island, Florida
5 to 12 May 1893

We arrived the next afternoon, bone tired. Old Tom Moore greeted us at the dock. He had the place in better shape than Whidden ever had, a validation of my decision to employ him as the new caretaker. After the previous night's hardship, the sunny ambiance of the islands helped to alleviate our worries as everyone trudged up the hill to the two bungalows at the top.

Mario and Useppa were in Rork's bungalow and he was staying in the caretaker's cottage at the north end of the island. Maria and I were finally alone in my—now *our*—bungalow. I was greatly relieved to see her enchanted by the island and our home, and knew then my other, greater fears about melding our lives were unfounded.

Our true wedding night was that first night at Patricio Island. It was as if there was a touch of Divine help to overcome the traumatic stress of the evening before. A cool easterly breeze sailed through the gumbo limbo trees around the bungalow, the moon streamed through the window to bathe the bedroom with a magical silvered light, and the scent of gardenias and jasmine perfumed the air. It was a perfect scene for romance.

Maria's poignant question, "When will this madness end, so we can live in peace?" had but one true answer, even in that idyllic setting.

"It ends when they think we aren't a threat anymore."

Recognition of this stark fact would be too much for most men or women to cope with, and I was thankful it did not demoralize her. To the contrary, it seemed to steel Maria's determination not to let others, no matter who or where, ruin our love. And once resolved, we were free to get on with life.

The next week at Patricio Island, so long a place devoid of feminine sounds and sights, was the most delightful since Rork and I brought the place ten years earlier. Days were filled with fishing action in the bay, relaxing sails among mangrove islets, and glorious sea bathing on the Gulf beaches of Lacosta Island. Evenings were spent on the verandah, eating freshly caught seafood, telling outrageous sea stories, listening to Old Tom singing his gospel songs, Rork sounding the conch shell at sunset, drinking Cuban rum and French wine, and gazing up at the glittering stars until the amber moonrise over Pine Island captured our gaze.

It was a time of love and laughter, for the cares of the world outside of the islands seemed unable to penetrate our refuge. Gradually shyness faded and contentment reigned as idiosyncrasies only learned by marriage were accepted and embraced.

On the final morning of our joint honeymoon on the island, the youngsters told everyone at breakfast they had an important announcement. The sun glinted off his spectacles as Mario cleared his throat and stood to emphasize his point. "We were discussing our rather unique situation last night. After weighing all factors, we are not going to Cuba. I have decided to become an American citizen, and to practice law here in Florida. As a bridge between the two cultures, I believe I can do good work for the Cuban exiles here, and also for the cause of freedom back on the island. Tampa is a growing city, so that is where we will live and raise our family."

"An excellent idea!" I exclaimed, without adding that it removed a huge weight from my heart, for Maria and I had been terribly worried about the two of them living in Cuba. The incident at the Key West wharf had been a warning to the wise.

Maria put a hand to her heart in joy, rising to embrace them both. Rork slapped Mario on the shoulder in delight. "Good decision, lad."

Useppa came over and sat in my lap and kissed my cheek, Just like she did when a little girl. What she said next, I have cherished ever since. "Daddy, I've never been happier than right now. You and mother were the best parents anyone could ask for. Thank you for all you've done for me. And for *our* children, Mario and I want to be parents just like you and mother."

"Well said, Useppa," murmured Rork.

Maria saw that I was overcome, unable to utter a word in reply. She tenderly held my hand. "I am so proud to be your wife, Peter Wake. Thank you for asking me. I love you."

I drank in the sight of my happy and healthy family. The scenery around us was fresh and alive with the promise of a new day's beginning. We could and would handle anything heading our way, for each of us had proven ourselves on the hard road to get there, at that time and place, together.

Later in the morning, while the others finished packing for the journey, I took a walk along the path of crushed shells that follows the little ridge line of the island. At the south end, I stopped to gaze out over the gumbo limbos and oranges and sabal palms, to the bay beyond. It is a beautiful vista, a balm for the eyes that I conjure when far away.

Maria arrived beside me and looked out over the scene. Our hands found each other. "Your mind seems to be a thousand miles away, Peter. What are you thinking of?" she asked.

"Assassins," I replied, omitting the rest of my thoughts—that that disreputable category had included me on occasion. It was something I rarely admitted to myself, and never to anyone else, certainly not the woman I wanted, *needed*, to love me. The darkest corners of one's past are best left in the shadows.

She was silent a while, then said, "Assassins? But you were smiling when I walked up."

"Well, dear, I was thinking about what Martí whispered to me, just before the wedding got under way."

"Yes, I remember that. I saw you with him in deep conversation and wondered about it at the time. Was it about the man who tried to assassinate him? What did he say?"

Martí's assassin. I had never told Maria the real story of the "new friend" she saw emerging from the box wagon the morning she left the Tampa Bay Hotel. I'd never told anyone about the man, now with a new name, quickly proving to be one of Martí's most trusted men inside Cuba. Only Martí and Rork knew.

The brief scene with José inside the church went through my mind. I'd just asked him how "our mutual friend" was doing. Martí leaned close and grasped my hand. His usually hard eyes had softened, for what he had to say didn't just apply to the man who tried to kill him. "Even assassins can redeem their honor and live in peace, Peter. Remember that, my friend."

He was right. They can indeed.

Lt. Commander Sean Wake, U.S.N.
U.S.S. Brooklyn
European Squadron

26 June 1903

My dear son Sean,

Well, now you know what actually happened from December
1892 to May 1893—a turbulent time in my life and career. You
know of the great mistake in judgment that led me astray to Mexico,
resulted in diplomatic contretemps with Germany, and nearly made
me too late to warn Martí about the poisoning. And I have also been
candid about the inexcusable lapse in discipline when I gave in to
temptation and struck Norton Gardiner.

I want you to learn from my mistakes. The lesson is simple:
recognize your prejudices and do not allow them to cloud your
assessment of conditions or men. I did, and was extremely lucky the
terrible consequences were never realized.

It is the inner man's mind and soul that ultimately determines
the outer man's success and happiness. My mind and soul were in
damned bad shape before I met Maria that summer of 1892. Her
love enabled me to live again, not merely exist—something I thought
lost forever when your mother died in '81. I hope someday you'll
meet such a lady. Do not hesitate when you do.

Now that you know what happened, you may wonder about the
aftermath regarding some of the more intriguing figures. Captain
Blau ended up retiring in 1898 after a disagreement with Tirpitz.
His Kaiser has grown even more obnoxious in world affairs—bad
things are ahead with him. Rear Admiral Walker retired in 1897
and became a leading proponent of the hot foreign policy topic of our
day, an Isthmian canal project. I am glad to say that Gardiner ended
up getting the better of us all—in 1896 he left the navy and became
a "remittance man" in Pago Pago.

The Cuban-Spanish connections turned out rather grimly.
Boreau and Marrón have been dead for five years now, but that's
another story for another time. There is good news regarding the

Pedrosos. They still live in the same house, are still active in exile affairs, and still make cigars during the day. Sadly, my friend Don Vicente Ybor died in back in 1896. He is still known as "the Great Benefactor" in Tampa.

The night of our wedding party was the last time I saw my dear friend José Martí. You may recall that he was killed in action against Spanish troops in Oriente, Cuba, in May 1895. Of all my memories of him, I prefer to remember José the way he was that night, smiling and laughing as he danced with Maria. The world is so much poorer without him.

And what of the assassin I tried so hard to thwart? He too was killed at Oriente in 1895, leading the Cuban liberation forces against the Spanish army in their fight for freedom. The man I saw nearly lynched as a criminal ended up dying with honor for a noble cause. Cuba is free.

So what exactly did Martí say to the assassin when alone with him that night at the Pedrosos' house? No one knows for sure, but a moral lesson is there for each of us: we can all change from bad to good.

I know I did in 1892.
With the greatest love and respect from your father,
Peter Wake
Rear Admiral, U.S.N.
Presidential Naval Aide
The White House
Washington, D.C.

Endnotes by Chapter

Chapter 1: The Unpleasant Truth
In 1908, President Theodore Roosevelt designated several islands in Charlotte Harbor and Pine Island Sound, including Patricio Island, as a wildlife refuge area. Today Patricio is off limits to the public.

Chapter 2: The Summons
U.S.S. *Bennington* was one of the earliest steel warships in the U.S. Navy. She was well known and respected for her design. Unfortunately, in July 1905, (twelve years after this story takes place) the ship suffered a catastrophic boiler explosion, killing sixty-six members of her crew and injuring almost fifty others. Eleven sailors earned the Medal of Honor for their heroism. The ship was removed from service afterward, sold in 1910 to the Matson Line, and used as a water barge at Honolulu until 1924, when she was scuttled offshore. At Fort Rosecrans National Cemetery in San Diego there is a 1908 memorial obelisk to the ship.

Chapter 3: The Reason
U.S.S. *Chicago* was the largest of the first three steel ships commissioned in the U.S. Navy in the 1880s, and already obsolete by the mid-1890s. She served in various duties until 1923, when she was decommissioned and used as a receiving/supply ship at Pearl Harbor. She sank while under tow in 1936.

John Grimes Walker (1835–1907) served in the U.S. Navy from 1850 until 1897. He saw extensive combat with Admiral David Porter on the Mississippi River and in coastal North Carolina during the Civil War. A highly respected officer, he commanded the main operations bureau of the navy from 1881 to 1889, and had several important squadron commands in the 1890s. Wake served under him in ONI from its inception until 1889, before joining him in the North Atlantic Squadron in 1890.

Joaquín Crespo (1841–1898) was head of state for Venezuela from 1884 to 1886, and from 1892 to 1898, when he was killed in battle during another civil war. As president, he was known for his dictatorial style; ruining the foreign credit of the country; taking large loans from Germany which Venezuela could not repay; and for the 1895 dispute with Great Britain over the boundary with Guiana, which was arbitrated by President Grover Cleveland, who found in favor of the British.

Chapter 4: The Enigma
The southern telegraph line from Key West stretched south to Havana, thence Jamaica and Mexico. The northern line stretched underwater to Sanibel Island, crossing the tip at Point Ybel, then across San Carlos Bay to Punta Rassa on the mainland. From there it went to Punta Gorda and up the Peace River Valley (along the rail line) to Bartow, Tampa, and to the east coast. The original brick cable station building can still be seen at Punta Rassa.

Chapter 5: The Message
A copy of this German Naval Code Book is still in existence,
inside the code archives vault at the National Security Agency
at Fort Meade, Maryland. I have been privileged to have been
granted access to it. For more detail on exactly how Wake
captured the Germans' code book at Samoa, read *Honors
Rendered.*

The Caste War of the Yucatán Peninsula of Mexico, between
the Mayan separatists and the federal government, smoldered
and periodically erupted from 1847 to 1901, when the Mexican
Army finally occupied Chan Santa Cruz with a large permanent
garrison. The last armed skirmish was in 1935.

Porfirio Díaz (1830–1915) was president of Mexico three
times: for two weeks in 1876, then from 1877 to 1880, and
finally from 1884 to 1911, when he was forced into exile by
the Mexican Revolution. He died in Paris in 1915 and is buried
there.

Dzul was a charismatic leader of the Mayan independence
movement in the 1880s and 1890s. Though there are many
stories, not much detail is known about him by the outside
world.

Chapter 6: The Enemy
S.M.S. *Gneisenau* was commissioned in 1880. She served the
Imperial German Navy around the world until 1900, when
she sank in a storm when the engine failed and she struck
a breakwater near Málaga, Spain. Forty men, including her
captain, died.

Kaiser Wilhelm II (1859–1941) was on the throne from
1888 (at age twenty-nine) until 1918, when he abdicated in
disgrace at the end of World War I. He lived the rest of his life in
exile in Doorn, Holland. He was buried there.

For details about how Rork lost his hand and a false
replacement was fashioned, read the account of Wake and Rork's
1883 mission inside French Indo-China in *The Honored Dead.*

Chapter 7: The Motive

There are usually four hours in a naval watch, or working shift. The ship's bell is struck every half hour, thus there are eight times when the bell is struck, each one counting out an increasing number.

Chapter 8: The Hypothesis

There was considerable call in the 1890s for a canal across Nicaragua, especially since the French canal debacle in Panama. Recently, this idea has resurfaced.

U.S. presidential inaugurations were held on the fourth day of March after the election from the beginning of Washington's first term in 1789 until the beginning of Franklin Roosevelt's first term in 1933. This meant the outgoing president was a "lame duck" for five months. The Twentieth Amendment (ratified in 1933) changed the date to the twenty-first day of January.

Chapter 9: The Mission

The Monroe Doctrine was a foreign policy statement by President James Monroe in 1823 and reiterated by succeeding presidents after that. It was periodically ignored by various European countries, most notably when France occupied Mexico and Spain occupied the Dominican Republic during the U.S. Civil War. In the 1895 Venezuelan Crisis between that country and Great Britain, the British recognized the Monroe Doctrine's validity. Soon afterward, most European countries followed suit. Germany was the last to recognize it—after their crisis with Venezuela in 1902 and Theodore Roosevelt's thinly veiled threat to defend Venezuela from them.

Chapter 10: The Lady

Enrique Dupuy de Lomé became the Spanish ambassador to the United States on 30 September 1892. He remained in that office until he left under American political pressure in the spring of 1898, due to a letter he'd written in February to the foreign minister in Madrid, in which he called President McKinley weak and catering to the rabble, among other things. Cubans intercepted the letter and leaked it to the *New York Journal,* which published it—right after the battleship *Maine* blew up in Havana harbor.

Admiral David Dixon Porter (1813–1891) was the adoptive brother of Admiral David Glasgow Farragut, a famous Civil War naval officer, a formidable leader, senior admiral of the navy from 1870 to 1891, an accomplished author of history and novels, and mentor of Peter Wake.

Chapter 12: The Departure

The maritime wind force scale was designed by Irish-born Royal Navy officer James Beaufort (later Rear Admiral) in 1805. It standardized various previous reporting practices. The scale is still used today and goes from Force One, a dead calm, to Force Twelve, a hurricane, and includes descriptions of waves and effects seen on land. I have been at sea in a Force Nine, gusting to Force Ten, and do not recommend the experience.

Chapter 13: The Mystery Man

In the 1800s about 20 percent of Key West's people came from the Bahamas, many from the Abaco Islands there, which to this day are renowned for their sailors and boat builders.

Chapter 14: The Yucatán

La Guardia Costera is Spanish for "coast guard."

The Yucatán Channel is also known as the Yucatán Strait. The current is extremely fast, having been blown there for hundreds of miles across the Caribbean Sea by the trade winds. I know from personal experience it can be vicious in an opposing wind from the north against that current.

For more about Wake's ordeal when he relieved his captain from command in 1869, read *A Dishonorable Few.*

Chapter 15: The Ruins
Wake is using the 1885 version of *Principal Characteristics of Foreign Ships of War*, which is still available in reprint. It was used by all American naval officers. Later, they also used the famous British naval ship books begun annually by *Brassey* in 1886 and *Janes* in 1898.

Xel-ha is about five miles north of the more famous ruins at Tulum.

Chapter 17: The Required Visit
Blau's rank was the equivalent of a commander, and Eichermann's rank was that of a lieutenant, in the U.S. Navy.

Chapter 18: The Luncheon
Wake's perilous clandestine mission in Samoa is detailed in *Honors Rendered*.

Chapter 19: The Turning Point
Many people, particularly foreigners, referred to the U.S. capital as "Washington City" in the 1800s. This practice faded by the turn of the century.

Wake first met José Martí (1853–1895) in 1886 in New York City. This encounter led to a close friendship, for Wake admired the Cuban writer and orator. They also were mutually beneficial to each other, for Wake's intelligence activities inside Cuba coincided with Martí's pro-independence efforts. The initial phase of their relationship is detailed in *The Darkest Shade of Honor*, and their 1888 collaboration on a mission in Havana is described in *Honorable Lies*.

Chapter 20: The Ruse Revealed
The *Cuerpo Militar de Orden Público* was a Spanish paramilitary police battalion formed in 1875 and consisting of about four hundred men. It was stationed primarily in Havana and charged with maintaining law and order, and also counterinsurgency

operations. There is no record of Colonel Isidro Marrón and his clandestine special section of counterinsurgency agents. Wake and Marrón's unit clashed several times in the 1880s at Cuba, Florida, and New York City.

Chapter 22: The First Evening of the Rest of My Life

Senior officialdom in Washington hated the hot, humid summers and did their best to get out, from the inception of the place as the national capital in the 1790s until the 1940s, when modern air conditioning made it more bearable. The annual Congressional recess in August is a legacy of this practice.

For details on how Wake came to receive the legendary French award of the Legion of Honor for his mission inside Africa, read *An Affair of Honor*.

"*Doña*" is the Spanish feminine version of the honorific "*Don*." It is loosely equivalent to "Lady" in Britain.

Majorca is the largest of the Balearic Islands, a Spanish archipelago in the Mediterranean Sea.

Chapter 23: The Blunder

Wake's foreign medals are rare among officers in the U.S. Navy. *An Affair of Honor* describes how he was awarded France's Legion of Honor for his actions in Africa. For details about Wake's mission in Peru, read *A Different Kind of Honor*, which I am proud to report won the highest national literary award in the genre. For his mission inside French Indo-China, read *The Honored Dead*. His exploits in Hawaii are described in *Honors Rendered*.

Antonio Maura (1853–1925) and Práxedes Sagasta (1825–1903) were political leaders in Spain who favored a more lenient attitude toward the Cubans, who were dissatisfied with the Spanish status quo in Cuba. Maura, who was born in Majorca, ended up prime minister five times: 1903–1904, 1907–1909, in 1918, in 1919, and 1921–1922. Many of his descendants are famous. There is no record of Maria Ana Maura y Abad.

Sagasta was prime minister eight times between 1870 and 1903, including during the Spanish-American War, when he had to preside over the loss of Spain's last two possessions in the new world, Cuba and Puerto Rico.

The United States offered to buy Cuba several times from the 1850s to the 1890s. Spain declined each time. Martí did not want Cuba to become part of the United States—he wanted her to be a fully independent nation.

Chapter 25: The New Plan

The San Carlos Institute still exists at 516 Duval Street and is a fascinating place to visit, just a few doors down from Jimmy Buffet's famous Margaritaville restaurant. For more information, visit www.institutosancarlos.org and be sure to stop by when in Key West.

Martin Herrera and José Poyo were civic leaders in Key West and also leaders of the Cuban pro-independence movement. They were close friends of Martí and are regarded as heroes to this day.

Gardiner's future commanding officer up in Boston is an interesting figure in American naval history. Captain Thomas O. Selfridge, Jr., (1836–1924) was a well-known naval officer who had seen a lot of combat during the Civil War. Unfortunately, that included being aboard three ships when they were sunk by the Confederates: *Cumberland*, *Cairo*, and *Conestoga*—commanding the last two. This led some in the navy to call him a "Jonah," or bad-luck sailor. Others said he was in actuality the luckiest man in the navy to have survived at all. After forty-eight years of honorable service, he retired as a rear admiral in 1898.

Chapter 27: The Mysterious Cuban

Useppa's unusual name comes from the island where she was born in 1864. It is near Pine Island, and very close to Patricio Island, which Wake bought in 1883. All of them are on the southwest coast of Florida.

Read *The Darkest Shade of Honor* for more about Useppa's murdered fiancé.

The Duval Hotel no longer exists, but in the 1890s was a premier lodging and dining room located at 117 Duval Street. That's halfway between Greene and Front streets, on the east side of Duval, right next to where Bagatelle Restaurant (one of my favorites) is today.

Chapter 28: The Kiss

Sir Julian Pauncefote (1828–1902) was another fascinating character in history, working around the British Empire from the 1860s to the 1880s. His diplomatic career reached its zenith as a very successful British envoy and ambassador to the United States from 1889 until his death in 1902.

Chapter 30: Nothing Is Easy

You can read more about Wake's friendship with Mu'al-lim Sohkoor in *An Affair of Honor*.

Chapter 33: *Force Majeure*

Force Majeure is the French legal term for an unforeseen event that occurs due to an overwhelming force or act of nature. It has been well established in international maritime law for two hundred years. I have invoked *Force Majeure* myself, as master of a vessel needing refuge at a restricted dock during a storm in 1992. In the particular case described in this story, for Wake to employ it as a ruse was not at all professional or honorable—a notable lapse in his lifelong adherence to honor—and defendable only because Martí's life was hanging in the balance.

The code flags used are from the international code set of 1890. The signal meanings have changed since then.

Chapter 34: An Unusual Signal

Heliographs have been used as signaling devises by armies and navies from the 1700s until the modern era. Today, most people usually have a perfect *ad hoc* heliograph with them—a CD or DVD—in case of emergency. It can be used to signal for help by reflecting the sun and can be easily seen by searching aircraft or vessels.

Chapter 36: Rum and Ribald Songs
In my not so humble opinion, which is echoed by Wake, Matusalem is still the finest sipping rum of Cuba. Visit www.matusalem.com to learn more.

Chapter 37: The Night Race
Passage Key Channel is still a tough one for deeper draft vessels. The currents there constantly shift the shoals.

Egmont Key has some interesting historical structures still existing and is well worth a visit—though it is only accessible by boat.

Chapter 38: The Necessary Accoutrements
The town of St. Petersburg was founded in 1888 by Pyotr Alexeyevitch Dementyev, a Russian immigrant who went by Peter Demens when he got to Florida. Demens and his friend John Williams brought the railroad to the town. By 1892 it had a population of around three hundred.

The two large piers of Port Tampa are still in operation, but look nothing like they did in 1892, having been modernized. The two hotels on the wharves no longer exist. Much of the area has been landfilled in—Mr. Plant would hardly recognize it.

The nearby town of Port Tampa has several homes and buildings from the 1890s and a great little library. Its most celebrated former resident is the professional wrestler Hulk Hogan (Terry Gene Bollea), who grew up there. Just south of the port, Picnic Island still has the beach park (now a county park) that Henry Plant created for his workers and the tourists at his hotels.

A ship's donkey engine is a small engine used for powering

deck winches—weighing anchor, cargo hauling, line hauling, etc.

Chapter 39: The Goat Locker's Retribution
The term "Goat Locker" is from the early days of sail when chickens and goats (and the occasional pig) were kept aboard ship for fresh food. They lived forward in the ship, near the senior petty officers' quarters—hence the name. To this day, few aboard a warship are anything but respectful to a senior petty officer, for none want the retribution of those grizzled salts.

Chapter 40: The Train
In 1892, there were only two bridges across the Hillsborough River at Tampa—the Lafayette Street Bridge for vehicular traffic and the railroad bridge. Both had been recently built, and both still exist in modern forms. Lafayette Street is now Kennedy Boulevard.

In the 1890s, Ybor City was reachable by road, steam train car, and electric street car. It is still connected with downtown Tampa by an electric railway, which is great fun to ride.

Chapter 41: The Tampa Bay Hotel
This magnificent building still exists as a focal point of the University of Tampa. It is also an iconic image of the city of Tampa. It is very much worth a visit to the museum there to get a glimpse into the lifestyle of the elite during the "Gilded Age."

Chapter 42: Wonderful Potholes
A landau was a carriage with two bench seats for passengers and a forward seat for the driver and footman. Many had a convertible canvas top. Her Majesty, Queen Elizabeth II, still travels on state occasions in a landau. Of course, hers is quite ornate.

Chapter 43: The Enemy Around Us
Vicente Martinez Ybor (1818–1896), the founder of Ybor City in 1886, is still revered as a community leader and progressive

businessman whose ideas regarding employee benefits were well ahead of his time. Born in Spain, he moved to Cuba, and later immigrated to the United States in 1869, just before the Spanish authorities could arrest him for supporting the Cuban rebel movement. A self-made success, he was the inspiration for many Cubans and Italians who came to Ybor City to start a new life.

The Ybor Cigar Factory building was built of brick due to lessons learned in the Great Fire of 1886 in Key West—(read *The Darkest Shade of Honor*)—and still exists. Renovated to its original exterior appearance, it now belongs to the Church of Scientology.

Bolita (Spanish for "little ball") is a traditional Cuban lottery gambling game where one hundred small balls, each with a different number, are tossed around in a sack. This system is prone to cheating by weighing the balls and other means. The number drawn out is the winner. The number three ball Wake chose was the traditional lucky number for sailors. *Bolita* was and is illegal in Florida, and became a moneymaking vice for the Mafia in Tampa for decades. Since Florida began its official state lottery, *bolita* isn't as popular as it once was.

Many Cubans came from Galician families. Galicia is the area of northwest Spain.

Chapter 44: A Time for Blessings

Paulina and Ruperto Pedroso were born in the mid-1840s in Pinar del Rio (the western end of Cuba) and moved to Havana in 1860. Trained as cigar workers, they subsequently immigrated to Key West and came to Ybor City in the late 1880s. Martí always stayed at their home when visiting the Tampa/Ybor City area, and considered the childless black couple to be his surrogate parents. Throughout the 1890s, they were leaders of the independence movement. They returned to Cuba in 1910 and lived in a rent-free home for the rest of their lives, courtesy of the Cuban people who appreciated their work for Martí. Paulina died in 1925. The house in Ybor City no longer exists, but the plot of land where it stood is a private park dedicated to José Martí and Cuba.

Fire Station #2 no longer exists. The spot is currently occupied by the New World Brewery.

Chapter 45: The Brotherhood

Hillsborough Masonic Lodge is the oldest continually operating lodge in Florida, now in its 165th year. Many civic, business, and governmental leaders in Florida's history have been members of this lodge. It is no longer at the location by Fort Brooke. See their interesting website at: www.hillsborough25.org.

For details on how José Martí's brother Masons in Cuba helped Wake escape in 1888, read *Honorable Lies*.

Chapter 48: Messages Received and Sent

Boreau is the Spanish naval officer who tried to kill Wake in a "friendly" saber match turned homicidal at Havana in 1888. The reason? Wake killed Boreau's father, an agent for Colonel Marrón, in New York City in 1886.

A phaeton was a small carriage with a single bench seat that was designed for speed.

Chapter 51: ¡Viva Martí!

General Máximo Gómez (1839–1905) was born in the Dominican Republic, trained and served as an officer in the Spanish Army, then became one of the most famous leaders of the thirty-year Cuban fight for independence against Spain. It was Gómez who taught the Cuban Mambi (farmworker) cavalrymen their most terrifying tactic, the machete charge, which was so effective against the Spanish conscript soldiers. He declined the presidency of Cuba when she became free, saying that a Cuban-born person should have the position. Gómez is still revered among Cubans everywhere.

Lt. General Antonio Maceo (José Antonio de la Caridad Maceo y Grajales, 1845–1896) is my favorite military officer in Cuban history. Known by Cubans everywhere as *El Titan Bronce* (The Bronze Titan) for his black skin color and large size, Maceo rose through the ranks at a time when even the Cuban independence movement had many supporters who looked down on dark-skinned military officers. Like Martí, Maceo was an accomplished Freemason and believed in their creed of "Liberty, Equality and Fraternity." He was also a self-educated, sophisticated gentleman. From 1868 to his death in battle in 1896, he fought in over five hundred battles and was wounded twenty-seven times. The mere understanding that Antonio Maceo was present on the battlefield demoralized his Spanish opponents. When he was killed in battle on 7 December 1896, at Punta Brava (southeast of Havana), his bodyguard, General Gómez's son Panchito, defended his dead body and was also killed by Spanish troops.

Chapter 52: A Most Incongruous Turn of Events
The fire station, begun in 1888 as the Mirta Hook and Ladder Company (named after the youngest daughter of Vicente Martinez Ybor) doesn't exist anymore, but there is a historical marker about it across the street, commemorating Captain Frank Puglisi and his Cuban volunteer firemen.

Madrileo (or *Madrileño*) refers to a person from Madrid

Chapter 53: Drinking with an Apostle
José Martí was known by many people around the world, especially by the 1890s, as the "Apostle of Liberty."

Gideon Welles (1802–1878) was the secretary of the navy from 1861 to 1869. He is chiefly remembered for being a taciturn, demanding, and successful civilian leader of the U.S. Navy, and reviled as the man who abolished the grog issue for enlisted sailors in 1862. Wake didn't like him. President Lincoln nicknamed Welles his "Neptune." Thus, Wake cringes inside whenever his dear friend Martí calls him Neptune.

The reader will note that Martí, the Cuban, wasn't drinking

rum. He is the only Cuban I know of who didn't (or doesn't) enjoy rum. Martí did like gin, the drink the Brits made famous throughout the tropics as a refreshing antidote to malaria, because they mixed it with quinine. Martí, who was fluent in French from his studies and work there, was a devotee of French food, wine, and philosophy.

Vin Mariani was a very well-known French Bordeaux infused with six milligrams of cocaine per fluid ounce. The version exported to the United States had 7.2 milligrams of cocaine per ounce and was widely fashionable with the upper class in America, including former president Grant. In Atlanta, John Pemberton (1831–1888), a morphine-addicted Civil War veteran, created a cocaine wine that became quite successful until the Atlanta temperance laws of 1885 forced him to make a nonalcoholic version. That later became the legendary Coca-Cola, which contained five ounces of cocaine per gallon of syrup until 1903, when all cocaine was removed from the recipe.

Chapter 54: Discipline in the Face of Evil
The Hahnemann test (discovered by German doctor Samuel Hahnemann in 1787) was the common preliminary test for arsenic poisoning. The Marsh test, a more complicated evaluation, would be done next.

Ipecacuanha is a plant from Brazil used as an emetic to induce vomiting. Many people know it as ipecac. This is not the standard procedure used by doctors nowadays.

Chapter 55: Bloodlust
Las Nuevitas Hotel is no longer there, nor Teatro Ybor.

One of the symptoms of arsenic poisoning is hoarseness. In Martí's case, it was aggravated by the medicine given to induce vomiting.

Chapter 56: A Curious Redemption of Honor
The exact identity of the assassins is still unknown, though there

is still some conjecture in Cuba about their names.

To this day, no one knows exactly what José Martí said to his assassin in that room, for neither man ever publicly said. There is some conjecture that after receiving the man's request for forgiveness, Martí, a Master Mason, may have made the man a brother Mason, thereby cementing his loyalty even further. This would not be the normal route for a man seeking membership, of course, but there is a special exemption in the rules allowing it in rare situations.

Chapter 57: A Service to Humanity
Saul of Tarsus (approx 5–67 A.D.) was a notorious persecutor of the early followers and apostles of Jesus, even killing them, but later underwent a complete change of faith and converted, becoming known by his Latin name, Paul. As Saint Paul the Apostle, he was one of the most widely known leaders and martyrs of early Christendom. Much of the New Testament is attributed to him. Obviously, Wake's naming the assassin "Pablo" was a tribute to the belief that the very worst can become the very best.

Chapter 58: A Reunion with Love
Sean Wake, born in 1865 at Pensacola, was named after Peter Wake's best friend Sean Rork. Unlike his father, Sean Wake graduated from the U.S. Naval Academy. Commissioned an ensign in 1890, his career will last over forty years.

This Methodist church still exists at that location. With its beautiful interior woodwork and unusually buttressed exterior architecture, it is well worth a visit. I always go there for Sunday services when in Key West.

Chapter 59: That None Must Know
In the 1890s, Delmonico's had several locations in New York City; this was the most famous. This great eatery started in 1837, spawned a number of culinary firsts, and is fortunately still open.

It is currently located on Beaver Street in lower Manhattan. It is one of the iconic dining experiences of the city.

Charles Ranhofer (1836–1899) was a renowned French chef who immigrated to the U.S. in 1856 and helped to make Delmonico's the place to eat, and be seen, in New York City. He wrote *The Epicurean*, which is still the definitive tome on cuisine of the Gilded Age.

James Blount (1837–1903) was a Confederate veteran and Democratic congressman from Georgia from 1873 to 1893. He was chairman of the House Foreign Affairs Committee and opposed to adding any territory inhabited by nonwhites to the United States. Blount's report recommended not recognizing the coup and new government, not acquiring Hawaii, and repudiating the actions of the U.S. Consul there. The Democratic-controlled U.S. Senate delivered their own report, which recommended the opposite. President Cleveland ended up taking Blount's (and Wake's) advice and repudiated the actions of the previous administration. The coup-implemented government still stood in Honolulu, however, and Hawaii was acquired in 1898 by the next administration in office, led by President McKinley.

Hilary Herbert (1834–1919) was a Confederate veteran and Democratic congressman from Alabama from 1877 to 1893. He was chairman of the Naval Affairs Committee, a great supporter of the navy, and largely responsible for the congressional funding in the 1880s and 1890s to modernize the country's warships. Herbert was secretary of the navy from 1803 to 1897. He died in Tampa in 1919.

Born in 1837, Grover Cleveland was two years older than Wake and lived until 1908, the year Wake will retire. Cleveland's young wife Francis lived until 1947.

Chapter 60: By Order of the President

What we now call the "White House" was routinely called the "Executive Mansion" in the 1800s. President Theodore Roosevelt began calling it the White House early in his first term and the moniker stuck.

A "parasymphyseal fracture of the mandible" means Wake broke Gardiner's jaw at the chin. Routine recovery time is six weeks. Due to the state of dental medicine in the late nineteenth century, Gardiner very likely had underbite problems for the rest of his life.

The French and Russian agreement Wake refers to was signed in 1892 and became known as the Franco-Russian Alliance. It was made to counter the Triple Alliance, the 1882 pact between Germany, Italy, and Austro-Hungary. In 1907, France, Russia, and Great Britain, supplemented by Japan and Portugal, formed the Triple Entente as a counterbalance to the Triple Alliance. Thus the basic antagonists of World War I (1914–1918) were formed in bewilderingly complex turn-of-the-century Europe. The reader will note that the United States of America was not a party to any of this, though we got dragged into the war in 1917.

In 1889, President Cleveland promised Wake a promotion for his good work. Wake, jaded soul that he was, never thought that would happen, since it was merely the word of a politician.

Rork joined about two hundred other petty officers in being promoted in April 1893 to the new rank of Chief Petty Officer.

Chapter 61: Tears of Love

The failed uprising to which Wake refers was led by two brothers, Manuel and Ricardo Sartorius, at Holguín, Cuba. It was not authorized or supported by Martí and the Cuban Revolutionary Party. The Spanish authorities quickly defeated it.

The area of Tift's Wharf has been filled in and paved over. It is now called Mallory Square. Mallory's dock was next to Tift's. The square is named for Stephen Mallory, former U.S. senator from Key West in the 1850s and secretary of the navy for the Confederacy from 1861 to 1865.

Lowe's Dock is now the A&B Marina.

The Author's Final Word with the Reader

José Martí's poisoning in Ybor City at the hands of Spanish
agents is little known by the public and the subject of conjecture
by students of Cuban history. Mañach writes that the poison
was acid, but does not specify the type. Several of the symptoms
listed by Mañach, and those in Martí's letter to Serafin Sanchez
a month later, are similar to those of arsenic poisoning, however.
Arsenic would also be easier for the assassins to administer. To
my uncertain knowledge, 123 years later no one still knows for
sure.

In Ybor City, there are some with the opinion that the
poisoning occurred in 1893. Martí's letter shows it happened
in mid-December 1892, and this is confirmed by the esteemed
Centro Estudiantes Martianos (Center for Martí Studies) in
Havana, Cuba, who gave me the date of December 16, 1892.
Alfred J. López's exemplary new book on Martí also confirms
that it occurred in December 1892, and uses references from
Carlos Ripoll's *La Vida Intima y Secreta de José Martí* and Nydia
Sarabia's *Noticias Confidenciales sobre Cuba 1870–1895*.

The political situations in Venezuela, Mexico, Germany,
Washington, and Florida are described accurately in this novel.
The global German Empire was in its ascendancy, and had
serious designs on the Caribbean. Drake, Blau, Boreau, Gardiner,
and Marrón are fictional.

From the late 1880s, Martí was under constant surveillance
and threat of assassination by Spanish agents, even in the United
States. This he understood intellectually, but in his focused drive
to secure freedom for his people, dismissed operationally. The
assassination attempt in Ybor City changed everything. At the
insistence of his closest confidants, Martí's subsequent travels
incorporated much more attention to security. He was, after all,
the voice of freedom.

I am saddened to report that José Julián Martí Pérez was
killed in action with the Spanish army on May 19, 1895, at Dos

Rios in Oriente Province in eastern Cuba. If only he had lived, the path of history would have turned out much better for his people.

Still, in the incredibly complex forty-two years of his life, this intriguing visionary of the human condition, advocate of universal freedoms, speaker of truth to tyrants, and compassionate poet of life, managed to change the world's view of individual freedom and responsibility. Amazingly, this triumph has not faded in all these years. To the contrary, Martí's ideas have become the goal of those aspiring liberty everywhere.

To this day he is revered by Cubans everywhere, as well as people from many other cultures, all of whom long for what Martí saw should be, if only mankind could rise above greed, jealousy, fear, and dogma.

His aficionados include me.

Robert N. Macomber
(hecho en Cuba)

Acknowledgments

Projects of this complexity require a lot of research and I am profoundly blessed to have a wonderfully diverse crew of experts (the Subject Matter Advanced Research Team: SMART) who helped me understand the facts and the flavor of the places, people, and events in this novel. Most are longtime readers of the Honor Series—true Wakians—and thus are part of my renowned SMART Wakians. I am very loyal and appreciative to these fascinating people. Here are some of them.

For insight into signals intelligence, the German language, and latter nineteenth-century German reports regarding the Caribbean, I send my sincere thanks to two of America's unsung heroes: Ron Kemper and Rich Rolfe, formerly of the NSA. For guiding me through the historical code vault at NSA and allowing me to peruse the Imperial German Navy code book of 1891, with attendant explanations and details, I thank Rene Stein, chief librarian at the NSA Cryptologic Museum at Fort Meade. RADM Tony Cothron U.S.N. (Ret), former Director of the Office of Naval Intelligence, has also helped with understanding many subtle factors in the Intel world over the years.

For the information about the Caste War of Mexico, I thank three dear friends with intimate knowledge of Yucatán: Reverend Ann McLemore, and authors John (Bing) and Jane Grimsrud. For first introducing me to the Yucatán by sea in 1987, and engendering a lifelong love for its people and culture, I thank the legendary Truman Morris (R.I.P.), my captain aboard the sailing vessel *Remote*.

For the information about Ybor City, Tampa, and Port Tampa, I have several people to thank—Elizabeth McCoy and Carl St. Meyer, from the very informative staff at the Ybor City State Museum; Dave Parsons at the Hillsborough County Public Library in Tampa; and Vickie Jewett at the Port Tampa Library.

For intense crucial efforts to unravel the mystery surrounding Martí's poisoning in Ybor City, huge thanks go to my dear friend Ela Lopez Ugarte, Editor-in-Chief at the Centro Estudiantes Martíanos (Center for Martí Studies) in Havana—one of the foremost Martí scholars in the world and an absolutely charming lady. Ela provided conclusive documentation (the January 1893 letter from Martí to Serafin Sanchez) showing that it happened 16 December 1892. For translation of some of the documents revealing details of the poisoning, I thank Mario Cano, Esquire, of Miami—a gentleman of the United States, Spain, and Cuba, who appreciates history and integrity.

For my understanding of Martí and the wonders of the Cuban culture and history, I thank Martí scholar and actor Chaz Mena, *mi tío* Raul Laffitte, the entire extended Laffitte family, Roberto Giraudy, George Alcober, Kiko Villalon, my father Robert Charles Macomber, and many others over the last sixty years.

For insight into the intriguing brotherhood of Freemasonry, my thanks go to Ted Connally of the Tropical Lodge of Southwest Florida, Justo Orihuela of the Grand Lodge of Cuba, and Charles Prosser of the Hillsborough Lodge of Tampa—good men all. I am very proud to have been designated a "Friend of Freemasonry."

For ship handling, thanks go to some real masters whom I've observed performing that difficult art: Captain Paul Welling, U.S.C.G.; Captain Chuck Nygaard, U.S.N.; Commodore Ronald Warwick, R.N.R.; and Captain Ullrich Nuber, German Merchant Marine.

The actual writing of the novel was begun at a refuge I've come to rely upon, Mark and Christine Strom's beautiful "Maramonte" in the high mountains of western North Carolina. Thank you for letting me hide out and work.

Perspective, critical analysis, and unfailing positive support have come from my business manager, morale officer, and loving wife, Nancy Ann Glickman, who also researches the astronomy and ornithology in my novels. *The Assassin's Honor* would not have been accomplished without her.

Editing a novel as complex as this is not an easy task, and I am very grateful for the patient and insightful editorial work by one of the best in the business, Helena Sznurkowski Berg.

As usual in my projects, I have done a lot of reading. Much of it was facilitated by the wonderful team of "biblio-sleuths" at the Pine Island Library, led by their boss, Randy Briggs. I'd put these folks up against any library in the world—they have never failed in locating and obtaining my requests for sometimes bizarre materials.

The bibliography of research materials used in this project is listed below. I urge my readers to peruse them and learn more about Florida, Cuba, Mexico, the Caribbean, Europe, the United States, and the U.S. Navy during those tumultuous years of "The Gilded Age."

About the Imperial German Navy in the Caribbean:

By Order of the Kaiser, by Terrell D. Gottschall (2003)
Germany's Vision of Empire in Venezuela 1871–1914, by
    Holger Herwig (1986)

About the Caste War of Mexico:

The Caste War of Yucatán, by Nelson Reed (2002)
The Caste War Route, webpage by John Grimsrud (2007)
  http://bicycleyucatan.wordpress.com/felipe-carrillo-
  puerto-tihosuco-and-valladolid-yucatan/

About Key West:

City of Intrigue, Nest of Revolution, by Consuelo E. Stebbins
  (2007)
Key West, Cigar City, USA, by Dr. Loy Glenn Westfall (1997)
Key West: The Old and the New, by Jefferson B. Browne
  (1912)
A Sketch of the History of Key West, Florida, by Walter C.
  Maloney (1876)

About Tampa and Ybor City:

The Tampa Daily Journal (newspaper), (6 February 1891)
The Tampa Daily Journal (newspaper), (14 December 1892)
Tampa: In Civil War and Reconstruction, by Canter Brown, Jr.
  (2000)
Ybor City: The Making of a Landmark Town, by Frank Trebín
  Lastra (2006)
The Ybor City Story 1885–1954 (*Los Cubanos en Tampa*, by
  Jose Rivero Muniz), translated by Eustasio Fernandez
  and Henry Beltran (1976)

About the U.S. Navy in the latter nineteenth century:

The American Steel Navy, by CMDR John T. Alden U.S.N.
  (Ret) (1972)
A Century of U.S. Naval Intelligence, by Captain Wyman H.
  Packard U.S.N. (Ret) (1996)
*Characteristics of Principal Foreign Ships of War: Prepared
  for the Board on Fortifications, Etc.*, Office of Naval
  Intelligence (1885)

Coaling, Docking, and Repair Facilities of the Ports of the World, Office of Naval Intelligence (1909)

Conway's All the World's Fighting Ships 1860–1905, Editorial Director Robert Gardiner (1979)

Masked Dispatches: Cryptograms and Cryptology in American History, 1775–1900, (Series I, Pre-World War I, Volume I) by Ralph Weber, National Security Agency (1993)

The Naval Annual of 1891, edited by T. A. Brassey (1891)

The Naval Aristocracy, The Golden Age of Annapolis and the Emergence of Modern American Navalism, by Peter Karsten (1972)

Naval Customs, Traditions, and Usage, by LCMDR Leland P. Lovette U.S.N. (1939)

The Naval Officer's Guide, by CDR Arthur A. Ageton U.S.N. (2nd edition, 1944)

The Naval Officer's Guide, by VADM William P. Mack U.S.N. (Ret) and Captain Thomas D. Paulsen U.S.N. (9th Edition, 1983)

Naval Shiphandling, by Captain R. S. Crenshaw U.S.N. (Ret) (4th Edition, 1975)

Navalism and the Emergence of American Sea Power 1882–1893, by Mark Russell Shulman (1995)

The Office of Naval Intelligence: The Birth of America's First Intelligence Agency 1865-1918, by Jeffery M. Dorwart (1979)

United States Cryptologic History, The Friedman Legacy: A tribute to William and Elizebeth Freidman, National Security Agency (1992)

U.S. Cruisers 1883–1904: The Birth of the Steel Navy, by Lawrence Burr (2008)

Watch Officer's Guide, by ADM James Stavridis U.S.N. and Captain Robert Girrier U.S.N. (15th Edition, 2007)

About New York City and Washington, D.C.:
The Epicurean, by Charles Ranhofer (1894)

Every-day Life in Washington, by Charles M. Pepper (1900)
Grover Cleveland, by Henry F. Graff (2002)
New York Songlines: Virtual Walking Tours of Manhattan StreetsNew York City (website), by Jim Naureckas www. nysonglines.com
Repast: Dining Out at the Dawn of the New American Century 1900–1910, by Michael Lesy and Lisa Stoffer (2013)
Victorian America: Transformations in Everyday Life 1876–1915, by Thomas J. Schlereth (1991)

About José Martí:
Cuba: or the Pursuit of Freedom, by Hugh Thomas (1971)
History of Cuba: the Challenge of the Yoke and the Star, by Professor José Cantón Navarro (2001)
Insurgent Cuba: Race, Nation, and Revolution, 1868–1898, by Ada Ferrer (1999)
José Martí: Cuban Patriot, by Richard Butler Gray (1962)
José Martí: A Revolutionary Life, Alfred J. López (2014)
Las enfermedades de José Martí: un reto vencido, an essay by Rolando López del Amo, published in *El Historiador* (2011)
Martí: Apostle of Freedom, by Jorge Mañach (1950)
Noticias confidenciales sobre Cuba 1870–1895, Nydia Sarabia (1985)
Nueva y humana visión de Martí, by Carlos Márquez Sterling (1953)

Maps and Charts:
Gulf of Mexico—Yucatan Channel, U.S. Office of Coast Survey #C (1880)
Gulf Stream—Caribbean, Gulf of Mexico, Atlantic Ocean, Lt. Mathew Fontaine Maury, U.S.N., U.S. Office of Coast Survey (1852)
Key West, Sanborn Fire Insurance Map (1892)

Key West Harbor and Approaches, U.S. Office of Coast Survey #469 (1896)

Tampa Bay, U.S. Office of Coast Survey #177 (1888)

Tampa Bay, U.S. Office of Coast Survey #177 (1895)

Tampa and Ybor City, Sanborn Fire Insurance Map (1892)

Tampa, Port Tampa, and Ybor City, Sanborn Fire Insurance Map, (1895)

Upper Caribbean Sea and Gulf of Mexico, American privately published chart with U.S., British, French, and Spanish survey data (1860)

Yukatanmeer, Westlicher Teil, German chart of the Yucatán east coast and the western Caribbean Sea (1992, with data from 1913)

And finally, I thank my dear readers around the world, the Wakians, for their loyalty, enthusiasm, and spreading of kind words about my work. You are the best readers an author could hope for, are very much a part of my life, and keep me motivated and ready to embark upon the next project in the Honor Series. Other authors have told me how jealous they are of the fun we have together.

And so the adventure continues. . . .

Onward and upward!

Robert N. Macomber

The Boat House

St. James, Pine Island

Florida

For a complete catalog, visit our website at www.pineapplepress.com. Or write to Pineapple Press, P.O. Box 3889, Sarasota, Florida 34230-3889, or call (800) 746-3275.

The Honor Series of Naval Fiction (in order of publication)

At the Edge of Honor. This nationally acclaimed naval Civil War novel introduces U.S. Navy officer Peter Wake, who in 1863 battles the enemy in Florida and social taboos in Key West when he falls in love with the daughter of a Confederate zealot.

Point of Honor. Winner of the Florida Historical Society's 2003 Patrick Smith Award for Best Florida Fiction. In 1864 Wake searches for army deserters in the Dry Tortugas and finds an old nemesis in Mexico.

Honorable Mention. In 1867 Wake chases a strange vessel off Cuba, liberates an escaping slave ship, and confronts the enemy's most powerful ocean warship in Havana's harbor.

A Dishonorable Few. In 1869 Wake heads to turbulent Central America to face a former American naval officer turned renegade mercenary.

An Affair of Honor. In 1873 Wake runs afoul of the Royal Navy in Antigua and becomes embroiled in a Spanish civil war.

A Different Kind of Honor. On assignment in 1879, Wake witnesses history's first battle between ocean-going ironclads and runs for his life in the Catacombs of the Dead in Lima.

The Honored Dead. On what at first appears to be a simple mission in French Indochina in 1883, Wake encounters opium warlords, Chinese-Malay pirates, and French gangsters.

The Darkest Shade of Honor. It's 1886 and Wake meets rising politico Theodore Roosevelt, befriends José Martí, and is engulfed in the most catastrophic event in Key West history.

Honor Bound. In 1888 Wake travels deep into the jungles of Haiti to discover the hidden lair of an anarchist group planning to wreak havoc around the world—unless he stops it.

Honorable Lies. In September 1888, Peter Wake has five days to rescue his two captured operatives from a dungeon in Spanish-Colonial Havana.

Honors Rendered. Peter Wake is sent in 1889 to the South Pacific to avert a war with the Germans.

Assassin's Honor. With command of a new warship in 1892 and the love of a fascinating lady, Wake is finally happy—that is, until he is ordered to prevent an assassination.